THINGS HAVE A HABIT

Peter Green

2015

ISBN: 1508974489

ISBN 13: 9781508974482

Cover photograph and design by **Peter N. Karalekas**

DEDICATION

This book is dedicated to Susan, my very best friend in the whole wide world.

ALSO BY PETER GREEN

CHAPTER 1

Crawford Taylor is not your ordinary shylock, no sir. None of your hook-nosed Fagins or Semitic stereotypes here, if you please. Crawford Taylor is your modern day shylock. He's suave and handsome and cool and elegant in his charcoal gray Armani suit and black Prada slip-ons. He's Harvard-educated with a grace and style you see all the time on the pages of *GQ.* Think George Clooney here only younger and without the gray hair. Crawford Taylor is perfectly tanned and dark-haired from people, they say, that go all the way back to the Mayflower. He carries himself like a leading man. Center stage. Head high. And the spotlight is always shining on him, even if it's not.

Crawford is upset. Payment is due. Not just due, very due, and a lot of money is at stake. A guy he was doing well with has been giving him the run-around.

And payment is due.

And nothing is forthcoming.

Gillie Fader is a giant of a man. He's six foot four and three hundred and forty five pounds of solid muscle that he hones every day in the gym in the basement of his apartment building in the City. He makes his living by intimidating people, but he's not your usual run of the mill heavy. Gillie is polished and smart and rarely has to use the Louisville Slugger he always takes with him on his missions to set people straight. His clean-shaven head gleams like a highly polished floor. His blue eyes are clear and hard. His face is featureless. Not fat. Or round. It just doesn't stop as it melds into his shiny bald head. He looks like a pink Easter egg with ears that are stuck on the side, but no one would tell him that to his face.

It's Monday afternoon. Crawford and Gillie are meeting at their favorite rendezvous, the bar in the Carlyle Hotel on Madison Avenue, to discuss Crawford's problem.

"I've made a mistake," Crawford admits woefully.

Gillie raises an eyebrow.

"I let it go on too long," says Crawford.

"How long?"

"Six months or so."

Gillie says, "I'm surprised at you," like he was talking to a naughty child.

Crawford shrugs and gives him a 'what are you going to do,' look.

"You'll have to pay him a visit," he says.

Gillie wants to know when.

"Now."

"You told him?"

"I did," says Crawford. "I didn't want to, but I did."

Gillie raises another eyebrow.

"The guy was going to make me a lot of money," says Crawford by way of an explanation, "I thought it would be okay."

"But it's not," says Gillie.

"No, it's not," says Crawford and digs out a cashew from the dish of nuts the bartender put in front of them.

Fee is not discussed. It's 10% of whatever Gillie collects and he gets first dibs. They've worked together before, these two. Crawford gives him the necessary information. What the man looks like. Where he lives, that sort of thing. Then he finishes his drink, puts a fifty on the bar, shakes Gillie's hand and says goodbye.

Gillie orders another scotch, pops a couple of peanuts in his mouth, takes out his cellphone and calls the guy.

"We're having trouble with your account," he says when the man picks up.

"Who is this?" says the man.

"I'm a business associate of Crawford Taylor," says Gillie. "He asked me to give you a call and see if we can work something out."

"This is very inconvenient," says the man in a nervous whisper. "I can't talk to you now."

Gillie agrees that it is indeed very inconvenient.

"How about we have a cup of coffee some place and talk it over?"

The guy says, "Where?"

"You tell me," says Gillie.

"Do you know Columbia?"

Gillie says he does.

"There's a diner in the middle of town."

"When?" says Gillie.

"Monday," says the man.

It's Tuesday.

Gillie says, "Tomorrow."

The guy says no.

"I'm afraid it will have to be," says Gillie firmly. "Mr. Taylor was very specific on this point. He says he wants this situation resolved quickly."

Gillie doesn't talk like a heavy. His soft voice has a Noo Yawk twang to it with a syrupy inflection that always seems to be selling something. You'd have to see him to know what he was all about.

"Friday," says the guy. "How about Friday?"

"Tomorrow," says Gillie. "I'll be at the diner at 3 o'clock. I'll wait fifteen minutes. If you don't show I'll come and find you and I don't have to tell you what will happen if I have to do that," he says and ends the call.

His drink arrives. He pays the bill, scarfs down a handful of peanuts, washes it down with his scotch, and leaves.

Austin is the name of the man Gillie Fader is talking to. He's the man who owes Crawford Taylor all that money. Austin looks like an accountant, which is what he is only he's higher up the food chain. He's a CFO to be exact. He's thin and wiry and wears thick, black-framed glasses that make him look older than he is, an asset for his line of work and the position he holds. His face is pinched and sallow and his mousy brown hair is graying and thinning prematurely, more so recently because of all the pressure he's put himself under. He stares at the phone then tries to call Gillie back, but the number is blocked. Nor does it come up on the screen the way it's supposed to when you press caller ID. How does he do that, Austin wonders? Then he wonders why he cares since his world is falling apart around him.

Austin has two thousand dollars to his name. Crawford Taylor wants twenty-five, and that's just a payment. Austin owes him another hundred on top of that, and that includes the vig and the late fees. He hocked his Rolex and his Dunhill lighter yesterday, gifts from Shirley from before they were married, and that's the last of it. He's tapped out. So are his friends. And relatives. And anyone else who's helped him out along the way. That's how he's managed to make his payments up until now hoping things would get better, but they haven't. And time has run out.

Conner Malloy thinks this is the best day of his life. Things could not get any better. Brie the Bartender is lying naked beside him. He's got a Quick Pick worth three thousand dollars in his wallet, and the icing on the cake was a call from Gillie Fader wanting him to go on a collection gig with him. Conner gets five hundred for punching some guy's lights out, or not depending on how the thing goes down. He gets paid either way and it's the kind of work he really enjoys.

Conner mutters, "Some fuckin day," and takes another hit off the roach in the ashtray on the bedside table. Then he wakes up Brie for another roll in the hay before he goes off to meet Gillie for a different kind of fun.

The way it works is Conner stays in the car with the Louisville Slugger while Gillie meets with the "client" in the diner. That's what they call them these days. Clients. Like they're in the real estate business or something. It's always a diner because they're everywhere and they usually have the same kind of layout. That way there are no surprises, like a back door by the bathroom or something of that nature. And Gillie likes to give his spiel over a cup coffee as opposed to a parking lot or some other outdoor venue. He says it's a civilized way of doing things and it makes him feel more like a businessman.

Sometimes, after Gillie's said his piece, the guy says fuck that and walks out of the meeting. The clients usually drive to these things. That's why Conner is waiting in the parking lot. In case the person flees the interview, or not enough money changes hands. This first meeting is called a tune-up. It's a brief seminar on the concept of prompt payment. Pain is usually inflicted to demonstrate how serious they are about getting paid and to establish an understanding with the client that this sort of thing can escalate into injuries that take a lifetime to recover from.

The ride to Columbia is pleasant and trouble free. Giant shapes of Kudzu-draped trees that look like scary green monsters line the Saw Mill River Parkway. As they get farther north the foliage begins to turn and every now and again there's a tree with bright orange leaves, a warning winter's not far behind.

The car is Conner's. It's a black Saab that's spotless inside and out. He parks in the diner parking lot.

Gillie goes inside.

Two minutes later Austin arrives. He parks not far from Conner and goes inside too.

Conner recognizes him from the description Gillie's given him.

Gillie's in a booth. He nods to Austin as Austin walks in.

Austin slides into the booth.

They order coffee and wait for it to be served. There are no introductions, handshakes or smiles. Austin has never done business with anyone who looks so scary before. He thinks he must've stepped into a fright movie. He thrusts the envelope containing his last two thousand dollars at Gillie and watches as the huge pink face falls as he peaks inside.

"What the fuck is this?" Gillie growls.

"That's it," says Austin.

"What's it?"

"All I've got."

"The fuck it is," says Gillie with a look that would terrify a Marine. "You've got kidneys, don't you? And eyes? See what I'm saying here, Austin? Those items are worth a lot of money these days. We can get a half a million for your heart alone. If you decide to take that direction, and I highly recommend that you do, we'll get our hundred and a quarter, take a small percentage to cover expenses, and the wife and kid will get the change." He holds a hand to heaven like he's a latter day preacher. "I give you my word on it," he says solemnly like giving his word will make all the difference to the pitch. "It's the honorable thing to do, Austin. A nice touch, if you want to think about it that way."

Gillie's purr makes it all sound so enticing. He peeks inside the envelope again and frowns.

"You're a dead man anyway based on this latest contribution. May as well make the best of a bad deal is how I'd be thinking. Go out like a man. We'll even get you something extra for your kidneys to show there's no hard feelings. Eyes too if you like. Your old lady will end up with more than a million after we're done slicing up your ugly carcass. It's not such a bad deal all things considered. Especially since you turned out to be such a skank and all."

Austin blinks not quite believing what he's hearing. It's a horror movie he's stepped into, he's sure of it. He stands up, bends over the table and leans into Gillie's huge pink face.

"It's all I've got," he says angrily, "and all you're gonna get. This has cost me a fortune and I've got nothing left. Tell Crawford not to be so greedy, I'm cleaned out."

Austin sidles out of the booth and marches out of the diner trying to look confident and unconcerned. He heads for the parking lot where a beefy looking man is leaning on his car hefting a Louisville Slugger.

Austin knows where this is going. He pulls out the 'just in case' gun he brought with him just in case, and pops Conner twice in the chest.

Pop.

Pop.

And Conner goes down.

Gillie is still in the diner paying the check. There's no one in the parking lot to see what happened. No one comes rushing out to see what's going on. No one runs into the parking lot from the street to check out the noise. There are no witnesses to what took place.

Austin gets into his car and drives away.

The last thought to enter Conner's brain before the blackness engulfs him is, "This is some fuckin day!"

CHAPTER 2
TUESDAY
THE PARKING LOT

A customer from the diner, a chubby looking single woman of forty-three, bloated and gaseous from an extended three-course lunch, stumbled on Conner Malloy's body as she went to retrieve her car from the parking lot. Her blood-curdling scream brought the customers, waitstaff and kitchen crew tumbling out of every doorway to see what had happened. When they saw Conner lying on the ground a dozen of them reached for their cellphones and called 911. A surreal chorus ensued as they all reported what they saw, answering the same questions in the same way to twelve different dispatchers at the very same time.

Eddie Smith was the first cop to arrive on the scene. He was cruising the downtown area as part of his regular patrol and was just around the corner when the call came in.

The small town of Columbia is nestled in the northern hills of Westchester County not far from the Hudson River. There's a main drag where the stores are and a number of side streets full of old houses converted long ago into apartments and offices. The shops are small; none of your Gaps and Banana Republics here, thank you very much. There's a deli, a diner, a couple of pizza parlors and a bunch of other small businesses. Property values have increased very slowly in this neck of the woods and the trains don't stop here any more. The station was converted into a library a long time ago. The bowling alley and the A&P closed a couple of years back and so did one of the three local colleges. On the plus side, the Higginbottoms recently sold their farm to a developer who is chopping it up into five-acre lots to grow McMansions for the newly rich.

Eddie secured the crime scene, held the gawkers at bay until help arrived, and when it did he worked the crowd to see if anyone saw what happened.

Nobody did.

It was beginning to look like the shooter got lucky. No one saw anything. Heard anything. Or knew anything. The three monkeys would've been proud.

Det. Jimmy Dugan arrived not long after Eddie.

Jimmy is Columbia's only Detective. He's a paunchy fifty-three, five foot nine, with stringy grey hair that needs cutting and combing. There's a twinkle in his green eyes and his chubby shopworn face has a look of intelligence and sensitivity. He wears an Inspector Gadget raincoat that has seen better days and black loafers that could do with a polish. In fact everything about Jimmy could do with a polish, but looks can be deceiving.

Jimmy and Eddie stood next to the body that was sprawled face up on the black asphalt. Its glazed eyes stared up at nothing.

Jimmy looked him over.

"Know him?" he asked Eddie.

Eddie is the same age as Jimmy with a little more hair and a much bigger gut. He's taller too with more of a Rod Steiger, *In The Heat of the Night*, look about him, all messy and paunchy with his police cap perched on the back of his head. Eddie played the line in Brooklyn from eighth grade through high school holding back defenses so Jimmy could run through them and get all those awards. That's how long they've known each other.

They both went into the NYPD, only at different times. Jimmy's star rose quicker than Eddie's. Eddie never got out of the ranks on account of he's not so smart. Not stupid you understand, just not detective material. He joined the Columbia police force three years after Jimmy did not knowing he was there. What are the odds on that? Eddie is still in a uniform and every now and again he helps Jimmy out on an investigation.

There were two bullet holes in the dead man's chest. Leaves had settled on his stomach. Autumn was here and every now and again a gust of wind brought a fresh shower of leaves that landed on the body.

A Louisville Slugger lay by his side.

Eddie said he didn't recognize him.

"I checked the crowd," he said, and looked over at the growing gathering of people. "Diner patrons mostly, and staff, and a couple of people from the street. No one had anything to say. The lady who found him is in the prowler." He looked at his notebook. "Her name's Nancy Drake. She says she was going for her car when she saw him lying on the ground. She was gonna give him a hand till she realized he was dead. According to everyone else she screamed the place down."

Jimmy looked down at the body.

"He looks surprised, doncha think?"

"What does that mean?"

"Like he wasn't expecting it."

Eddie took a quick peek then looked away. Bodies gave him the creeps and the occasional nightmare.

"Most people look surprised when they get popped," he said.

"They do," agreed Jimmy, "but this guy looks even more so. To me he does, anyway. Like it was something he wasn't counting on." He looked around the parking lot. "You think his car's here?" There were fifteen cars in the lot. "Run down the numbers, Eddie and see what we got."

The crime scene crew arrived just then, and the Medical Examiner. And a lot more people. Then the press showed up; a couple of TV crews, and some reporters. And more cops. The place was beginning to look like a three-ring-circus.

The ME headed for the corpse without greeting Jimmy or Eddie, who had moved away from the body.

The ME was a project of Jimmy's.

"What's up Doc?" he said in a Bugs Bunny voice as the ME scurried by.

The ME tensed. You could see his shoulders bunch up somewhere around his ears, but he continued on his way. He was a prissy little man with a narrow point of view and no sense of humor. He was born in Columbia and distrusted anyone who wasn't. He wore an old-fashioned, double-breasted pinstripe suit, and a thin bow tie. His oily gray hair had a razor sharp side part and was cut in a short back and sides and he wore steel-rimmed glasses that made him look remarkably like Harry Truman.

They don't like each other these two going back to when Jimmy first came to Columbia looking for peace and quiet and a new beginning. Instead he got the ME who made him jump through hoops until Jimmy got all Brooklyn on him and told him to go fuck himself. The ME backed off after that, but neither of them forgot what happened back then.

The ME knelt down beside the body, opened his bag of tricks and got to work. Five minutes later he put his tools back in his bag, straightened up and, without making eye contact with anyone said in a high-pitched squawk, "Two bullets in the chest. Death was instantaneous. No more than an hour ago. The slugs are still in him. You'll have to wait for the autopsy to find out what kind of gun was used."

Like they didn't know that already.

Then he was gone. Making his way to his car. Pushing through the crowd using his bag as a battering ram.

The crime scene crew, two men and a woman sent from the County office, were dressed in white coveralls and blue booties. They spread out around the body and began to shoot pictures, take measurements and samples, and look for clues.

Jimmy said to the woman, "Do you see a wallet?"

She said they were about to turn him over. When they did, she gingerly fished out a grungy looking brown leather wallet from the back pocket of the man's jeans.

They all crowded in to see.

Eddie had his notebook ready.

There was a driver's license. The photograph matched the body. Conner Malloy from Windsor Terrace. Brooklyn, N.Y.

Eddie said he thought that Windsor Terrace was somewhere out by the Greenwood Cemetery.

Only Jimmy knew what he was talking about, everyone else thought that Brooklyn was a foreign country. Greenwood Cemetery might as well have been on the moon.

There were five crisp hundred-dollar bills in the wallet and a bunch of singles, a lottery ticket and some business cards from various people.

Jimmy took out his cellphone and called Det. Morgan Flynn, his buddy at the 23rd precinct in the great City of New York.

Morgan picked up on the first ring.

"What?" he said. Not one for niceties.

They'd worked a couple of cases together over the years and they both had a taste for Jewish deli. It was nice to have things in common besides the job. They spoke once in a while when they needed help.

Like now for instance.

With Conner Malloy from Brooklyn lying dead from gunshot wounds in a parking lot in the middle of Columbia.

Jimmy gave Morgan Conner's details and the little they knew about him, which was nothing.

"See if someone's heard of him, Morg. I think he might be dirty."

"Now why would you say a thing like that?" said Morgan sarcastically. "Doesn't everyone from Brooklyn hang around a parking lot in East Bumblefuck with two bullet holes in his chest and a baseball bat by his side?" and hung up.

No one from County was there. That was not how it's supposed to work in Westchester. If there's a dead body in a small district like Columbia the County detectives show up like flies on bad fruit and take over the case. It was standard procedure because small police departments like Jimmy's don't have the resources to conduct an effective investigation of a major crime. Murder is considered a major crime. That's what the Westchester Criminal Investigation Department was set up for.

The CID.

And they hadn't arrived yet.

The Chief of the Columbia Police Department made his entrance looking like someone from central casting. He was square-jawed and rugged with steely grey hair, an immaculate uniform, and shoes so highly polished they looked like they were new, but were not. The Chief looked like he was ready for his close-up. The Chief always looked like he was ready for his close-up. He strode purposefully towards Jimmy and Eddie, who looked shabby by comparison. They always looked shabby by comparison, today being no different than any other.

"I just heard from County," the Chief boomed in a baritone rumble he'd perfected for microphones, sound bites, and re-election campaigns. "They want you to take the case."

Jimmy was surprised. This had never happened before.

"They've got too much going on is what the big guy told me. Too busy chasing scofflaws if you ask me," said the Chief and raised his eyebrows in a Groucho kind of way. "Anyway, it's a big compliment, don't you think?"

Jimmy did. He'd had trouble with a couple of CID detectives in the past. Smith and Monahan. Also known as Laurel and Hardy because they were a big guy and a little guy and just as dumb. They were two bullies who thought they knew everything but didn't, and had an act that was something out of an old-time movie. Jimmy solved three cases from under their noses and made them look bad in the eyes of their bosses, earning him their eternal enmity and, or so he thought, the rest of the Westchester CID. So yes. This was a very big compliment.

The Chief thought the media would eat it up. It was a story within a story, and he couldn't wait to announce it to a press that was eager for any sort of insight. He'd frame it in such a way as to garner most of the credit for himself. How, because of him, County decided to let bygones be bygones and use the man best suited for the job: Det. Jimmy Dugan. A man he's worked with for more years than he cares to remember. Rooting out crime and protecting Columbia's citizens. Standing up for what's right. Arm in arm. Shoulder to shoulder. Jimmy and the Chief, the stuff of movies ladies and gentlemen. Cue the music, bring on the choir and please pass the tissues. He strode purposefully towards Jimmy and Eddie.

It's what the Chief did whenever the press were involved. Pumped himself up as big as he could, employing a style and rhetoric only a bad actor would have the nerve to use. Ah yes, re-election is just around the corner my friends and it's stuff like this that's kept him in office for years.

"Anything you want is yours the big guy said to tell you," said the Chief, eying Eddie's shirt that was struggling to get out of his pants. "You can have Eddie for as long as you want," he sniffed. "County says it's picking up the overtime."

"Huh," said Jimmy.

Eddie smiled.

CHAPTER 3

GILLIE FADER

Gillie Fader watched Austin march out of the diner seemingly unafraid, his head held high, his chest thrust out and his stomach abnormally sucked in. Trying to look like a guy who was in control of a situation he was not, with right on his side because he was tapped out, or so he says, and he's got nothing to lose, or so he thinks.

"Self-righteous bastard," Gillie muttered to himself.

It was guys like Austin that got up Gillie's nose. Guys that had everything and when they couldn't pay up they thought they were entitled to a break because that's what had happened to them before. There was always someone there to bail them out. Gillie'd never had that kind of luck, spending most of his life out on one limb or another with no one to catch him if he fell. He was thinking how much he was going to enjoy taking Austin down a peg or two. That's why Conner was waiting for him in the parking lot. That's how they did it with guys like Austin. Guys who thought they were in control of the situation and marched out of a meeting like their shit didn't smell.

Conner blocks his escape.

Gillie comes from behind.

Then they muscle him into the car, drive him someplace quiet and show him the error of his ways. They'll give him choices he never thought possible.

"What do you want broken?" they'll ask him like they were negotiating a business deal. "We've got to break something," Gillie will explain to him in his syrupy purr. "That's how it goes in situations like these."

Then Austin will have to decide what he can afford to lose the use of for a while. An arm? A leg? Something. No free ride this time, no sir, and no one around to bail him out. This is the big time we're talking about here where you

13

have to pay the piper one way or another. And isn't that what life's all about if you really want to think about it?

Gillie finished his coffee, threw a ten on the counter and headed for the door. That was when he heard it. That's when they all heard it. A blood-curdling shriek and a scream that seemed to go on forever.

Everyone tumbled out of the diner to see what was going on, pushing past Gillie who hung back. Sensing trouble. Positioning himself for a quick exit. He peered over the crowd and saw Conner lying on the ground with his dead eyes looking skyward.

Austin wasn't there.

Gillie walked away from the diner, up the street, and headed for a super-market they passed on the way in. He needed a car. A supermarket parking lot was the best place to get one. He could've taken a cab to the station in the next town over, but that would have meant people would see him. Stealing a car, he thought, was the lesser of the two evils. Though to think no one would notice a six foot five, three hundred and fifty pound man was a lot like saying you wouldn't notice someone walking down the street in a gorilla suit.

People leave their cars unlocked all the time. It's a modern day phenomena. Gillie thought it was because they lived in the suburbs and they thought they were safe. Sometimes they even left the keys in them. Go figure.

There were no keys this time, but the third car he tried, a shiny black Lexus, was unlocked. It amazed him how little regard people had for their stuff, espe-cially a fifty thousand dollar riding machine like this one. People were lazy he supposed and thank goodness for that, or he'd have to walk home.

Getting the car started wasn't a problem. He'd been boosting cars all his life. It took a second to cross the wires and then it was a sweet ride home, but a rotten substitute, Gillie thought gloomily, for a piss poor day. Conner was dead. Money was owed. And by who? That rat-faced deadbeat Austin, that's who. He couldn't believe the guy had the balls to pull something off like this. He took out his cell-phone and called Crawford to tell him the "good news."

Crawford Taylor was good with numbers; he was gifted that way, but he was always working on it. Gifts and talent were no substitute for hard work and prac-tice. He honed his skills playing poker, which was how he spent his time in col-lege, cruising through by getting people who owed him money to do his papers for him. Halfway through his senior year his parents were killed in a car crash. He was the only child of only children and there were no uncles, aunts, or cous-ins and the grandparents were long gone. He found himself alone in the world, but his father and mother left him plenty of money to compensate. A house in Bronxville; a million dollar life insurance policy on each parent; a half a million dollar stock portfolio, and his father's IRA that was worth another million. He sold the house as soon as the will was out of probate and sat on the money for a while. That's how lucky he was. He sold the house at the peak of the market and looked like a genius. When prices bottomed out he bought a magnificent penthouse on Central Park West for a song.

Timing's everything.

By then he was twenty-five and worth four million dollars, but that didn't generate enough income to support the lifestyle he acquired. You'd think four million would be enough for anyone, but these were the days of drugs, sex, and rock and roll and Crawford indulged himself in all three vices in a never-ending cycle of parties, nightclubs and beautiful women. The concept of work and weekends eluded him. One day led to another in a constant supply of twenty-four hour periods with names that had no significance for him.

Eventually it became clear he was spending more than was coming in and he'd have to do something about it, so he hooked up with a couple of college buddies and set up some card games. They were small affairs at first, but very quickly, as word got around, they became bigger and more ambitious.

It was at these games that Crawford began to loan out money.

When the pots got bigger people bet over their heads, and when that happened he was there to help them out. After all, what are friends for? They were short-term loans at short-term prices. A thousand for a week was eleven hundred. Done and done again. Some loans were bigger, ten grand for eleven payable in a month. The money came in and went out as regular as clockwork and turned out to be a nice living, along with his card winnings. More than enough to cover his coke and booze and all the extras he liked to indulge himself in.

Pretty soon the boys expanded to two games a week and still the money poured in, but then came a downturn in the economy and someone decided they weren't going pay him. This was a muscular looking ex-jock who thought he had no need to fear the puny Crawford Taylor. He was the first person ever to hold out on him, politely at first, but the longer it went the more confident he got, deriding Crawford at the table and finally refusing to pay him altogether. Word got around. A few more of Crawford's customers decided to hold out on him and see what happened.

One of Crawford's partners had deep roots in the Brooklyn underworld. Gillie Fader was the name his partner came up with to take care of Crawford's problem.

The jock paid up as soon as he got out of the emergency room.

Everyone else paid up without the need of medical attention.

Eventually Crawford gave up the card games and went into loansharking full time. And once in a while he'd call on Gillie's expertise to help him out with someone who didn't think the rules applied to them.

When Gille told Crawford what happened to Conner he was furious. He liked Conner. He'd only met him once, early on, when Gillie wanted Crawford to approve him. He said it was only right, what with Crawford being the client and all. Crawford thought it was very respectful the way Gillie did it and made it him feel like he was some sort of Don. Gillie making it clear that if Crawford didn't like Connor he'd get someone else. But Crawford did like him. He was impressed by Conner's obvious loyalty to Gillie. He could never pull that off, the loyalty thing. Money was the leverage he had on people and he didn't give a damn whether they liked him or not.

And now look what had happened.

Austin going Billy the Kid on them, drawing down on Conner and shooting his way out of a beating. Now what the fuck was that all about?

"No one saw you?" Crawford asked Gillie.

"I don't think so," said Gillie.

"No one knows you were with Conner?"

"I don't see why they should. I never told anyone where I was going or what I was doing, I never do. And Conner was in the parking lot. I was in the diner."

"What about when you got out the car?"

"There was no one around. I checked."

"Then you left."

"Then I left."

Crawford thought it made sense. The worst-case scenario was they could trace Conner to Gillie, and then to him, but it didn't look that way. No one saw them together, so how could anyone make the connection? Gillie had used good sense getting out of Columbia quickly and with any luck that would be the end of it. He'd keep an eye on it, but he felt safe. That was all he really cared about any way. Sorry about Conner and all that, but can anything lead back to me? That was his only concern.

"You've got the two grand Austin gave you?"

Gillie said he did.

"And you're short the five you paid Conner?"

"And Conner," said Gillie.

"And Conner," said Crawford. "So what do you want to do about Austin?"

"Kill the fucker," said Gillie without hesitation.

"And forget about the money?"

"I'm not out a lot," said Gillie.

"I am," said Crawford angrily. "A hundred and twenty five grand to be exact. More now with the clock ticking."

"So what do you want to do about him?" said Gillie.

"He's got a wife and a kid up there, so he can't just up and leave. And he's got an important job in the City; controller, treasurer, something like that. He's got a scam he did well with for a while. Then he got caught short. That's how he got to me. I'm thinking of giving him a little time to run it again. Maybe it'll work this time. Then we'll get our money back and some more besides. Then you can kill him."

Gillie liked it.

"What's the scam?"

"He kites checks."

"Boy," said Gillie. "I haven't heard term that in a while."

"You know what it is?"

Gillie did. Writing a check with no money in the account to cover it.

"What does he do?"

"He tells his boss he needs money to cover a check he's got to write for a real estate investment. He says his partners' checks have been deposited in his bank account, but they won't clear for a couple of days. He gives the boss a post-dated personal check, then he writes a company check for the same amount, gets it certified, and deposits it in his account as cash. Then he buys hundreds of thousands of out-of-the-money calls that are about to expire and cost next to nothing."

"Out-of-the-money calls?"

The stock market was the only thing that baffled Gillie. Everything else he had a handle on.

Crawford explained.

"A call is an agreement that gives an investor the right, but not the obligation, to buy a stock, bond, commodity, or other instrument at a specified price within a specific time period. Calls are traded on the options market. If the underlying, in this case stock, goes up the value of the call goes up too. If the stock goes down, the call goes down and becomes what they call, "out-of-the- money." If they're out-of-the-money and close to their expiration date they go for a song. Austin buys them, holds them till they go up, and sells them for a profit."

"And his boss believes him about the check being for a real estate investment?"

"He does. Austin says the property is in foreclosure. He says he's got a guy at the bank who tells him when the house is going on the block and he's got to have a certified check when he goes to the auction in the event he gets it. The boss always gets his money back, so there's never been a reason to say no or not believe him."

"And Austin never buys property, only out-of-the-money calls?"

"Correct."

"How does he know they're gonna go up?"

"He's good with the charts and trend lines and all of that stuff. He says he's made a fortune over the years and I believe him. Of course a market that went straight up didn't hurt any. You could've used a dart and still made money."

"So what went wrong?"

"The market took a hit is what went wrong and Austin's hundreds of thousands of worthless options turned out to be just that. Worthless. He couldn't cover the check he wrote and he's got nothing put by for mistakes and bad decisions. If his boss found out the check was worthless, he could go to jail. Kiting is a felony in this great country of ours, so I loaned him the money to cover it."

"How did he get to you?"

"There's a golf club I like up there. The clubhouse is on top of a hill with a bar that looks out on this incredible view. Austin's a boozer. I'm at the bar. Austin's crying in his soup. One thing leads to another, need I say more?"

He did not.

"So we wait?" asked Gillie.

"I think so," said Crawford. "Too many people are watching right now. I'll call Austin and see if I can calm him down and we'll take it from there. "

By the time Gillie finished talking to Crawford he was almost in the City and was faced with a conflict of sorts. He could drive the car to a chop shop he knew on Queens Boulevard and pick up a couple of grand, but when the guy got busted, and they always got busted, he'd rat him out in a New York minute. People will do anything to save some time in the can and who can blame them?

Or he could ditch it, and then it would be someone else's problem.

He went for option number two and, after wiping the car down, left it unlocked on 97th St. between Second Avenue and Third and walked the rest of the way home. Steaming over the loss of Conner and thinking about what he was only going to do to Austin when the time came.

CHAPTER 4
THE PARKING LOT

A breeze had picked up. Flurries of leaves swept across the parking lot sounding like an army of tiny tap dancers. Jimmy crunched through them as he walked over to Eddie's cruiser to talk to Nancy Drake, the witness who discovered Conner Malloy's body.

Nancy Drake had pulled herself together after her screaming fit and was now looking like she was having a good time. It was not every day she was the center of attention. She was thinking how this would keep her in stories for weeks to come. A reporter tapped on the window only to be shooed away by the policeman standing by the car. The implications of her newfound fame were only just beginning to dawn on her. When you're single, plump, in your forties and not much is going on in your life, things can get pretty boring. Her social life was non-existent and the few friends she had were centered on the church. She was already planning what she was going to tell them on Sunday and how she'd gussie it up a little to make it sound more dramatic. People were sure to want to know what happened. Weren't they?

"How're you doing?" said Jimmy as he slid in next to her on the back seat of the cruiser.

He left the door open so they could see and be seen; you can't be too careful these days. A friend of his was recently accused of touching a witness inappropriately in the back seat of a cruiser while he was conducting an interview. Jimmy couldn't believe it was true. He'd known the man for years and it didn't seem possible. He also didn't want the same thing happening to him.

He handed her his card.

Nancy Drake scrutinized it suspiciously then put it in her purse, a small black thing that seemed to emphasize how large she was.

"I'm fine," she said primly, shoving a strand of hair behind a surprisingly delicate ear. The skin on her face was stretched out, as was everything else about her. She wore bulky clothes she must've thought disguised her figure, but you'd have to be blind not to see she was fat.

Jimmy took out a pen and notebook from his inside pocket.

"Can you tell me what you saw?"

He gave her a reassuring smile.

She fussed with the strand of hair again. It was something she did when she was nervous.

"Well," she said in the type of phone husk men fall in love with without any idea what the person looks like. "I finished lunch and was going back to work. I'm a receptionist for an architect," she explained and gave him the address and the phone number. "When I got to the driveway I saw him lying on the ground. I went over to help him and then I realized he was dead. Then I screamed." Her face went dark as she relived the moment. She looked like she was going to start screaming again.

Before she could start up Jimmy asked her, "And you knew he was dead because...?"

"His eyes were open and sightless. They had that glazed look about them and there was no blinking. He just stared up at nothing. It was all soooo creepy. Then I noticed the holes in his chest. Oh my God," a chubby hand went to a chubbier cheek. "I never saw anything like that before in my whole life."

"Did he say anything?"

Her eyes went wide.

"Lord no. He was dead, I just told you that. How could he talk to me if he was dead?" She said it like it was the dumbest thing she ever heard. Her lower body gave an indignant shuffle like a duck ruffling its feathers.

"Did you see anyone in the area, Mrs. Drake?"

"It's Miss," she said primly and checked on the strand of hair again.

Jimmy said he was sorry. He could see why this delicate flower wasn't married by now or was ever likely to be. Not for nothing was he a detective.

"Did you see anyone in the parking lot, Miss Drake?" he asked. Trying hard to hang on to his attitude.

"I didn't see a soul."

"A car coming out of the driveway?"

"No."

"Someone getting in a car?"

"No."

"Someone sitting in a car?"

She shook her head, which made her many chins wobble.

"Maybe a car idling?"

Another jiggling of chins.

"Did you hear a noise that could have sounded like a gunshot?"

"No."

"A car backfiring?"

"No."

Jimmy scratched his head and stared at his notebook.

"Anything else you think might help me here?"

She couldn't.

"I just started screaming when I realized he was dead," she said as if that explained everything.

Jimmy thanked her and said if there was anything else she could think of he'd appreciate a call.

"I'll have someone drive you home."

"To my office," she said imperiously.

"To your office," he echoed.

As she was maneuvering out of the back seat Jimmy asked her, as an afterthought, "Did you see anything unusual take place inside the diner?"

That stopped her. She fell back into the seat, which made the springs squeak and the car shake.

"As a matter of fact I did," she said.

Jimmy waited.

"There was an altercation at one of the booths. One man stood up while the other one stayed sitting. The man standing leaned into the other one and said something I did not hear, but you could tell that he wasn't very happy, then he marched out of the diner."

"Who wasn't happy?" Jimmy asked her, to be clear.

"The man standing up," she said irritably.

Jimmy thought he and Miss Drake were not destined for a lasting relationship.

"Just the two of them at the table?"

"Yes."

"When was this?"

"Just before I paid my bill."

"How long between the man who left and you leaving?"

"Two or three minutes. Not much more."

Jimmy wrote it all down.

"What did the man left sitting do?"

She thought about it.

Then, "He watched the man leaving with a look of disgust on his face."

"Could you describe the two men?"

She could. She gave him a detailed description of a huge man with a shiny pink head and a vague one of the other guy. She told Jimmy she was fixated on the large gentleman, which is why she could describe him so clearly.

"He was enormous," she said in a tone laced with a certain amount of respect. She had an affinity for people who looked like herself. Big people. She also said she'd managed to catch a whiff of his cologne.

"Do you know what it was?"

She did.

"Givenchy."

He was thinking Old Spice or something like that. This was a new one.

"How do you know?" he asked.

"My boss wears it all the time, he must take a bath in it." Her pug-like nose wrinkled up in disapproval. "The office reeks of the stuff."

"Huh," said Jimmy, fascinated by her chins that wobbled every time her head shook. He wondered if she could feel them moving?

He was finished with her after that. He arranged for someone to drive her wherever she wanted to go and went to find Eddie to see what he'd come up with.

CHAPTER 5

JIMMY DUGAN

Jimmy Dugan is from Brooklyn. He was born there, grew up there, and was a cop there. A good one too. He was hot back then. In Brooklyn. Where he was a Detective. Williamsburg Division. Jimmy Dugan. Thirty-five. Five-foot nine, all muscle and moxie. Hotter than a pistol. Walking through the building with that swagger of his. Wetting a finger and touching his ass. SSSSS, that's how hot he was. With the slicked back hair, and sharp looking suits, and his fancy ties. He had a big thing for ties.

They put him in an elite squad, courtesy of the captain.

"Part of your education, kid" he told him. "One day you'll be running the place."

That's how hot he was.

It's a steamy afternoon in August. The sun's beating down. There's been no rain for days. Everything is dry. And dusty. And hot. Jimmy is out with his partner named Curtis.

"Don't be calling me no Curt," he told Jimmy their first day out together. "IT'S CURTIS."

Curtis is a large black man elegantly turned out with a knife-edge crease in the trousers of his dark mohair suit and a highly polished shine on his Bally shoes. Jimmy looks good too. He always looks good. Wearing all black today. Black slacks, black open-necked shirt, black sport coat and black slip-ons. They all look like that, the other members of the unit. Sharp. Hot. Gelled. And hungry.

The lieutenant looks even sharper.

The squad is an anti-crime unit targeting areas that might lead them to bigger fish. This time it's the fences. Jimmy and Curtis were sent to interview one working out of a pawnshop on Broadway underneath the El in Williamsburg. It's what they call a go-see. A roust. To let the guy know they're there and to push him just a little. The whole unit in their fancy-looking clothes and heavily styled hair are out doing the same thing.

Shaking the fences to see what falls out.

The place is a grimy storefront next to a laundromat on a block crammed with people of every persuasion. Chassids and Puerto Ricans. Mexicans and Russians. Chinese and Slavs. Black and white. Straight and gay. Salt and pepper and everything in between. The melting pot in all of its glory. Rushing this way and that like rats in a lab experiment. The three-ball pawnbroker sign hung outside the store. The window is crammed with musical instruments, some hanging from the ceiling, some piled on cases. All of them are dusty and cobwebbed. Tarnished trumpets and dull trombones lie in a pile on the floor. Guitars are tumbled one on top of the other in a rudimentary display. A banjo, the only clean instrument in the window, has a special place close to the glass.

Inside is the same. Boxes piled high in every direction. Instruments wherever you look.

At the back of the store is a counter with a grill. Behind that, sitting on a stool wearing a dealer's green visor and a jeweler's glass in one eye, is the man they've come to see. Murray Fisher. Caucasian. 45, looks older. Five feet seven, looks shorter. 160 pounds, looks fatter. Gray hair. Balding. Brown eyes. Pasty white. Murray Fisher. Owner. And fence.

Murray the Fence, seeing the obvious cops come storming into his place of business, decides to do the only thing his addled brain can come up with on such short notice. He draws the gun he's got ready for the robber he's sure will one day hold him up. It's registered and legal this gun, and has never been fired. Until now, that is. Because Murray the Fence takes aim at the cop in the front. The thin one. The white one. The one not in a suit who's beginning to make a move of his own.

Jimmy's the man in front. The one Murray the Fence is taking aim at. Jimmy Dugan. Our Jimmy. Out there in front. Just ahead of Curtis, not Curt. Screaming at the top of his lungs, "Gun. Gun," and drawing his own weapon as he leaps horizontally. Falling. Falling. Onto a pile of boxes. Squeezing off a shot as he falls.

At the same time Murray the Fence pulls his own trigger, but Jimmy's not there. He's lying in a pile of boxes. The pawnbroker's bullet goes between Jimmy and Curtis not Curt, bounces off a tuba and settles in a squeezebox that makes a plinking-plonking sound.

The shot Jimmy gets off slams into the fence's shoulder and puts him out of action.

It was a close call. The closest Jimmy's ever had.

Back at the station house he's debriefed, shrunk, and offered some counseling. Then they send him home telling him to take tomorrow off and take more time off if he thinks it's necessary.

He drives home listening to the Dave Mathews band at full blast, adrenalin pumping through his brain and wild thoughts charging through his mind. Images flash on and off of the pawnbroker and that filthy store. Murray the Fence. Whoever heard of a guy called Murray the Fence drawing down on him like he was Gary fucking Cooper?

On top of the rush and the trembling in his belly, he's horny. He can hardly believe it. He could've been shot or maimed and there he is with a big old hard-on. He laughed out loud and his mind went to Vicki. His Vicki. Beautiful Vicki. Home from work early these days. Maybe there now? Waiting to comfort him and hold him in her arms.

His brain is speeding like a meteor. His dick is as hard as a rock.

They rent a walkup in Park Slope where the streets are quiet and the neighbors are decent. Jimmy and Vicki. In their two-bedroom apartment with the drop living room and the big bay window. The two of them make out pretty good. She's a teacher. He does okay as a cop. High school sweethearts married ten years now. No kids, though. She wants them, he doesn't. He doesn't tell her this. He says he wants them too, just not now. But he doesn't want them. Ever.

He finds a spot at the top of the street, parks and hotfoots it to their building. Bounds up the stairs. Opens the door and bursts into the apartment with an expectant look on his face and a big erection in his pants.

And there she is, Vicki his high school sweetheart. The love of his life. Married ten years now. In their bedroom. On their bed. Naked as a babe, in the arms of his best friend. Who's not heard his entrance. And continues to pump himself wildly into Jimmy's horror stricken wife.

He fell apart after that with the booze and the screw-ups and the gradual letting go of everything he worked so hard to achieve. Until he hit rock bottom. And then, because of a captain who had a soft spot for him, he picked himself up and turned things around. He dried himself out, got some counseling, and when he'd pulled himself together looked for somewhere new to start over again.

Columbia fit the bill.

Jimmy's still Columbia's only Detective. He's looking dumpy and round these days and thin of hair, but he's clean and sober. Traveling through life now with Mary Harwood, his lady friend, and Lucy her twelve-year old daughter, and enjoying a way of living he never thought possible.

CHAPTER 6
AUSTIN

Austin stared at the mountain of a man sitting across from him in the diner, with his massive pink head and his mean looking eyes. What was he going to do, Austin wondered?

Gillie Fader peered into the envelope then back at him with a look of disgust and told Austin he didn't think he was going to survive very long based on this latest contribution. Then he proceeded to give him a friendly lecture on the value of his body parts. How it was the right thing to do, to let him sell them off to square his debt and set up his family in a responsible manner for when he was no longer with them.

Right.

That's all he wanted was to have his organs harvested so his shopaholic wife and idiot son could live high on the hog when he was dead and buried.

Fuck that.

And fuck them.

Austin stood up abruptly, leaned over the table, looked into Gillie's large pink face, and gave him the first words of the speech he'd been working on all week. Ten seconds into his presentation he realized he was talking to a brick wall. There was no point in going on, so he slid out of the booth and left the diner, doing his best to look casual and unconcerned. It was his John Wayne moment. The bravest thing he'd ever done. His head up high, his stomach sucked in, and a walk that projected confidence and control.

Or so he thought.

When he got to the parking lot there was a tough looking goon leaning on his car with a baseball bat in his hand and a look on his face that said this was the part of it he really enjoyed. Austin figured one swing of that bat and it would all be over. He was still in his John Wayne mode, adrenaline speeding through his body and his heart racing a mile a minute.

Out came the 'just in case' gun he brought just in case and shot the man down. What else was he going to do? What would you have done? Then he got into his car, drove out of the parking lot onto Main Street, and headed home to wait for the police who, he was sure, were on their way to arrest him. Someone must have seen what he did? Or got his plate number? Or heard the shot? Or saw him throw the gun in the woods on his way home? But they never came, the police. And no one saw him do any of those things. Not in the parking lot, or in the driveway, or out on Main Street. No one heard anything either. Not the shot fired, or his car starting up. And for those few moments when the crime took place and the time after, Austin might just as well have been invisible.

After a while, when it was clear that no one was coming to arrest him, he calmed down, poured himself a drink and stretched out on the couch. He took a big gulp and was beginning to think he might have gotten away with murder when the phone rang.

"Austin?"

Austin knew that voice. He waited. And listened.

Crawford Taylor waited too. Feeling his way.

Then he said, "Austin?" Softer this time.

"That guy was gonna beat the shit outta me," Austin shouted down the phone. "What did you expect me to do?"

"You could've shot him in the leg," suggested Crawford. "Why'd you have to kill him?"

Austin never thought of that.

"I guess I panicked," he offered. "You ever have someone come at you with a baseball bat? A Louisville Slugger no less."

Crawford said he hadn't, but he said he could see his point. Then he cranked out a song and dance routine that was both sympathetic and pleasing to Austin's freaked out ears, ending up with, "So, what do you want to do about it, Austin?" in a soft purr like they were talking about getting from point A to point B, and certainly not Austin having just shot and killed someone.

Austin was defiant.

"I've got no more money," he said angrily. "You've sucked me dry you greedy bastard."

"That's what Gillie told me you said," said Crawford calmly. Not rising to the bait. Imagining what Gillie would only do to him when he set him loose. "I'm not sure you were seeing things properly when you told him that," Crawford suggested.

"Is this another one of your pitches to sell off my body parts, because if it is you can shove it up your ass along with that fucking baseball bat."

Crawford made some more sympathetic clucking sounds to let Austin know he was still on his side and had nothing but sympathy for the situation he'd found himself in. But murder was murder, he told him, and to look the other way on something as serious as that would require a great deal of money.

"When was the last time you pulled off that scam of yours?" Crawford asked him gently.

Austin made him wait for an answer, not because he didn't know it, but because he could feel the conversation beginning to shift in his favor and he wanted to savor the moment.

He could see the way clearly now. He'd known it all along, really. Long before he shot the guy in the parking lot and certainly now, listening to Crawford's reasonable tone about going to the well again. It's what money can do for you. Make problems like this go away. That's what Crawford was telling him here. That if he made the right bets, and he thought he could this time because it was one of those moments when the indicators were kicking in and there were 'buy' signals galore, he could get Crawford off his back and even end up with a little something for himself when it was all over.

"What's it gonna take to make this go away?" Austin finally said. Not angry any more. Calm, cool, and collected now. Confident he was a master of the universe once more and in control of the situation. Invincible. And able to leap tall buildings in a single bound.

"This guy you shot," said Crawford like he was suddenly Mother Theresa. "He's got a family, you know. A wife and kids. A mortgage too is what Gillie's been telling me. What do you think something like that's worth in the scheme of things, Austin? Depriving those poor children of a father, and a wife of her husband and the food he put on the table? What sort of compensation package are those folks entitled to because of these unforeseen and terrible circumstances?"

Austin grinned a wolfish grin. His nose was actually twitching. He could smell a win on the way and he was trying hard to control his excitement.

"A quarter of a million to the family," he said. Sure he could pull it off now. All of it. Three hours had gone by since he popped that guy in the parking lot and there were still no cops banging down the door. The news shows were saying they had no suspects and they kept cutting to the scene of the crime and their reporters for updates.

How creepy was that?

Seeing the crime scene over and over again was like some bizarre version of Groundhog Day. Every time they cut to the parking lot he could see what happened a little more clearly. And the more he thought about it, the more he realized there was no one in the parking lot except for the goon and himself. No one was there when he shot that guy. And no one saw what he'd done.

"Plus what you owe me," said Crawford grinning his own wolfish grin now. "And the vig, and my outside contractor's fee. Say a half a mil all told," which was going to be mostly profit since Conner Malloy had no family that he was aware of let alone any mortgage payments to make, and Gillie's cut would barely make a dent.

"Done," said Austin without hesitation. "But I'm going to need a little time to pull things together."

"Absolutely," said Crawford graciously. "Take all the time you need." There was a pause, then, "Let me ask you something, Austin."

"Yes?"

"Why didn't you do this in the first place?"

"Run the scam?"

"Run the scam."

Austin couldn't come up with an answer that would satisfy Crawford, but it was all about timing. And right now the timing was just about perfect.

CHAPTER 7
THE PARKING LOT

The lights came on in the parking lot. It was still light and the bulbs seemed dim. Jimmy wondered how they were going to illuminate the place when it got dark, which was happening quickly, but the darker it got the brighter the lights got, so that answered that question.

The parking lot was a kaleidoscope of uniforms, cameras, microphones, equipment and legal pads, in constant motion. Two sites were taped off, Conner's body, and a large area around his black Saab. Additional lights were being set up. Red and black wires snaked from floods to generators. Two technicians from the morgue were smoking cigarettes in the front of their black van parked in the driveway, bemoaning their fate. They'd been denied permission to remove the body. It looked like it was going to be a long night. There was still a large crowd held back by barriers set up by the traffic people. Cops were everywhere. And more press. And not ten minutes ago a convoy of Troopers augmented the gathering with their lights on and their sirens blaring to make sure everyone was aware of their arrival.

Eddie found Conner's car through Conner's drivers license and a quick call to the DMV. He had the techs go over it before he and Jimmy took a look inside. The interior was spotless. Not a fleck of dust or dirt. The techs said it looked like there'd been a passenger. They found fresh prints on the passenger side and marks on the side window where the person rested their head. There was also an indent on the passenger seat where, judging by the size of the impression, it looked like someone big and heavy sat. Probably male, they said. Women generally leave something of themselves. A fragrance. A tissue. And they'd found nothing of that sort. They were running the prints and sent scrapings from the smudges on the passenger window for DNA testing. The results would take a while, was what they were told. That's how backed up they were. There was nothing in the glove compartment or the side pockets that could help. And there was no registration or insurance. All this Eddie reported to Jimmy as they stood by Conner's black Saab in the semi dark.

"And no clue to lead us to the perpetrator of this terrible crime," Jimmy asked?

"'Fraid not," said Eddie.

"And the car's not stolen?"

"It's Conner's."

"What's the deal with no paperwork?" Jimmy wondered.

"A precaution against trouble?"

"If they got stopped for a traffic violation there'd be trouble. If they ditched it we'd find him through the vin number and you were able to find the car through his license. I don't get it."

"Everyone's got a procedure," said Eddie sagely. "You go on a job you go as clean as possible."

"So how come the wallet?"

Eddie had no answer for that, so he moved on.

"What did Mrs. Drake say?"

"It's Miss," said Jimmy in the same tone she'd used on him.

"No need to get snippy."

"That's how she said it to me. 'It's Miss.' All prim and proper."

"What did you say?"

"I repeated the question."

"With an attitude?"

"What's the point?"

"And a smile?"

"I think the smile had gone by then."

"What did she say?"

Jimmy turned his collar up to ward off a breeze. The sun had gone down behind the tree line. It was getting cold.

"She said she saw the body and screamed. End of story."

Eddie was about to ask more questions.

Jimmy cut him off. He knew where Eddie was going. They were the same questions Eddie always asked at the start of an investigation. Jimmy had been waiting for them.

"She didn't hear anything. See anything. Or know anything," said Jimmy. Grinning. "I asked her all that and a lot more besides."

Sometimes Eddie forgot who the detective was.

Like now, for instance.

Eddie would be shooting off questions like a machine gun if Jimmy hadn't stopped him. Eddie implying, though he didn't mean to, that Jimmy hadn't thought of asking these questions himself. Eddie's face got serious at times like these, then out poured the questions. The face was the tip-off and Jimmy waited for it with great anticipation. Then, after the first rush, Eddie would realize he was out of his depth and go back to being a uniform.

Jimmy thought it was funny, especially because it happened as regular as clockwork.

"She said the big guy was wearing Givenchy cologne."

Eddie said he never heard of it.

"Me either. I bet you can get it in the City. Have someone make some calls, Eddie. See if they can find out who carries the stuff. Then we'll figure out what to do next. That's it from the techs?"

"They said they're gonna be a while. They might have something for us later. If not you'll get their preliminary report first thing in the morning."

Jimmy told Eddie what Miss Drake said went on in the diner. How she saw two guys fighting and how he thought it might have something to do with what happened.

"Let's see if anyone else saw what she saw."

Eddie hitched up his trousers, tucked in his shirt, and followed Jimmy up the stairs and into the restaurant.

CHAPTER 8
AUSTIN

When his wife got home Austin was lying on the couch out cold, reeking of liquor. 'Shirley from Great Neck' was back from shopping. Her favorite pass-time. She was good at it too. And there was always that look on his face to look forward to when he saw how much money she'd spent. But here now was Austin, lying drunk on the couch. Or stoned. Was he stoned? It was so hard to tell these days. Either way he was out of it. And where was their son, she wondered? At a friend's house, she hoped, and not witness to this little episode.

She called out, but there was no reply.

Austin stirred on the couch.

"He's out," he slurred.

She gave him a withering stare.

"You think this is the way to behave with a teenager in the house?"

Their son was sixteen. He spent most of his time at a friend's place. At least that's what he told them.

"I told you, he's out," said Austin thickly. "Anyway the sun's over the yardarm somewhere, isn't that what they say?"

She looked at him like he was crazy.

"Who says?"

"The Brits. They're always saying something like that. The sun's over the yardarm so pour me some gin, what, what."

Austin reached for his drink and gulped it down.

She was appalled.

"What if he sees you like this?"

"He's out," he snapped. "How many times do I have to tell you?"

She looked at him with disgust and loathing because this pig of a man she wanted to annoy with her extravagant purchases had managed to turn the tables and spoil her fun.

"Anyway," he humphed, "it wouldn't be the first time."

"Or the last," she muttered.

"What's that?"

She decided not to fight. He was too far-gone to make any headway. She'd take another run at him when he sobered up. She took the decanter and the ashtray with the roaches and cigarette butts off the coffee table and into the kitchen.

Austin was standing now. Swaying. But standing.

"Where ya been?" he wanted to know.

Then he saw the packages and nodded like he knew it all along. He wondered how much she'd spent this time? She was like his shylock, Crawford Taylor. The nut was probably the same. The only difference was there was no vig. He wondered whether he should pop her too, but only for a second. Then he considered telling her the fix he was in. The money part, not the dead guy, but he decided against that too. He knew what she'd say. Her face would scrunch up because it's hard for her to concentrate on anything that isn't about shopping, hair, or nails. Then she'd say without an ounce of sympathy or compassion, "I thought you were so hot," and probe and poke, and look for a chink in whatever he told her. Then she'd slip it in someplace like a knife. Like a dagger to the heart.

"Daddy too," she'd say sweetly.

Talking about that fat fuck of a father of hers who wouldn't give you a tissue if your nose was bleeding, and who went around telling people he was a self-made man, which he wasn't. He got a free ride when his wife died and left him a fortune.

When Daddy met Austin he thought they were kindred spirits. Goldbrickers who came from nothing and married into money, but he was wrong about Austin who was desperate to make his own way. And that's what he told Daddy in the heart-to-heart they had not long after the wedding.

"Don't come to me for any money," said Daddy like it was something Austin did all the time, "I don't have any."

Which was a lie, because he had tons of the stuff, but only for himself.

Austin told him not to lose any sleep over it because he was planning to make his own, and walked away from him in disgust.

Shirley once told him how much his success meant to Daddy and how it gave him bragging rights at the club, bragging being all the old man was good at any more. She told him this little nugget after a marathon session in the sack about

35

a year before the kid was born, like they'd ever do anything like that again now. She was brittle and delicate and oh so perfect these days like that girl on the Regis show. Kathy Gripper? Kelly Lee? All skin and bones like a good fuck would spit her in two.

And how did Austin make all this money everyone's sure he has? He stole it, of course. Not outright, but by slight of hand, and, even if he says so himself, a dazzling brilliance at kiting checks and buying out-of-the-money options and making a fortune. In all the years he's been doing it, he's never been wrong. Until now, that is, when the shit has well and truly hit the fan. Because against all the indicators that worked so well in the past, and the oscillators, and trend lines, and the levels of support, and every other fucking thing he used to contribute to the success of his scam, the stock market tanked on him and he had to turn to Crawford Taylor to loan him the money to keep out of jail.

CHAPTER 9
THE DINER

The diner was an eye party of chrome, Formica, and shiny aluminum, and it had the atmosphere of a time gone by. They still used the old Hamilton Beach mixers, and the faded red lollypop stools at the counter had cracked plastic cushions that were patched up with black masking tape. The tables and counter tops were covered in a green Formica edged with dull, fluted metal. There were glass cases full of desserts and cabinets with sliding doors behind the counter that featured small boxes of cereal, bowls of fruit salad, displays of yoghurts, and containers of milk. There was a pass-through to the kitchen and hustle and bustle wherever you looked. The smell of food was pervasive. Not one thing, but a melding of all things edible dominated by the aroma of brewing coffee and freshly baked bread.

Things were getting back to normal. Customers were being served and there was a clatter of cutlery and dishes as tables were being cleared or set up.

The far end of the counter was where the regulars sat, five of them. And there was plenty of chatter going on in that neck of the woods as they nursed their coffees and nibbled their Danish. They were there every day, this bunch of old farts, for hours on end especially now that the weather had turned cool. What else was there to do?

They liked to hang out at different places at different times of the day: the library for the papers and the facilities, then either the bowling alley or the OTB office, and always ending up at the diner. They were retirees with too much time on their hands and worn down and jaded to all the nice things life had given them. Their faces were set in a permanent mask of discontent and misery. They were in their late seventies and looked grizzled and scuzzy with unshaven faces, thinning gray hair, and balding pates.

Jimmy ambled over to them with a friendly smile so as not to spook them.

Eddie brought up the rear with his own version of the same tactic, but a friendly smile was something Eddie was not very good at, so he did the best he could.

It wasn't like they all knew each other, but they did, sort of, to nod to or to raise an eyebrow at. Columbia was a small town, and everybody bumped into everyone at one time or another, especially if you went to the diner two or three times a week. Like Jimmy and Eddie here. Regulars too in their own way just like these good old boys.

"How's it going?" said Jimmy.

Five gnarly heads bobbed up and down like rabbis on the High Holidays, cautiously waiting for the next question. Their bodies were tense and they leaned forward anxiously.

Jimmy gave the guy closest to him a bigger smile and clapped him on the shoulder.

Henry was his name. A reedy looking man in a worn out sports jacket and baggy, brown trousers. His open-necked shirt had a collar that was fashionable twenty years ago, exposing a scraggly chicken's neck and a pointed Adam's apple that bobbed up and down to a rhythm of its own making. His comb-over from the back of his head to the front did nothing to disguise the fact that he was a balding old geezer who had no idea how silly he looked. All that was missing was a gold medallion around his neck, but his ring and his watch more than made up for it. They were gaudy things designed to impress if you were a pimp or a gang-banger, but on this man they looked ridiculous.

"What did you see, Henry?" Jimmy asked him.

Henry blinked.

The others watched intently. Wondering what he'd say. Wondering what they'd say when their turn came.

"Outside?" said Henry.

Referring to the body in the parking lot.

"No," said Jimmy. "In here."

Henry went into a small performance after that. He took a sip of coffee while his Adam's apple bobbed up and down at warp speed. Then he rearranged the things in front of him, a fork here a knife someplace else. Then he dabbed around the corners of his mouth with a napkin while he formulated his thoughts and considered his answer.

"I'm not sure," he finally croaked in a voice that suggested too much smoking.

"What's that mean?" said Jimmy.

Henry looked at the gang for encouragement then back at Jimmy.

They had just been talking about it when Jimmy and Eddie came in. What they saw. What they didn't.

"We think," said Henry cautiously, looking at the others.

They nodded for him to go on. Glad they weren't on the hot seat.

Henry lowered his head conspiratorially and said in a throaty whisper, "We think there was a fight at one of the tables."

"Which one?"

Henry pointed to a booth by the window.

Jimmy looked.

"Go on," he encouraged.

"Well," rasped Henry, "There was this one guy who looked like a pink bowling ball with ears stuck on the side, and there was this other guy sitting opposite. He suddenly stands up, leans into the bowling ball all angry and mad, says something none of us can hear, then leaves. Storms out, more like it. You know when someone's trying to look tough and they're not? That's how this guy looked."

Jimmy looked at the others.

They looked back at him. Nodding. All eyes saying this is exactly what happened and please don't ask us anything else.

Jimmy said, "Did they come in together?"

No one knew.

"How long were they sitting there?"

No one knew that either.

"The one that stood up, does anyone know him?"

Five grey heads shook as one.

"What about the bowling ball?"

More head shaking.

"Any idea what the fight was about?"

Henry said they didn't.

"But you think they were definitely fighting."

Five emphatic nods.

Jimmy made a couple of notes then he looked at them like a general inspecting his troops.

"I need your help on this one, fellas," he said grimly. "This is a murder investigation we're working here. Serious stuff." He introduced them to Eddie who they already knew, everyone being regulars and all. "Eddie's gonna take your statements and write down what you saw and anything else you think might help us. Some minor detail you don't think is important could make all the difference to our investigation. At this stage everything's important. Whatever you tell Eddie will be very helpful I can assure you, so please don't hold back."

The gang of five puffed themselves up like toads on their lily pads. Fannies rearranged themselves discreetly. Necks stretched out just a little. Five scraggly faces looked smug with pride. Then, quite suddenly, awkwardness descended on the group like a cloud on the Fourth of July. They weren't used to praise, this bunch, and they didn't know how to conduct themselves after it was laid upon them.

Eddie, seeing the sudden change in mood, stepped up and ordered them a round of coffee and doughnuts. That loosened things up and pretty soon they were falling over themselves to tell him what they saw.

CHAPTER 10
JIMMY AND MARY

Jimmy worshipped her. Mary. The woman he was living with. The way she wore her hat. The way she sipped her tea. The way she was with Lucy. And the way she cared about people and only saw the good in them. It's a remarkable quality considering everything she's been through. He was sure if they sat down with Hitler she'd find something nice to say about him; what nice manners he had, something along those lines. She always found nice things to say about everyone, whereas he, cynical bastard that he was, only saw the bad. Because of what he was he supposed. A cop. Someone who questioned everything whether he liked to or not.

He still didn't understand what she saw in him. Mary. He was short and dumpy and certainly no Matthew McConaughey. She was taller, and younger, and very attractive. With bleached blonde shoulder-length hair. Sparkling gray eyes. A warm smile and a trim figure that reflected the six miles a day she spent on her treadmill keeping her five foot seven frame in perfect working order.

Their first date was three years ago in an Italian joint on the outskirts of town. She smiled at him all night, laughed at his jokes and helped him through his awkward pauses. He couldn't believe his good luck when she said she'd go out with him again. And again after that.

Pretty soon they were inseparable.

A year ago his cat died. Felix, the orneriest cat in the world. The next day he put his house up for sale and moved in with them. He couldn't do it before. He had to wait until Felix passed. The poor animal was deaf, blind, and dying. He didn't think it was right to move him to a new environment while that was going on, so he waited. When he finally moved in, his life changed in ways he never thought possible and he became part of something he'd never had before. A family. His family.

Mary loved him. He wasn't so sure how Lucy felt about him, but as soon as he settled in she trailed after him like a puppy dog, telling him things she never told anyone else before. Not even Mary. Or so she said. Making up for lost time was Mary's take on it, and a confirmation of sorts about what a nice guy Jimmy was.

He blushed when she told him this.

He's not so good with compliments.

Mary's not either.

She delivers food for Food From Friends, an organization that provides meals to senior citizens and the needy. She gets uncomfortable when people praise her for doing it. On a couple of glasses of wine she might go off on a jag to whoever's handing out the compliments. Telling them, if they'd pissed her off, "All I do is deliver food. It takes a couple of hours once a week and it's no big deal. Nurses, doctors and first responders are the people who deserve the praise. You praise me for delivering food and I feel guilty because I could do so much more."

She'd only say it when she was a little buzzed and even then the person had to press all the right buttons. Jimmy loved watching their faces as they ran the gamut from polite to surprise to a sense, from their body language, that they were desperate to get away from her.

Then there was Lucy, all twelve years of her, who just entered middle school, with shoulder-length auburn hair that was always put up in a ponytail. Re-arranging it was a full-time occupation and conversations always included a number of maneuvers to tighten it, smooth it, adjust it, and then start all over again. It was a tic of sorts and annoying as hell, but Jimmy never said anything. It would've been a mistake and would have destroyed the rhythm of the thing and whatever was going on would stop. And what would be the point of that? So he ignored it. And bit his lip. And in return for his patience, she would tell him the most amazing things.

She was five feet tall. Lucy. And trim with the beginnings of some lady parts. She started wearing a training bra two weeks ago and got her period the week after Jimmy moved in.

Welcome to the deep end, buddy.

Lucy was the self-appointed designated driver in charge of dragging Jimmy into the twenty-first century with his computer, I Pad, and the mysteries of the Internet and the information highway. And what an education that's turned out to be. Finding his favorites from years ago. Stuff he hadn't heard since he was a kid. The Drifters. Jackie Wilson. And watching his TV programs. *I Spy, Star Trek* and his new old favorites, *The Wire* and *Homicide.*

You could re-live your whole life if you wanted to.

Who knew?

Then there was her music.

"Listen to this," she'd say as she rearranged her ponytail.

Or, "Whatcha think of that?"

Sharing her music with him. Sharing everything with him. It was like he'd come from Mars it was all so new to him. And sometimes he'd hate it. The music. Her clothes. Even the language she used. But that's not the point, is it? Doing it together is the point. Sharing with her is the point. Not like in his day when no one gave a shit.

Once in a while he'd tell her the music was crap, but it had to be really bad for him to do that. And maybe he shouldn't have. Shades of his father, who always criticized his music and everything else for that matter, but Jimmy said it with a smile and she never seemed to mind. And that was another thing about this learning process. There were no rules. No convention. No book to tell you how to do it or what to say. He just tried to go along and share in the fun without letting his age and his prejudices get in the way.

"Listen to this," she'd say.

'If You Needed Me,' by Townes Van Zandt.

Really great, he thought.

"Really great," he told her.

Then they went through the versions.

Lots of them.

On YouTube.

On a rainy Saturday afternoon.

The two of them.

Up in Lucy's room.

Listening to music.

And each other.

Becoming friends.

Something neither of them ever had before.

CHAPTER 11
THE DINER

Jimmy excused himself from Eddie and the gaggle of bobble-heads and went over to talk to a waitress standing at the other end of the counter. Her name was Pat, an ample woman with touches of Irish, Chinese and Philippine running through her blood. She was dark with short, curly chocolate colored hair, a round face with doll-like features and long brown eyelashes. Pat had two kids and was trying for a third. Her husband was Puerto Rican with touches of Mexican and African in him. Each child was a different color with different features. Bets were being made as to what the new one would look like. Everyone knew what Pat was doing because she made no secret of it. They cheered her when she arrived and serenaded her with fist pumps, rude gestures and an occasional chant when she left at night.

Jimmy gave her a smile, made some small talk then asked her, "Did you wait on the ones who were fighting?"

"I did," she said.

The stress of the situation brought out a Gaelic lilt that she must've got from her Irish mother and didn't jibe with her Filipino features.

"What were they fighting about?" he asked.

"I don't know."

"What did you hear?"

"I didn't."

"A word?"

"They stopped talking whenever I got close."

"You must have heard something?"

"I did not."

"Do you know them?"

"I don't," she said.

"Have they been in before?"

"Not to my knowledge."

"Were they friends?"

She shook her head.

"That was not my impression."

"Enemies?"

"I dunno. The one that stood up gave the Buddha an envelope."

"The Buddha?"

"That's what the big one looked like. A big pink Buddha."

"What then?"

"The Buddha didn't look very happy with what was inside."

"Did they come in together?"

"No. The Buddha came in first, then a couple of minutes later the other one showed up. That's when he gave him the envelope."

"What do you think was inside?"

"Money."

"You saw it?"

"He was counting something. What else would it be?"

"And you think the Buddha was unhappy with what was there?"

"I do."

"Because?"

"Steam was comin out of his ears. Little things they were, like someone stuck em on the side of his head like Mr. Potato Head."

"You think he expected more?"

"I do."

"And the other one, the one who gave the Buddha the envelope. He left?"

"He did."

"And the Buddha?"

"Finished his coffee, paid the bill, and also left."

"How soon after the other one?"

"Pretty soon. A couple of minutes, that's all."

"Did he look surprised when the guy walked out on him?"

"He stared at him with a look between contempt and amusement. Like he thought the guy was an asshole, you know what I mean?"

Jimmy did.

Her description matched the one Miss Drake gave him and what the gang of five saw and all the other people they spoke to after that.

Everyone described the big guy the same way. He'd grabbed everyone's attention because he was as big as a house with a bowling ball for a head. The other one, the one who walked out, didn't catch anyone's eye because no one was looking at him. Everyone said something different about him. He had black hair. Someone said brown. Another said fair, but she could've been wrong. He was fat. He was thin. He wore a grey suit. He was wearing jeans. Nothing jibed. He might as well have been invisible. It's not that no one saw him, it's that no one saw him clearly because no one was paying attention to him. It was the Jolly Pink Giant with a bowling ball for a head they all had their eyes on.

Jimmy told Eddie to order up an artist and see if the witnesses could come up with a likeness. He figured they wouldn't get anything until tomorrow afternoon at the earliest, and that was only if they were able to get an artist quickly.

"If you have any trouble call County," Jimmy told him. "They promised us everything."

"Got it," said Eddie.

"Don't let em give you the run around."

"I got it," said Eddie.

"Tell em…"

Eddie cut him off.

"I got it," he said, and was about to say something snarky when they both got calls on their cellphones.

Eddie's was from the sergeant telling him about a black Lexus that was stolen from the supermarket parking lot. How witnesses said they saw a huge man with a head like a pink melon in the area.

Jimmy's call came from the Chief, telling him the same thing.

CHAPTER 12

AUSTIN

Austin purchased his first house a long time ago. He bought it using "the scam" before it ever became a scam. He was two years in at the company, a successful women's fashion house in the garment center, and not running the money side of things. The comptroller. The CFO. Whatever you want to call it.

Not there.

Yet.

Austin was CFO Miles Carter's assistant back then. He was a single kid living in a one-bedroom apartment in a six-story walkup on the Upper East Side. The best little whorehouse on Second Avenue is what they called it. His friends. His buddies. Austin had lots of buddies. He was a magnet for good times, great parties and even better dope, but he was good was our Austin; you had to give him credit for that. And even though his life was a carnival he managed to squirrel away some money and find a house to buy in Riverdale.

A foreclosure.

People were losing their homes back then. There was a recession on and there were bargains to be had. Someone tipped Austin off about a foreclosure auction on the steps of the Bronx Court House. That's how they did it in those days. You needed a certified check for a dollar over what the bank was owed. Fifty thousand plus a dollar is what you could get a house for providing no one bid against you. Austin had it, too. The money. Some of his own, some from the family, and some from a couple of partners, but the checks had to clear and that would take time. He needed the money now. That day. That afternoon. That's when the auction was. Not many people would be there, his buddy at the bank said, and there were lots of houses to be sold. Meaning Austin had a clear shot at the one he wanted.

Austin went to Miles Carter and showed him the checks from everyone. They're all good, he told him, but they'll take a couple of days to clear. Would the company float him $50,000 against these checks? He'd give the company his own post-dated check for $50,000 and they could deposit it in a couple of days when the checks from his investors cleared.

Miles Carter went to Mal Finklestein, the owner of the company, to get his okay. Mal liked Austin. He was grooming him to take over Miles's spot when Miles retired. It was a question of confidence as far as Mal was concerned and it gave him an opportunity to show Austin how much he trusted him.

"What's to lose?" Mal asked Miles. "We've got his check, don't we? I just don't see Austin sacrificing his future on a stunt like this."

Mal thought it would also buy him some loyalty, something he was always trying to cultivate with key employees. It didn't work out that way with Austin, but it took Mal a long time to find that out.

A company check was certified for $50,000. Austin deposited it in his bank account as cash, then had a check of his own certified to the bank selling the property at the Courthouse. He got the house like his bank buddy said he would and he lived there until he got married.

CFO Miles Carter did not deposit Austin's check for $50,000 for a couple of days. Between that and the regular clearance time, it took six days before Austin's check cleared and the company got its money back. For six days Austin had a $50,000 bank balance that wasn't his. He wondered what he could've done with it. Bet on a horse? Go to Atlantic City? Or maybe play the stock market?

Over time these questions became an obsession with him. What could he have done with that money? It took him a couple of years to come up with the answer. In the meantime he took some courses on the stock market, something he knew nothing about but thought he should, and fell in love with a technical approach to investing that employed charting and all its variations. Bar charts. Point-and-figure charts. Head-and-shoulders patterns. Double tops, triple bottoms, candles and hammers, and indicators and trends. His professors at The New School pounded some basic rules into him and told him if he adhered to them he'd probably make out all right.

Preservation of capital is of paramount importance.

Do NOT fall in love with a stock, or its name, or the business it's in.

Remember they're numbers. If the number doesn't do what it's supposed to, sell it.

Which gets you back to rule number one: preservation of capital. It's better to lose a little and play again than get trapped in a stock that keeps going down and lose your liquidity.

And in time, the decisions Austin made concerning the stock market were rarely wrong. And then, for a long time after that, he was never wrong at all.

So now it's two years after Austin bought his first house when he used the scam before it became a scam. The stock market had become an obsession and it was one of those rare moments when all the charts and indictors and everything else he used were screaming 'buy, buy, for God's sake buy.' So Austin went back to Miles Carter, who still hadn't retired as the CFO, the comptroller, whatever you call it, but was seriously considering it, and ran the same story by him. He'd found another house in foreclosure. He and his partners had the money. Everybody's checks were in the bank, but they would take a couple of days to clear. He needed fifty thousand dollars for the closing. Today. Now. Just like last time, two years ago. Would the company float him a certified check for the $50,000 against his post-dated check for the same amount and hold on to it for a couple of days until his investor's checks cleared?

Miles went back to Mal Finkelstein to get his approval. Mal was only too happy to help Austin out. Again. Because, as he said to Miles like he was talking to a two year old, he'd been right all along, hadn't he? Austin had turned out to be a stellar employee and a valuable member of his inner circle.

"Last time there was no problem," said Mal with an, 'I told you so,' attitude. "And look what happened then? Nothing. That's what happened."

The $50,000 sat in Austin's bank account for five days before his personal check to the company cleared. Kudos to Mal Finkelstein for trusting him again. And high fives and salutations to Austin who, during that five-day period, used the money to buy thousands of out-of-the-money General Motors calls he thought would double if the stock did what he thought it would, only he was wrong. Neither did he double his money. Instead he quintupled it with a day to spare and walked away with a two hundred thousand dollar profit.

Kiting is what it's called. Writing a check against money that's not there. It's against the law and if you get caught you can go to jail.

Over time Austin amassed an impressive portfolio of assets, lived a lifestyle that reflected his amazing success, and spent it as fast as it came in. His beloved wife, Shirley from Great Neck, helped him do this with unprecedented zeal and a great deal of passion.

Eventually Miles Carter retired and Austin took his job, the CFO, the comptroller, whatever you want to call it. And every now and again Austin went to his boss Mal Finkelstein and asked him to cover a check for one of his so-called property investments.

Like now for instance.

Austin asking Mal to cover a post-dated, personal check made out to the company for $250,000 for a couple of days. Another real estate deal, Austin told him. Only this time it was a record breaker. How could it not be if Austin was going to pay off that bloodsucking bastard Crawford Taylor, and have enough money left over for himself?

CHAPTER 13

MAGDALENA
TUESDAY

She was waiting for Mary at the front door. Magdalena. The door was open. Ajar really, and Magdalena was sitting on a chair just inside the threshold waiting for her 'Food From Friends' delivery. Tuesdays and Fridays were the days it came. Mary had been coming on Tuesdays for a couple of years now. Friday was someone else.

She was almost toothless, Magdalena. There was a stump on the top of her mouth and two on the bottom that stuck out of her maw like stained yellow pegs. Her messy, white hair straggled to her shoulders in a greasy disorder. Her face was lined and waxen from old age and no sun. She was small, a bag of bones really, and wore a not-so-clean housedress. Not dirty, but faded and looked like she'd been wearing it a while. She was short, Magdalena, a little less than five feet, and had small pointed ears that looked like they were made of parchment. She wore support stockings on her legs and threadbare slippers on her feet and there was that smell of an old person about her that was stale and medicinal.

She always said no when Mary offered to bring the food inside. Three days worth, some of it frozen and heavy for a bent over ninety-two year old who used a walker to get around.

"That's okay," she'd say with a gummy smile. "Put it on the tray on my walker and I'll take care of it."

Not wanting strangers in her house, Mary supposed and liking her privacy. Mary could understand it. She'd probably be the same way when she got that old. She hoped so. And brave, like Magdalena. Living in the backwoods, isolated and defenseless except for a caregiver who came every day for a couple of hours to keep an eye on her. Maintaining her independence and not rolling over and letting people who didn't know her control her life.

But not this time.

This time Magdalena said yes when Mary offered to bring her food inside. Coyly and shyly, with a fluttering of eyelids like a young woman giving it up.

Mary figured she had something on her mind. That was the reason for the invitation. She squeezed past her with the packages and headed for the kitchen.

There was a picture of a much younger Magdalena on the wall in the hallway. She was taller then, and gorgeous. Stunning really. At the beach in a black one-piece bathing suit, back arched, breasts thrust out, and her blond hair blowing in the wind. A hand shaded her eyes as she stared off into the distance. She looked like an ad for something invigorating like one of those posters the Nazis used for their Aryan sales pitch. Not that Magdalena was German. She was from Hungary and crossed the border into Austria after she and her husband got the call during the '56 uprising.

"They're coming," said the person on the other end, and hung up.

That's all you had to hear. They knew people who didn't heed the call and were never seen again. They left that minute, with the clothes on their backs and whatever they could carry, and walked the hundred and fifty miles to the Austrian border. Crossed over. And were interred in a refugee camp and eventually granted political asylum in the United States.

The kitchen was dimly lit. There was a bare bulb of low wattage in the ceiling and a window over the sink that gave no light because it faced north and was shaded by shrubs. Mary cleared a spot on the table that was home to boxes of tea, magazines, medications, cooking utensils, dishtowels, junk mail and bills. The appliances were old as were the cabinets and what furniture Mary could see. She felt like she'd stepped into a time warp. Everything was from an era where televisions had rabbit ears and computers were yet to be invented. Her mind captured everything she saw, every detail, like it was a camera. Crud on the stove, click. Worn out linoleum, click. Sink with dried suds and dirty plates. Click, and click again.

This was how she lived, Magdalena. It was a private affair as far as she was concerned. Her dust. Her whatever. And here now was a stranger. Standing in her kitchen. Checking things out. Examining her. Judging her. This was why she hated strangers coming inside her home. They always looked like they were looking up her skirt, but this time she needed something, so this time it was all right.

"I'll put it away," said Magdalena from behind her.

Still asserting her independence.

Then came the story, but not right away. They still had another ritual to go through that usually took place at the door. Mary would ask her how she was, and Magdalena would answer, "All right I suppose," and look weary and resigned. "What am I going to do?" she'd say and her shoulders would sag and her eyes would slip away from Mary's leaving the rest unsaid.

And so it was today.

What was she going to do? What could she do? Trapped in this impossible situation. Head stuffed with memories. House filled with more. Living in a wasted body that barely obeyed her commands. Hanging on. Enduring. Wondering if each day was going to be her last. So, whenever well-meaning people like Mary asked her how she was, she'd shake her scraggly head in a resigned recognition of her own reality and wish they'd mind their own business.

But not this time.

This time Magdalena wanted something, so after the rituals were dispensed with she got to the reason she'd invited Mary inside. Her caregiver. Somebody new, she explained. Replacing someone who'd been with her for a long time and knew her ways and habits. The new caregiver came every day for a couple of hours and was asking questions she shouldn't ask, about things that were none of her business. All of this Magdalena told Mary in a heavily accented rant punctuated with flying spittle and a rattling of her walker. How uncomfortable this made her feel, these questions. And how vulnerable she felt because of them, her being so old and alone and ripe for the picking.

Magdalena was working herself up into a froth and putting on a show for Mary. Exaggerating her plight a little so Mary would take some action, which she did, of course. Telling Magdalena she'd send Jimmy over to check things out, which put a gummy smile back on Magdalena's ancient face.

Jimmy had been there a couple of times before, at Mary's insistence, when Magdalena was worried about something and he was able to put her mind at rest. She liked him and broke out a flirtatious routine whenever she saw him that was obsolete and heavy handed. For someone else it might have been embarrassing, but Jimmy always played along with her and got a kick out of it. It's not every day you get a ninety-two-year old coming on to you.

CHAPTER 14

THE PARKING LOT

It was getting dark. That was the trouble with the fall; it got dark early. They hadn't even had the daylight savings switchover yet and look how gloomy it was. It'll start to get dark at four when that happened, thought Jimmy and shuddered at the thought of it. Every year it got darker sooner or so it seemed to him.

He and Eddie were sitting in Eddie's cruiser smoking cigarettes and drinking coffee out of Styrofoam cups they got from the diner.

Eddie had calmed down in the question department. After that first rush, he couldn't think of anything else to say. It was always like that. Eddie trying to show Jimmy how smart he was, only to find out he wasn't. That's when he went back to being a uniform and was glad of it.

Jimmy was enjoying their cigarette moment. He'd given up smoking a long time ago, but every now and again he'd have one with Eddie, usually when they were starting something new. You'd think they'd do it at the end of the investigation as a celebration of sorts, but this was the routine they came up with and this was what they were sticking with.

"So whaddya think?" said Jimmy.

He cracked open his window and blew the smoke out.

Eddie shrugged. He was already out of his depth and had no idea what to think. He had good news though, so he stuck with that.

"I'm meeting with the artist tomorrow morning, 8:30 at the station house. I got Kelly Blake. Remember her? We used her on the last thing."

Jimmy said, "The one you thought played for the other team?"

Kelly Blake was a police artist. When they worked with her last, she had a man's haircut that set off Eddie's right wing prejudices against gays, lesbians and anyone who did not fit the mold.

"That's her," said Eddie. Not caring which team she played for any more. "I've got a schedule all figured out. With any luck, we should be done by lunchtime."

Jimmy was pleased. They were moving along nicely.

"Nice work, Eddie."

Eddie beamed. He loved the praise.

"Did you get any more off the bobble heads?"

"Nah," said Eddie. "They kept saying the same things in different ways to keep the coffee and doughnuts coming. They'll be back tomorrow bright and early for more freebies."

Jimmy chuckled.

"I've got to be in Brooklyn tomorrow afternoon to check out Conner Malloy's apartment. I spoke to the locals. A detective's gonna meet me there. If you're done with the artist, I'd like you to come with me."

Eddie looked like he was panting. He really was like a puppy.

"Before we do that I've got to make a stop at one of Mary's clients. She's an old lady living in the back and beyond with a new caregiver, who, she says, is asking too many questions. Mary says the caregiver's probably just trying to make conversation and the old lady's got the wrong end of the stick. She told her I'd stop by to check her out. I've been there a couple of times before when she got a bee in her bonnet about something or other. It's just to calm her down and to please Mary. I can't imagine this caregiver's up to no good. Those people are like angels the way they take care of the old people. It won't take me long."

Eddie said it was fine.

They sucked on their cigarettes.

Jimmy asked him again, "So, whaddya think's going on?"

Eddie had no idea and turned it back on Jimmy.

"What do YOU think's going on?"

Jimmy took another hit on his cigarette before answering. He looked like something from a black and white movie. Sitting in the dark, a street lamp highlighting his silhouette, and smoke leaking from his nose and mouth as he spoke.

"The one who walked out owed someone some money. Whatever he gave the big guy wasn't enough. The big guy and the dead man are together. A team. Collectors. Something like that. This is a routine they've done before. One waits in the parking lot in case there's trouble. The big guy is the 'meet and greet' man. If all goes well nothing happens and everyone goes their separate ways. This time the money wasn't right. There was a fight, an exchange of words, something. The one who stood up goes for his car. Conner Malloy's waiting for him in the parking lot with the baseball bat. The guy gets scared. Pops him. And leaves.

Baldy comes out. He's the sweeper. He's supposed to come up from behind. Get the guy in the car. Take him someplace and work him over. This time it didn't work out that way because Conner got popped. Baldy sees him on the ground and needs to get out of Dodge. I bet you a dime to a dollar he lifted that car that was pinched from the supermarket, which, I forgot to tell you, was found in the City on 90th and Third ten minutes ago. I just got the call from Morgan."

"Why?" said Eddie.

"Why what?"

"Why steal the car? Why not take the train?"

"He probably didn't want anyone to eyeball him."

"He's as big as a house and he thinks no one's gonna see him?"

"It's the same logic as Conner carrying his wallet and not having any paperwork in the car."

Eddie said he supposed so.

"How do you come up with this?" he said knowing not for the first time that a uniform was all he could hope for. He was amazed how Jimmy put all that together from the same stuff he heard, and he'd managed to get none of it.

"I'm just guessing," said Jimmy not wanting to make Eddie feel bad.

"Yeah," said Eddie wryly, "but your guesses are usually right."

"We need to find the big man to get us to the guy he was talking to. I bet the picture of him you get from the artist tomorrow will be pretty accurate. Everyone had their eye on him because he's so conspicuous. I gotta believe there's someone who knows who he is in the City. Morgan will come up with something. You'll see."

"And then?"

"We'll peck our way along like we always do."

Eddie liked that.

Jimmy took another hit on the cigarette, blew the smoke out of the window then stubbed it out in the ashtray.

"I'm going home," he said and drained his coffee, stretched, and yawned. "We'll start up again in the morning. We should have all the reports by then. Maybe there'll be something we'll be able to hang our hats on. Wear civvies tomorrow, Eddie. I want you to look nice when you go around with the artist."

"How early?" Eddie asked.

"7:30."

Eddie shuddered.

CHAPTER 15

JIMMY

Mary was waiting for him at the front door when he got home. A porch fixture bathed her in a soft light.

"We've got a problem," she said as he got out of the car and walked towards her. "I tried calling you, but the voicemail kept picking up and your message box was full."

Jimmy looked sheepish. He'd turned his phone off after he got the call from the Chief about the stolen car and he never turned it back on again. He did that a lot. He hated the thing. People always calling him at their convenience and interrupting his life. A conversation. A dump. Anything. So he turned it off all the time and usually forgot to turn it back on, which pissed a lot of people off. He was still getting used to the idea that Lucy and Mary needed to get in touch with him whenever they had to. He wasn't so concerned about the people he worked with, or anyone else for that matter.

"The County guys put me in charge of a case," he said by way of explanation and gave her a peck on the cheek.

"So you turned your phone off?"

"I was in the middle of something."

It was another lame excuse.

She looked at him like he was crazy.

"Of what?" she wanted to know.

"A murder."

"A murder? How awful. Anyone we know?"

"Someone from Brooklyn."

"And you're running it?"

"I am."

"No Laurel and Hardy?" She was talking about Smith and Monahan, the County Detectives he was always running afoul of.

"County says they're backed up and those guys are still on leave, so they gave me the ball."

"That's a big deal."

"Yes it is," said Jimmy and smiled modestly. She wasn't mad at him any more, but there was still that look on her face. "Why were you calling me?" he asked.

They were inside the house now.

"Can't you smell it?" she asked him.

He could not.

He hung his raincoat on the rack in the hallway.

"Marijuana," she said and looked like she was going to burst out crying.

Jimmy looked like he'd been slapped.

"I caught Lucy smoking it," she said.

"Where?"

"In her room."

"You went in?"

Lucy's room had become a DMZ where you could only go in if you were invited. Signs expressing this concept were posted on her door in a variety of ways including a skull and crossbones, warnings about booby traps, and a list of dire punishments if the edict was disobeyed.

"I could smell it all over the house, that's why I went in."

He still couldn't smell anything.

"What did you do?"

"I took it away from her and told her to stay in her room till you came home."

"I'm the heavy?"

"You're the cop."

"And the heavy."

"And the heavy."

It was Mary's house. She owned it. She was rich after Jimmy found the money her dead husband was stealing from her and got it back. Jimmy paid his fair share though. He insisted on it, otherwise he wouldn't have moved in with them. When he did there was a surprise waiting. Mary had turned one of the bedrooms into an office for him. They'd found an old wooden desk with lots of draws and cubbyholes and a beat-up old Eames chair. Lucy set up a monitor, printer and his computer and tied the sound to the huge, wooden speakers he was so proud of, placing them on either side of the room. The sound was remarkable. Even better was the bay window overlooking the garden in the back of the house. His garden. The garden they handed him the minute he walked in the door and was still trying to get into shape.

He filled the room with his favorite stuff. Weirdly shaped gourds he grew at the old house. Books he loved, his vinyl record collection and Grundig turntable. There were pictures, toys, and bits of wood from places only he remembered. Model planes hung from the ceiling and photographs were stuck on the wall with double-edged tape. There was even a sheep's skull he picked up when he was out West. The room looked like a junk shop, dust and all, which was just the way he liked it, that and a commitment from Mary never to go in and clean the place, which she broke immediately. How much dirt is a woman supposed to tolerate in her own home?

They ate together five nights a week. Or tried to. That was the routine. It took him a while to get used to it. He used to believe family eating was a holy experience where no one talked and you concentrated on the job at hand. That's how it was growing up in his house. You cut, chewed, and swallowed your food and God help you if you made any noise doing it. Mary put paid to that notion after their first dinner together. She went to a lot of trouble and thought it would be a celebration of sorts, but Jimmy wolfed down his food without saying a word and couldn't wait to leave the table. The next night Mary didn't go to as much trouble, but made sure there was plenty of conversation. And so it went. Jimmy got to love it, especially the laughter. Eventually. Because he'd never seen anything like it before, and it took a little getting used to.

It was at dinner that Jimmy chose to talk to Lucy about the marijuana.

"Where did you get it from?" he asked her when the food was on the table.

Lucy stared into her plate.

"Is this the first time?"

Lucy pursed her lips.

"This is not good, Lucy. You're twelve years old and getting stoned. I don't like it and neither does your mother." They'd never had this sort of conversation before. He was sure he was destroying the nice thing they had going since he'd moved in, but he had to go on. "Where'd you get it from?" he asked.

No answer and an aggressive rearranging of her ponytail.

"At school?"

Her body language said yes, but she said nothing.

His face was stern, also something he'd never done before.

"I'm going to have to talk to the principal about this," he said.

Lucy squirmed.

"Please don't do that," she pleaded and looked at him with doughy eyes.

Jimmy changed his tone to something softer. Not so confrontational.

"I'm a cop, Lucy. And marijuana is against the law. My job is to uphold the law. Corny, but true. You've put me in a bad spot here. Don't smoke that stuff any more, please. It's not good for you at your age."

Mary gave him a look.

"At any age," he corrected himself. "It messes up your mind and distracts you from things you're supposed to be doing. You tried it? Good for you. Now no more, please. But I'm still gonna have to speak to the principal. There's no place for drugs at school. He has to be told about this."

Lucy made with the eyes again.

"If I tell you where I got it will you promise not go and to see the principal?" she said softly.

"I can't do that."

"What will you do if I tell you?"

"Catch the kid who sold it to you."

She frowned,

"And if not?"

"If you don't tell me?"

She nodded.

"I'm going to your school no matter what, Lucy. I have to. That's my job."

Nobody spoke for a while. Knives and forks scraped plates. There were chewing noises. And drinking. And a stifled burp.

Then, without looking up, Lucy said in an almost whisper, "Martin Rogers."

"What about him?"

"He sold it to my friend. She gave it to me."

"You bought it from her?"

"No. She gave it to me."

"Why would she do that?"

"She's my friend."

"Yeah, but why did she give it to you?"

Lucy screwed up her face.

Jimmy said, "Well?"

Lucy undid the ponytail, smoothed her hair back into a hank and retied it.

"I wanted to try it," she said. "All the other kids have tried it. I'm the only one who hasn't. My friend was doing me a favor. Everyone knows you're a cop, so they keep things away from me."

"What things?"

She shrugged.

"What things?"

She looked into her plate some more.

Then she said, "Whatever's going around."

"Like what?"

She sighed and smoothed her hair again. Her eyes flew around the room while she searched for the right response and finally settled on his in surrender.

"One time someone had some Ecstacy. Another time it was booze. Always there's beer."

Jimmy's eyes widened.

"Whaddya mean always?"

"Always."

"Where?"

"The golf course."

Jimmy and Mary exchanged looks. They'd talked about this before. The golf course. Where the kids met every Saturday night before moving on to whatever was going on in the neighborhood. Or not. Some kids stayed there all night drinking and carousing and making noise. A big knot of them that grew and contracted and broke off into smaller groups reforming like a swarm of bees, only it was a mass of teenagers. Older kids. Juniors. Seniors. And kids from the middle school. All jumbled together for the weekend. Connecting. Hitting on. Smoking and drinking and anything else they weren't supposed to do. What else was there to do in a small town? And what were they going to do about it? Jimmy and Mary. What could they do about it? Chain her to the bed? Keep her indoors for the rest of her life? It's what the kids did these days. It's what they did when they were that age.

"Who gave it to you?" asked Jimmy.

Lucy gave him the look again.

Jimmy didn't press.

"But Martin Rogers sold it to your friend?" he asked her to be sure, and to keep the kettle boiling.

She looked into her lap.

"Is Martin in your grade?"

She shook her head.

"No. High school. A junior, I think."

"And?"

Silence.

"And?"

"I heard he sells it at school."

It was a small school district. The middle school and high school were in the same building. Everyone saw everyone. Everyone knew everyone. Like on the golf course. Or at a party. Or at school. What would you like? Weed? Molly? Booze? Drugs and alcohol seeped in and out of the kids like an oil spill, with no age requirement. A kid he once busted told him you could get anything you wanted in the schoolyard. Anything. And if you couldn't get it there, you could get it on the golf course. They tried, Jimmy and the boys, to close things down. Raiding the golf course. Watching the kids scatter. Coming up with a couple of six packs and a bottle of Captain Morgan. The next time they came up with less. He gave the school a heads up, but they needed a name or something specific, they said, to take any action. Jimmy had neither.

Till now, that is.

"Did you like it?" he asked Lucy.

"Not particularly."

"So you won't be doing it again, will you," said Jimmy.

A statement. Not a question. With the appropriate expression.

She looked at him. Then her mother. Then back in her plate.

"Here's the thing," Jimmy said kindly. "When you're high you're vulnerable, especially if you're not used to it. You're not in control of the situation. Sometimes you're around people who'd like to exploit that. I see it all the time. It's not very pretty. They take photos and make you do all sorts of stuff you'd never consider doing if you weren't high. We're talking about good old American boys here. They get a girl all liquored up. Or stoned. And then they take advantage of her."

She shook her head. It wasn't like that.

"I know, I know," he put his hands up in surrender. "These are people you trust. I gotta tell you Luce, it's really not a good thing when it happens. Pictures show up on the Internet. Or cellphones. Reputations are destroyed in a heart-beat. All of it done by people you trusted. Girls too, it's not just the boys. Someone who doesn't like you, or is jealous of you, and you're not thinking right. That's when they take advantage of you and it's you that let it happen. You let your guard down." He was piling it on to scare her, but the truth was it happened all the time. "Stay away from the stuff, Lucy. Please. The same goes for alcohol. Don't get in a situation where you're not in control and not aware of what's going on around you. When you're high, you're not in control. Your senses are dulled. Your judgment's off and you're easy prey for people who want to do you harm."

Lucy kept her head down, but she was listening. They could see that.

Then Mary took over. She told Lucy she was grounded. They'd do some stuff together, but there was to be no hanging out with her friends for a while.

"You do something wrong, there's got to be consequences," she declared.

Lucy's eyes went up to the ceiling. She huffed and puffed and did a number with her ponytail, but she went along with it without throwing herself around. Grateful there were no hysterics from the parentals.

It was the first bad thing to happen since Jimmy moved in. The first issue they had to deal with as a family. A unit. And, miracle of miracles, it didn't turn them against each other and no one tried to rip anyone's head off. Jimmy would've bet against it, but everything worked out. They all stayed friends and there was no lingering attitude or uncomfortable silence. It even brought them closer which took them all by surprise. That's not what would have happened in his family. His father would've beaten the shit out of him, and if his mother didn't agree, she'd have got a thumping too.

Jimmy said he'd try and keep Lucy's name out of it when he went to the school and that was the end of it. Case closed. They went on after that as if nothing happened.

Chatting about this.

And that.

And this again.

Then came dessert.

Apple pie, oh my. And ice cream.

Jimmy's put on a few pounds since he moved in.

Say five or ten, but who's counting?

CHAPTER 16

WEDNESDAY MORNING

Driving to work was a pain in the ass. It was cold and drizzling and miserable, and the roads were covered with wet slippery leaves. Twice Jimmy got stuck behind a school bus and three times behind cars that drifted into his path. It happens a lot, this drifting business. They're usually old farts crawling out of their driveways, and they never seem to go any faster than twenty, and he's left dawdling behind them chewing his cheek and trying to control his temper. You'd think they'd let him pass before they crawled out of their driveways because there's no one else on the road. There's never anyone else on these roads, but they don't. Ever. He's put the light on his roof a couple of times, but when they pulled over they looked like they were having a heart attack, so he stopped, not wanting anything like that on his conscience. And there's no place to pass them unless you want to take your life in your hands, so he's learned to be patient, but it's still a pain in the ass.

By 11:00 he had the report from the crime scene people, which included a forensic report, a report about Conner Malloy's car, and a one-page document covering all cogent details about the crime scene. The DNA reports on the hair and the smears found in Conner's car would take a while, they said. The lab was backed up. The prints in the car were from Conner Malloy and one other person they could not identify. Those prints were not in the system. What they had on the passenger was nothing unless they were lucky when the DNA report came in. No one was very optimistic. If their prints weren't in the system was the general conclusion, their DNA probably wasn't either.

The Autopsy report came in from the ME. The toxicology screen found traces of marijuana, Percocet, and cocaine in Conner Malloy's system. He died from two gunshot wounds to the chest. Big surprise. Both bullets came from a snub-nosed thirty-eight. The ME had the bullets examined. They found a partial thumbprint on one bullet and an almost complete forefinger print on the other one. The prints were run through the system and came up blank. The ME's report said the prints were good enough for identification purposes should a suspect ever be apprehended.

Jimmy objected to the word 'ever.' It was judgmental and implied a certain lack of confidence in the investigator, like he'd never be able to come up with a 'suspect.' It was a dig if you wanted to look at it that way, which Jimmy chose to, but consider the source. It was the ME who wrote the report, and the ME's choice of words, and since Jimmy didn't give a rat's ass what the ME thought he didn't take it seriously. But it rubbed him the wrong way.

Score one for the Doc.

At 12:00 noon Eddie and the artist walked into his office.

"How's it going?" said Jimmy, and gave them a welcoming smile.

Kelly Blake was the same artist they'd worked with on a previous case. She was in her late thirties and wore a shiny grey pantsuit that looked like it had seen better days and black shoes that were scuffed and in need of a polish. She'd grown her hair longer since Jimmy saw her last. It was to her shoulders now and loose and wavy. With her hair this way she didn't look like she played for the other team, which is what they thought last time they worked together, in fact quite the opposite. She also looked like she was not in the best of moods.

Jimmy figured Eddie must have said something off base, breaking out his right wing charm where all insults should be forgiven unless they were directed at him. He probably told her she didn't look like a dyke anymore, and she would have been forced to respond. Then Eddie, who's not so good with the words anyway, probably fucked up royally.

Jimmy was sure that's what happened. Their body language said he was right. Two people who spent the morning together in close proximity should be showing some sort of camaraderie; instead they were barely speaking to each other. She wouldn't even look in Eddie's direction.

"Whatcha got?" said Jimmy. Still smiling. Not wanting to get into it.

He pointed to the two chairs on the other side of his desk and motioned for them to sit down.

After they'd gone through the niceties, Kelly handed him a manila envelope. Inside were two likenesses. She'd gotten a clear picture of the Melon Man. Everyone, she said, described him in great detail because they were all paying attention to him. Not so the second guy. The one Jimmy made for Conner Malloy's murder. No one really paid any attention to him even though they said they did. What they remembered, she told him, was nothing, and they all said something different. He was tall. He was short. He was fat. He was thin. They couldn't even agree on the color of his hair or what he was wearing. The image Kelly Blake managed to come up with could fit a million guys.

Eddie ran the Melon Man's picture through the DMV and all the other data banks. The man did not exist. He had no driver's license. No record. No passport. He'd never been in the military, or any other place that needed a photo ID or fingerprints.

But they did have a credible picture of him thanks to Kelly Blake, and that was something to go on.

Jimmy thanked her and, after a little more small talk, said she could go.

After she left he said to Eddie, "What did you say to her?"

"How do you know I said something?"

"I'm a detective."

"I told her how great she looked."

"And that made her mad?"

Eddie looked uncomfortable.

"What else?"

Eddie looked uncomfortable.

"You told her she didn't look like a dyke anymore, didn't you?"

Eddie looked uncomfortable.

"Didn't you?"

Eddie nodded. Shyly. Like a kid caught stealing porn.

CHAPTER 17

THE CAREGIVER

They arrived at Magdalena's house the same time as the caregiver. Jimmy timed it that way. Eddie fell in behind her when she made the left onto Magdalena's road. It wasn't hard to pick her out. In the ten minutes they were waiting, hers was the only car that took the turn.

Eddie followed her past woods and meadows, and scattered neighbors. At the end of the road was a clearing, and there was Magdalena's house. Eddie parked the cruiser next to the caregiver's in the gravel driveway.

A patrol car was not Jimmy's usual ride. They're intimidating and make people uncomfortable, especially if someone's up to no good; it tends to rattle them and put them off their game. Or not, because it was entirely possible this hard-working caregiver was just doing her job and trying to make conversation with Magdalena who got the wrong end of the stick and thought she was asking her inappropriate questions.

Jimmy thought the elderly were a suspicious lot at the best of times. They don't like new people, their judgment's not what it used to be, and they're inclined to make mistakes. Like now for instance, with Magdalena getting herself all worked up about someone who was probably only trying to make nice.

On the other hand, Magdalena's suspicions could be well founded and the caregiver was on the make. It happens. Either way, according to Mary, Magdalena was scared out of her wits. That's why Jimmy was there, to calm her down and give her some peace of mind. That was the fine line Jimmy was walking here. That's how delicate a mission he was on.

He reached for the box of pastries he'd hidden underneath his raincoat on the back seat of the car. Eddie would've scarfed them down if he knew they were there. He bought them from Angelo's across from the station house. Napoleons and éclairs. It's a well-known fact that sweet, sticky desserts drive old people crazy. Mary said she sometimes brought them for Magdalena as a special treat. It's why Jimmy brought them today.

Magdalena opened her front door as Jimmy and the caregiver got out of their cars.

Eddie stayed in the cruiser, happy to watch from the comfort of the car and listen to an oldies' station.

Jimmy walked towards Magdalena with a big smile on his face.

"Mary said to drop these off," he said and handed her the box of pastries.

"For me," she said coquettishly. Transforming herself in the blink of an eye from the tough old broad Jimmy thought she was to an adolescent flirt who batted her eyes and planted a come-hither smile on her wrinkly old face.

You could see what a fox she used to be. She had all the moves only they were dated and obvious. She reminded him of a silent movie actress with those overdone mannerisms and exaggerated facial expressions, but you had to give her credit for trying. For breaking out the old soft-shoe shuffle and the song and dance routine. Stuff she's been doing all of her life to survive and get by.

He thought she put on a good show and reciprocated in kind, telling her how terrific she looked and laying it on nice and thick. Saying how he hoped she enjoyed the pastries and spending some time going over each one to make conversation and stretch things out.

Magdalena beamed and fingered the box like they were the crown jewels.

It made him realize how much this dog and pony show really meant to her.

He turned to the caregiver, all smiles.

"And you are?" he said and held out his hand.

She'd been standing to the side watching the proceedings.

She reached out to shake Jimmy's hand.

Her hand was thick and meaty and Jimmy's hand was lost inside of it.

"I'm Mrs. Glotz's caregiver, Kathy O'Brien," she said.

You'd never think she was Irish to look at her. She had mocha skin, and thick African lips. Jimmy figured her to be in her early forties.

"My Irish mother married a trumpet player from Harlem," she said reacting to Jimmy's puzzled look. "When he walked out on us we went back to being O'Briens.

Kathy O'Brien was a big woman. Not fat, but tall, and broad, and very large. Jimmy could see how that might be intimidating for Magdalena, who was small and frail. Kathy also seemed to be a no-nonsense type who was not easily taken in by Magdalena's machinations. Jimmy figured this was a turf war plain and simple, and

Magdalena was trying to establish the dominant role in the proceedings. That's why she'd conned Mary into sending him around; to bolster her position against this very large woman. Jimmy hoped that by showing the flag it might encourage them to try a little harder to get along. To compromise. To perpetuate the grand experiment that is the human condition, and try and find the middle ground.

But Jimmy bet against it. He'd seen this movie before.

"You're just the person I'm looking for," he said to her.

Kathy's face showed no signs of concern or surprise. No tics or tells to suggest she was guilty of anything or had something to hide. She stood there with a bland look on her face waiting to hear what he had to say.

"My friend's mother is sick," said Jimmy. "He needs someone to help take care of her and here you are. It's another Festivus miracle," he said referring to a 'Seinfeld' episode he saw recently and chuckling at his own joke.

Kathy O'Brien had no idea what Jimmy was talking about and looked at him like he was crazy. Magdalena was having the same sort of reaction. Both of them wondering, what is this Festivus?

Jimmy carried on like nothing happened.

"Do you have a card?"

Kathy fished around her handbag and came up with one.

"My plate's full right now," she explained. "Mrs. Glotz took my last slot. I'm here every afternoon for two hours and I've got a couple of other people I've been looking in on."

"Seven days a week?"

"That's right."

"Boy you people work hard."

She gave him a resigned smile that said, 'you don't know the half of it.'

"But you've only been with Magdalena for a short time?"

"That's right. This is my second week. A patient I'd been with for a long time passed away. I was with him full time. This is something different for me. The agency is short staffed and I'm helping them out, but I'm sure they'll be able to fix your friend up with someone. The number is on the card. If you wouldn't mind, tell them I sent you. It'll get me some brownie points."

"I'd be glad to, thanks." He glanced at the card and put it in his top pocket. Then he turned to Magdalena. "Is there anything you need?" he asked and looked at his watch, indicating the show was over and he had to move on.

She fluttered her eyes and gave him a gummy smile. No, she said wistfully and thanked him for his concern. She didn't need anything. Jimmy, bless his heart, had seen to everything she required. Evening up the score and making sure the bossy Kathy O'Brien knew she was not alone. That there were people out there who cared about her. People she could call on should the need arise and she was not ripe fruit ready for the picking. Not her. Not Magdalena Glotz who walked across the Hungarian border with just the clothes on her back. Not today, anyway.

The pastries were just a bonus.

Jimmy turned back to Kathy O'Brien, shook her hand again and fished out a card of his own.

"Call me if you need anything and please don't be shy. I can be here in ten minutes and I can call on all sorts of resources should they be needed."

Kathy gave him a confident smile and said she hoped it wouldn't be necessary.

Jimmy waved and climbed into the cruiser.

Eddie put the car in drive.

"How'd it go?" he asked as he maneuvered out of the driveway and got back on the road.

"I don't like her," said Jimmy.

"Why not?"

"Nothing you can put your finger on. She doesn't like cops though, that's for sure."

Eddie understood. It was a radar cops were equipped with. A sense. A feeling. And it didn't have to mean anything. Lots of people don't like cops for no other reason than that they don't like them. It doesn't mean they're criminals or have anything to hide. But if they don't like cops, cops don't like them in return and that's how Jimmy felt about Kathy O'Brien.

Eddie too.

"Why?" Jimmy asked him.

"Same as you. From where I sat, especially when you were talking to the old lady, you could see it plain enough. There was a body language you were probably too close to catch and when you weren't looking at her she had this look on her face."

"Like what?"

"Evil, skeevy, dislike and hatred, all rolled into one. And it was only there for a second while your attention was on the old lady. Then it was gone."

"Huh."

"You think she's trying to steal her money?"

Jimmy thought about it. There was definitely something about her that gave him the creeps, especially now that Eddie had added his two cents. But what did it mean? That she didn't like cops? Maybe her brother got busted, or she'd had some trouble herself along the way and that's what he was picking up.

"I don't think so," said Jimmy and cracked his knuckles, something he was not allowed to do at home because it drove Mary crazy. "The woman's a professional. I don't see her ruining her reputation by nicking whatever Magdalena's got to steal, and the pickings are kinda slim anyway. I think she's just trying to do her job. Magdalena's one tough cookie, though. I'd hate to go up against her. She'd be better off with a younger person. Someone she can tell what to do. The large and experienced Kathy O'Brien does not appear to be such a candidate and that's probably the root of the problem right there."

And maybe that's what he was getting a sense of here; that Ms. Kathy O'Brien didn't like Magdalena very much either.

CHAPTER 18
CONNER MALLOY'S APARTMENT

When they got on the Saw Mill River Parkway to go to Brooklyn the leaves were falling and the trees were changing color. By the time they got to the City the trees were all green and there wasn't a dead leaf to be seen on the ground. That's how much colder it was in Columbia.

When Jimmy pointed out this phenomenon to Eddie, Eddie said, "Who gives a shit," which ended any more discourse on nature's mysterious ways and Jimmy's observations about them.

The route they took was Eddie's. Eddie the Driver. Eddie the Route Man. It was his life's work this driving business, which is why Jimmy never drove any more. He used to, but that was a long time ago. All they did was fight because Eddie kept second-guessing everything he did. Why would you go that way? Why didn't you go this way? Whatever route Jimmy took was never any good because Eddie's way was always better. After a while it got to be annoying and who cared anyway, so nowadays he let Eddie drive and have all the fun. Like zooming up to cars going slow in the fast lane and giving them the lights and the siren. Punishment, he said, for fucking up the traffic flow. Then there was the running commentary Eddie kept up on everyone's driving skills. "Look at this guy," he'd say. Or, "what an asshole that guy was." Jimmy was used to it and didn't pay attention. Instead he stared out the window and took in the scenery gawking like a tourist at Manhattan's magnificent skyline and noting the changes that had taken place since his last visit. The City was a living, breathing organism. If you blinked once everything changed. If you blinked twice it had changed again.

They met the NYPD detective outside Conner Malloy's apartment building on the edge of the Windsor Terrace section of Brooklyn hard by the Greenwood

Cemetery. Realtors had come up with a new name for the area. Greenwood Heights, which enabled them to raise property values and rents for the privilege of living in this newly invented neighborhood. Conner's apartment was on the second floor of a five-story walk-up on a street full of the same sort of buildings. Some of them were unkempt and on the verge of becoming slums. Others were in the middle of million dollar renovations. Gentrification is the name they give to this process. Pushing out the locals is another.

First come the artists who are always willing to take a risk for space and price. Then come the bargain hunters, the restaurants, the boutiques and small galleries. Once they're successfully planted and given time to mature come the speculators, and the money, and the expensive remodeling. The process tops out with knockdowns and new apartment buildings and hey presto, you've got yourself a new, upwardly mobile, freshly minted neighborhood and fuck the people who've lived there for generations and can't afford to live there any more. Greenwood Heights has got a ways to go yet, but the process is well underway.

It was the detective's first day on the job. He couldn't be more than twenty-six, he couldn't be. But he was. Det. Frank Simmons was thirty-five and perfectly turned out in his brand new blue suit, crisp white shirt, striped blue tie, and shiny black Oxfords recently purchased from the Coat Factory along with another four outfits for his newly acquired position. He came from the army they found out later, two tours in Iraq and one in Afghanistan. Fast tracked to the NYPD Detective Program for retiring MPs. A nice thank-you from a grateful New York for services rendered to the nation. Not like the Viet Nam vets who came back with their heads down and were vilified and spat upon. Not like those poor folks and thank goodness for that.

Now this - his first day on the job babysitting out-of-towners who looked like they couldn't fight themselves out of a paper bag. Someone's got to do it, he supposed, but why did it have to be him?

Conner Malloy's super was an unsightly middle-aged man who wore bib-overalls that smelled of liquor and sweat and had a face and head that badly needed shaving. They showed him their badges and explained the situation. The super reacted the same way everyone did when they found out someone they had dealings with had been murdered, and could offer them no information that shed any light on the matter. He let them into the apartment then scurried back to whatever he was doing before, but not before he put a call in to a man who promised him five hundred bucks for a heads-up should an apartment open up in this rent-stabilized building.

The apartment had a living room/kitchenette, a bedroom and a bathroom. It was a bare bones affair with very little furniture: a bed, a table, two chairs, a TV resting on a blue plastic milk crate, and nothing on the walls or the floor except for scuffmarks, cracks, and cobwebs. The one bare window faced the next-door building and offered nothing in the way of light or view. Conner's whole life appeared to be strewn on the table, with the exception of his wallet, which they knew he'd taken with him. There were a couple of paycheck stubs, a box of checks, assorted change, some bank statements, bills, junk mail and last Saturday's *New York Post*.

The paychecks were from a local bar called Bogey's. Det. Simmons knew the place; he was a Brooklynite after all. Born, bred, and current resident.

Jimmy wondered if anyone knew who Bogey was any more?

Det. Simmons didn't.

Jimmy asked him.

The bar was a couple of blocks away. The owner had to know who Bogey was because the entire wall space, including the corridor to the bathrooms and the kitchen, was covered in posters from Humphrey Bogart movies. It was the only motif the place had. Other than that the bar, tables, chairs, booths and tin-plate ceiling was just like any other local watering hole.

Det. Simmons showed a guy behind the counter his badge and asked to speak to the manager who was a twitchy sort of a guy who squeezed them into a booth at the back of the room. He confirmed that Conner Malloy was on the payroll and had worked there for two years.

"He's a bouncer four nights a week. He's supposed to be here now for a meeting," said the manager irritably and looked at his watch. "I was just about to call him. What's this about?"

Det. Simmons said, "Conner Malloy was shot dead yesterday outside a diner in Columbia. Doesn't anybody watch the news here?"

Apparently they did not. Neither did anyone know where Columbia was.

The manager appeared to show no remorse for the loss of his employee. Neither did he show any emotion. He didn't like Conner was the truth of the matter. Conner the swarthy. Conner the popular. Conner the man who appeared to get laid more times than the manager brushed his teeth. He was sorry the man was dead, of course, but the truth of the matter was he was glad he was gone. There were plenty of bouncers around and a lot of them were ugly, which was the new job requirement for anyone seeking such employment at Bogey's.

Brie the Bartender, who was leaning on the counter and listening in on the proceedings, began to sob. Since she was the only one who seemed to have any reaction to Conner's death, the people in the law enforcement business thought she might be a love interest of Conner's.

Brie's sobbing pissed off the weasely manager royally. He got a little twitchier because it was clear that something was going on in his world he had no knowledge of, and with Brie the Bartender of all people. The same Brie the Bartender he'd been fixing to make a move on of his very own. Brie, who he'd worshipped from afar, was sullied forever now he knew she'd succumbed to the charms of Conner Malloy who, if these officers were to be believed, would never be able to beat him to the trough again.

They asked the manager a lot more questions none of which he had the answers to, so they dismissed him not unkindly and had Brie the Bartender take his place.

She was still sniffling and snarfling, but had managed by then to get herself under control. She told them she'd been with Conner two nights ago. And no, this to Det. Simmons, they were not a regular item. And yes, this was the first time she'd slept with him. And was that important, she wanted to know? And if so, why?

No one could give her a satisfactory answer.

Jimmy asked her if anything unusual happened at the sleepover.

Brie blushed thinking Jimmy was asking her something of a sexual nature since, by her reckoning, there'd already been one inappropriate question. But then she realized what he was after and, following a spirited honking into what was left of her tissue, she said, "He got a call in the morning that made him very happy."

"Did he say what it was about?" asked Jimmy.

"No."

"Whaddya think it was about?"

"He said a guy he liked working with had a job for him."

"And?" said Jimmy.

"That's it."

"He didn't say what sort of job?"

"No.

"Or who the guy was?"

"No."

"Or where the job was?"

"No."

"What time was this?"

She told him.

"Did you speak to him after he left the apartment?"

She shook her head.

"And you haven't heard from him since?"

"No."

"And when you didn't hear from him for the last couple of days you thought what?"

"He was supposed to work tonight. I figured we'd see each other then. It's not like we're living together," she said defensively.

"And no idea where he was going or what he was going to do?"

She shook her head.

"And no names?"

"No. No names."

She had nothing more for them.

It turned out neither she, nor any of her co-workers, knew very much about Conner Malloy or what he did with himself when he wasn't working at the bar. Not where he came from. Or whether he had any relatives. Or friends. He kept himself to himself, did his job, and on Monday night did Brie the Bartender. End of story.

Contact information was exchanged with everyone at the bar. No one saw Conner's death as having anything to do with Bogey's. No disgruntled customer bearing a grudge or anything like that. There hadn't been any trouble for ages. Apparently Conner did his work well. There'd been no difficulties with co-workers and neither did anyone recognize the picture the artist came up with of the Melon Man.

Jimmy gave a copy to Det. Simmons and asked him to show it around the station house and post it on the board.

Det. Simmons said he'd be glad to. The twitchy manager had a last piece of wisdom for them as they were walking out the door.

"And anyway," he said disdainfully, laying bare the falseness of his sorrow for the dearly departed Conner Malloy, "who'd ya think's gonna schlep all the way up to Columbia, wherever the fuck that is, to whack him?"

Meaning Conner Malloy was of minor importance to just about everybody with the exception of Brie the Bartender and every other good-looking woman in the borough of Brooklyn.

Outside on the street Jimmy asked Det. Simmons if he could order up the records for Conner's phone to see if they could get a line on who called him that morning.

Det. Simmons took out his cellphone. It took him a while, but finally, after getting to the right person, he was told he'd have them by tomorrow, or the next day, or maybe the day after that. Det. Simmons vowed to pass them to Jimmy the minute he received them.

They all shook hands.

Jimmy thanked him for his help and he and Eddie went to retrieve their car.

Det. Simmons, once the duo turned the corner, ducked back into Bogeys and, under the pretense of having another couple of questions for Brie the Bartender, asked her out on a date.

Jimmy and Eddie met up with Det. Morgan Flynn at the Second Avenue Deli, which was situated, strangely enough, on First Avenue on the Isle of Manhattan.

Eddie couldn't help noticing that for a Jewish deli there didn't seem to be any Jewish people there except for the customers. The people in the kitchen looked South American, the waitstaff was Korean and the person that seated them was African-American. What's up with that, he wanted to know? No one had an answer for him, but the food was delicious and that was all that counted. The corned beef was to die for, so was the kreplach soup, the sour pickles, and even the coleslaw that can sometimes be a bit soggy in the best of places.

Jimmy was in heaven.

Morgan too.

Eddie wasn't so over the moon, but appeared to be having a good time hanging with big boys, chomping on his pot roast with a side of potato pancakes and applesauce. Italian food was his thing. You'd have to go to Brooklyn to get a smile on Eddie's face where food was concerned.

"So whaddya got?" asked Morgan and crashed his mouth into the side of his six-inch thick corned beef sandwich and hacked off a chunk.

Jimmy told him how he thought Conner Malloy and the Melon Man were a team. How he thought if he got to the Melon Man he could get to the man he was sitting in the diner with. The man he pegged for Conner Malloy's killer. He handed Morgan a copy of the sketch of the big guy.

Morgan stared at it and shook his head.

"Nah. Don't know him. I'll spread the word though. Shouldn't be hard to place a man as inconspicuous as this." He chomped on a pickle then poked at Jimmy with what was left of it. "So you got nothing? That's what you're telling me?"

Eddie almost choked on his pot roast.

Jimmy squirmed.

"Well, I wouldn't put it that way."

"How would you put it?"

Jimmy stroked his bottom lip.

"I've got Conner's phone records coming," he said defensively.

"That's it?"

"And someone must know who the Melon Man is. It's not like he's your average looking person."

"What makes you think he's gonna tell you what you want to know when you find him?"

"My unbridled optimism."

"What else ya got?"

"My secret weapon."

"What's that?"

Jimmy made him wait. He took another bite of his sandwich and a big slug of orange soda.

When his mouth was finally empty he said, "You!" and they all put their hands together in silent prayer.

CHAPTER 19

THURSDAY

THE CHIEF

First thing Thursday morning Jimmy went in to see the Chief to bring him up to speed on Conner Malloy's murder investigation.

The Chief was a beefy looking man with piercing blue eyes, a flat pockmarked nose and a meaty face made larger by a fresh crew cut, and darker by the scowl that spoiled his central casting appearance. He sat behind a desk that was neatly arranged and he looked like he was trying to control an oncoming heart attack. He had just gotten off the phone with the president of the local school board, Dr. Arnold Bender, a man the Chief has tussled with before.

Last night Dr. Bender's son was issued a desk ticket for possession of marijuana, a Class 'A' misdemeanor with a required court appearance. Dr. Bender wanted the Chief to tear the ticket up as a personal favor. Tear it up? Where did the man think he was, Chicago? While the Chief was a number of things, including a major publicity hound, he believed in the sanctity of the law for all of Columbia's citizens, not just the common folk, so he said no.

And they had a fight.

And things were brought up that shouldn't have been, like how Dr. Bender never supported the Chief in any of his reelection campaigns. The call ended with the Chief telling Dr. Bender how he was sending someone over to speak to the kid about where he got the stuff. Which set off another round of righteous indignation from Dr. Bender, who quickly climbed on his high horse and in a tone he liked to use on secretaries, waiters, and anyone else he regarded as not up to his intellectual standards and station in life, began to berate the Chief in no uncertain terms, threatening not only to endorse someone else when the time came for the Chief's reelection, but to make sure the rest of the school board went along with him. And all the other boards he was on, and everyone at his golf club, where he was a very big mucky-muck. And anyone else he knew now or was ever likely to know in the future.

The Chief had his own way of handling discussions of this sort employing, when it was his turn to speak, a raised voice technique that sounded like a drill-master with a toothache and ending up in a delicious crescendo of outrageous rhetoric honed from years of experience in matters such as these.

Then he slammed down the phone.

It was Jimmy's misfortune to enter the office just after this last part. He found the Chief trembling with rage and himself the target of the Chief's righteous indignation.

"I want you to go over to that son-of-a-bitch's house right now and talk to his kid," the Chief said angrily, then he explained who the kid was and what had happened.

"Who gave him the ticket?" asked Jimmy.

"The new guy."

"Mr. Officious?"

Mr. Officious was a rookie cop, a no-nonsense kind of guy who was a little tightly wired.

"That's him," said the Chief whose face had taken on a disturbing shade of red.

Jimmy wondered if he was going to explode. An image of brain goop hanging from the ceiling crept into his mind.

"The kid's gotta be in school, Chief. Let's wait for him to get home."

The Chief's steely blue eyes bored into Jimmy like a comic book villain. This was not the answer he was looking for.

"I want you to go over to this guy's house right now," he barked. "Talk to them. Talk to the kid if he's there. Shake him up. Shake them up. Show that Dr. Bender he can shove his fancy titles up his ass and how, instead of helping his kid, he's managed to push him deeper in the shit. Take Eddie with you and pump it up. Show 'em the flag and read 'em the riot act."

The Chief seemed suddenly to be having a good time.

Jimmy had seen this act before, when someone stepped over the Chief's line and tried to pull rank on him. It was the one thing they had in common. Small towns like Columbia have a pecking order and people like Jimmy and the Chief are always bumping up against it. Like now for instance, when a so-called big-shot thought he could push the department around.

Jimmy handed the Chief the pictures the artist came up with.

The Chief stared at the one of the Melon Man.

"What about the other guy?"

"Everyone fixated on the big guy. The second man's picture could fit anyone."

"What else you got?"

Jimmy told him about his trip to Conner's apartment and the phone call Brie the Bartender said Conner got.

"I'm waiting on his phone records."

"Won't show you anything," said the Chief caustically. "It's from a throwaway. Count on it. That's it? That's all you got?"

Jimmy thought the Chief must have been talking to Morgan.

"We're distributing the big guy's picture. He's so conspicuous, someone must know who he is."

"Then what?"

This was deja vu all over again. First Morgan, now the Chief, not to mention the ME's nasty dig in his report about his detecting abilities. Jimmy was thinking no one seemed to have very much confidence in him.

"I'm hoping he'll lead me to the other guy," he said. "The one I think is the shooter."

"Good luck with that," the Chief sniffed. "Personally, I don't see it happening. Like I said, you got nothing." Then a sort of panic set in. "What am I gonna tell the CID people, Jimmy? Those guys have always been gunning for you. Now you've given them your head on a platter. What have you been doing all this time?" Then he bore down on him, exchanging Jimmy for Dr. Bender and getting his rocks off on poor Jimmy's sorry ass. "You're gonna fuck this up for me Jimmy, I just know you are. And who's it gonna come down on when it's over and done with, answer me that will you? Not you, oh no. It'll be me they hang out to dry. I'm gonna look like a complete asshole by the time this is finished. I can only imagine what the press is gonna do with it."

Jimmy stiffened. It's why they never got along in the first place. Everything always came down to the Chief's image with the press.

"This case is two days old, Skipper," Jimmy said coldly. "I don't see what the problem is. I'm sorry Dr. Bender pissed you off, but don't go taking it out on me. Me and Eddie will take a ride over to the doctor's house as soon as we're finished here and see what we can find out. Now on this other thing. I say we send out a press release with the picture of the big guy and see if we get anything back. You know how these things work, Chief. You plug away and poke around and see what comes up. That's what we're doing here, poking around."

It didn't take much to get the two of them riled up and now they found themselves on familiar ground. Jousting with one another. Glaring at each other. It was a routine they'd been through a thousand times before. All they needed was a ring and a referee and they'd be good to go, but it wouldn't get that far. It never did. Each of them played out their appointed roles and then it was time to take the pot off the boil.

Jimmy looked away first. After all, the Chief was his boss.

And the Chief, always sensitive to the way the wind was blowing, gave a stiff nod acknowledging the bout was over.

He picked up the phone and summoned his secretary and the three of them collaborated on the press release. When it was finished the secretary was instructed to send it out to everyone and their uncle and put it on the wires. Jimmy told the Chief he'd let him know how things went at Dr. Bender's house and walked out of the office.

CHAPTER 20

THE BENDERS

Jimmy and Eddie drove over to Dr. Arnold Bender's house in Eddie's patrol car. Eddie was in uniform at the suggestion of the Chief who thought a uniform and the patrol car would add to the drama of the visit and piss the Benders off mightily.

It was a miserable day. No rain, but the thick cloud cover was dark and threatening and made everything feel gloomy. The weather reports said it would clear up later, but who can believe them?

On the way over, Jimmy told Eddie about Mary catching Lucy smoking dope."

"How old is she?"

"Twelve."

"That's when I tried it."

"Me too," said Jimmy.

"Whatcha gonna do?"

Jimmy blew the air through his teeth and sighed.

"Well, she's grounded, that's the first thing. She says she got it from a friend who bought it from a kid at the high school."

"Got a name?"

"I do."

"Good," said Eddie. "Let's go over to his house and beat the shit outta him," and meant every word of it.

Jimmy shook his head. They couldn't do that.

"I'm going to speak to the principal and see what he has to say about it. Lucy said the kid sells it on school grounds. Maybe we can close him down and put him out of business."

"If the school cooperates."

"I don't see why they shouldn't."

It was Eddie's turn to sigh.

"I hope so," he said though he didn't sound very confident. He'd been chasing kids smoking dope for too long to be optimistic about anything regarding drugs in Columbia. If the kids weren't doing it, the parents were and cooperation was at a minimum. "Did she like it?" he asked.

"She says not."

"They all say that."

"I did," said Jimmy.

"Me too," said Eddie. "And she swore she'd never try it again?"

"She did."

"That's what I said when I got caught."

"Me too," said Jimmy glumly.

Dr. Bender's gated house was a magnificent affair built in the '30s and full of brick and dark wood porches, weathered furniture and shingled roofing. The lawns were sweeping and perfect in texture and color. There were no weeds to be seen anywhere, no thanks to the agronomist the Benders just hired at the expense of Jose who'd been tending their lawns for the last five years, but didn't have a title.

The gate opened when Eddie identified himself.

They drove up a short driveway that led to the house and parked.

They were greeted there by Mrs. Bender, a scrawny looking woman in her mid to late forties with a face that was once pretty but was now lined and pinched and showed signs of a general dissatisfaction with everything around her. She came out of the house and walked quickly towards their approaching car. Her shoulders were hunched and her arms hugged her body in a manner that suggested she was either cold, or insecure, or both.

She reached the patrol car before Jimmy could get out.

When he rolled down his window, she wanted to know what they wanted.

When Jimmy told her about her son's ticket, she paled. She was already on the chalky side so her face took on a ghostly appearance. She immediately went on the attack.

"There must be some mistake," she said tersely and regarded Jimmy with a withering stare.

Jimmy said there was no mistake and asked if they could come inside to talk to her son. Jimmy could see she didn't know about the ticket and was dealing with the situation the only way she knew how. Fight, deny and obfuscate.

When she'd finished flustering and blustering, Mrs. Bender told them to stay in the car until her husband, who she said she was about to call, arrived.

"And you want us to wait in the car?" said Jimmy, to be clear.

She said that was so and set herself up in an imperious pose that was supposed to cower them into submission and put them in their place.

"Not come inside the house and talk to your son?"

"He's at school," she snapped.

"And not come inside," Jimmy repeated, adding a dash of sauce to his tone, "and offer us a nice cup of coffee while we wait for your husband to arrive. Not that?"

"Not that," she agreed and gave them a firm nod to emphasize the point.

Jimmy thought about it. Choosing not to invite them inside was her right of course, but he didn't care for the message it sent or the way it was given. She was being rude and confrontational and he had no intention of sitting in the car like a jackass waiting for Dr. Big Shot to show up.

"And you're not prepared to answer any of my questions?" he asked her.

"Not until my husband comes."

"Tell you what," said Jimmy. "What time does your son get home from school?"

"Five o'clock."

"We'll be back then. You can have your husband and your lawyer present, but no one else. I'll be asking your son questions regarding the ticket he got for possession of marijuana at approximately 9:30 last night in the parking lot of the Columbia Library. I'm telling you this to be sure we're on the same page here. I'm also telling you for the record, and my report, and in front of Patrolman Eddie Smith who is acting as a witness in this regard."

Mrs. Bender face appeared to get paler if such a thing was possible.

Jimmy got the distinct impression that life was not all peaches and cream under the Bender roof.

She said she'd see them at 5:00 and walked away from the cruiser, head bowed, arms wound tightly around herself, back inside the house and closed the door behind her.

CHAPTER 21

THURSDAY
SHELLY BARTON

Mary stopped by the Columbia Senior Center to talk to the director about a new client she was delivering food to. Maybe there was something she should know about him, or perhaps they wanted her to be on the alert for something he was dealing with? The Senior Center was a lifeline to a lot of the seniors in the neighborhood who had no one else to look out for them. The Food From Friends volunteers were a useful means of communication for some of those people.

The Senior Center's main feature was its large social hall where meetings and functions took place: the bridge club, cardio fitness sessions, lectures, socials and the occasional party. A cozy corner had some armchairs, a couple of sofas, and a bookcase full of board games, puzzles and DVDs. A big screen television also lived at this end of the hall. Today everything was stacked up or pushed to the edges of the room and the entire floor space was taken up with cartons, racks of clothing, old electrical appliances, hundreds of books and records, pots, pans, and sets of dishes and cutlery. There was some furniture, a few rugs, glasswear and crockery. It looked like a big tag sale only no money was changing hands, just a bunch of seniors who were picking their way through the stuff and making piles of their own to take home.

Mary asked an old lady she knew what was going on.

"These are Shelly Barton's things," said the woman sweetly.

"Doesn't he need them?"

"Oh no," said the lady said sadly. "Poor Shelly passed away a little while ago." She was clutching a mint condition frying pan and was having a hard time containing the look of triumph that kept creeping onto her face while she was talking about something so sad. "The new owner gave the Senior Center permission to distribute Shelly's belongings."

Mary used to bring food to Shelly Barton until one day a few years ago when she came to make her delivery and no one answered the door. Usually she'd hear him shuffling around as he made his way to the front door. This time there were no sounds and no feeling there was anyone inside, which made no sense since Shelly Barton was close to ninety and couldn't drive any more. She walked around the house, but couldn't see inside. The curtains were closed. There was no sign of life and the mailbox was stuffed with three days' mail.

She reported all of this to the Senior Center.

They called the police who found Shelly lying on the floor of his kitchen unable to move. He'd been like that for days, he told them. He heard Mary when she came with his food, but he was too weak to cry out. He was in the hospital for a long time after that. When he came out he had a full-time caregiver living with him, so there was no need for the Food From Friends deliveries any more.

Shelly Barton lived in a forested section of Columbia close by the Putnam County border, in an old vacation cabin community built in 1948. A selling point back then was that no colored or Jews were allowed to live there. There's a photo someplace of the billboard advertising that very sentiment along with the name of the sub-division and what a great place it was to live in. You've got to wonder what folks are talking about when they say they yearn for "The Good Old Days." They must have forgotten stuff like this unless, of course, they don't like blacks or Jews.

The Bartons bought the house in the 60's as a weekend home when no one cared too much if you were Jewish, but if you were black there was still some resistance. Black being much easier to spot than a white Jew. They used it as a weekend home, Shelly and Judy, and lived in the City in those days. She was a schoolteacher. He worked for the MTA. Between them they made out pretty good. No kids though. They tried, but it didn't work. Was it her or was it him? Who knew back then? Maybe his plumbing was faulty? Either way they never got it checked out and left things to fate, which chose to leave them childless.

They retired in the '80s on comfortable pensions, packed up their apartment on the Upper West Side and moved to the cabin in the country where they lived in blissful happiness until the day Judy collapsed from a heart attack.

An ambulance came and collected her.

She died in the hospital five days later and Shelly Barton was alone. Their relatives were all gone and they'd outlived their friends and never made any new ones.

All of this Shelly told Mary the first time she delivered food to him. He invited her inside and showed her Judy's handbag hanging from the chair where she'd left it. He never moved any of her things, he told her. They were exactly the same as she left them the day they took her to the hospital.

Mary saw him once a week for a year after that and he never invited her inside his house again.

What was interesting about Shelly was his face. If you only saw that part of him you'd never know he was close to ninety. It was a stark contrast to the rest of him that was frail and bent over from a curvature of the spine that got worse as he got older. What skin Mary could see was covered in lesions and blotches, but not so his face - that was clear and translucent and blemish free. He had a full head of silvery gray hair, a thin angular nose, high cheekbones and thin lips that were always fixed in a sardonic smile.

Mary was taken by his resilience in the face of so much pain and adversity. He had an assortment of ailments that kept him going backwards and forwards to one hospital or another and he seemed to take it all in stride. Peering up at her from his bent over position when she asked him the obligatory, "Is everything all right?" And, "Is there anything you need?" as if to say, "I'm fine thank you now get the hell out of here." Though he was far too polite to ever say such a thing.

Now poor Shelly was dead. Finally. He'd hung on longer than he should have, the old lady told her, and endured an ending that seemed unfair for someone who was so nice.

And now they were picking over his things at the Senior Center like scavengers at a rubbish dump.

Mary called Jimmy the minute she got home and was pleased to see he'd left his phone on, for a change.

"Do you remember Shelly Barton, that guy I used to deliver food to?"

Jimmy said he did.

He and Eddie were just pulling out of the Bender's driveway.

"Turns out I didn't do him any favors," she told him, talking about that time she saved Shelly's life.

"It was the right thing to do," said Jimmy.

"Yeah, but I heard that last stretch was very painful. He was alone, except for a caregiver. You know that, right? No family. Or friends."

Jimmy said he did and shuddered at the thought of it. The idea of being alone when he got old terrified him.

"So guess who got it?" she asked.

"Got what?"

"His house."

"I have no idea."

"Yes you do."

"Why's that?"

"Because Shelly Barton's caregiver was Kathy O'Brien and he left the house and everything else he had to her."

"The same Kathy O'Brien who's taking care of Magdalena?"

"The very same."

"Huh."

CHAPTER 22

JIMMY AND EDDIE

On the drive back from the Bender's house Eddie kept saying the same things over and over. How not to be invited in for coffee while they waited for the husband was the height of rudeness as far as he was concerned, and how he'd never seen anything like it in all the time he'd been in Columbia.

Jimmy didn't like it either. It sounded like more of the same dish the Chief had been served this morning by the good Dr. Bender.

"We'll get 'em next time," he said confidently. "Things have a habit……"

Eddie wasn't so sure. He thought they'd been disrespected.

Jimmy agreed with him.

Eddie didn't like it.

Jimmy didn't like it either.

"It would be nice, when we go back, if we could get Dr. Bender's kid to come up with a name."

Eddie said not to hold his breath.

"Maybe Dr. Bender will make him tell us."

Eddie looked at him like he was nuts.

"You really are an optimist, aren't you?"

Jimmy realized how ridiculous he sounded.

"I'm living with a pair of them," he explained. Meaning Lucy and Mary. "It must be contagious."

Eddie grunted.

"Speaking of which," he said wondering if this newfound optimism of Jimmy's had completely warped his mind. "You really think Lucy's not gonna try that stuff again?"

Jimmy sighed.

"Not really."

"What did you say to her?"

"Not enough."

"Did she get it?"

"I hope so. Time will tell."

"So you think she'll try it again."

"I do," said Jimmy sadly. "We did, didn't we?"

"We did."

"So why wouldn't she?"

They kicked over the living with a teenager thing for a bit. How Jimmy never imagined how difficult it was going to be. Lucy getting her period, training bras, feminine mood swings, and now this. "Talk about getting thrown in the deep end."

"But you love it."

"I do," said Jimmy. "I never thought I would, but I do."

Eddie mumbled something about how he'd take his chances staying single.

They parted company at the station house and agreed to meet up later for the return trip to Dr. Bender's. Jimmy was anxious to see if there was any response to the press release on the Melon Man, but there was none. Early days, he told himself. And it was. Just a couple of hours, but he'd hoped for a quick break.

Oh silly man.

There was nothing from Morgan either.

So far his critics were batting a thousand. He had nothing.

He got to work assembling the murder book for Conner Malloy.

The murder book is a complete record of an investigation from start to finish, or in this case for as far as he'd got. Reports, interviews, notes, even theories and speculation, all went into the murder book in a chronological order.

Thus far Conner's murder book was looking pretty thin!

CHAPTER 23

DUPREE JOHNSON

Dupree Johnson and Jimmy were sitting in the Shanghai Palace, a Chinese restaurant just off Main Street in the heart of Columbia. They usually met for lunch the first Thursday of every month, unless something came up sooner. It was nice for both of them. They got to touch base and chew the fat and once in a while Duprec had some information to pass on to Jimmy.

Like now for instance.

Dupree was a gangly looking dark-skinned man with a lopey stride and a face that was making a comeback. It used to have the look of a doper, all sucked-in and cadaverous with watery eyes and yellowish teeth. Now the teeth have been capped, the eyes were sharp and focused and his face had filled out nicely. He was once a basketball player with a lot of promise. That was in high school. He never made it to college. The acclaim was too much for him and he succumbed to the temptations of an early success. Weed messed up his timing. Smack messed up his mind. Until he got himself cleaned up, thanks to Jimmy, and became the young phenom who was sitting across from him now, wearing designer clothes and sipping on Chinese tea.

They always sat in the same booth and ordered the same things. Wonton soup, pepper steak and fried rice for Jimmy. Egg drop soup, spare ribs well-done, egg roll and chicken chow mein for Dupree. The waiter put their order in as soon as they walked in the door, such was the regularity of their routine.

The Chinese noodles were particularly good. Dupree sloshed them around in the duck sauce and scarfed them down like someone was going to take them away from him.

"Remember my cousin Lamont?" he said between mouthfuls.

Jimmy said he did.

A while ago, Dupree and Lamont had gotten themselves mixed up in an attempted robbery that had nothing to do with them. Jimmy helped them get out of jail.

"Lamont's still on the street," Dupree went on. "He does a few bad things every now and then, but we don't have to get into that." He took a sip of tea to wash down the noodles and smiled gratefully as the waiter brought over another bowl of them and more duck sauce. "Him and me were talkin the other night an he's tellin me this wild tale about some light-skinned princess he's been bangin. Princess might be a little strong in this lady's case 'cause he says she's over forty and built like a truck. He says he picked her up in a bar a little while back. Seems the girl likes to get high and laid and high some more, so they get themselves a room someplace and Lamont obliges her on all counts.

"Well sir, she gets herself a little too high, if you know what I mean, and tells Lamont some stuff she shouldn't have. Like how she lives with old folks and gets them to be her friends, then persuades them to leave her their stuff when they're dead and gone.

"Lamont hates scams that have anythin to do with the old folks. He's got a soft spot for them, probably cos he's got no folks of his own. He loves my Moms more'n I do is what I keep tellin him, an I think it's true. You know he lives with her, I told you that didn't I?"

Jimmy said he did.

"Funny cos the dude will do anythin else, and I do mean anythin, and not even bat an eyelid. Shows to go you, you can never tell nothin about peeps. There's always some good in there someplace."

Jimmy had to smile at that. Dupree turning philosopher along with all the other things he's managed to pull off since he straightened himself out.

"Anyway," Dupree went on, "as Lamont's tellin me this stuff he's gettin all worked up. His eyes are buggin outta his head and his mouth's all a froth. If I didn't know better I'd a thought he was fixin to take me out right there! Course he had a little somethin before we hooked up an you know how that goes."

Jimmy did.

"So there's Lamont steamin like a kettle an itchin to tell me the rest of the tale 'cos now he's got a big hate on for this bitch, her havin crossed a line she never knew existed, an all he wants to do is beat the shit outta her. By the third date he says they're really gettin down and dirty. She's snortin smack like she's been doin it all her life and she's gettin sloppier by the minute, tellin him more and more stuff about how she's been rippin off the old folks and how much she stole from them. Tryin to impress him I s'pose and showin him how smart she is.

"Lamont's no genius, but he's got street smarts up the kazoo. His brain kicks in like they just threw the switch and he helps her along with a couple more hits so's he can get to the bottom of things 'cos he's beginnin to see a business opportunity here.

"She tells him about how she just made a big score and she's retiring. Says she's tired of wipin their asses and puttin up with their shit while she's waitin for them to die. She was out celebratin is why she was at that club where they met.

"So now Lamont's beginnin to get itchy. He hates the sight of her, but he wants to know where the money's at 'cos he'd like to get his hands on some of it, so he doubles down on the dose, fucks the life out of her and, when she's wanderin around on cloud nine, he gives her the third degree and records it.

"She's all giggly and coy and high as a kite, her judgment's way off and for some reason she's still lookin to impress him. So she tells him how she kills them."

Jimmy blinked.

"Kills them," Jimmy repeated. To be sure he heard it right.

Dupree nods.

"S'what I said, man. Kills them! Well sir, that sobers Lamont up real quick. So while she's passed out he gets her particulars outta her bag and asks me to take a look at her. Which I do 'cos I can. Lamont's still figurin how he can get his hands on her money. I'm figurin this is somethin you'd wanna know about." He handed Jimmy a manila envelope full of everything he'd found out about her.

Dupree's a computer geek if you can believe it. How is such a thing possible, this child of the streets, this one time junkie? Dupree was Jimmy's snitch after he helped get him and Lamont out of jail, but not any more. It's not like Dupree was a bad source, his information helped an innocent man go free, it's because the C note Jimmy paid him for snitching pushed him back over the edge. The next time Jimmy saw him he was filthy, bedraggled, and strung out. Jimmy was so upset he said he wouldn't give him any more money no matter what information he had. He thought Dupree's relapse was his fault and he wanted to get him into a detox program to make amends.

Dupree said he didn't want to go and was pissed off at Jimmy for getting all guilty on him and not giving him the money he thought he was entitled to.

It took a lot of persuading, but by the time Jimmy got him to the facility it dawned on Dupree that he was finally going to get clean. Not like when he was in jail where he went to all the meetings then went right back into the yard and got whatever he needed to get high. No sir, this was the real deal, Neal. The last time he was straight was in high school, so now he was scared on top of everything else, not knowing what to expect and thinking it could only be bad.

Only it wasn't. Not really.

There were a couple of tough nights shivering and shitting and puking his guts out, and then it was all over. Hi Ho Silver. He was surprised how quickly he was able to get his shit together, and the rehab people did the rest. They signed him up at the local community college for some computer classes and that's where he took off. This was a time when the economy was booming, where anyone who could work a keyboard could get a job and if you had any ambition just about anything was possible. In a short time Dupree went from being a penniless junkie to the P. Diddy of Ossining and an employer of people just like him, misfits looking for a second chance. Fixers, programmers, and anything else you might need computer-wise. Pretty soon he moved out of his Mom's house into one of those apartment buildings that overlooked the Hudson in what used to be called the "white section," but was now integrating in lightening fashion.

He was living large now, Dupree.

Living the dream.

Only in America folks, only in America.

The waiter cleared their dishes and brought back a plate of cut-up oranges and a couple of fortune cookies.

Jimmy's said, "A positive attitude is your best asset," a philosophy he believed in except for those dark days when he didn't.

Dupree's was, "A dear friend is in trouble," which turned out to be closer to the bone than he cared for.

"I need to speak to Lamont," said Jimmy spraying a mouthful of cookie crumbs Dupree's way.

Dupree brushed the crumbs off his sleeve.

"Easy James," he said looking alarmed. "I just had this bad boy cleaned."

He pulled out his phone and hit the auto dial.

Lamont picked up right away. An exchange took place, Dupree explained what was up and that Jimmy wanted a word with him about his girl friend and the things she told him.

Lamont gave him a loud mouthful.

It was so loud Dupree had to pull the phone away from his ear.

It was so loud Jimmy could hear Lamont saying "motherfucker" over and over as clear as a bell.

It was so loud that everyone in the restaurant could hear it too.

When Lamont finished his tirade, Dupree handed Jimmy the phone.

CHAPTER 24

LAMONT'S GIRLFRIEND

She lived in Tarrytown, the woman Lamont Dubois was partying with. She picked him out as soon as she walked into the club. He was leaning against the bar, braids to his shoulders, tats up his arms, sucking on a beer. He was just what she was looking for: thirtyish, boney, with plenty of tread left on him and looking to hook up. Her instincts said he was an animal, which he was. Lamont. And well hung, which she found out to her delight as she slow danced with him in a corner of the room. He was rough and raw and ready to go. Not hot to look at, but then she was no J Lo herself. She was big and broad and just out of her thirties. Something happened to her face along the way. She used to have a look about her, a hard to describe something that attracted the boys, but those days were long gone now. Lately she'd become jowly and severe. It was the nature of her business, she supposed, telling people what to do all the time and backing it up with an attitude, pursed lips and frowning.

After a while it sticks.

She was getting out of the business. Finally. She was home free and financially independent after seventeen years of hard work and no conscience. Sounds like a jail sentence, doesn't it? She spent two to four years with each patient depending on how sick they were, working her way in with them and fetching and carrying for them until they were dead. 'Til death us do part. Like a marriage vow of sorts only she got to choose the dying part. There were no shortcuts either except at the end when they started to dribble and looked like they weren't going to make it. And they weren't were they, so what's the big deal? They were only going to get worse. That's when she got antsy and wanted to get out of there, so she cut to the chase and put them out of their misery. Hers too, if you want to think about it that way.

Her first was the best, isn't that always the way? She was young and frothy back then with big tits and a cute ass, just out of nursing school and working for an agency. He was her first assignment. Arthur Motzny: a seventy-eight year old codger with a congenital heart condition and a constant hard on.

How was that possible, she wondered?

Her first day on the job with him he put his hand up her skirt.

She leaned over to fluff up his pillow and he reached right in there and copped himself a feel. And she let him. Not a flinch on her part. Just a parting of her legs so he could get to where he was going. She looked him in the eye while he was doing it, too. Saying, without having to, you better be nice to me Mr. Motzney or you won't be doing this any more.

And he was, Arthur, generous and kind. And one day six months later, after she'd performed the most remarkable blowjob on his grizzled but still active member, he told her he was leaving everything he had to her.

"Who else am I gonna leave it to?" he asked her.

She had no answer for him. She'd never given it any thought up until then. She was just a kid out of school on her first assignment, and more than happy with Mr. Motzny's generosity and his lusty behavior. Nothing else ever crossed her mind, but now it did.

He'd outlived everyone, he explained to her and was alone in the world with no family or friends.

She was overwhelmed by this sudden turn of events and reciprocated in the only way she knew how by performing creative feats of a sexual nature on his frail and withered body until he got sick one day and had to have some surgery. There wasn't much left of him after that. She still fucked him, but not very often because it wore him out. The last time they did it he couldn't catch his breath and his eyes looked like they were going to pop out of his head.

Then he passed out.

She'd fucked him to death if you want to think about it that way, but just to be sure she put a pillow over his face and that sealed the deal.

It wasn't like she planned it. It just happened, when that thing took over. That out of body experience she can't explain, even to herself, like something switched off inside of her and someone else showed up. She was surprised she could do it so easily. There was no remorse or regret, it was just something that had to be done. She was no murderer was her opinion of herself. She was more like a facilitator who helped poor Arthur on his way.

Helped them all on their way if you cared to look at it like that and in the final analysis she'd have to admit that she rather enjoyed it. That feeling of control.

That power over life and death and the idea she could snuff it out whenever she felt like it. Yes sir, she was going to miss that aspect of her career, but nothing else. The rest of it was hard fucking work and good riddance to all of that.

That's why she was out partying.

She was celebrating her retirement. She was rich. And high. And in a motel room with Lamont, fucking each other's brains out.

Then higher still when Lamont broke out the smack.

The last time she did heroin was a lifetime ago when she was young and skinny and eager to fuck. Living at home then, eighteen or so, not much more. How she loved that white powder and sex. Now here she was with Lamont. Pushing her to the edge, then farther still. To places she'd never been before with this animal of a man. Pumping himself into her like a fucking jackhammer. And orgasms! So many. Like she'd never had in her life before.

She couldn't remember what happened after that. Only that she woke up in her own bed. Alone. Now how did that happen, she wondered? He must've taken her home. Must have. Or not. She can't remember. Her mind was a blank. After the sex she must have passed out. Must have. What did she say? What did she tell him? But it didn't matter, did it? Because he called her soon after she woke up and quickly there was a next time, and a time after that. Each time was as good as the last. No. Better.

The wildness, the wetness, and that sweet sweet release.

She thought she would never feel that way again. Or do those things again. But it's like riding a bike, she supposed. And hadn't she proved that with Lamont? Adding a couple of new tricks to her repertoire. Showing Lamont a move or two. And he her. Who'd have thought it was possible at this stage of the game? And that endless supply of H Lamont had: that delicious white lightening to make your orgasms complete.

What happened after that second hit was the part she could never remember. Waking up in her own bed, wondering what she'd said, or done? And how the fuck did she get there?

But Lamont knew.

The fourth time they hooked up he recorded it and gave Dupree the disc along with her address and social security number he got from her purse while she was passed out on the bed.

That's what was in the envelope Dupree gave to Jimmy at the Chinese restaurant - a video of Lamont's lady friend whacked out of her mind answering all of Lamont's questions.

How she just killed a man. How she put a pillow over his face like she did all the others. There was a long rant about how she was doing them a favor. How they were on their last lap and fading fast. A kindness, she called it. She was doing them a kindness. Instead of living a life wracked with pain, discomfort and hopelessness, she helped them out and on their way. They were going anyway, weren't they? She was just speeding up the process and what's wrong with that, I'm asking you?

Just what the fuck is wrong with that?

Eagerly telling all of this to Lamont after he finished pumping her full of himself and his heroin. Spilling the beans. Answering his questions like she was on '60 Minutes' and he was Steve Croft.

Her name is Kathy O'Brien, the woman Lamont was hooked up with.

The woman who was whacked out of her mind on smack.

The same Kathy O'Brien Jimmy met at Magdalena's house.

The same Kathy O'Brien who owned Shelly Barton's house and all of his earthly possessions.

CHAPTER 25

THURSDAY AFTERNOON

Jimmy got back to the office in a state of high anxiety. The envelope Dupree gave him was a treasure trove of information and the recording Lamont made was mind blowing: Lamont asking Kathy O'Brien a zillion questions of a specific nature.

What she did? And how did she do it?

And she. Kathy O'Brien. Out of her mind on heroin telling him the most extraordinary things. Bragging on it. Boasting on it like she was proud of what she'd done. Her accomplishments. How she'd managed to put her nest egg together and what she did to get it. Five murders. And what she had to endure to achieve her goals. Groped, fucked and generally disabused by some of her patients. She might as well have been a slave to them, she slurred. Ordering her around like she was a skivvy. Get this. Get that. Tote that barge. Lift that bale. No please or thank you. Like she was dirt on their shoe.

Why? Lamont wanted to know.

Because they were paying for her services, weren't they? They didn't have to be nice if they didn't want to, and some of them didn't want to. The older they got, the worse they became. The bad ones. The men. She only did men.

All of this she told Lamont in a mumbling ramble fueled by booze and heroin.

But she got the last laugh, didn't she? She always got the last laugh after she got them to sign over their stuff to her for a hand-job and a peak or whatever else it was that they wanted. Whatever. Whenever. She didn't care. Whatever it took to get them to sign.

And after that it was business as usual until things fell apart for them. Because people were watching, she husked sounding suddenly paranoiac. Not relatives or friends, she whispered, because they had none. They were all alone, she made sure of that before she started up with them. It was the Senior Center and the social workers who were always looking over her shoulder, so she had to be careful, but when her charges started to go south it was all so easy. Especially the ones she didn't like. Easy. And fun, too.

Lamont gave her some more scotch. You could hear the ice cubes tinkling as she sucked it down. Then there was a couple of deep sniffs as she snorted some more heroin.

Then she told him how she liked to drive them crazy. The bad ones. The ones that were horrible to her. Taunting them. Teasing them. Remember this, she'd say? Or that? And she'd remind them what they did to her when their health was good and all their parts were working. Not like now when they were falling apart. Now was payback time and payback's a bitch isn't it? Then she'd do something awful to them to drive them crazy.

"That was the best part," she giggled. "Watching them spaz out. Arms flaying. Trying to speak. Or beg. But they were too far gone to pull it off and they'd shit their diapers in frustration and fear."

When she had enough of torturing them, she'd kill them.

Even the nice ones. Yeah, yeah there were a few nice ones. Like Shelley Barton, the last one. But even the nice ones got to be too much. So she killed him too.

Put a pillow over his face while he slept. Not even a struggle, he was so weak.

"It was all soooooo easy," she crowed.

Jimmy went through the rest of the stuff Dupree put together. Bank records and credit card reports. Information from off shore banks in the Cayman Islands. Information on the real estate she owned. Balance sheets. Valuations. Profit and loss statements. Bottom line, Kathy O'Brien owned five houses worth approximately two and a half million dollars with a rent roll of $12,000 a month, soon to be $15,000 when she got Shelly Barton's house leased out.

Someone who was able to get information like this is called a hacker, but it would be unfair to lump Dupree in with that category. He didn't do it all the time, only when he could do a little good with his skills. It was a white knight sort of thing to make up for all the bad things he'd done before he got himself straight.

Dupree pushing back against evil with this second chance he'd been given.

Like now for instance.

Exposing a serial killer and laying the foundation for shutting her down.

Jimmy was horrified.

None of the material was admissible in court because it was illegally obtained, but he thought he had the basis for an investigation.

The first thing he did was to look at the official record of Shelly Barton's death. The death certificate said Mr. Barton died of natural causes. There was no autopsy. Then he called Mary and asked her to find out if Kathy O'Brien was still going to Magdalena's and told her why he wanted to know.

Two minutes later she called back to say that Kathy O'Brien did not show up for work today. A substitute arrived and informed Magdalena she was her new caregiver. Magdalena was thrilled, according to Mary, because this person was younger and smaller than Kathy O'Brien and seemed willing to see things Magdalena's way on just about everything.

Jimmy fished out the card Kathy gave him and called the agency. They explained that the Magdalena posting was a temporary one and saw nothing wrong in Ms. O'Brien taking some time off. She'd been with a patient for a number of years who had recently passed away. It was usual after such an event for the caregiver to take a rest. Such situations, they explained, were traumatic for the caregiver, since they usually became emotionally attached to the patient and it took them a while to get over it. And yes, they said, they were sure Ms. O'Brien would return to the agency once she was rejuvenated and refreshed.

After that Jimmy called the DA's office in White Plains and spoke to an ADA. Ms. Karen Blum, the newest addition to the department and the next one up in the bullpen. She was a rookie. Their only rookie, budgets being what they were these days. She was 28, right out of law school. Bright, and sharp, and fresh as a daisy.

Based on what he had, then she corrected herself, what WE have, she thought a judge would most definitely authorize an exhumation to see if Shelly Barton had died of asphyxiation. She put Jimmy on hold while she cleared it with her boss who got on the phone and put Jimmy through a third degree to make sure the rookie wasn't getting ahead of herself.

This was Karen Blum's first case. Her boss had to calm her down she was so excited. When she got back on the phone Jimmy said he'd send her the package Dupree gave him with the understanding he had no idea where it came from or who sent it to him.

She told him she could live with that and said she'd be in touch.

The five properties Kathy O'Brien owned were in different places in the metropolitan area. Columbia, Scarsdale, and Manhattan in New York; Fort Lee, New Jersey; and Greenwich, Connecticut. Jimmy had someone check the records in those places to find the names of the previous owners and obtain copies of their death certificates, wills, and the dates of their filing. He also got them to compile a record of Kathy's employment for the last seventeen years and to get the phone number for each place and a contact name.

Jimmy thought he should bring the Chief up to speed on these fast moving developments and took a walk down the hall to tell him what was going on.

The Chief was sitting at his desk working through some paperwork. He thought Jimmy had come to report on his visit to Dr. Bender's and looked up expectantly.

"Not that," said Jimmy.

"What then?"

Jimmy told him about Kathy O'Brien.

When he finished the Chief said, "We should nail this source of yours on hacking charges, Jimmy. Scoop him up so we have something to show for our trouble at the end of the day. The DA's office will get all the ink on the killer if, in fact, that's what she is, and we'll get nothing unless we look sharp and get the hacker and beat them to the punch."

This was not what Jimmy was expecting. Only the Chief would see everything through the prism of publicity. He shifted from one foot to the other; his heart sped up and a pulse in his neck began to make an appearance.

"That's not the point here Chief. Kathy O'Brien is who our focus is on."

The Chief scowled.

"Your source is a hacker isn't he, and he's ours. What part of that don't you understand, Jimmy? Round him up and charge him before they do."

Jimmy took a step back and a deep breath.

Was it him? Maybe it was him? He willed himself to calm down.

"Am I missing something here, boss?"

The Chief gave off one of his exaggerated sighs.

"This is what I heard, Jimmy," he said testily, "and feel free to correct me if I'm wrong. You've got a doper who told a hacker a story. The hacker's got info that means jack shit in court and he broke the law getting it. That puts you in a spot, since you had knowledge of a crime and you, so far, have done nothing about it. On top of that you've got a rookie ADA who doesn't know her ass from her elbow telling you stuff she probably can't back up. Did I miss anything?"

He stuck his chin out at Jimmy. Challenging him. Ready for another fight.

This was one of those moments when everything can change in the blink of an eye. Jimmy's been here before. Lots of times. When his mouth gets the better of him and he says things he shouldn't. Things you can't take back. Out of anger. Or spite. Or just plain stupidity. And then he ends up fucking up everything, including himself. So now he took another deep breath and silently counted to ten. Let's hear it for maturity and the influence of the Mary.

Then he said politely, "I think you have, Chief. I'm an instrument of the DA on this one. They're conducting an investigation into Kathy O'Brien based on information I passed on to them. I'm not looking for permission here, boss. I'm just trying to fill you in on what's going on."

The Chief thought about that.

He was angry and he wasn't thinking right. The fight with Dr. Bender had given him a headache and it still hadn't gone away. Jimmy was getting on his nerves. Jimmy's source was getting on his nerves. In fact everything was getting on his nerves. He swallowed hard and rubbed his temples and thought, on re-flection, he might have gone too far.

He changed his tone and put a nicer look on his face.

"What will you do?" he asked.

"They think there's enough here to get a judge to sign off on exhuming Barton's body."

"Why?"

"The Medical Examiner's report says Barton died of natural causes. And in fairness, why would you think a ninety-two year old man was murdered, so why would you waste time and money doing an autopsy on him?" Especially, thought Jimmy, if you were a lazy bastard like the ME was.

The Chief was having the same thought.

"The ME didn't do an autopsy?" he asked with a touch of incredulity.

"He did not," said Jimmy. "They'll do one now if they get the go-ahead from the court. I think it'll prove Mr. Barton died of asphyxiation. In fairness to the ME, if you weren't looking for the signs you'd never find them."

"What signs?"

"Red blotches on the eyes."

The Chief fiddled with his stapler as he digested everything. It was time to jump on the bandwagon before it was too late.

"Did you speak to the Lamont guy?"

"I did."

"And?

"He confirmed what my source said he told him."

The Chief scowled as he tried to figure out what Jimmy just said.

"Will Lamont testify?"

"I think so."

Jimmy was counting on Lamont's hatred of scams involving old people, though he hadn't discussed it with him yet.

The Chief calculated the angles. What was good, what was bad? How he would look? What kind of blowback would there be if Jimmy was wrong? And where the glory was if he was right? His brain went through the permutations like a computer on crack and his head doubled down in the throbbing department.

"So what's the plan?" he finally asked.

"Pull her in, I suppose."

"What's the rush?"

"If the media print the exhumation story she might see it and run."

"What does the DA say?"

"We'll be lucky if we can get a conviction no matter what."

"Why's that?"

"Our chief witness is a heroin sniffing ex-con who makes his living on the street. It's a weak point don't you agree?"

The Chief did.

"Why do it at all then?"

He poked about in one of his drawers for the aspirin bottle.

"To shine a light," said Jimmy. "Sometimes it's the best you can hope for in these things is what the DA says."

The Chief changed his manner to that of a coach and modulated his tone to that of a father. There now to offer Jimmy guidance and advice through whatever obstacles might present themselves on the difficult road ahead.

"Wait until they've dug up Barton would be my thought," he offered. "A day won't make any difference. By the time the story gets out you'll know if he was murdered, and if he was you'll have scooped her up already."

Jimmy agreed. In fact the DA had said as much.

The Chief was pleased he could make a contribution and that Jimmy concurred. It meant they were friends again and he could begin to maneuver for a piece of the pie.

"What about that other thing?" he asked. Meaning Dr. Bender.

"We're going back at 5:00."

Jimmy told him how Mrs. Bender wouldn't let them inside the house.

"She asked you to wait in the car?"

Jimmy nodded.

"Not come inside for a cup of coffee while you waited for his nibs?"

Jimmy nodded again.

The Chief scowled.

These people were really beginning to get on his nerves.

CHAPTER 26

THE BENDERS

It was dark. And cold. Jimmy and Eddie were on the way back to the Bender's for round two. Eddie was still in uniform, driving. Jimmy was about to tell Eddie the Kathy O'Brien story when he got a call from Det. Simmons in Brooklyn telling him he was faxing over the telephone logs for Conner Malloy's phone. The bottom line was the call they were interested in, the one Conner got the morning he was killed and Jimmy hoped would lead them to the Melon Man, came from a throwaway just like the Chief had predicted, and there was no way to trace it.

"Shit," said Jimmy and hung up.

He didn't need to explain to Eddie what Det. Simmons said.

Eddie'd figured it out.

"So we got nothing," he complained.

"You're beginning to sound like rest of them," said Jimmy and stared out the window for the rest of the ride.

When they got to the Bender home it was Dr. Bender who greeted them at the door. He was a beaky little man in a three-piece dark suit with shiny shoes and silver hair. He was all black and white and short and there was a penguin quality to him that was hard to ignore. He was furious and wanted to know the meaning of this harassment and did they know with whom they were dealing?

"I'm the head of the School Board, the chairman of the Planning Commission, and I'm on the board of the Library and my country club."

His tone was loud and dictatorial and grated on Jimmy's nerves.

"Why can't this just go away?" Dr. Bender wanted to know and put a flipper to his brow like a headache was fast approaching. "I don't understand," he said shaking his head in theatrical wonder. "All the community service I do and the work I've put into this town, not to mention the money I've coughed up. All that and I can't catch a break here? It's not like the kid held up a liquor store."

The thing about the badge is that it cuts through all of this crap and levels the playing field. Sometimes it even tilts it your way depending on who you come across. Like now for instance. With Dr. Bender thinking he could beat them back with his lofty manner and various titles.

Jimmy smiled at him. It was a thin, gruely looking thing with no humor in it.

"I'm assuming you're Dr. Bender?" he said ignoring the rant. "Good evening, sir. I need to ask your son some questions about the ticket he received last night at the Columbia Library for possession of marijuana. I am a detective with the Columbia Police Department," he showed him his badge. "I have given your wife forewarning of this meeting. Should you choose not to produce your son at this time, I shall have a warrant sworn out and have him arrested and taken to the station house and we'll question him there. Which would you prefer, sir?"

Jimmy gave him the stare.

Eddie too.

A *CSI Columbia* moment - all attitude, minus the close-ups. Jimmy and Eddie facing down the bad guys using cop talk in a tone that was sometimes hard to beat.

Dr. Bender backed down immediately and invited the boys inside.

He led them to a huge family room in the back of the house with walls of wood, thick rafters, a cathedral ceiling, bay windows with colonial grilles, cozy plaid furniture, and a fireplace, big and blazing.

Mrs. Bender was waiting there.

So was their lawyer who stepped forward, introduced himself and handed Jimmy his card.

"The boy's a minor, Detective," he said, opening up first in an authoritative manner. Not at all impressed with this rumpled-looking detective and his equally disheveled-looking mall cop assistant. "He has certain rights, you know."

Jimmy gave him the gruely smile and rubbed his hands together like he was cold. Which he was. The weather had taken a turn for the worse and no one had warned him about it. Not the radio or the TV. It was supposed to clear up according to the morning report. Instead it had turned windy and was much colder than when he left the house. And he had no topcoat.

What Jimmy wanted to do was stand closer to the fire, which they did. Jimmy and Eddie. Edging nearer to the blaze without being invited. They were cold and the Bender gang was not being very hospitable. The boys were from Brooklyn where territory was measured in inches. A block. A yard. And in this case a fire, which is where they staked out their claim, parking themselves in front of it, and spreading their hands out toward the blaze to warm them.

Jimmy turned to face the Benders and their attorney.

"Look," he said reasonably. "We need to tamp this thing down as quickly as possible. That's my job," he looked at Eddie, correcting himself. "Our job. To enforce the law and protect the kids. I need to know where he got the stuff? Who sold it to him? And who was there? I need to know those things so I can work an investigation. Move along the chain. And close it down as quickly as possible to protect the kids. Our kids. Don't you see that? We are not the enemy here. We rely on leaders of the community like you to set the example. We count on your support. We don't expect to be obstructed or watch you throw your weight around to impede our investigation. Either way your son is going to have to answer these questions and please don't think if you play for time we'll lose interest. We won't. I won't. This is an important issue we're dealing with here. If nothing else you must realize what a good story this is. The media's going to lap it up."

"Is that a threat, detective?" this from Mrs. Bender, looking all prim and proper in a black sweater, black pants and a single strand of pearls around her once elegant, now scrawny, neck. She was a leading member of Team Bender now, establishing a position, or trying to, of confrontation and bullying in tone and intent. What else was new with people like this?

"It's a nothing Mrs. Bender," said Jimmy and gave her a blank stare. "It's how these things work. Folks like you think the rules don't apply to them." He looked around at the opulent surroundings. "The press evens that up for us. Like now for instance. You've threatened my Chief. You threatened me. All of this is in regard to the ticket your son received. And what was that ticket for? Possession of marijuana. And whose son is he? The head of the School Board. And what was the head of the School Board's reaction to this unfortunate event? Threats, obfuscation, and a lack of cooperation. You see where I'm going here, Dr. Bender? This story's a local reporter's dream come true."

"It is a threat," said the lawyer not quite hopping up and down, but close enough that you couldn't tell the difference. "It is most definitely a threat, and in front of witnesses too. You're gong to be very sorry you made it, Detective. I can promise you that."

"It's nothing of the sort counselor, you're the one who's issuing threats here. Mr. Bender threatened my Chief. And what you just said was most definitely a threat directed at me."

"It's Doctor," this was from Bender.

Jimmy paused and looked at him.

"Excuse me?"

"It's Doctor not Mister. You called me Mister."

"This is what you're worried about," said Jimmy incredulously. "Your title? Your kid's in trouble here, don't you get that? Let me ask him a few questions and I'll be on my way. You can be there and so can your attorney, but he must cooperate and so must you. No coaching. Or attitude. I just need him to answer my questions."

They folded quicker than he thought they would, but then they didn't.

Son Jason didn't.

He was a skinny sixteen-year-old bag of bones, six feet tall and still growing, in worn out jeans, a grubby Grateful Dead tee shirt, and a 'what me worry' look on his spotty face. And yes, he told them, he's bought weed at the Library. Not that night though.

"Just weed?" asked Jimmy.

Jason nodded.

"But if you wanted something else. Coke? Crack?"

"Anything."

"Anything?"

"Anything."

"Huh. What's the name of the guy you buy from?"

That's when he clammed up. He didn't even look at his lawyer. He just said nothing.

"Is it the same guy all the time?

Nothing.

"Any one else you know buys from him?"

Nothing.

"Could you give us a description?"

Silence.

"Where did you buy the joint you were smoking when you got the ticket?"

"I don't remember."

"You mean you won't tell me."

"I mean I don't remember."

"At school?"

There was a pause, which led Jimmy to believe that's where he got it, but then Jason shook his head.

"C'mon Jason. Help me out here. You got it from school didn't you?"

The lawyer stepped in.

"You're badgering the boy Detective. I can't allow that."

"We're not in court now counselor so I would respectfully ask you to back off. My sense is that young Jason here knows exactly who he gets his drugs from and it would be very helpful if he would pass that information on to me." He turned back to Jason. "Jason?"

But Jason would not help. He stared sullenly at Jimmy without saying another word.

Jimmy knew he'd get nothing else from the boy. They were just rousting the Benders any way. Showing them the flag. Driving them crazy. Telling them in their own way not to fuck around with the Department. All the same Jimmy thought they'd have to spend some more time on the Library, things were getting out of hand there.

But then he decided to take another run at it. They'd pissed him off, these people, with their lofty manner and their shit doesn't smell attitude, especially the boy. So he came at it from a different direction and moved closer to the fire, both physically and metaphorically.

"This is not a slam dunk when it gets to the judge, you know that don't you? I've seen plenty of times where counseling and probation have been ordered."

"It's an appearance ticket not an indictment," said the lawyer like he was talking to an idiot.

"Not in our court," Jimmy shot back. "We take drug possession very seriously here. You of all people should know that, Doctor." He looked hard at Dr. Bender. "A lot depends on what sort of cooperation we receive in our investigation. Remorse is taken into account. The arresting officer will be in attendance and I'll be there too. Quite frankly, the report I'm going to write will be less than favorable based on this interview."

"Is that another threat, Detective?" this from the lawyer using the same imperious tone.

"It is not another threat, sir. I have made no threats. Patrolman Smith will verify that. No sir. This is a fact. I am required by law to provide the court with a report of what took place here. It will include Dr. Bender's tirade to my Chief, Dr. Bender's soliloquy when we arrived here, and his son's current lack of cooperation."

Jimmy saw Dr. Bender smirk.

"You see something funny here, Dr. Bender?" A pulse started up in his temple. He really didn't like this guy.

Dr. Bender couldn't resist. His lawyer shook his head warning him not to, but a bully's a bully and they just love to throw their weight around. The smirk became a cocky grin.

"The Judge you say?" said Dr. Bender. "Would that be Judge Spillinger?"

Jimmy nodded.

"Well sir, Judge Spillinger is one of my dearest friends, my golfing partner, a Lodge brother and my college roommate."

Jimmy returned Dr. Bender's grin, only his was a 'don't fuck with me' sort of thing that lingered a little longer than it should have.

"Yes sir, that Judge Spillinger. I hope you're not hinting at some special treatment you're expecting from the judge because of this relationship?"

The smirk was back on Dr. Bender's face and then the curtain came down.

"I think this meeting is over, Detective," he said.

And that was the end of it.

Back at the station house Jimmy was fuming.

So was Eddie.

The Chief could see the anger rising off them like steam from a volcano as they marched into his office. After they told him what had happened he tried to impress them with his own version of outrage, but it didn't come close to the boys' Brooklyn dander.

A little while later, after they'd finished their ranting and raving, the Chief asked Jimmy what he thought they should do next.

"Plan 'B'," said Jimmy like it was a no brainer and flopped himself down on one of the Chief's chairs.

The Chief didn't know there was a Plan 'B' and wondered what this Plan 'B' consisted of.

Eddie didn't know either. He sat down next to Jimmy, eagerly looking forward to the next part of the show.

There they were.

The three co-conspirators.

The Three Amigos.

All for one and one for all.

On this one at least.

Eddie and the Chief were looking at Jimmy expectantly. Waiting in barely concealed anticipation for the details of this Plan 'B.'

Jimmy smiled at them benevolently.

"We'll set Connie on em," he said.

And then his co-conspirators smiled too.

CHAPTER 27
CONNIE

Connie Fieldstone worked for the local newspaper. He was their only full-time reporter, just as Jimmy was Columbia's only detective. They had that in common, only Jimmy didn't do weddings or bar mitzvahs. Jimmy found Connie at La Manda's, an Italian restaurant in Elmsford known for the best pizza in Westchester and a signature dish called Chicken Scarparo that has a sauce to die for. But Connie was having none of it. Instead he sat at the bar working on a Johnny Walker Black with a beer chaser.

This was not the first drink of his day judging by the brightness of his nose and the bleariness of his eyes.

Connie was older than Jimmy. He was in his early sixties and looked shop-worn and frayed. His unshaven, saggy face resembled that of a tired old blood-hound, and his stringy, yellowing hair was long and messy. He wore jeans and loafers and a hounds tooth jacket over a brown crew neck sweater and white shirt. All of it looked slept in, including the loafers.

They'd not seen each other since the last big case Jimmy worked on. They spoke on the phone once in a while, Connie calling for a quote or a perspective on something or other, but nothing face-to-face.

Jimmy was surprised Connie wasn't at the diner after Conner Malloy was shot. He was even more surprised at the way he looked now.

"What happened to you?"

He sat down on the stool next to him.

"I'm afraid you've caught me at rather a bad time, old chap," said Connie.

He had English roots and they popped out every now and again. Usually when things weren't going so good.

"How's that?"

"The economy's in the crapper and the paper's cutting back," said Conner miserably. His big droopy eyes drooped even more and, because the lighting in the bar was so dim, he looked like he was about a hundred and eight. "Everyone's being laid off. It's just a matter of time till they call my number."

"Why weren't you at the diner?"

"They sent a cub to that one. A getting-his-feet-wet sort of thing. They're priming him for my job if you ask me. You'd have to be blind not to see it the way things are. They can get three people for what they pay me." He took a slug of his scotch and shook his shaggy head sadly. "It's just a matter of time," he said into the glass.

"Wasn't Hearst publishing your book?"

Connie reported about a local gangster Jimmy pursued in his last big case. Hearst, who owns the paper Connie works for, asked him to write a book about it.

"They were," said Connie and raised his bloodshot eyes to meet Jimmy's.

"What happened?"

"Nothing. That's what happened. Nothing."

Jimmy asked the bartender for a Coke.

Jimmy's a recovering alcoholic. He was pleased to see that the bar didn't arouse any longings in him. That was a measure of how happy he was these days.

The bartender, a ringer for an extra in any Mafia movie you've ever seen, grabbed a glass from a shelf behind him and sprayed Coke into it from a nozzle under the bar.

He handed it to Jimmy who touched Connie's glass, took a swig and raised his eyebrows. Waiting for more.

"They gave me a small advance." Connie continued. Fingering his glass. Trying to decide whether to take another slug. Or not. 'Not' won out, but not for long would be Jimmy's bet. "By the time I got the book done the economy was falling apart and everyone was downsizing, especially in the publishing industry. People out of work don't buy books. It's the first thing they cut back on my contact at Hearst told me, like I didn't know that already. Sales are nose-diving. Bookstores are closing. They said I could keep the advance figuring, quite rightly I might add, that I'd spent it and it would cost them more to get it back than they gave me in the first place. I still had the manuscript, I never handed it in, and ended up publishing it myself."

"I know," said Jimmy. "We bought it."

Connie perked up at that.

"Did you indeed. Did you like it?"

"Very much."

For a brief moment it seemed to cheer Connie up, but then the long face returned.

"I'm sorry," he said morosely. "This is not a very good time for me."

"I can see that," said Jimmy and gave him a sympathetic grin. "Maybe I can help you out with that."

"Oh?" said Connie and downed what was left of his scotch, chasing it with the beer. It seemed to settle him.

Jimmy told him about the Dr. Bender saga.

Connie looked hopeful.

"I need a favor," said Jimmy.

"Anything."

"I need to find out who his kid bought the weed from. Maybe coming at Dr. Bender from a different direction will shake him loose. Something to remind him how vulnerable he is to public opinion without actually saying it."

Connie rallied and everything about him changed. His back straightened, the frown left his face, and ten years disappeared from his soggy features.

"Mmmmm. This has the makings of something quite interesting, dear boy," he said excitedly. "It would be jolly nice to go out with a bang of sorts."

"Not one story, Connie. Two," and Jimmy told him about Kathy O'Brien and how they were waiting on permission to exhume Shelly Barton's body to see if he was murdered."

Connie jiggled on his barstool with uncontained glee.

"This is bloody marvelous, James. I can't thank you enough. It's been so long since I had something good to get my teeth into I was beginning to think I was all washed up. Especially with this latest cull that's going on at the office." To celebrate he ordered them another round. "I'll go and see Dr. Bender tomorrow, first thing. I'll tell him I'm doing a piece on drugs in the community. That there have been a number of drug-related incidents involving high school students and the trouble the police are having getting cooperation from the parents. I'll ask him for his take on the situation, given that he's the head of the school board. What does he think parents should do? What advice can he give them? And so on. And so forth. He'll have to give me the official line on these issues, which, of course, is one of cooperation and support. That will put him in direct conflict with the position he's taken with you regarding his naughty offspring. This makes him very vulnerable in the event the story gets out about his boy's evil transgressions. My guess is he'll act accordingly and get the boy to tell you what you want to know. Dinner is the bet, sir, that says you'll be hearing from the good Doctor by the close of business tomorrow."

"I'll be happy to pay up," said Jimmy and downed his soda. "I'll need you to hold back on the O'Brien story until we get the results from the autopsy, providing we get permission to dig him up. If you print it beforehand Kathy might see it and make a run for it. If it's a go, I'll let you know. I have to think about you being in on the arrest, but there's nothing to say you can't be hanging around the station house with a photographer when we bring her in."

"A photographer?"

"You're working the drug thing, right? Go and interview the desk sergeant and take his picture. He'll love it. No one ever writes anything about him and he's got a million stories to tell. I'll let you know when to be there."

"Brilliant."

"It is," said Jimmy. "Isn't it?"

CHAPTER 28

FRIDAY MORNING

Jimmy's day was off to a good start. The few traffic lights he hit were all green, which was a very good sign. Usually he caught red lights eighty percent of the time. Eight times out of ten. It defied logic. And we're not just talking about the local lights. We're talking about red lights everywhere. Eight out of ten. And don't think he hasn't tried shaving those odds. Sneaking up on them. Slowing down. Tucking in behind someone going very fast. It didn't make any difference and the results were always the same. Everything else in his life was in perfect balance. Living with Mary was going fine. Lucy's marijuana issue had worked out well. He was busy at work and he was loving this new life of his. This family. This warm and fuzzy feeling he's been floating on ever since the day he moved in with them. Everything was going perfectly, except for those fucking red lights. Eight times out of ten. Now what the fuck was that all about?

When he got to the office there was a pile of papers on his desk. Wills, death certificates and a sheet of pertinent information about Kathy O'Brien and her five victims. All of them, according to the death certificates, died of natural causes and because the people were so old, no autopsies were performed. All of them changed their last will and testaments at least two years before their deaths and named Kathy O'Brien as the recipient of their estates. No one came forward to contest these wills and all the assets were now in Kathy's possession.

There was also a message from ADA Karen Blum to call her about Shelly Barton's autopsy. Jimmy had a knot in his stomach as he punched out her number. The green lights had made him feel optimistic, but this was the moment of truth and he steeled himself for bad news.

Karen picked up on the first ring.

"We got the okay," she said without preamble.

"Great," said Jimmy and pumped a fist.

"We'll know if he was murdered by the end of the day."

Jimmy was about to say something flowery, but she'd already hung up.

He didn't take offence. Social skills are nothing they teach you in the DA's office. Setting boundaries. Establishing positions of authority. Making sure everyone knows who's in charge. Those are the things they drum into you over there. Karen Blum was just following orders. If anyone happened to be listening in on her conversation, they would've been proud of her. On the other hand, Jimmy didn't give a shit.

Luckily for Jimmy the Conner Malloy murder case had faded into the background because there was so much else going on. Nothing had come in from the press release they sent out about the Melon Man and Morgan hadn't been able to find out anything about him in the City. He told Jimmy not to call him any more.

"If I get something, I'll let you know," he growled after Jimmy's fifth call and hung up on him.

The Kathy O'Brien thing had distracted the Chief, so there was no needling coming from that direction. But bottom line, everyone was right. He had absolutely nothing on the Conner Malloy murder.

Just before lunch, Jimmy got a call from Connie Fieldstone reporting in on his interview with Dr. Bender. He thought it went well. He'd gone to Bender's office in White Plains and was treated, he said in all seriousness, with the solemnity and respect a reporter of his caliber was entitled to.

"Bender gave me all the right answers," he said cheerfully. "How cooperation from the public was the key to shutting these things down and how he'd really encourage parents to cooperate with the authorities. Then he did five minutes on how great the Police Department was and what a good job they've done keeping the community safe and drug free."

"Sucking up now to us now," said Jimmy. "The Chief'll get a kick out of that one."

"Everything he said is the opposite of the position he's taken with you."

"It is, isn't it."

"My guess is you'll be hearing from the good Doctor by the end of the day."

"So where do you wanna eat?" said Jimmy. Talking about the bet they made.

"You ever dine at La Mandas, that place where you found me last night?"

Jimmy said he had not.

"Well you're in for a rare treat my friend," said Connie and made a date for the payoff in the event that he was right. "By the way, I didn't detect any signs the good Doctor thought we were in cahoots."

"Cahoots?"

"Aren't we in cahoots?"

"We are I suppose," said Jimmy, "But I never considered it cahooting."

"What would you call it?"

"Cooperating."

"Cahoots," said Conner firmly and ended the conversation.

Jimmy went in to tell the Chief how plan 'B' was shaping up. How Dr. Bender told Connie nice things about the job the Department was doing keeping drugs out of the neighborhood, and the cahooting thing.

The Chief didn't like the last bit.

"We're in cahoots with him, my ass," he said angrily. "How about we threw him a bone and gave him a story that isn't over yet? And how about we gave him the inside track on another developing situation? The drunken bum should be grateful we're letting him have first peek at these unfolding sagas and giving him a chance to resurrect that failing career of his. Son of a bitch better spell our names right when the time comes," he harrumphed. "What did you tell him?"

"All of that," lied Jimmy, "and a whole lot more besides."

Jimmy got the call from Dr. Bender later in the day. Dr. Bender told Jimmy how sorry he was for his arrogant behavior the night before and would he please come to the house as quickly as possible because son Jason had something he wanted to tell him. And no, in answer to Jimmy's unasked question, his lawyer would not be in attendance.

Well done, Connie, and one dinner at La Manda's coming up.

Jimmy rounded up Eddie and they were at the Bender house thirty minutes later. On the way Jimmy told Eddie the Kathy O'Brien story.

Eddie was about to start up with the questions, but Jimmy cut him off.

"Let's see if Shelly Barton was murdered before we get crazy," he told him.

"But you think he was?"

"I do."

"Why?"

"It's an odd thing to crow about if it's not true. Kathy bragged to Lamont a whole lot. And about the others too."

Eddie thought that made sense. He was about to start up again but Jimmy cut him off again, anticipating the next question.

"I don't think there's anything we can do about those other people, Eddie. It's too long ago. Barton, on the other hand will show signs of suffocation if that's what Kathy did to him."

"How's that?"

"Red splotches on the eyes," said Jimmy. "It's a clear indication."

"And if they're there?"

"We scoop her up. If we dug up the other people their eyes will have gone, along with everything else. They've been in the ground too long. Eyes are the first thing to go, you know that don't you?"

Eddie did, but he didn't want to think about it or even talk about it. The whole thing gave him the creeps.

"You think she was fixing to make Magdalena victim number six?" he asked mischievously. "Boy, Jimmy," he said without waiting for an answer, "you sure didn't see that coming. I hope you're not losing your touch."

Jimmy chose to ignore him.

They were treated much differently at Castle Bender this time; offered coffee this time and invited to sit close to the fire that was still blazing away. Jimmy figured they had to go through at least a cord of wood a week the way they were burning the stuff. He wished he had the contract. Whoever did had to be making a fortune off of them.

Jason Bender was obsequious today. Not the arrogant schoolboy today. Dressed nicely in khaki trousers and clean white shirt today, and bowing and scraping and acting all humble and contrite.

Jimmy liked the old Jason better. At least it was honest.

The name Jason gave up was the same one Lucy had given him. Martin Rogers. The same kid who sold Lucy's friend a joint on school grounds.

"Where's he get it from?"

Jason didn't know.

"And you bought it from him on campus?" asked Jimmy to be sure.

He did.

"Who sells it at the Library?"

Jason didn't know. He didn't know anything that went on at the Library; he was just caught smoking a joint there. That's why he got the ticket, but that's not where he did his business.

"You buy it at school."

He did.

"From Martin Rogers."

That's right.

"He only sells it to you?"

Jason squirmed. He was moving into serious snitching territory here and he was not very comfortable about it. He could feel his father's eyes boring into him. The same father who stood up for him so nobly the night before and now, for some unknown reason, had reversed his position and thrown him to the wolves.

"Others too," he said dejectedly.

"Like who?"

"I don't know." He stole a glance at his father who was still glaring at him. He sighed. "Look I don't know who he sells it to, but I can tell you this. He's the go-to guy on campus for weed."

Dr. Bender looked relieved.

"He's the only one that provides this service?" asked Jimmy.

"The only one I know of."

They went back and forth on it a couple of times, but nothing else came up.

Dr. Bender went through another round of apologies.

Mrs. Bender never made an appearance.

Jimmy said he'd have a statement printed up for them to sign and that everything that happened yesterday would be forgotten. Eddie would bring the statements over for their signatures as soon as they were done.

Dr. Bender looked like he'd just won the lottery and laced his gratitude with so many compliments you'd have thought Jimmy came up with the cure for the common cold.

But he got what he came for.

A name.

Martin Rogers.

Eddie dropped Jimmy off at the station house to pick up his car. Jimmy was going to tell the Chief what happened at Fortress Bender, but the Chief was gone, so Jimmy decided to go home too. On the way he pulled over to take a call from ADA Karen Blum who was reporting in on Shelly Barton's autopsy.

"Murdered," she said before Jimmy could say a word. "Absolutely no doubt. We're putting together a warrant for Kathy O'Brien's arrest. I'll fax it to you as soon as it's done. You can scoop her up first thing in the morning."

"Yes ma'am," said Jimmy, but she'd already hung up.

Jimmy couldn't remember the last time so many things had gone right for him in a single day. Even the lights were still cooperating on the way home. It was a perfect ending to a perfect day, but not quite, or so it seemed, because the best was yet to come. When he got to the house he was greeted with mouthwatering smells that were emanating from the kitchen. Mary informed him that Lucy was staying at a friend's house, something about a class trip tomorrow and they were leaving early in the morning. She also told him she'd fixed him his favorite dinner: meat loaf, roast potatoes, corn and gravy and promised him a dessert he'd never forget.

CHAPTER 29
SATURDAY
KATHY O'BRIEN

When the police came to her door Saturday morning, Kathy couldn't imagine what they wanted. She was so secure in her sense of invincibility that it never occurred to her that they were there because of Shelly Barton.

It was early in the day. She was still in her bathrobe, a pink fluffy thing that was faded and frayed. It was the first thing she'd made up her mind to replace when she rode off into the sunset. She wanted one from the hotel. The Ritz Carlton in Grand Cayman. They were in all the rooms. Big white fluffy terry-cloth things you sank into and made you feel like a million dollars. She thought it would be a symbolic start to her new life and she couldn't wait to have one.

The pudgy detective showed her his badge. He was the same old-school cop she met at Magdalena's the other day. She knew he was trouble the minute she laid eyes on him. He said he'd come to bring the old cow some pastries, but that was just bullshit. He'd come to lay the fear on her was what that was all about. Warning her not to get any ideas. That the old bat had friends and not to steal the silverware or anything else for that matter. "Fuck that" was her first and only reaction. She was only there as a favor to the agency because they were short staffed. She quit at the end of the day without telling Magdalena and told the agency she needed time off because she was exhausted and emotionally run down from the death of Shelly Barton.

Jimmy was accompanied by a female police officer, a pretty little thing who looked like she should still be in high school. They invited themselves in, and then Jimmy pulled out a laminated card from his inside pocket and read Kathy her rights and told her he was arresting her for the murder of Shelly Barton.

Kathy had to sit down to catch her breath she was so stunned.

When she pulled herself together, the policewoman accompanied her up to her bedroom where she got dressed and, on the policewoman's advice, put some toiletries and a couple of essentials in a small traveling bag.

Her mind was racing as she tried to figure how they found out. She could only come up with one conclusion: Lamont Dubois. She must have told him when she was high and he went and ratted her out. Who would've thought that low life would run to the cops? It was that second hit of H that did it, she was sure of it. She could never remember anything that happened after that.

While Kathy was upstairs, Jimmy called Connie to give him the heads up. Connie was suitably grateful and said dinner was now on him; still at La Mandas, and still on the date they'd agreed upon, but now it was his treat.

When they got Kathy to the station house Connie was in the middle of interviewing the desk sergeant. The photographer had positioned himself in a corner and was shooting Connie talking to the sergeant with the entrance to the station house in the background. When Jimmy marched Kathy through the door the photographer already had them in focus and was able to get off some nice shots. Then Connie got to ask her the questions he and Jimmy had rehearsed earlier, thus enabling Connie to break the story ahead of the competition and making him a big hero in the eyes of his editor.

Kathy O'Brien was ushered downstairs to the cells where she was fingerprinted, photographed, mouth swabbed, and given her one telephone phone call.

The person she called was Crawford Taylor. The same Crawford Taylor who sent Gillie Fader and Conner Malloy to collect his money from Austin at the Columbia Diner, four days ago.

She'd known Crawford for years. She was his nurse when he had a disc removed, and his gall bladder taken out, and after his knee replacement that took longer to heal than anything else. She nursed him back to health the only way she knew how by using her body and her mouth as instruments of a therapeutic technique she'd perfected all by herself and was proud to call her very own.

"If you ever need anything call me," Crawford told her every time she left his employ, but she never had any cause.

Now she did.

Crawford told her not to worry about a thing and sent her a lawyer and put up the money for her bail. That's when she knew everything was going to be all right; Crawford Taylor never bet on losers. And because of his kindness she was back on the street as quickly as the law allowed, which was Monday because the courts were closed over the weekend.

She was arraigned and entered a plea of not guilty.

There was a big fight over the question of bail.

The DA argued that bail should be denied because she was a flight risk and she had the resources to make an escape.

Kathy's lawyer argued that his client had never received so much as a parking ticket. And, up until this outrageous and unfounded charge of murder that had been leveled against her, she'd been a model citizen who earned her living by taking care of the elderly when they'd reached the stage in their lives they couldn't take care of themselves. In that regard, her lawyer continued, she had a spotless record without so much as a word of complaint about the performance of said duties.

The judge agreed with the defense and bail was set at $400,000. Kathy was required to surrender her passport and a date was set for a preliminary hearing.

The lawyer told her he could get her off, but it would cost her a half a million dollars and a great deal of patience because the wheels of justice worked terribly slow. It didn't sound English the way he said it, but what did she know.

When she got out she went to see Crawford Taylor. Kathy told him about her finances and put up her houses, five including Shelly Barton's home, as collateral for the bail money and the lawyer's fees.

Crawford didn't ask her where she got them from or how, but he had a pretty good idea.

Then the bottom fell out of the real estate market.

CHAPTER 30

MONDAY

An ancient dilapidated barn sat close to the road in the corner of a vast field of six-inch corn stalks, all that was left from the fall harvest. From a distance it looked like smoke was pouring out of the front of the barn. As Jimmy got closer he saw that what he thought was smoke was actually hundreds of barn swallows zooming in and out of the barn's open doors.

He pulled over to watch.

Clouds of the birds wheeled and swooped in massive formations that disappeared inside the barn and poured out a few seconds later, going through the same procedure again and again, giving the impression, from a distance, that it was smoke that was billowing out of it.

He'd passed the barn a hundred times before and never saw so much as a sparrow hanging around. Was it some feathered ritual, he wondered? Or maybe they were in heat; did swallows get in heat? He didn't think so. Maybe it was their swan song before they headed south for the winter? Or was it a food thing? Some bug they liked that was only available at this time of the year in this particular barn?

It was a remarkable sight to see, as he sat in the car looking into the sun with shafts of sunlight streaking through the gnarly leafless trees. And there stood the ancient barn, stark and forbidding, as swarms of frenzied birds careened in and out of its open doors.

Jimmy thought it looked like a scene from a Tim Burton fantasy.

Then his phone rang, which broke the spell.

It was Morgan Flynn. Calling to say that they got him. Well, not got him exactly. They'd identified him. The big pink man in the diner when Conner Malloy got popped.

It was Morgan's partner, Tim Mathews, who actually got him.

Timmy they called him. Timmy from Brooklyn. Timmy from Brooklyn was plugged into the life. He was not dirty himself, but he was a useful go-between for an exchange of ideas between the two worlds whenever it was called for. Like now for instance, where Timmy wanted to know who the big pink yeti was. They were Timmy's cousin's these people. And high school buddies. And guys he'd known all his life from the neighborhood. And they were the ones who got him, that jolly pink giant who was better known as Gillie Fader.

Everyone on the other side of the fence knew who he was. How could you not? He was the giant sack a shit who thought he was a big shot with his airs and graces and his fancy looking suits, and no one liked that. No one in the life that is, especially Timmy from Brooklyn's friends, because they knew where Gillie came from. The street. Just like them. And you don't see them putting on airs and graces, do you?

Gillie Fader, they said, was an upscale collection man who, when he deigned to come to Brooklyn, walked around the neighborhood like he had a stick up his ass. He sometimes partnered with the late Conner Malloy, but he was working a single these days, for obvious reasons. Who were his clients? They didn't know. Who did he work for? No one knew that either. But they did have an address for him and Morgan said he'd check it out as soon as he could find the time. He was working eight cases right now, he said irritably, and was just a little distracted.

Jimmy thanked him for his trouble and ended the call.

Then he grinned.

Maybe he didn't have 'nothing' on the Conner Malloy case after all.

When he got to the office Jimmy made some calls to Kathy O'Brien's previous employers. They weren't employers exactly; they were agencies that acted as a broker for Kathy's nursing services. Over a seventeen-year period she had worked with five of them. One for each murder, thought Jimmy. Each agency, when contacted, was shocked at the murder charge that had been leveled against her, especially the most recent agency that got her the job with Shelly Barton. That person gave Jimmy an earful about what a saint she thought Kathy was and how he'd rue the day he thought she could possibly commit such a heinous crime.

When he asked the agencies if they were aware that Kathy received the proceeds from the estates of one of their patients, they said they were not. But it didn't surprise them; it wasn't unusual. The bond, they explained, between patient and caregiver can become intense, especially if they've been together for a long time. And if the patient had no family left, which was often the case, it was their way of saying thank you for services rendered.

Jimmy asked each agency to fax him whatever records they had regarding Kathy's time with them, which they said they'd be happy to do. He was looking for complaints and misdeeds and some sort of pattern that would help him build the case against her. He'd had no luck so far, in fact quite the opposite. She looked like such a tough cookie but based on what he heard from her last employer she clearly had a soft side and was very good at her job. He supposed you'd have to be if you were going to get your patients to leave you all their stuff, especially if you added a quotient of sex to the proceedings, which is what she told Lamont she liked to do.

After getting a cup of coffee from the coffee machine, he called to make an appointment to see the Columbia High School principal. His secretary said he'd be available in an hour. Jimmy took Eddie and his cruiser along for effect. For shock value. And to let the kids know there were consequences for bad behavior.

The principal was a gangly looking man with a thin face, a high forehead and thinning sandy hair. He wore an unbuttoned, double-breasted suit that hung on his thin frame like it was a size too big for him. Jimmy didn't understand the unbuttoned look. David Letterman did the same thing; wore a double-breasted suit and kept the jacket unbuttoned. It never looked good as far as Jimmy was concerned, not that he was an expert about such things. The materiel flapped all over the place and it looked messy and unflattering. Just like it did on the principal here. But even if he buttoned it up, Jimmy suspected, the jacket would still look too big on him.

Jimmy didn't like the man, and up close he liked him even less. He thought he was pompous and aloof. When Lucy started at the Middle School, the High School principal gave a speech to the parents about how tuned in the schools were drug-wise. The High School and the Middle School shared the same campus, which was why the High School principal gave the speech and not the principal of the Middle School. There's always a pecking order in everything.

He told the parents how he knew everything that went on inside the school and on the school grounds and that there was absolutely nothing to worry about in that regard.

But Lucy told Jimmy during their marijuana bust-up that whatever drugs you wanted you could get on campus. It made him mad, especially because the principal had been so arrogantly confident that he had it under control. Dr. Bender's son Jason told him the very same thing. If the kids knew where to buy the stuff, why didn't he? Jimmy would have liked to ask him that, but he needed his help, so he didn't.

The principal peered at Jimmy and Eddie through wire-rimmed glasses and talked in a manner that suggested he didn't think they were very smart. Jimmy told him what Jason Bender and Lucy said, without mentioning her name, that Martin Rogers was selling marijuana on school grounds. He said he wanted to search Martin's locker and his backpack.

The principal said he didn't see why not, but he'd have to check with the superintendent and get back to him. The way he said it was annoying. His head was tilted upwards and was slightly challenging; his eyes were dismissive and he used a tone that lacked surprise or any sense of urgency.

Jimmy said that wouldn't do. Their visit was highly visible and there was the likelihood that if they waited too long Martin that would clean out his locker before they got to it.

There was an awkward pause while the principal decided how to react to that. He was, of course, firmly on the side of the law; he just had a thing about being told what to do on his own turf, especially by this dumpy looking detective and his scruffy looking assistant.

Finally he picked up the phone, punched out the school superintendent's number, and ran the thing by him.

Jimmy could hear how the conversation was going, especially the principal's lack of urgency, and was beginning to simmer.

When he couldn't stand it any more he said irritably, "Now."

The principal put his hand over the receiver, astonished at Jimmy's interruption, and said, "I beg your pardon?"

"Now," repeated Jimmy, his temper rising. "I want you to do it now. Tell the superintendent I can get a warrant if he likes. And if I have to go that route I'm going to station Officer Smith outside Martin's locker till I return so no one gets into it."

"You can't do that," said the principal, his jaw jutting out like he was on a parade ground.

He'd taken his hand off the receiver. The superintendent could hear the back and forth between them.

"Do what?" he pleaded down the phone.

"He wants this done now," said the principal petulantly. "If not, he says he'll place a policeman by Martin's locker until he comes back with a warrant."

Jimmy leaned over and snatched the phone from the principal.

"Sir," he covered the mouthpiece with his hand and turned to the principal. "What's his name?"

The principal glared at him, shocked at this blatant act of disrespect, but nevertheless managed to rise above it and mouth, "Dr. Lichtenfeld."

Jimmy started over.

"Dr. Lichtenfeld, this is Detective Jimmy Dugan with the Columbia Police Department. I'm conducting a drug investigation. Two witnesses have identified Martin Rogers, a student at this school, as someone who is selling drugs on campus grounds. I need to search that boy's locker and his backpack or have someone do it for me. I believe I have the right to request this and quite frankly I'm surprised at the hostility I'm receiving in that regard. We're all supposed to be on the same side here. You should be outraged that this boy is selling drugs in your backyard. You should be leaping at the chance to set an example and show the students the consequences of these actions." Jimmy was getting going now. He kept thinking about Lucy and how the school was not living up to their responsibility.

"I was at that speech the principal gave a couple of weeks ago to the incoming Middle School parents," he said letting his anger get the better of him. "How he knew everything that was going on in the school drug-wise, and there was nothing to worry about." Jimmy stared at the principal. His eyes were harsh and unforgiving. "Well guess what, he doesn't, and neither, it seems, do you. Either cooperate with me now or I'll be forced to go to a judge and obtain a search warrant. If I go that route I can assure you something like that is bound to go public."

"What do you mean 'go public'?" asked the superintendent.

"Well for one thing there's a reporter sniffing around the neighborhood asking questions about drugs in our area. Who's doing what? What's the cooperation like? His name is Connie Fieldstone. Do you know him? He's with the *Gazette*."

Dr. Lichtenfeld said he did not.

"He's got his head around the idea that people who should be helping the police, aren't. Check with Dr. Bender. He's the president of your School Board, isn't he? He'll tell you what it's all about. I understand he's already been interviewed."

Dr. Lichtenfeld said he'd be right over.

Jimmy said they'd be waiting.

The principal couldn't decide which he was more annoyed about: Jimmy snatching the phone from him so rudely, his criticism of his finely constructed and magnificently delivered speech to the parents of the incoming Middle School class, or that a reporter might actually say some terrible things about him.

The superintendent was in his late fifties. He was tall, dark, and balding and wore grey flannel trousers, a blue blazer, a white shirt and a striped blue tie. He was new to the post. Jimmy had had a good relationship with his predecessor and thus far he was not impressed with his successor. But he was mistaken.

Dr. Lichtenfeld turned out to be a nice man. He was charming, polite, and anxious to help in any way he could. Jimmy had read him wrong. The principal got him all wound up with his superior attitude and condescending airs and it had clouded Jimmy's judgment.

The superintendent was determined to get to the bottom of things and apologized profusely for seeming to get off on the wrong foot.

"This drug thing is everywhere," he said, worry creasing his already furrowed brow. "I just hate it. Anything that helps keep it out of our schools is fine with me. Protocol says it's up to us to open Martin's locker, but I think it would make an impression on the student body if you came along too."

Jimmy liked this. He was pleased to finally find someone who thought the way he did. The principal, it was his feeling, did not.

They all trooped down to where Martin Rogers' locker was located and were met by the janitor, a wiry looking Eastern European in bib overalls and a shock of unruly, black hair. He'd brought along his bolt cutters and cut through Martin's padlock in one swift and practiced move. It would seem that this was not the first time he'd had to perform this particular maneuver.

The locker yielded fifteen dime bags of marijuana.

The superintendent told the principal to have Martin Rogers brought to the principal's office and to call his parents and tell them what was going on: that drugs were found in Martin's locker and the police wanted to question him on school grounds. They could only do so with a parent present. They also had the right to bring an attorney with them.

Martin Rogers looked like every other male student in the school. Torn jeans, a black hoodie, and sneakers so dirty it was hard to tell who made them. His hair seemed to be his point of pride. It was piled high in a '50s pompadour and loaded with product, which couldn't have helped his advanced case of acne very much.

When he came to the principal's office, he was without his backpack.

The superintendent asked him where it was and sent someone to fetch it. Inside they found three dime bags of marijuana and a bunch of loose joints.

Mr. and Mrs. Rogers arrived at the school fifteen minutes later. They seemed like nice people. She was a little on the thin side and nervous as she gnawed at her nails and fiddled with her ends of her heavily streaked hair. Mr. Rogers seemed to be more in control. They did not bring an attorney. Mr. Rogers had high hopes he could wangle his kid out of it, whatever it may be, with a smile and an elaborate soft shoe shuffle. It was the way he dealt with all things of a serious nature, with mixed results.

In this case he didn't improve his average any.

Once the parents arrived, Jimmy read Martin his rights and advised the parents he was charging their son with possession of marijuana with intent to distribute on school grounds. The parents were dumbstruck. Martin was in shock and looked like he was about to burst into tears. Jimmy had Eddie cuff him and they took him to the station house where he was photographed, fingerprinted, and processed. After that they all gathered in the interview room: Martin, his parents, and the attorney they called the minute they realized what was going on.

On the law enforcement side was Eddie, who stood by the door, and Jimmy, who informed them the interview was being filmed and recorded and could or would be used as evidence in the event of a trial.

Martin was charged with a variety of drug infractions and then Jimmy went to work on him. Who did he get it from? Who were his contacts? And who did he sell it to?

Martin, for his part, held nothing back, responding enthusiastically to Jimmy's caution that the judge's decision, when it came to sentencing, would rely heavily on the level of Martin's cooperation. The jewel in the crown of this wealth of information Martin supplied turned out to be name of Martin's partner-in-crime.

Jimmy was surprised that there was another layer in the enterprise. He thought Martin was a solo and the tip of the triangle, and by closing him down it would clean up the school. Not so, as it turned out. There was one more level to be revealed, and this was where the Rogers' attorney stepped in and took a hand. Explaining to Jimmy that this was Martin's first offence and sending him to any form of juvenile institution would not help matters. Martin came from a fine home and this should be considered an aberration in his behavior. His grades were good and his participation in school programs was exemplary. In return for this final, and most important piece of information, the attorney asked for a commitment from Jimmy that probation would be the way to go and that he would recommend such a course to the DA's office.

Jimmy said he had no problem making such a recommendation with the understanding that he couldn't guarantee the DA or the judge would go along and that everything was predicated on the information being good. Jimmy said some sort of community service should also be part of the deal.

All parties eagerly agreed to this, with the understanding that the judge was the wild card in the equation and that no one could speak for him. All the DA could do was inform him of Martin's guilty plea and the bargain they had struck and hope the judge went along with it.

He usually did.

Mike Kenner, a Columbia High School freshman, was the name Martin Rogers gave Jimmy. Six months ago Mike found the combination to his father's safe while he was poking around his office. When he opened it he found an Aladdin's cave that was full of weed. That's when he called Martin Rogers and the two of them went into business together.

CHAPTER 31

MONDAY AFTERNOON

Jimmy called School Superintendent Lichtenfeld and filled him in on what had happened with Martin Rogers at the station house. How he was released on his parent's recognizance and the deal that they came up with pending the judge and the DA's agreement. And how he told them that Mike Kenner was his partner-in-crime. Jimmy asked the superintendent to have Mike's locker searched and go through his backpack as quickly as possible. He should also call Mike's parents, explain the situation and tell them to come to the school. Jimmy and Eddie would be there as soon as they could.

Jimmy ordered up a search warrant for the Kenner home specifying Mr. Kenner's study and his safe, based on the information provided by Martin Rogers. After that he went in to see the Chief who was sitting at his desk reading a report, looking his usual immaculate self.

He looked up as Jimmy walked in and drew first. Why was that, Jimmy wondered? Why did everybody have to be so confrontational? And it wasn't just the Chief who did it. That school principal had raised his hackles for no good reason. Everyone trying to assert themselves. Everyone trying to make sure you knew where you stood in the pecking order. Like the Chief here, who was coming out swinging. Not waiting to hear any of the great news he'd come to tell him. Just wanting to step on Jimmy's toes so he knew who was in charge, as if Jimmy didn't know already.

"What's going on with the Conner Malloy shooting," said the Chief brusquely. He put the report down and stared at Jimmy with a look of bored sufferance. "The Westchester CID's on my ass and they're getting antsy, Jimmy. What's he doing, they want to know? Why's it taking so long, they keep asking me?"

Diggety poke. Pokety dig.

Jimmy rolled out his strong-armed act, the one where he sounded like he didn't give a shit because he didn't give a shit. He gave the Chief a thin smile that imparted these feelings without having to say them.

"Tell em the person we've been looking for, the guy in the diner sitting with the man I think is the shooter, is somebody called Gillie Fader. I just got the call from Morgan this morning. Gillie's not in the system, but we do have an address for him. Morgan's going over there as soon as he can. It's been confirmed that Gillie Fader is a collection man though no one seems to know who for. Gillie and Conner were at the diner to collect a payment from the shooter and something went wrong. Hopefully Gillie can throw some light on that and point us in the right direction."

The Chief grunted something noncommittal.

Then Jimmy told him about Dr. Bender's son. How he helped him get to the bottom of the drug thing at the school by identifying Martin Rogers as his supplier, and, in turn, Martin Rogers identifying Mike Kenner as his partner in crime. And how he was getting a search warrant for Mr. Kenner's safe based on what Martin Rogers told them.

The Chief provided the first smile of the meeting. Oozing satisfaction.

"That'll teach that Dr. Bender not to fuck around with us," he said contentedly.

Jimmy agreed.

"On another subject, boss," said Jimmy with a cheeky grin. "Connie Fieldstone wants to interview you."

Connie wanted no such thing. Jimmy made it up to mess with the Chief and wind him up. He was tired of everyone pissing on his shoes at the drop of a hat and went for a little sport to cheer himself up.

The Chief looked like a man who was as close to arousal as someone could get without being obscene. His face was flushed and his eyes had a dreamy look about them as he contemplated the possibilities of this unforeseen, but very welcome, piece of publicity

"He wants to bring a photographer with him. That's all right isn't it, boss?" said Jimmy giving it another twist. "The paper's giving him a lot of space on this one. Sounds like it's gonna be good, doesn't it Chief?"

It certainly sounded good to the Skipper. It was as if someone shoved an air hose up his ass he puffed up so quickly.

"Absolutely," he declared and beamed at Jimmy like they were life-long buddies. "You tell him I'll be ready for him the minute we sew it all up, cameraman and all. You might want to suggest some location shots, Jimmy. The public loves to see me out and about." Then he changed his mind. "Maybe not," he said, and shook his head gravely. "Maybe not." Then his face clouded over with concentration like he was planning the Normandy landings as he worked the thing through. "Maybe we should give him a free hand on this one and not try to micromanage him. Yeah, that's it. Tell him that for me will you, Jimmy. Tell him," said the Chief magnanimously, "he can do whatever he likes."

Jimmy gave him a mock salute and strutted out of the office with a mischievous smile on his face and a bounce in his step.

Five minutes later Jimmy and Eddie were in the cruiser, driving back to the school for the same reason as before, and this time with the enthusiastic concurrence of the school superintendent. For the theater of it. And to show the kids what happens if you break the rules.

Mrs. Kenner was waiting for them in the principal's office along with her recalcitrant son, Mike. Both were perched on their chairs looking uncomfortable and ill at ease.

Mike was a shifty looking boy with shoulder length hair, and Gap'd out like he was one of their ads. He reeked of privilege and no discipline and looked like one of those kids parents throw stuff at in lieu of effort and affection.

The school superintendent was there along with the principal who was feeling sorry for himself because his world was being turned upside down. He was a Princeton man, and the principal of a high school, and he thought he was entitled to a lot more respect than he was getting from these two policemen who were prancing all over his school like they owned the place.

Mrs. Kenner looked like she'd been dragged through a hedge backwards. There were dark circles under her watery eyes, her bleached blonde hair was a frizzy mess, and her expensive clothes were disheveled and uncoordinated. She was in her mid to late-forties and moving towards fat, but not quite there yet. Her face had begun to stretch with the exception of her medically altered nose that looked like a small island in a sea of heavily made-up, pudgy flesh.

And it wasn't just this business, Jimmy surmised, that had thrown her into such a tizzy. She looked like her world was falling apart and this was just one piece of it.

He introduced himself and handed her one of his cards.

She took it and shoved into her handbag without looking at it.

"My husband's at work," she explained in a tremulous voice. "He works in the City." She looked at her watch. "He should be here soon."

She said it in a manner that suggested she didn't care if he was there or not.

Mike Kenner munched on his nails and kept his eyes glued to the floor. His stringy black hair formed a curtain around his face.

They'd found ten dime bags in his locker and a dozen in his backpack. No contest. Nolo Contendere. The boy was in deep shit and he knew it. He was terrified not just of them, but also of his father. Things were bad enough between them, but this: raiding his stash and bringing the law down on him. He'll never forgive him for that. Never.

Fuck, fuck, fuck.

The superintendent and the principal stood side-by-side behind the principal's desk looking like back-up singers at a recording session without the microphones.

Eddie assumed his usual position by the door, took out his note pad and prepared to make notes.

Jimmy positioned himself in front of Mike and went through the usual explanation about how his cooperation or lack of it would weigh heavily on the judge's decision regarding his sentencing.

Mike kept his head down and didn't say anything.

"Tell us about your dad's safe," said Jimmy.

Mrs. Kenner sat up in her chair like she'd been hit with a cattle prod.

"What are you talking about?" she spluttered.

She didn't know, that much was clear. Jimmy figured it was one more nail in the Kenner's marriage coffin. When he told her what they'd been told was in her husband's safe, her shoulders slumped and she began to whimper. Her world was falling apart around her and things kept getting worse. She looked at Mike, pain and hurt etched on her bloated features. Tears streamed down her face that cut deep lines in her makeup, and snot bubbles pulsed under her nose.

"How could you?" she blubbered.

Jimmy handed her a tissue.

"You know how things are between me and your father. Why would you make things worse for me? How could you?" Then quieter and puzzled, and almost to herself, "How could you?" as she tried to comprehend this unforeseen betrayal from her only child.

Mike Kenner gave them the same story Martin Rogers had.

He got the combination of his father's safe while he was poking around in his office, opened it, and found a lot of marijuana inside. How he went into business with Martin who was always looking for ways to make some extra money. This last was said with a touch of disdain for his partner who, Jimmy surmised, was lower down in the order of things and not nearly as rich. Martin was the salesman;

Mike was his supplier. The stuff they'd found in his locker was backup. The stuff in his backpack was going into his locker. They were supposed to meet up at the end of the day to transfer it all to Martin's locker.

Mike Kenner was a freshman. Martin Rogers was a junior. The two rarely saw each other during the day because they had different schedules. Mike heard the police were on campus, but he never made the connection. Word about what was going on in the higher grades only reached the freshmen by rumor. Each grade had their lockers in a different part of the school. Juniors and freshmen never mixed on campus, so Mike didn't get the word, which answered Jimmy's question as to why Mike Kenner didn't clean out his locker and backpack after they'd rounded up Martin.

Jimmy decided to move the proceedings to the station house. After obtaining his cellphone number from Mrs. Kenner, Jimmy called Mr. Kenner and identified himself.

"Change of plan, Mr. Kenner," he said into the phone. "Please meet us at the station house not the school."

Mr. Kenner insisted on speaking to his wife.

Jimmy offered her the phone.

Mrs. Kenner shook her head and shrank away from it like it was a hot coal.

Jimmy told Mr. Kenner that Mrs. Kenner did not wish to speak to him. He went on to tell him they were on their way to the station house to process Mike and charge him with possession with intent to distribute marijuana on campus grounds. Jimmy did not mention Mr. Kenner's safe or the search warrant he'd obtained to look inside. He thought he'd save that for later. He also stationed an officer outside the Kenner home in case Mr. Kenner decided to go there first. The officer was told should that be the case, to bring Mr. Kenner to the station house and not allow him inside. If Mr. Kenner resisted, the officer was instructed to arrest him for obstruction, cuff him, read him his rights, then bring him down to the station house.

CHAPTER 32
MONDAY AFTERNOON

Austin Kenner swept into the station house with a confident flourish. A cape would have been appropriate here and a fanfare of some sort, that's how dramatic he looked. He'd taken his last hit of coke as he got off the Taconic State Parkway and threw the empty vial out the window. He was in full command of his faculties and in Captain Marvel mode. Untouchable. Sure beyond a shadow of a doubt that this was going to be easy. The kid got caught with drugs, big fucking deal. What were they gonna do, lock him up and throw away the key? I don't think so. They'll suspend him from school for a while and the cops will give him a ticket, that's what they'll do. That's what they did when he was a kid.

This was not going to be a problem, especially on a day like today. Because today was the day the stock market rebounded from an oversold position and Austin had called the turn and placed his bets accordingly. The Dow Jones Average rose a record amount after being down two hundred and fifty at the opening, which caused the shorts to panic and bid everything up, including Austin's thousands of out-of-the-money options that were now worth millions. His millions. Enough to pay off his boss Mal Finkelstein and his shylock Crawford Taylor, leave Shirley and the kid a little something to be going on with, and disappear for good.

No sir, this was not the day to fuck around with Austin Kenner. Today was his day, and little Mikey would have to suck it up and suffer the consequences of his actions, just like he did when he was a kid. Like they all did when the shit hit the fan. Suck it up, kid. That's the only way you're gonna learn.

These were the thoughts that were swirling around Austin's coked-up brain as he swept into the Columbia Police Station in his $2,500 ankle length camel hair coat, his $3,000 bespoke suit, his $350 Sulka shirt, and his $150 silk tie. Such was the confidence good nose-candy can give you. There was not an ounce of fear he would be connected to Conner Malloy or his murder, that's how cool he felt, and how invincible he thought he was. He'd not shaved or cut his hair since that terrible day. He looked different now. Slightly. And anyway, the trail had gone cold, that's what all the papers said. And there was this great win he had under his belt today. He was rich. Again. And hot as a pistol. And there was no way his snot-nose kid could possibly ruin a day like this for him.

Oh foolish man.

The desk sergeant greeted Austin with a welcoming smile and asked a passing uniform to escort him to the interview room where his wife and son were waiting for him, along with Jimmy and Eddie.

Jimmy introduced himself as Austin walked in the door, handed him his card and offered him a seat at the metal table next to his wife and child.

Eddie stood in his usual position by the door, notebook in one hand, and pen in the other.

Mrs. Kenner did not lean forward to accept Austin's proffered cheek peck. His puckered lips hung in the air without making contact and looked slightly ridiculous.

Mike Kenner did not look up or acknowledge his father's presence save to shrink inside his skin and disappear further behind his curtain of hair.

Austin Kenner exuded wealth and a confidence he had no right to feel.

Jimmy loved the man for his arrogance. His perfection. His perfectly gelled hair, perfectly fashionable unshaven face, and the way the room filled up with his perfectly delicate fragrance. He sat down at the table and leaned back in his chair to enjoy the show.

Austin removed his camel hair coat, carefully draped it over the back of his chair and sat down next to his wife. He crossed one leg delicately over the other and adjusted the crease in his trousers accordingly.

Then he took a deep breath as if he was about to sing a beautiful aria and said in a voice that was tinged with command and control, "Now what's this all about, Detective?"

Jimmy beamed at him. Art for art's sake, you had to admire a man of this caliber who thought his shit did not smell and was in control of the situation. In a world full of assholes, this guy had to take the cake. He gave Eddie a glance.

Eddie's face had the trace of a smirk, but you'd have to know him to know it was there.

Jimmy looked at his watch. It was getting late. It was time to put on a show of his own.

"Mr. Kenner," he said solemnly, "your son has been charged with possession of marijuana with intent to distribute on school grounds, a class 'C' felony that requires a court appearance. You'll be informed by mail as to the time and the date. He's already been processed and he'll be released on parental recognizance as soon as we've finished up here.

A soft moan escaped from Mrs. Kenner's lips.

Austin tried to put his arm around her to comfort her, but she angrily brushed it away. It put a slight dent in Austin's confidence factor, but no more than that. The coke was percolating nicely through his body and he still felt like he was master of the universe.

"On another matter," said Jimmy and he reached into his inside pocket and produced a copy of the search warrant he'd obtained. He handed it to Austin. "This gives us the right to search your house for drugs, Mr. Kenner. Specifically your study, and your safe."

That fine line of euphoria and control that coke can give you faded in the blink of an eye. In its place arrived terror in the form of a rapid heartbeat, a flush to the face and a tightening of Austin's sphincter. He fingered the document, looked at it without reading it, and then he looked back at Jimmy. Uncomprehending. Blindsided. Having no sense of his vulnerability until this very second.

He managed to stammer out a, "Wwwhat?" but no one took any notice of him. Instead Eddie stepped forward. Helped him to his feet. And guided him out of the door, through the station house, and into the back seat of his cruiser.

Jimmy told Mrs. Kenner and Mike they were free to go. He'd see them at the house or not, it was up to them. Then he joined Eddie in the cruiser.

'Eddie'n the Cruiser.' Sounds like a rock'n roll band, doesn't it?

Austin was dumbstruck. His brain was paralyzed. But by the time they got to the house he had regained a modicum of his senses and stiffened.

"You're not going into my house until my lawyer arrives," he declared and punched out the man's number on his cellphone.

Jimmy frowned and headed for the door.

The uniform stationed there in case Austin showed up, joined him.

Eddie stood next to Austin.

Jimmy turned and said to Austin, "Open the door or we'll break it down."

Austin finished talking to his lawyer and snapped his phone shut.

"He'll be here in half an hour," he said like that explained everything.

Jimmy tried the handle. The door opened.

Austin made to stop him.

Jimmy waved the warrant in his face.

"You don't want to be doing that Mr. Kenner. If you put one finger on me I have the right to lay you flat, or Taser you, or have this officer wrestle you to the ground with who knows what consequences. Call your lawyer, he'll tell you we're within our rights and to step aside."

Austin wilted like a dying rose and followed them indoors.

Eddie brought up the rear.

The uniform led the way and found Austin's study at the back of the house, where they all assembled.

The study was small with a window looking out onto the garden, some filing cabinets with papers piled on top, and pennants and framed sports memorabilia on the walls. A desk and an accompanying chair faced the window. Next to it was the safe, an old-time cast iron affair, three feet by three feet and three feet deep with a dial and an ivory handle on the door.

Austin was a pasty white, a shadow of the man who had breezed so airily into the station house not one hour ago.

His wife and son were nowhere to be seen.

Jimmy figured they'd gone for pizza.

"Open the safe, Mr. Kenner," he said.

Austin said he wouldn't.

"Open the safe Mr. Kenner or I'll cite you for obstruction and call in an expert who will open it any way he sees fit. Explosives would be my guess," he said eying the safe. "Collateral damage is hard to predict with those things. This warrant authorizes me to do anything necessary to fulfill its mandate. The fine print says the penalty for obstruction is severe. Are you getting what I'm saying here, Mr. Kenner?"

Austin capitulated and with a trembling hand spun the dial backwards and forwards a couple of times, pulled on the handle, and the safe popped open. The smell, a heavy skunky fragrance, was overpowering and took over the room.

Before they did anything, the uniform took pictures of the interior of the safe with his cellphone.

Jimmy snapped on a pair of rubber gloves and looked inside. On one shelf was a large sealed plastic bag full of marijuana, the source of the strong odor. On another were some bottles of pills and several small plastic bags of a white powder. The uniform photographed it all. After that they went through Austin's desk and found a couple of rolled up singles with a white powder residue. All of it was photographed by the uniform and put in evidence bags.

Jimmy took a look around the rest of the house. He checked out the bedside tables and the bathroom cabinets and, apart from a bunch of vials of Ativan, Valium, and Ambient, all prescribed for Mrs. Kenner, there was nothing more to find.

The uniform labeled the evidence bags and put them in one large plastic bag to be sent to the lab.

Eddie never left Austin's side.

Austin looked like he'd been in a fight. His fashionably unkempt hair was unfashionably mussed up in a style that was unrecognizable. Greasy strands of it fell into his face. His tie was loose. The top button of his custom made shirt was open. He looked rumpled and crumpled and no longer in control. Someone had taken away his cape and confiscated his attitude.

Jimmy said, "Cuff him, Eddie." And to Austin, "Mr. Kenner, I'm arresting you and charging you with possession of a controlled substance with intent to distribute." He read him his rights. "Take him to the station house Eddie and process him. I'll tell his lawyer where to find him," he looked at his watch. "According to Mr. Kenner he should be here any minute."

When they were gone Jimmy called Connie and gave him the story.

When he was finished he said wryly, "Oh, and I blew some smoke up the Chief's ass this morning for a little sport. I told him you wanted to interview him for the 'drugs in the neighborhood' article." Jimmy chuckled. "You should've seen him puff himself up when I mentioned your name. He got all Brian Williams on me and began to look at me sideways like he was staring into a camera."

"Sideways?"

"His body went one way while his head went another like Brian Williams does on the Nightly News."

Connie said, "I see," but he did not. He never watched the Nightly News, or any other news for that matter. He got all his information from the Internet.

Jimmy said, "If you get over there now, you'll be in time to catch Eddie bringing Austin in. You can explain your presence there by asking to see the Skipper for the interview. I'll tell Eddie to slow it down so you can get your pictures as he comes in. Throw the Chief whatever bone you like."

Connie was profuse in his thanks and claimed Jimmy was single handedly resurrecting his career.

"A meal at La Manda's, delectable as that might be, dear boy, is not nearly sufficient to cover my debt to you. By the time we dine together at that extravaganza for the taste buds, I'll have come up with something more appropriate to express my gratitude for your extraordinary display of friendship."

Jimmy was not so good with the praise.

He mumbled something about it not being necessary and ended the call.

CHAPTER 33
MAL FINKELSTEIN

Austin Kenner's boss Mal Finkelstein was a garmento cliché. He sported a year round 'out of a bottle' tan, which had an orange tinge to it that made him look not unlike someone who painted his face with a mild solution of iodine. He wore dark suits and shirts that were open one button too many to show off his chest and the gaudy medallion that sat in his greying thatch. He was too loud is the thing, and flashy, and given to wild statements and tall boasts. But he's done well, has our Mal, and received a great deal of help along the way. It didn't hurt that his daddy was rich, or that his mother was good looking. Or that his daddy's daddy was even richer. It was a well-heeled family that Mal came from and the tricks of the trade he learned along the way were of a type that only money can make work. Top locations, fabulous publicity, and the most amazing press kits.

The best, the best, only the best.

Mal Finkelstein was a born showman who was blessed with a winning way and the gift of the gab. He could sell anything was what they all said about him, including himself. He was a leading man and a self-promoter who was only too happy to mug for the cameras and hang out with the bright lights at the best places in town. He's had three wives and a couple of kids along the way and at the ripe old age of fifty-four you'd think by now he'd be able to stand on his own two feet, wouldn't you? But it takes a lot of money to live the way he does. You've got to sell a lot of dresses to pay the four grand a month he spent on coke alone. Then there's the alimony. And the child support. And the booze, and the broads, and the ring-a-ding-ding. And that was Mal's problem right there. He thought he was Frank Sinatra. Playboy hip, Sinatra cool. But he was a long way from that, talking that cheap scat the way he did, like he was in *Ocean's Eleven*.

The original, not the remake!

The family wondered where it came from, this coarse way of doing things. They were third generation money and believed in taste and style and the idea that understatement was the smartest way to play it. Having money was cool they thought, but one should be very discreet about spreading it around.

Not so our Mal. The more he got, the flashier he became. And brazen. And fearless. And incredibly loud.

Mal Finkelstein honed his skills when he got out of school by working in his uncle's showroom on Seventh Avenue, selling appealing lines of women's clothing to the top buyers in town. Bloomingdale's, Bergdorf, people like that. Building a network of contacts and patiently waiting for his time to come and the opportunity to show the family what he was made of.

His break came a couple of years later when he met Billy Conway at a popular City nightclub where they got into one of those all-nighters that was fueled by coke, and scotch, and a lot more coke.

That's where it all spilled out; those hopes and dreams Billy harbored and had managed to suppress until this stranger with the endless supply of cocaine came along and pried them out of him. How good he was. How talented he was. And if he could only get a shot. A chance. And how, not for the first time, he'd created a fabulous line of women's clothing and how hard it was to find the money to get it going.

When they adjourned to Billy's tiny apartment on the Upper East Side it was not for sex, Lord no. It was because Mal wanted to see what Billy's bragging and lofty claims were all about.

A little while later they were watching the sun come up from the roof of Billy's building, champagne flutes in hand and expressions of awe and expectation on their weary, but happy, faces.

The champagne was Mal's idea. Billy had a bottle in the fridge. Mal insisted they bring it with them to the roof.

"The rising of the sun is symbolic of the future that's about to dawn for us," he said sagely and a little wobbly from the night's proceedings.

Billy said he didn't get it.

Mal said, "You will."

He thought Billy Conway's designs were out of this world and the two of them were sitting on a gold mine.

And then, as the first streaks of the sun peaked through the smoke stacks on the Queens side of the East River, they clinked glasses and Billy heard the words he'd been waiting to hear all of his life.

He was going to be a star.

And they went forth from that place to an attorney of Mal's choosing and formed themselves a corporation. Mal put up the money for a fifty one percent share of the new company and that was how Mal's run as a Garment Center superstar began. How it finishes is an entirely different matter. Billy Conway is long gone now. He was just the first in a long line of partners Mal has used and abused along the way.

These days he's hanging on by a whisker.

"I've turned into Jack Lemon," he told the hooker who was blowing him as he sat at his desk in his office that overlooked 7th Avenue. "Did you ever see, *Save The Tiger?*"

She stopped what she was doing and looked up at him like he was crazy. Her lipstick was smeared and her hair was disheveled from Mal's guiding hands that had been pushing and pulling her head for maximum effect.

"Is that a National Geographic show?" she wanted to know, feigning an interest that was part of her job description and why they paid her the big bucks for what she did.

It pained him to realize how old he was getting when only he understood his frames of reference. He told her to get back to finishing what she began, but that, he knew, was what was happening to him. He'd turned into Jack Lemon.

Save the Tiger was a '70s movie about the seamy side of the garment business that won Jack Lemon the Oscar. Mal thought he was even beginning to look like him. All worn around the edges and hustling more than he'd ever done before.

And for why?

And for what?

One more season, that's what. That's what Jack Lemon kept saying all through the movie. One more season, and doing whatever it took to make that happen. And isn't that what he's doing now? Working with the shylocks and doing all manner of creepy things. And if the new line's a dud they're going to find him floating face down in the river.

That's something he did not tell the hooker.

And it's not like he doesn't know what he's doing. The line is good, of that he's sure, and this could turn out to be his finest hour. Could be. But it takes a whole lot of money to launch a new line. And luck. And a great deal of moxie.

It was the smart play, this new line of his. Everyone said so. You were competing with yourself, but not really. And it's not like he came up with the concept himself. Gap, Banana Republic and Old Navy are all owned by the same company and compete with each other, don't they? Not really. Each line is aimed at a different market with different price points and locations. That's what Mal's doing here; going from mass-market to a grade higher. Aiming for different stores. Neiman Marcus, Bergdorf; that level, those types of locations. Whatever Calvin Klein does for his stuff Mal's doing for his, and more. Advertising. Promotions. The works.

Money, money, money honey.

He was maxed out at the bank, borrowed to the hilt, and he'd called in every favor he was ever owed. And he was still short.

The family was out of the loop on this one, that's why he was short. No money was coming from that direction, no sir. He stormed out of the house a year ago after his father spoke to him like he was a three-year-old and his mother said they were putting in an accountant to keep an eye on things. They said they expected him to run the business the way you're supposed to instead of stealing everything for the house he was building in the Hamptons. And there'll be no more running up expenses the business can't afford. And cut out the drugs. All of this said to him with that look of disdain they could muster at the drop of a hat.

No sir, not after they spoke to him like that.

He told them to shove their money where the sun doesn't shine and stormed out of the house and hasn't spoken to them since.

What else could he do?

What would you do?

Mal met Crawford Taylor at Balthazar, a fashionable restaurant in the East Village. Mal was with a bunch of models picking at some finger food at the end of the day. Crawford breezed by them. One of the models knew him, called him over and invited him to join them. After dinner, they all went back to Crawford's apartment for a nightcap and paired up, then tripled up, and in Mal's case quadrupled up, and a good time was had by all. In the morning the girls left and Mal and Crawford went for bloodies at PJ Clarke's on Third Avenue. That was when Mal brought up the subject of money to his newfound buddy who, he thought, might be someone he could sell a bill of goods to. An investor. An angel. Someone he could con three hundred grand from and maybe a little bit more. So it wasn't a moan-fest Mal laid out that morning for his newfound friend, but rather a sales pitch so elegant that Crawford had to marvel at the shear artistry of the softest sell he'd ever been exposed to.

Crawford smelled blood. He let Mal give him his best shot without biting or showing any interest. Instead he pressed the friendship thing and invited Mal to a charity event at the Whitney where, he told him, they were sure they would find some ladies they would be able to orgy with later on in the evening.

The following day the boys met up at the Boat House in Central Park where Crawford baited his own hook, finally showing an interest in Mal's pitch and asking him questions like, what's the money for, and things of that sort.

Mal's ears pricked up as he finally heard, after three days of socializing and general debauchery, a softening of Crawford's tone and a general shift in his point of view.

It was then that the bargaining began.

Crawford said he could get him $350k for 55% percent of the company plus 10% interest on the $350k until the principle was paid off. $8k a month for four years plus $3k a month interest, an $11,000-a-month nut.

Mal was incredulous.

"Are you crazy? I pay you all of this money and you're still my partner when it's over?"

"Right."

"I don't think so."

"Why not?"

"I can't afford it."

"Sure you can," said Crawford with a grin.

It was then that Mal realized who Crawford was. A shylock. And he was the player who was being played.

It took a week of back and forth until they settled on a six-month note for $350,000 at 35% interest to be paid in its entirety including compound interest when the note matured. The total came to six hundred thousand give or take and Mal had to put the business up as collateral. If payment was late when the note came due, Mal would be out on his ass, but he would still be liable for the six hundred thousand plus interest that accrued on a daily basis until it was paid in full.

Done, and done again.

There was nowhere else to go.

What was he going to do?

What would you do?

Mal figured he'd have the six hundred thousand and a lot more besides from the initial orders they'd write at the launch and from the follow-up publicity he expected to receive.

They'd been working on this launch for over a year and this was the last lap. Mal's designer was very hot, his latest discovery, fresh out of FIT and looking for a job when Mal found him. He had no idea how good he was, but Mal did. And was willing to throw the dice for one more season based on nothing more than instinct. To show everyone he still had it. That eye. That flare. That unique ability to spot a winner and have the balls to run with it.

"The loan from Crawford is just a tide me over. A stopgap measure."

"I'm not worried about it," he'd say if he told you what he'd done.

But he should have been.

Not long after Mal got his infusion of Crawford Taylor's cash he found himself exposed to a major bit of schmoozing from his CFO Austin Kenner, asking him to cover one of his post-dated checks. Again. A real estate deal, he said, like the last time, and the time before that.

Mal thought Austin seemed a bit sweaty on this one. Twitchy was how he'd describe him. But they were all a bit twitchy what with the new line coming out on Friday and all that went with it. It was annoying and presumptuous and a pain in the ass for Austin to ask him to cover a check at a time likes this. Everything was on the line for this one and there was absolutely no margin for error. Mal thought Austin was treating him like he was his personal banker, a quarter of a million dollars this time, but what was he going to do? Say no? And it's not like he doesn't have it. Or that Austin doesn't know he's got it. He's the CFO for God's sake and it's just sitting there staring him in the face.

His war chest.

Every penny accounted for.

Every dollar begged.

Borrowed.

Or stolen.

So why take a chance when every penny counts, you might ask? Because it's not like it's the first time that this has happened, and Austin's checks have always cleared in the past; fifteen of them over a twenty-year period. And because they're friends or so he thinks, which makes it even harder to say no. And Austin stands to benefit if the launch goes well. Getting a piece of the action, a share, something of that sort that will keep him happy for years to come. And Austin knows this because it's all they've been talking about for the last six months. So why would he put something like that at risk? He wouldn't. That's the answer to that question. He would not. So it's business as usual as far as Mal's concerned. And annoying. And so fucking pushy, but that's okay. Really. Because it's only for a couple of days, isn't it? That's what Austin said. It's just for a couple of days.

Like the last time.
And the time before that.
Right?
Right.

CHAPTER 34

TUESDAY
CRAWFORD TAYLOR

Just like that everything was falling apart and stocks were in a free fall. There was a rally yesterday, a technical bounce they called it, but they were going down again today. Crawford wondered if Austin was able to take advantage of it. He certainly hoped so because that would put him back on the plus side and it had been a while since he'd been able to say something like that. Real Estate smelled like garbage. Everything except for gold, diamonds and platinum were going down like a stone dropped from a great height. Every day someone else was late for a payment. People you couldn't imagine were telling him sob stories you'd never believe and guys that Crawford had been doing business with for years were holding out on him.

He was keeping Gillie Fader busy. Gillie was doing a solo now. Cracking heads for Crawford with his Louisville slugger, a new one this time, because the old one was still sitting in the Columbia Police Department evidence room. And doing things for Crawford he used to have Conner do for him.

"Because," as Crawford explained to him at their regular meeting place in the bar at the Carlisle, "I've got to get in there first, Gil. These people owe everything and everybody, that's why they came to me in the first place, so I've got to be the first in line or I'll get nothing. You've got to make them understand that, Gil," and he chuckled. "Look who I'm talking to. If you can't make them understand that no one can. Take anything they offer you. Jewelry. Art. Even the rings on their fingers."

It was early in the day.

They were having coffee at the bar, and muffins. Bite sized blueberry muffins. Crawford's favorite. He nodded to the bartender and pointed at the empty basket for more.

Then he said to Gillie, "I've got another problem."

Gillie gave him the look. One eye raised the other in a squint.

"A friend of mine got herself jammed up. I helped her out and put up some funds for her release and, if things go right, her exoneration. In return for said favors, she put up a bunch of houses as collateral."

Gillie nodded. He knew where this was going, but he didn't. Not really.

Crawford took a sip of coffee.

"I don't have to tell you what's going on out there, Gil. The property market has disappeared over night. Even if I could sell her houses they won't cover what she's going to owe me by the time this is all finished, what with the vig and the lawyer's fees. You know what those bloodsuckers are like?" he said self-righteously like he wasn't one of them himself. "I'm going to suggest a different way to her, Gil. I'm going to tell her that for twenty-five grand she can make her problem go away."

"What problem's that?"

"There's a guy that will testify that my friend told him things she shouldn't have. His testimony, along with a recording he made of her telling him these things, and the autopsy evidence they already have, will do her in. And if it doesn't, by the time this is over the lawyers will have cleaned her out anyway. If the guy disappears so does their case. I like this lady, Gil. I've known her for a long time and I'm not interested in cleaning her out or watching some shyster do it instead of me."

Gillie nodded like he understood, which he didn't because Crawford was the coldest bastard he ever met. This was a side of him he'd never seen before.

"Interested?" asked Crawford.

"For twenty-five?"

"Why not."

"Nothing for you?"

Crawford said not this time.

"When?"

"I'm seeing her after we're finished here. She'll listen to me. And it's not like she's innocent when it comes to killing people, so what I'm suggesting is not likely to freak her out."

Then he told Gillie how Kathy O'Brien made her money.

Gillie was impressed.

"She's going to end up broke by the time this is over and I don't want to see that happen. This is not a done deal yet, Gil. You understand that, don't you? I'm just laying the groundwork here."

Gillie said he understood.

They finished their coffee.

Crawford threw a fifty on the counter and they left together.

On the street Crawford said he'd be in touch as soon as he knew something, and they parted company.

A little while later Crawford met up with Kathy O'Brien at a hotdog stand by the boating lake in Central Park. The sun was shining and the air was crisp and fresh. Trees were beginning to turn and the different colored leaves sparkled in the sunlight.

It had happened overnight.

One day the leaves were all green and the next, after a killing frost, they'd begun to change. You'd never think on such a beautiful day like today the markets were crashing and people were jumping out of windows.

In the time it took Crawford to get to Kathy from the Carlisle, the Dow had dropped another five hundred points.

"This is going to break you," he told her as they strolled around the boating lake.

Tourists were snapping pictures like they never saw a duck before.

"The half a mil the lawyer wants to get you off, plus what you're going to owe me, and real estate prices the way they're headed, you're going to be wiped out."

She was shaken to the core. Everything she'd worked so hard for was going down the drain. When it was over she'd be lucky if she could support herself what with all the bad publicity she'd been getting. Her picture was on the front pages of all the newspapers and the TV was full of it. She wore dark glasses and a scarf over her head to disguise her appearance.

Crawford said, "If we get rid of the witness, what's his name?"

"Lamont."

"If we get rid of Lamont they've got no case. Am I right?"

She nodded.

He'd taken her by surprise. Not about getting rid of Lamont, but because he'd used the word 'we,' and was willing to go this extra mile for her.

"You'd do that for me?" she asked him.

"I would," he said. "You've helped me out on more than one occasion and I'd like to return the favor. I can count on one hand the people who've been nice to me and you're one of them. Come to think about it, you might even be at the top of the list. I've got a guy that will do the job for you for twenty-five k. This way you'll be able to keep your houses and live off the income like you planned."

She was struck by what a bizarre moment this was. They were walking by the Alice in Wonderland sculpture at the north end of the lake, surrounded by tourists, and mothers, and nannies with kids in strollers. Children big and small were climbing all over the Mad Hatter sculpture, posing for pictures.

And there they were.

Walking by this menagerie of young and old and fantasy, discussing having Lamont whacked.

"What about what I owe you?" she asked.

"Once we get this guy off your back, they'll drop the charges so there'll be no more interest on the bail money, which I'll get back. You'll be out about forty grand by the time you're done. You own those houses outright. A bank will loan you forty grand on them in spite of what's going on out there. You give me the forty and we'll be quits. Your payment to the bank will be nothing. Two bills a month, not much more. And you'll be able to live happily ever after like you planned until Lamont came along and fucked everything up for you."

She agreed.

Of course she did.

It was a no brainer.

CHAPTER 35

WEDNESDAY

Lamont Dubois was not a stupid man. No sir. Just because life had dumped him on the edge of society, it by no means took away from his smarts. When word came down that a big ole pink dude with a bowling ball for a head was asking for him, Lamont's first thought was that no good could come of such a meeting. He'd heard about this man from the street. How Mr. Pink was the same dude that had something to do with the shooting at the Columbia Diner. The idea that the Jolly Pink Giant was looking for him suggested trouble might be on the horizon, so Lamont did the only thing a smart man like him would do under the circumstances. He went home and got his friend Smith and Wesson and with the gun tucked into the waistband of his pants he thought he would have nothing to worry about.

He was only half right.

Not long after Lamont teamed up with Smith and Wesson, Gillie Fader discovered him coming out of a coffee shop off of Main Street in the middle of Ossining.

They startled one another.

Gillie was not expecting to find Lamont so quickly.

Lamont was surprised at how big the Pink Man really was and how the fuck had he tracked him down so fast? Then he surprised Gillie even more by drawing down on him and putting a big hole in his left shoulder.

Gillie dropped to the pavement.

Lamont strode over to him.

Gille lay on the ground clutching his bleeding shoulder and looked up at Lamont defiantly.

Lamont made to shoot him in the head, but instead said, "Stay away from me you pink pile a shit or next time I'll blow your fuckin head off."

Then he straightened up. Blew down the barrel of the gun. Stuffed it back in the waistband of his pants. Stepped over Gillie, and strutted down the street like Wyatt Earp after the OK Corral. He figured enough people had seen what had happened to elevate his street creds by several notches. He was sure the corner boys would be giving him free hits tonight just to listen to his story.

By the time the cops showed up, the Pink Man had disappeared and Lamont Dubois never existed. People said they hadn't seen anything and had no idea what they were talking about.

Such was life on the street of Anyhood, U.S.A.

Gillie could not believe his misfortune. It felt like a hurricane had torn his arm off, only it was still there. Dangling by his side. Useless. And there was a hole in his shoulder he could put his fist through.

He had to get out of there.

People were standing around watching him. Fascinated. Fixated. But no one offered to help him.

Gillie staggered to his feet, lumbered to his car and drove away. The pain was excruciating. He used his knees to steer while he wadded his handkerchief and shoved it in the hole to staunch the bleeding. When that didn't work he took off a sock, no easy task when you're driving a car in terrible pain, and shoved it into the hole as well.

For a moment he thought he was going to pass out.

Then it passed and he was able to think clearly and assess his options. He couldn't go back to the City because the doorman would take one look at his shoulder and call 911. But he did have a bolt hole - a house upstate his grandmother left him when she died. He'd managed to keep it in her name by the astute distribution of American currency to such personages that were willing and able to make things like that happen. No one knew about it. He kept it well stocked with food and stayed there every now and again to get away from it all or when the heat was coming down on him.

Like now for instance.

It was deep in the country close to the Massachusetts border. There wasn't a neighbor for miles, so there'd be no one around to see the state he was in when he got up there.

He called Crawford on the number he'd been given for emergencies. It connected him to a throwaway Crawford threw away the minute he got off the phone. That's why they're called throwaways. Gillie told him the witness he was supposed to take care of was alive and well, while he was on death's door with a hole in his shoulder that was leaking blood like a burst pipe. He told Crawford about his grandmother's house, where it was, and how to get there. He told him to get someone up there as soon as possible because he thought he was dying.

Crawford said he'd send Kathy O'Brien.

Gillie said he wasn't so keen on Mrs. Kervorkian taking care of him. He'd noticed that none of her patients did very well by the time she'd finished with them.

Crawford said it was her, or no one.

Gillie said okay.

What else was he going to say? He really thought he was dying.

Lamont called Dupree to tell him about the shootout as soon as he thought he was safe and the cops weren't after him.

"Like fuckin Wyatt Earp," he bragged. "I tole you what I said to him when I stepped over him, didn't I?"

Dupree said he did.

"And you shot him in the shoulder?"

Lamont laughed.

"I was aimin for his belly, Dupree. Ain't had much practice with that thing. Fuckin bullets cost a fortune."

He'd rather spend the money getting high, but he never said it.

Dupree said, "You figure his blood's still on the street, Lamont?"

"Most def."

"A lot or a little?"

"A lot, man. I popped that mother pretty good. He went down like Goliath, I tole you that, right?" He laughed. It was more of a giggle really. "There was a big crash and the earth shook like there was an earthquake or sumpthin. Blood was pourin outta his shoulder like ketchup at a fixin's bar."

Dupree could hear how the story was taking off in Lamont's mind. By tonight it would have taken on epic proportions.

"Why was he lookin for you, Lamont?"

"Damned if I know Dupree, damned if I know." Then he chuckled some more, "He won't be lookin for me no more though."

Dupree called Jimmy as soon as he got off the phone with Lamont and told him what had happened.

"I don't get it," said Jimmy when he finished.

"What?"

"The connection between Gillie and Lamont."

Dupree said, "You're sure it's the same guy?"

Jimmy said he couldn't believe there were two bald headed pink gorillas that were wandering around the neighborhood.

"What's Lamont got to do with him?" he wondered.

Dupree said he didn't know.

"You think Lamont's left out some significant detail here, Dupree?"

Dupree said he'd be surprised.

"Lamont tells me everythin that's going on in his life. Never holds back nothin. Tell you the truth, James, I wish he would if you know what I mean?"

Jimmy did. He wouldn't want to hear it all either.

"Kathy O'Brien's the only one who profits from Lamont's death, unless there's something else going on here we don't know about. He's our whole case against her. Nothing holds up without his corroborating testimony. I wonder if she set this up, and if she did, how the hell does she know Gillie Fader?"

"Ask her," said Dupree.

"I will," said Jimmy.

Dupree said he thought Lamont would be strutting the streets tonight like Superman on crack. "Reapin the creds that are so rightfully his," he said proudly.

Jimmy quite didn't see it that way, but he kept that to himself.

"Imagine?" said Dupree incredulously. "A stranger comin on Lamont's patch and figurin he's jus gonna roll over an take what's comin to him. Fuck that, man. Big insult to Lamont and the whole damn neighborhood. Corner boys be buyin Lamont hits tonight and treatin him like royalty for defending the turf. Dupree better make hay while that sun's shinin, James, 'cos tomorrow they won't even remember his name."

Jimmy called Det. Calum McHugh a friend of his in the Ossining Police Department. Calum was a Scotsman with a strong accent who came to America as a drummer with a punk rock band and parted company with them because he wouldn't get as high as they wanted him to. He went into the army after that, made sergeant with the MPs and got his citizenship. After the military he became a detective in the NYPD for a while, then moved north and joined the Ossining police force.

He had his stint in the NYPD in common with Jimmy and every now and again they'd trade war stories over a cup of coffee and a donut.

Jimmy told him about the Lamont shooting.

McHugh checked the sheet.

"We've got an anonymous 911 reporting a shooting at 1:45pm outside a coffee shop in the middle of town. Officers investigated and found nothing. They asked around and no one saw a thing."

Jimmy said there should be blood traces on the street. It hadn't rained and it was a bloody wound. "It should still be there unless someone washed it away."

McHugh said he'd send a crime team over there to check it out. He'd call back if they had something, which they did because the blood was still on the pavement when they got there. The cops that answered the anonymous 911 missed it. Or weren't looking for it. Or couldn't be bothered. Or any of the above.

McHugh said he'd have to look into that, but that was an internal affair.

The techs lifted enough blood for a DNA comparison with the stuff taken from the passenger side of Conner Malloy's car. They said it would them take a couple of weeks to come up with a result, that's how backed up they were.

Uniforms canvassed the area again, but came up against a wall of silence. Again. No one saw anything or heard anything.

Jimmy wasn't surprised. People didn't want to get involved. He couldn't blame them. Word gets around quickly in a small town. Cooperating with the police can get a person in a whole lot of trouble.

He checked the hospitals for gunshot wounds. There were a lot, but none of them were his guy.

Then he got a call from Morgan. He was at Gillie Fader's apartment in the City. Gillie was not there. The doorman said he'd seen him earlier in the day, but not since then. If he showed up, the doorman said he'd call them. He said he was only too happy to perform his civic duty and also collect the ten spot Morgan had promised him for the information.

Crawford Taylor could not get over the fact that things always seemed to fall into place for him. It had been that way since his parents died. He always got good cards, and always bet on the right horse. And, even though things were falling apart all around him, there was this little nugget that confirmed what a lucky man he was.

An hour before Gillie Fader called him with his tale of woe, a source in the NYPD told him that Gillie had been made. An artist's picture placed Gillie in the Columbia Diner where Conner got popped and it was about to be circulated. Gillie was a monster of a man and it would be easy to identify him. It was just a matter of time until someone put a name to the picture and they caught up with him. Crawford was sure when that happened Gillie would shop him in a heartbeat, and why shouldn't he? Honor amongst thieves went out the window years ago, if it ever existed in the first place. Crawford had his doubts. These days you ratted out whoever you could as quickly as you could in return for less time in the slammer.

The same source called later in the day to say they'd put Gillie's name to the picture, and that sealed the deal. So when Crawford asked Kathy O'Brien to take a drive upstate and take care of Gillie, that's exactly what he meant.

He wanted her to take care of him.

Crawford met Kathy on the promenade of the Carl Shurtz Park over on the Upper East Side where the East River joins the Harlem River, or parts company, depending on the direction of the tide. It was late in the day. The shadows were getting longer and the park was full of kids in strollers, big dogs on short leashes, old ladies with nurses, joggers, power walkers, skateboarders, pretty girls and ugly old men. The flowerbeds were all but dead except for a brave marigold here and there and an occasional aster that had managed to survive the killing frost. Brightly colored leaves dropped like a gentle snowfall and there was a chill in the air.

Kathy said she wasn't so keen on taking care of Gillie the way Crawford wanted her to. Not that she was squeamish or anything like that. It was just that she thought she was finished with that part of her life. And that, she explained, was where her head was at right now. In retirement mode.

Crawford explained the situation to her in harsher terms. How it was Gillie who was working on her contract to kill Lamont when he got popped and it was Lamont who did the popping. How, when the cops took Gillie down, which was just a matter of time because they'd identified him and knew where he lived, he'd add her name to the package he was going to assemble in return for a better deal.

She had to agree with him. How could she not?

They'd come to Gracie Mansion at the northern tip of the park. It was the mayor's residence, but the current mayor didn't live there. He was a rich dude and lived somewhere else, but held some City functions there. It was as if the President of the United States didn't live in the White House, he just showed up for the formal stuff.

Kathy said, "I still need Lamont done."

Crawford said, "I can do that."

"And the forty I owe you is still the same? $25,000 for the hit and $15,000 for my bail and the lawyer?"

"Correct."

"But now I'm doing a hit for you."

"For us."

"For us," she agreed. "But still," she persisted, "it should be worth something, don't you think?"

"I'm spending $25,000 to have Lamont done for you. And the fifteen is for bailing you out."

She thought about that.

"How about this," she said. "I'll split the forty with you and do the hit for free. Twenty grand in all."

"Almost for free," he corrected her.

"Almost for free," she agreed.

Crawford thought about it and gave her a fixed lip smile.

"Seems fair." He said.

But just to be sure she said, "And my properties will be free and clear?"

Crawford nodded slowly and gave her the fixed lip smile again

CHAPTER 36

THURSDAY

Columbia has changed. It's no longer the lilywhite WASP's nest it was when Jimmy took up residence there twenty years ago. The downtown area is dotted with small boutiques. There are some art galleries. A couple of fancy coffee shops have opened up. And there are no big chains like the Gap or J. Crew in the vicinity. They'd been banned long ago. "To keep the identity of the town in its original form," was the way they worded it on the ballot. It passed unanimously, though of late a petition has been circulated for a Starbucks on the outskirts of town.

The people have changed too.

Jews moved in and built a Temple. Then another one. There are some African-Americans, and Asians, and South Americans, and gays. Yes gays. The place has taken on a whole new version of a cosmopolitan mix. A little of this and some of that sprinkled together with salt and pepper, and a touch of mocha.

And so it was on this crisp and sunny morning that Jimmy, flush with his victory against Austin Kenner and his drug dealing son Mike, decided to try his luck and get a cup of coffee at one of the new coffee houses that had opened up on Main Street. He'd tried the place before, but it hadn't worked out so well. The choices were too many and he didn't know the language. "Mocha express with something and foam" he heard people say with no understanding of what they were talking about. When it was his turn to order he got flustered and asked for the first thing he could see on the menu on the wall. It was the wrong choice and, after taking a couple of sips, he threw it in the garbage on his way out. But recently Mary had introduced him to lattes and armed with this new information, he decided to give the place another shot.

He ordered his coffee from the pretty young girl behind the counter with an authority he did not feel, and was pleased with the result. He was hoping for some applause for this minor victory, but no one was paying any attention.

Mary would've clapped.

Back on the street, coffee in hand, he passed a pair of hand-holding lesbians walking in the opposite direction.

One was in her early thirties and very attractive, wearing black jeans, a black shirt and a black embroidered leather jerkin.

Her partner was in her early twenties and was darkly complected with cherubic lips and a well-cut bob that framed her beautiful face to perfection.

She was drop-dead gorgeous.

So much so that Jimmy couldn't take his eyes off her and found himself staring at her longer than he should. Taking her all in, in her black tights and black crewneck sweater that hugged her seductive curves like a second skin. He marveled at her beauty and the picture they made, these two, so happily carefree and so obviously in lust.

The younger one had a look of absolute satisfaction planted on her face.

The older one too, but there was something else there as well. A gait. A strut. A pride on her face that she'd snared such a prize that was clearly the envy of everyone they passed.

Every head turned to watch them pass as they bounced up the street with a body language that screamed they were on their way home for some more.

They were all Jimmy could think about as he walked to the station house sipping his latte. What those two had been doing and what, pretty soon, they were going to be doing again.

And that's when it hit him.

How that type of sexual frenzy was a thing of the past for him. He'd never thought about it before, but seeing those two so ripe and so full of lust, brought it all home to him. The way things were when he and his ex-wife were that age and sex was all they did and all they ever thought about. Touching. Groping. Fondling. They couldn't get enough of each other. And seeing those two marching up the street with those dreamy looks on their faces made him realize how much time had gone by. How much older he'd become. And how that urgency that centered on sex and all of its variations had gone from his life. It had nothing to do with Mary. Their love life was great and they certainly had their moments. But it was different now.

Not like those two lovebirds who wreaked so much of their passion.

Those days were long gone for him now and he only just realized it.

When he got back to the office there was a pile of faxes on his desk. They were Kathy O'Brien's employment records from the agencies she'd worked for. Where should he start, he wondered, the oldest agency or the most recent? Whatever direction he took could either be a waste of time, or the fastest way to a clue. He went with the oldest, The Durham Agency, because he'd already spoken to the most recent and they seemed to be her biggest fans. This was seventeen years ago when she was fresh out of school. It was a thin file. Kathy's first assignment with them was a man called Arthur Motzney. When she'd finished with him not only was he dead, but she ended up with his house and all of his money. Now what was that all about, he wondered? Beginners luck?

Jimmy found someone at the agency who remembered her from back then and she pulled up her file so they could go through it together. Kathy stayed with Mr. Motzney for nearly three years. There were a lot of reports on her time with him because procedure dictated the client was required to file them every month. They were perfect. More than perfect. Mr. Motzney described her in glowing terms. How great she was. And caring. And so on. And so forth. One almost got the feeling he was in love with her, he wrote about her so reverently. Then he died. And she got all his stuff.

"Everyone knew it," said the woman on the phone. She had a scratchy voice and sounded like she needed to clear her throat. "We were all pleased for Kathy. All the caregivers hope it will happen to them. Well. Not all of them. That's not fair. But some of them are only in it for the money and try very hard to ingratiate themselves with their patients so they get left something. Very few are able to pull it off. The interesting thing about Kathy was that she wasn't even trying."

"How would you know that?"

"She told me."

"When was that?"

"When Mr. Motzney told her what he was going to do."

"He told her?"

"He did. She came to me and asked me what she should do about it."

"What did you tell her?"

"To say thank you."

She cleared her throat. Finally, after a long hacking noise. Then it sounded like she was spitting into something.

Jimmy grimaced.

"After he died," she continued, "she did a couple of short term placements, then she left us."

Jimmy reeled off the names from the fax. Three of them.

Yes she remembered them too.

Jimmy thought she must have a photographic memory. Either that or she had nothing else going on in her life.

"The reports we got about her from them were simply glowing," croaked the woman. "Frankly the agency was sorry to lose her."

"Why did she leave?"

"I don't know."

"Why do you think?"

She gave out with a phlegmy cough. There was another spit into something and another grimace from Jimmy.

Then she said, "I have no idea."

And that was the end of the interview.

It was not what he wanted to hear. There were no recriminations and no hint of any wrongdoing, even though Kathy got Mr. Motzney's house and his money and she'd admitted to Lamont that she killed him.

She also managed to do it four times after that.

"Things have a habit" is what Jimmy's father always used to say. It was the only thing he ever taught him, that and to stay out of his way when he was drunk. What his father meant by that was if you can only hang on long enough things have a habit of working out.

Like now for instance.

The trail for Gillie Fader had gone cold and so had the investigation into Conner Malloy's murder. According to Morgan, Gillie never showed up at his apartment and hadn't been seen since the shootout with Lamont, assuming it was Gillie that got shot. No hospital had treated him and no unexplained corpse had turned up anywhere. Hertz had a record of a Gillie Fader renting a car four days ago from a mid-town location that had not been spotted, returned, smashed up, or abandoned, even though it was supposed to be back yesterday. It had simply disappeared along with its supposedly damaged driver.

The Chief still had the faintest of glows from closing the case of the high school drug business, the arrest of Austin Kenner for possession of controlled substances with intent to distribute, and the accompanying media attention along with Connie's up-coming piece on him. But in spite of such a plethora of good fortune, the Chief was not a happy camper. The Westchester Criminal Investigation Department was driving him crazy about the Conner Malloy murder. They'd taken to calling him two and three times a day to stick the knife in. Taking a delight in his obvious discomfort while enjoying Jimmy's failure to solve the case and getting their jollies watching the Columbia whiz kid come up with nothing. Payback's a bitch, so eat shit and die. That'll teach you to fuck around with the Westchester CID's star players was implied without saying so, but told to the Chief in a variety of subtle and not so subtle ways.

The Chief then quickly passed on their sentiments to Jimmy by memo, voice message, email and the occasional phone call.

And so it was with great pleasure that Jimmy, not long after he'd consumed his delicious latte and recovered from the realization that he'd suddenly become an old fart, took a call from the waitress he'd interviewed at the Columbia Diner the day of the Conner Malloy shooting. Her name was Pat, and Pat from the Diner was about to save the day.

"Is that you, Jimmy?"

Jimmy said it was.

"That guy you caught with the weed in his safe, his picture's on the front page of the paper today."

"I know."

"He was the one who was sitting with the big fella in the diner the day that guy got shot. He's the one who marched out."

"You're kidding."

"I kid you not."

"You're sure?"

"And why would I be calling you if I wasn't?"

Jimmy said he was sorry

"I owe you one, Pat."

"I've already got a husband. And it turns out I'm pregnant. So I can't imagine what you meant by that last remark."

Jimmy called the lab and asked them to see if Austin Kenner's prints matched the partials from the bullets the ME dug out of Conner Malloy. They had Austin's prints on file from his drug bust.

Twenty minutes later the lab called to say they were a match.

Jimmy went looking for Eddie, found him holding court by the coffee machine, and saddled up to haul Austin Kenner in for a line-up just to be sure.

They got a couple of uniforms to put on civvies, grabbed a guy who was delivering pizza and recruited two men from the street who said they were only too happy to perform their civic duty. They told Austin to stand wherever he liked.

Pat from the Diner, Miss not Mrs. Nancy Drake, the lady who discovered Conner's body, and Henry, he of the dancing Adam's apple and a founding member of the scraggly gang of bobble heads at the diner, stood or sat behind a one-way glass with Jimmy and Eddie, studying the men.

They all picked out Austin as the man sitting with the Jolly Pink Giant at the diner, without any hesitation.

Jimmy charged Austin Kenner with the murder of Conner Malloy and just like that the case was closed.

CHAPTER 37
AUSTIN KENNER
WEDNESDAY NIGHT/THURSDAY MORNING

It was 11:30 Wednesday night by the time Austin got home from his drug bust. Everything took so long: fingerprinting, processing, and the interrogation. That's what seemed to take forever, the interrogation. Around and around they went, backwards and forwards. The same questions over and over again, covering the same ground. Who? What? When? And where? And that's all it was, but the chubby cop kept finding different ways to ask the same questions. When he'd finally had enough, Austin was arraigned, bail was set, and they turned him loose. It was the only part of the proceedings he was lucky about. Night court was in session, a rarity in these parts, but there was a backlog the court wanted to catch up with and he was able to get on the docket. Otherwise he'd have had to spend the night in jail.

When he got home - tired, bedraggled and all beaten up - she was waiting for him. Shirley from Great Neck. Overweight Shirley. Distraught Shirley. All that was missing was her sleeves rolled up and a rolling pin in her hand. She was yelling at him from the moment he walked in the door. She'd had plenty of time to rehearse and let fly with a stream of hysteria he found hard to deflect. He was worn out and drained and too tired to fight. What did she want from him?

"Can't it wait till morning?" he pleaded.

That opened the floodgates for another ten-minute diatribe on his responsibilities as a father and why did he have to smoke that wretched stuff.

"And coke?" she screamed. "You're doing coke now? How long's that been going on?"

She must've forgotten, because it was not so long ago she had a taste for those forbidden pleasures her very own self. When the kid was young. And went to bed early. And slept like a top. So together they could smoke that wretched stuff or sniff a line or two and reach such unbelievable heights of sexual exuberance that it was hard to imagine they were the same two people. Such was the level of their estrangement that even a peck on the cheek was received like a branding iron. On and on she badgered him until he threw up his hands in disgust and stormed upstairs to the guest room where he decided to camp out for the night and leave her alone with her misery and discontent. Safe in the knowledge that in two days his trades would clear and the proceeds would lie safely in his account. Not hers. Or a joint account. His account. One she knew nothing about. And then he was off to parts unknown; so long and goodbye. Fuck bail. And her. And the horse she rode in on.

He planned to go back to work tomorrow. It seemed only right since it was Mal Finklestein who had financed his upcoming freedom. There was much to close out and clear up so that when he rode off into the sunset he didn't leave Mal with a mess that needed sorting out. No sir, that's what loyalty was all about. He planned to clean up his desk and the books and leave Mal with his accounts in pristine condition, so the next guy could start up where he left off. That's what he planned to do and had the best intentions of doing so, but when the alarm went off in the morning he was so exhausted he hit the off button, rolled over and went back to sleep.

When he got up it was 9:30. The house was empty. A note on the kitchen table told him Shirley from Great Neck, along with their drug dealing offspring, had gone to the school for a meeting in the principal's office to sort out the boy's punishment. Those things were always in Shirley's column; she neither expected nor wanted him along to support them in their deliberations.

"Fuck em," Austin mumbled as he reached into the fridge for some orange juice. Truth to tell, he was feeling pretty good about everything. He'd spent the night in the belly of the beast and it was clear that no one suspected him of Conner Malloy's murder. There wasn't even a hint that they thought he was involved. And after all the backwards and forwards and incessant questioning, all the roly-poly cop could do was charge him with possession with intent to distribute and bail was set at $5,000. Big fucking deal. He'll be long gone by the time the case comes up, so who gives a shit. One more day and he'll be home free. One more day and his option trades will clear, the money will be his, and it'll be so long goodbye and good riddance. He scarfed down his orange juice and was about to hop in the shower when the doorbell rang.

And there was the chubby cop.

Again.

Accompanied by his uniformed sidekick.

And before he could say howdy doo, Fatty was reading him his rights and arresting him on suspicion of the murder of Conner Malloy. A wave of panic swept over him like a tsunami. His knees went weak and he thought he was going to throw up. What happened from last night to now? What changed? What had tipped them off?

They cuffed him and schlepped him out to the cruiser, one on either side of him, holding him up because he could barely walk his knees were trembling so much.

At the station house the desk sergeant held up the local newspaper as they walked past him on the way to the cells. He pointed to Austin's picture on the front page and called out, "Nice picture Mr. K."

CHAPTER 38

JIMMY

Jimmy decided to reap the creds that were so rightfully his on this one. As soon as Austin was re-processed and safely ensconced in one of their choicest cells, and even before he went down the hall to tell the Chief the good news, he picked up the phone and called Cpt. Phillips, the head of the Westchester CID.

It seemed that the Captain used the same playbook as the Chief did and drew first without waiting to hear why Jimmy was calling him, thinking it was to apologize for his lack of progress on the Conner Malloy murder investigation.

"What the fuck, Jimmy. How long is this thing gonna take you? We thought we were doing you a favor by giving you this case, you being such a hotshot detective and all, and you'd close it for us in a timely fashion. And whaddya got so far? Nothing. That's what your Chief keeps telling me. Some sob story about a guy called Gillie Fader you can't find and what he might tell you, if you ever do. It's because of you I'm still short-handed or I wouldn't have given you the case in the first place."

The last big case Jimmy handled resulted in the embarrassment of Smith and Monahan, the Captain's best case clearers, forcing them to take an extended leave of absence they still hadn't returned from. Such were the roots of the Captain's venom, which continued to spew out in an avalanche of thinly disguised insults and glee.

"Where do you go from here, Jimmy that's what I'd like to know? You're up shit's creek as far as I can see, and unless you can advise me otherwise I'm thinking of giving the case to someone else."

"That won't be necessary, Captain."

"And why's that, Jimmy? Some great lead you've come up with since this morning when I spoke to your Chief. I gotta tell you boyo, that's one pissed off boss

172

you've got yourself there. I'm surprised he hasn't busted you down to a uniform by now."

The Captain was clearly enjoying himself.

Jimmy got a kick out of it, too. There was nothing better than letting an asshole expose his assholiness. Like now for instance, where the Captain wouldn't let Jimmy get a word in edgewise and found more ways to dig a hole for himself than you'd think possible for a man of his caliber. Jimmy thought if he kept on digging like this he'd end up in China.

"Captain…"

"The more I think about it, now's as good a time as any," said the Captain. "I'm sorry, but I've made up my mind. You're a big disappointment to me Jimmy, a big disappointment. God help you when the Chief finds out. This is a black mark not just for you, but for the whole department."

"I said that won't be necessary," said Jimmy again.

The Captain didn't hear him. He was in love with the sound of his own voice and all the bad things he could beat Jimmy up with and drive him into the ground.

"The press are gonna love this one. It's not every day we take a copper off a case."

But Jimmy had had enough.

He yelled down the phone, "WE GOT THE GUY."

Silence. Dead silence.

"Are you there Captain? Did you hear what I just said?"

There was a long pause.

Then, "You got the guy?"

"I did, sir."

"When?"

"We just now brought him in. That's why I'm calling you. I wanted you to be the first to know."

A pause.

Then, "Ah."

Jimmy told him about it in excruciating detail. Teasing the story out and building it up so you'd think only *War and Peace* could be any longer.

When it was over, the Captain, shell shocked and flummoxed and worn out from listening, was forced to offer a "Nice work, Jimmy," before ending the conversation.

Jimmy pumped a fist and did the dance of joy behind the closed door of his office, then went down the hall to report the good news to the Chief, including a detailed description of his conversation with Captain Phillips.

The Chief was duly impressed with the way Jimmy put the good Captain in his place and was dazzled by Jimmy's ability to close so many cases in such a short space of time. The media, he knew, were just going to eat it up.

It was the DA himself who made the sojourn to Columbia to officially charge Austin Kenner with the murder of Conner Malloy and conduct the press conference thereafter. The DA was no slouch when it came to getting his picture in the papers and put the Chief to shame when it came to keeping his name in the public eye. The Chief managed to get himself in some of the shots, but he wasn't allowed to speak. The DA kept those honors for himself, he always did. His show. His rules.

Connie got the call along with the rest of the media for the press conference. But he already had the inside track thanks to Jimmy and was able to deliver a deeper and much more detailed piece than his colleagues, thereby continuing to resurrect his career and elevate his rapidly rising standing with his employer.

Austin was arraigned, pled not guilty, and denied bail because he was considered a flight risk, which was hotly contested by his lawyer who immediately filed an appeal. It was the worst possible scenario for our hero since he couldn't get to his money. To do so would have alerted his lovely wife, the fabulous Shirley from Great Neck, as to the whereabouts of said funds, and given her the freedom to spend them at will, which she would do with a passion, until she'd made a serious dent in his nest egg.

Then there was Crawford Taylor, who was supposed to be paid a half a million dollars at the end of the week. Austin was going to need all of that money for the best defense team money could buy and still have some left over for himself. His lawyer had lined up a dream team and Austin was getting positive vibes that they thought they could get him off with a self-defense defense. So no money for Crawford and no contact with him either. All Crawford could do was leave a message on Austin's cellphone telling him he was prepared to be patient for only so long, but in truth there was nothing he could do to get his money. He couldn't even get at Austin where they had him; he'd just have to wait him out.

And then there was poor Mal Finkelstein who was about to cash the postdated personal check Austin gave him for a quarter of a million dollars. The account was approximately $249,500 short! Austin planned to cover it with a banker's check when his money cleared, but now he couldn't. And fuck Mal anyway. He needed every penny to get out of jail and live happily ever after.

Austin gave his lawyer the power of attorney to pay himself, give the new defense team a handsome retainer, and put the rest of it in his escrow account where no one could get at it.

All four million dollars of it.

CHAPTER 39

KATHY O'BRIEN

After her meeting in the City Kathy O'Brien drove to that secret place of Gillie Fader's in upstate New York to, as her dear friend Crawford Taylor put it, take care of him. It took her a while to get there and it was late when she arrived. The house was in darkness. She put on a pair of rubber gloves before touching the door handle, not wanting her fingerprints to be on anything. The door was unlocked. She let herself in, groped for a light switch and flipped it on.

Gillie lay on the couch passed out.

The place was small, a cabin really: one big room with a fireplace, an open kitchen, and a couple of bedrooms. The smell was revolting. She figured he must have crapped his pants and didn't have the energy to clean himself up.

He came to when she walked in and groaned.

She went through a quick pantomime of pretending to put on the gloves figuring if he thought she came in wearing them he'd know she was up to something.

He'd lost a lot of blood. She might have been tempted to turn around and leave him to die on the couch, but he'd stuffed the wound with a towel and tied it up. It looked like the bleeding had stopped and it didn't look like he was going to bleed out any time soon. The wound could get infected, she supposed, and he could die from that. Or a fever; he was already very warm. Even shock, which he looked like he was in, would do the trick, but they'd all take a while to run their course and she wasn't prepared to wait around. And if she left him she ran the risk he'd be found. Or he'd call for help on a hidden cellphone. She couldn't take that chance, so she went ahead as planned, played the part of an efficient nurse, and got to work.

It was a through and through wound so there was no need to pretend she'd have to dig the bullet out. She was thankful for that. It took a while to get him "sorted", as an English friend of hers used to say, and make him comfortable.

All the time he drifted in and out of consciousness.

There was some small talk. Nurse talk.

Words of encouragement like, "Everything's gonna be all right," and, "There's nothing to worry about."

She gave him a shot for the pain and dressed the wound, bandaged him, and set things up like she was going to stay for a while.

When he asked her, in a moment of clarity, where her suitcase was she told him it was still in the car. She wanted to take care of him first, she said in the voice of a martyr. Then she'd see to herself.

She cleaned him up, got him in his pajamas, then into bed. No easy task when you consider how big he was and how dirty and smelly he was on top of that. The bigger they were the larger the dump was a truth she could personally attest to.

She couldn't just kill him. It went against the grain. She'd never taken a short cut in her life and she wasn't about to start now. There was a right way and a wrong way to do these things and she had her principles, just like with all of those old people she'd helped on their way. This was more of a coldblooded affair, but she still wanted to make him feel like everything was under control and he was going to make it.

The other thing was he was as strong as an ox, so if she cut to the chase too quickly it was possible he would not go easily. And might fight back. Then what would she do? Fight him off with her cheery manner and her rubber gloves?

So she took her time and played the part and lulled him into a false sense of security. Then she shot him up with some morphine, which did not put him out or cover the pain because he was such a big man. He was still drifting in and out and wincing and moaning and saying weird things, so she shot him up some more. And then, when she was sure he was out, went for the tried and true method and put a pillow over his face until he was dead.

She killed him. Murdered him in cold blood. For Crawford Taylor. For herself. For king and country and peace of mind. And any other excuse you can come up with. And it's not like she'd never done it before, but this one was different somehow. There was no euphoria or sense of power with this one. Or any other of those other delicious emotions she was used to feeling when she pulled someone's plug.

And she didn't know why.

Was it because she didn't know him? Or because Lamont was still walking around and she was pissed off at Gillie for being so inept? Or was it because it was just business, which was an end of things she'd never been on before?

"Nothing personal Sonny, it's just business," is what they said in *The Godfather* and she realized that was just how she felt about it.

Nothing personal Gillie, it was just business.

After it was done, she spent a lot of time cleaning up after herself. She took his wallet out of his smelly, crapped pants and was pleased to find it was untainted by his shit. There was a big wad of cash inside. She put it in her purse and put the wallet in a garbage bag she brought with her, along with the syringes, towels, cotton balls, and anything else she'd used to tend to his wound. His cellphone was on the coffee table and she put that in the bag too. Then she went through all the drawers and cupboards looking for anything else of value or that would identify him, but there was nothing more to find.

She vacuumed the place from top to bottom and put the bag in the garbage bag. She washed down all the surfaces with Windex and put the rags and the empty bottle in the garbage bag. She went through his car and took the rental agreement and removed the plates and put them all in the now full garbage bag, which she planned to dump someplace on the way home. She was proud of herself that she'd become such a professional. If all else failed, she thought, this could be a line of work she might be well suited for. When she was sure she'd done everything she could think of to protect herself, she turned off the lights and closed the door, removed her rubber gloves and put them in the garbage bag, got in her car and drove home.

CHAPTER 40
THURSDAY NIGHT/ FRIDAY MORNING

They'd finished dinner - Shepherd's Pie, apple pie and ice cream. And cleared the table. Lucy was in her room. Mary was cleaning up the kitchen. Jimmy was sprawled on the couch trying to get their program ready on the TV. *Inspector Lewis*. An English cop show they liked. They'd recorded it. Mary recorded it. Jimmy was trying to boot it up. Or put it on. Or get it on the screen. Anything. He was getting mad and began to push every button on the controller. This recorded three shows he didn't want and purchased a pay per view movie he'd never heard of and there was still no *Inspector Lewis*. Jimmy started to mutter. He was not so good with the new technology.

Then his phone rang.

It was Dupree.

"Lamont's missing."

"How long?"

"He never came home last night."

"How do you know?"

"He lives with my Moms. You know that."

Jimmy did.

"I can't get him on the phone."

"Maybe he's with someone."

"Nah. Lamont always checks in. Did you speak to Kathy O'Brien?"

"Not yet."

"See your picture in the papers all the time, James."

"It's been crazy."

"Yeah. Well. Way to go champ, but what we gonna do 'bout Dupree?"

"I need a picture."

"I'll send you a Jpeg."

"I have no idea what you just said."

"Still in the Dark Ages, big man? I thought Lucy was teachin you stuff."

"Small steps, Dupree. Small steps.'

"Gimme someone's email."

Jimmy gave him the clerk's email at the station house.

"Don't look good, James," Dupree said sadly. "This is the second time they went at Lamont."

"We don't know that for sure, Dupree."

"Yeah we do," said Lamont sadly and ended the call.

Lamont's picture was on Jimmy's desk when he got to the office the next morning. He asked the clerk to send it to Calum McHugh at the Ossining Police Department.

Two minutes later Calum called.

"He's disappeared," said Jimmy. "This is the kid who drew down on Gillie Fader who, by the way, has also disappeared. This is the second time they've taken a run at him. I think they might have been successful this time."

"Ach mon, you've got him dead and buried already."

"He's street-wise, Callum. Guys like him don't get lost, somebody loses them."

"And you want me to do what?"

"See if your guys have heard anything. Ask around. Show his picture."

"I'll see to it."

Jimmy thanked him and hung up.

After that he filed a missing person report for Lamont and put it on the wire along with his picture. Then he phoned Kathy O'Brien who did not pick up. He left a message for her to return his call.

Fat chance was his thought on that.

He spent some more time going through her employment records. This was the second agency she worked for. The Clarion Company. She was with them for five years. Again he got to someone who remembered her working for them, and yes, she said when Jimmy asked her, she was aware that one of her patients left her everything.

"Good for her," the woman said.

"Good for her?"

"She deserved every penny. He was just awful to her at the beginning. She was with him for four years, you know. Things changed after she was with him a year. But that first year. Oh my God."

"Huh."

"She had a couple of short term jobs before she got to that man and there were some more after he died. Then she moved on. I have nothing but good things to say about her. She was a saint. You got those records I sent you?"

Jimmy said he did.

"Well it's all in there as plain as the nose on your face. I wish all of our caregivers were like her."

He thanked her for her help then tried calling the people Kathy nursed. The short-term patients. A couple had died. One was in intensive care. There were some no answers and one livewire who remembered Kathy fondly. He'd had a disc removed and it was a long recovery. She was with him for a month.

"And she was just perfect," said the man wistfully.

"Huh," said Jimmy. Not hearing what he wanted to hear.

The next day, Saturday, 9:30am Lamont's body was discovered on the shore of the Hudson River in the weeds under the Tappan Zee Bridge. A fisherman discovered him and called it in.

When Jimmy got the call he said he'd like to see where Lamont was found.

"This is where bodies that were pushed, dumped, or have fallen in upriver, come to rest," said Det. Larkin of the Tarrytown Police Department.

He spoke slowly and deliberately with a minimum of inflection and was someone who could make a meal out of crossing the road. After much hemming and hawing he'd agreed to meet Jimmy at 4 o'clock. Now they were standing at the end of the road that serviced the marinas and restaurants that lined the Hudson River by the Tappan Zee Bridge. An iron trestle loomed above them. Traffic clanked and clunked like the percussion section of a motor pool. Some of the boats were already out of the water for the winter and were wrapped up in white plastic cocoons.

Soon they'd all look like that, thought Jimmy. Boatyards full of white pods like something out of a sci-fi movie, all waiting to hatch and take over the world.

"There's a place downriver where the same thing happens," said Larkin, a man who looked like he enjoyed his booze.

He had a bulbous nose pitted like a moonscape and covered in spidery blood vessels that extended like the minor tributaries of a road map. He was a big man who looked old and weathered and ready for retirement. His faded gabardine raincoat flapped in the breeze and a liver-spotted hand held his battered fedora to his head.

"Riverdale, I think. Or is it Spuyten Duyvil? It's got to do with the currents and the tides, is what the River Men say. Imagine working in a place where there are such people."

"Where are you from?" asked Jimmy.

"New Rochelle. We got plenty of boats and marinas there, but no fuckin 'River Men.' That's like some ancient thing from way back when and when you meet them you know why. Jeez. They look like something out of another world all lined and weathered and old. All they're missing is a yellow sou'wester and the hat that goes with it, but them ole boys know what they're talking about when it comes to the river. River Men," he shook his head like he still couldn't believe it. "Anyway, at first I never understood it when they told me, but then you see it for yourself. Not all the time, but most. Enough to be the first place you go to if you're looking for a body."

"Huh," said Jimmy.

"Your guy's got a lot of heroin in him," said Larkin and thrust a copy of the Medical Examiner's report into Jimmy's hand. "It's a slow day and you got lucky," he said in response to Jimmy's look of surprise. "Normally it takes a week, but we've got a lull." He said it like it was something to be ashamed of. Like they were supposed to be busy, but they weren't, and it was something they were going to be judged by.

"The ME jumped right on it. Says there were needle marks on his arm. My guess - your guy got high, fell in and drowned. End of story." He clapped his hands and held them up palms out like a croupier does when they change dealers. "Happens all the time," he said like he was starting to get bored. "Once a month at least, more in the summertime. Drugs or booze. It don't matter. They all end up the same way. Bobbing face down underneath the Tappan Zee Bridge."

"How long's he been dead?"

"What's the report say?" said Larkin sounding not quite so friendly any more. Jimmy looked.

"48 hours," he muttered.

"And how'd he die?" asked Larkin in a sing song 'I told you so,' voice.

"He drowned," said Jimmy.

He'd seen enough. He figured if he spent another minute with Larkin he'd have to throw him in the river for being such a smartass. He thanked him for his time, ignored the smug look on his face, and said so long.

When Jimmy called Dupree and told him what Larkin said, Dupree got mad.

"That's bullshit," he said angrily.

"How so?"

"Lamont didn't shoot."

"What did he do?"

"Snort."

"So? He could've still fallen in."

"I doubt it."

"How do you account for the needle marks?"

"Lamont hated needles. There's a story Moms tells 'bout when he was a kid and got a bad cut. They took him to the Emergency Room and wanted to give him a tetanus shot only they couldn't catch him. Skinny piece a wire ran em ragged. Doctors and nurses chasin him all over the place till they gave up and sent him home. Like I said, Lamont don't use no needles and neither did he fall in that river. He was pushed."

"By who?"

"The same people who went at him the first time."

"Not someone he pissed off in the neighborhood?"

"Could be, but I doubt it."

"Why's that?"

"A couple of days ago he was a hero."

"Maybe the corner boys gave him too much?"

"Are you kidding me? Lamont's a seasoned traveler when it comes to that stuff. I never saw anyone do more dope and still be able to think straight. No sir. It's too much of a coincidence. Three days ago someone took a run at him and now he's dead."

Jimmy couldn't disagree.

On the way home, he tried Kathy O'Brien again.

She picked up on the eighth ring.

Jimmy identified himself and said, "I need to talk to you."

"I don't have to talk to you if I don't want to."

"Yes you do. You're out on bail. I can go to the judge, cite non co-operation in an investigation and have it revoked in a heartbeat. Is that what you want me to do?"

Silence.

Then, "What investigation?"

"The death of Lamont Dubois."

"Lamont's dead?"

"He is." He couldn't read her reaction. Her voice showed a little surprise, but not much. That was the trouble with the phone. Face to face makes for a much better read.

"How'd he die?"

"He drowned. They found him in the river underneath the Tappan Zee Bridge this morning."

"Oh," was all she said. Then, "What's that got to do with me?"

"That's why I want to talk to you."

"Call my lawyer and set up a meeting," she said and slammed the phone down.

Jimmy called back, but she wouldn't pick up. Then he called her attorney who was, as luck would have it, working on a Saturday afternoon. He said he'd talk to his client and get back to him. When he did they agreed to meet in the attorney's office in Tarrytown on Monday. 10:00am.

CHAPTER 41

SUNDAY/MONDAY

Jimmy spent the weekend putting the garden to bed. He hated endings of any sort and though the fall had its pleasures, the bottom line was that the garden was finished for another year and now he had the winter to look forward to. He'd put a lot of work into the landscaping since he got to Mary's and created a bunch of beds that needed little or no work. It was a system he'd perfected in the old garden through years of trial and error.

Mostly error.

The garden was the only thing he missed about the old place. The last six months living there was a horrible time as he watched his ancient cat Felix sicken and die. By the end he couldn't wait to get out of there, but the garden. That was something else.

It was hard to turn his back on that.

Mary's backyard was a neglected child until Jimmy showed up and took hold of it. A small patch of grass surrounded the house. The rest of the property was scrub and wilderness that faded into the woods on all sides. It was claustrophobic until Jimmy cut down a bunch of trees around the edges to expand the space and increase the light, especially on the southern side. By the time he was finished the garden got seven hours of sun until it dipped below a tree line that was beyond his control.

He dug up the perennials from his old place and brought them over to the new garden. These were plants that had been with him from the beginning of his gardening experiments. Huge clumps of coreopsis, asters, bee balm and black-eyed Susans. Shrubs too. Hydrangeas and the like. And fruit trees that never gave any fruit till they got to their new home. By the time he moved in he'd collected over a hundred plants to be put into beds he had yet to create. All for free. And that was the best part of the exercise. They were his in the first place, so it cost him nothing and, for a cheap gardener, there was nothing better than that.

There's a lot to learn about a new landscape and it took him a while to get the hang of it, but eventually he managed to get everyone in the ground. A little bit, a little bit was how he went about things these days. Learned the hard way from the old garden where he rushed into everything like a lunatic and made every mistake in the book because he had no idea what he was doing and thought that he did.

So he took his time now. Correcting all the mistakes he made in his old garden. Getting each plant in the right spot. By the book this time, almost. Unheard of for him. It was a clear sign he was becoming a grownup, and the plants responded magnificently. He used logs from downed trees to make raised beds, added mulch that was plentiful on the property, and placed the plants and shrubs according to whim, design, and light.

Each bed was unique.

Like a canvas.

Eight of them.

And once they were in the ground the plants fought it out with their neighbors for light and space. And then, once they'd established themselves, filled out and provided more blooms than they'd ever done before. The fruit trees too. The vegetables thrived, and it was the best harvest he ever had. Tomatoes, potatoes, garlic, cucumbers, peas and peppers. And that was another thing he finally learned. Only plant the stuff you're going to eat. Hello? It doesn't take a genius, but for some reason he always planted melons and corn and things that didn't stand a chance. But not this time. This time he only planted the things that would grow in his new environment and gave every plant a healthy dose of compost when he planted them. The results were terrific and there was always fresh food to eat in the summer months whenever he came in from the garden.

And now the winter was on the horizon, that was something new to experience. That's what was great about a new garden, now dying or dead. You never knew what to expect. Unforeseen things happen that take on a beauty all of their own. Transparent shapes of dead flowers, ghostly clumps of leafless bushes, and skeletal displays of dried buds on stalks short and tall, all of them waiting for the snow to arrive and turn them into mounds of undulating white. In the end that's all that would be left of the garden, a dirty grey blanket that will stay on the ground till the spring.

That's what he had to look forward to.

Watching from the house.

Because it'll be far too cold to go outside.
And there's nothing to do out there anyway

Jimmy took Eddie to the meeting at Kathy O'Brien's attorney's office on Monday morning. Two on two. Jimmy didn't like to be outnumbered, especially when it came to lawyers. Eddie drove, as usual. Muttering about this driver or that and his lack of coffee. Coffee was a major contributor to Eddie's sanity. They used Jimmy's car this time. Eddie was in civvies. A sport jacket, grey slacks and an open white shirt. Jimmy looked good too wearing a freshly cleaned blue suit, a clean white shirt and a blue striped tie that was perfect in its selection. Mary's selection. She was beginning to have an effect on him. Not all the time, but on a day like today she had a lot to be proud of.

The lawyer's office was located in a private house off of Route 9 in Tarrytown. He was the firm's senior partner, so he had the best suite on the top floor of the building with a panoramic view of the Hudson River. One wall had floor-to-ceiling shelves that were filled with law books. Another wall had framed certifications along with some prints of nothing in particular. Under them were a number of filing cabinets with papers and folders piled on top. There was a teacart with a coffee maker and all the fixings near the door.

Kathy O'Brien was already there, sitting in a comfy armchair that was facing the window.

After handshakes and nods in Kathy's direction, Jimmy and Eddie were offered chairs on the other side the lawyer's desk.

The lawyer was a short mousy looking man in a dark three-piece suit with dandruff on the collar, a blue shirt, and a college tie. His crinkly red hair was neatly combed in a side part. His freckled face was full of consternation and face-tags a dermatologist should have removed long ago.

Jimmy found them a distraction. His eyes were drawn to them like magnets, especially the ones on his eyelids. He wondered if Eddie was having the same trouble.

The lawyer invited Jimmy to proceed.

Jimmy looked at Kathy.

"As you know Lamont Dubois was found floating in the Hudson River on Saturday."

The lawyer put a finger to his lips and told Kathy not to speak.

"Don't you worry," she said with an attitude. "I'm not going say a word."

Jimmy said to the lawyer, "Lamont Dubois shot a man called Gillie Fader last week in Ossining. Gillie Fader was coming to kill him."

The attorney feigned exasperation.

"What has any of this got to do with my client?"

"The person who benefits most from Lamont's death is your client."

"So what?" He got up, went over to Kathy and whispered something in her ear.

She whispered something back.

The lawyer said to Jimmy, "Lamont Dubois is a junkie. It sounds like he got wasted, fell into the river and drowned. It happens all the time around here. I still don't see what any of this has to do with my client."

"There's evidence suggesting he didn't fall."

"What evidence?"

"I'd rather not say."

"So. What? You think my client pushed him?"

Jimmy squinched up his face.

"Oh come on!" said the lawyer.

Jimmy put the composites of Gillie Fader on the lawyer's desk.

"This is the guy that took a run at Lamont. Do you know him Ms. O'Brien?"

They all looked in her direction.

Kathy got up and sauntered over to the desk and looked at the pictures. She said she never saw the man before in her life. She said it with all the conviction of a nun even though she'd killed him with her very own hands on Wednesday evening.

She didn't like Jimmy going at her like this, rattling her cage and trying it on. It bothered her. She could see how this guy with his folksy style and old school ways might be able to peck his way along and get from Lamont, to Gillie, to Crawford. And if he got to Crawford, he'd get to her. Without Crawford she was free and clear. With him she was vulnerable, especially with Fatso looking into every nook and cranny. Crawford would offer her up in a heartbeat, if they got to him. It had begun to gnaw at her, this idea she was at Crawford Taylor's mercy. And this visit by Chubby wasn't helping her confidence any.

There was more whispering between lawyer and client.

Then the lawyer said, "My client wants to end the interview."

Jimmy looked at her.

She nodded. Her face a blank. Giving nothing away.

Jimmy stood up and said, "Let's go Eddie."

"What was the point of that?" Eddie wanted to know when they were standing outside on the street.

Gusts of cold wind blew in off the river. Leaves clattered along the road and flew up into the air. They turned up their collars and hunched their shoulders as they leaned into the breeze and walked towards the car.

"I want her to know I'm on to her," said Jimmy.

"And are you?"

"No."

"So what's the point?"

"To shake her up."

"She's shook up all right. We've lost our big witness, we'll have to drop our case against her, and she's gonna be as free as a bird."

"So all I can do is annoy her, right?"

"She didn't look annoyed to me."

"I think it shook her up."

"I didn't see it."

"That's why I'm the detective."

"Why didn't you have her come to the station?"

"Because I've got nothing."

"So?"

"I like to have something on them when I do that."

Eddie grunted.

"I still can't figure it out, though," said Jimmy.

"What's that?"

"Any of it. What's the connection between Kathy and Gillie Fader? Or did she just get lucky and Lamont got wacked for a crime to be named later, some street thing that's got nothing to do with this. Or maybe he really did fall in the river? It happens all the time is what everyone keeps telling me. And where's Gillie Fader in all of this? He's got a hole in his shoulder as big as the Lincoln Tunnel and I still can't find him. He can't just up and disappear. None of it makes any sense."

"Unless he's dead."

"Then he would've showed up by now, wouldn't you think?"

Eddie agreed. You would.

"But she's lying," said Jimmy.

"Kathy?"

"Kathy."

"About what?"

"Everything."

"She knows Gillie?"

"Yes."

"How?"

"I just told you, I can't figure it out."

"And had Lamont done?"

"Definitely."

"By Gillie?"

"It's possible.

"Huh."

CHAPTER 42

MONDAY

AUSTIN

On the way back to the station house Jimmy called Austin Kenner's attorney and told him he wanted to speak to Austin about Gillie Fader. Austin was incarcerated in the Westchester County lock-up in White Plains as a flight risk from his upcoming trial for the murder of Conner Malloy. The meeting was set up for that afternoon.

The boys had some lunch at the Columbia Diner: grilled cheese sandwiches with fries and brown gravy for dunking. Coffee white. Coffee black. No dessert. Both were trying to lose weight. Then they headed out to White Plains.

Eddie drove. Cursing a new VW Beetle he thought was going backwards but wasn't; there was something about the design that made it look that way. Eddie's VW observation was a prelude to the main event. The VW cut him off and a long and repetitive aria of misery and complaint followed about how no one could drive any more and if he had the time he'd pull the guy over and give him a talking to.

Jimmy interrupted him with an explanation of his thinking about their visit to Austin to put an end to Eddie's rant because it was giving him a headache.

When he finished Eddie had some questions.

"How come you didn't ask Austin about Gillie when you busted him?"

"I did."

"What did he say?"

"He clammed up."

"Clammed up? What - are we in a Jimmy Cagney movie now?"

"He wouldn't talk, is that better?"

"Why do you think he will now?"
"I have things to offer."
"Why didn't you offer them before?"
"I didn't think I'd have to."

It was different for flight risks at the Westchester County lock-up. They were not considered prisoners; more like guests of the County. Security was light and they could do what they wanted within the confines of their small space that was tucked away from the main prison population. Getting a meeting on such short notice was not unusual either. Flight risks were innocent until proven guilty and they'd not been proven guilty of anything. Yet. So their lawyers had access to them as often as they liked. They still had to wear the orange jump suits though, with Westchester County Correction Facility written on the back of them, and that was not such a good thing because it made them feel like they were jailbirds, which they weren't. But neither were they free.

They met in an interview room that was solely reserved for Austin's section. Jimmy, Eddie, Austin, and his lawyer who looked old and wizened, but was neither. The room smelled stale and dank from constant use; too many bodies and not enough air. There were no windows in the room, just a vent and some strip lighting. There was a metal table and four folding chairs and cinderblock walls that were once white, but were now a dirty gray.

They say clothes make the man and in Austin's case that was certainly true. When Jimmy saw him last, even though he'd had the stuffing knocked out of him, he still looked imposing in his fancy clothes and expensive jewelry. Not so any more. His orange jump suit hung on him like it was two sizes too big and his face was pale and featureless. It was as if everything about him had disappeared into his orange prison wrapping and this skinny, pasty, other thing showed up.

Jimmy started Austin out with soft balls. Tosses, really. To test the waters and see which way the wind was blowing.

"Who did you owe the money to?" he asked.
"What money?"
"The money they came to collect."
"Who came to collect?"

Jimmy showed him pictures of Gillie Fader and Conner Malloy without naming them.

"Know them?" he asked.
"Never seen them before."
Jimmy stood up.

"C'mon Eddie, we're outta here."

The lawyer was alarmed.

Eddie was surprised.

Austin didn't know what to say.

"That's it?" said the lawyer.

"Look," said Jimmy. "I've got a dozen witnesses who place your client at the Columbia Diner sitting with this guy," he pointed at Gillie Fader's picture, "arguing with him and walking out on him. If your client wants to fart around, I'm off. On the other hand, I understand you're offering a self-defense defense. I can help you with that if you can convince your client to cut the crap and answer my questions. Cooperating with me might also help with his denial of bail thing, which I understand you're in the process of appealing."

The lawyer leaned back and appraised Jimmy.

"How can you help?" he asked.

"If I was to be asked in court, I would say those guys," looking at the pictures of Gillie and Conner, "were out to harm your client."

"You'd say that?"

"I would."

"Won't you be undermining the DA's case?"

"Not really," said Jimmy. "Your dream team is sure to ask me that on the stand. I'm just giving you a heads up on how I'd answer."

"In return for what?"

"Your client's got to tell me everything that went down, and no more cute answers." He shot Austin a look. "What happened at the Diner? What's the guy's name he owes the money to. How much does he owe him? He's also got to work with an artist so we can get a picture of him. I want all of that and anything else he can tell us."

They looked at Austin.

Austin stared at his hands in his lap.

Jimmy didn't like him. Everything about him annoyed him. Even this little performance was ridiculous and unnecessary.

"So who do you owe the money to?" he asked.

Without looking up Austin said, "Gillie Fader."

Jimmy sighed. His face tightened. He really didn't like this guy.

"Gillie Fader's this guy," he said angrily and waved Gillie's picture in Austin's face. "You sat with him in the Columbia Diner. He's not who you owe the money to. Gillie's a collection specialist. Great title, rotten job; you can get killed doing it. Witness his partner Conner Malloy's experience." He waved Conner's picture at him. "Don't fuck around with me, Austin. I've got plenty of other ways to find this out, then there's no deal. Talk to me now or take your chances. I'm the difference between walking and doing time. Ask your lawyer, he'll tell you."

The lawyer was nodding enthusiastically.

Austin thought about the consequences of what he was about to do. He was sure Crawford would set Gillie on him if he got out on the street. And if he ended up in jail, Crawford would pay someone to hurt him there. He was damned if he did and damned if he didn't. But he was already going stir crazy so anything that got him out of this place was probably a good thing.

After another long pause he said, "Crawford Taylor."

Jimmy shook his head and accused him of making it up.

Austin panicked

"It's the truth," he said realizing he might have cried wolf one too many times and now they won't believe him. He put as much sincerity in his voice as he could muster and looked Jimmy squarely in the eye. "His name is Crawford Taylor. That's the absolute truth."

Jimmy looked at Eddie who already had his notebook out and was writing things down.

"You met him where?"

Austin told him. Not about kiting a check with his boss Mal Finkelstein, which is how he got into this mess in the first place. Just how he met Crawford Taylor by chance at the bar at the Columbia Golf Club, drinking the night away and pouring out his heart to him.

"Why did you need the money?"

"I gamble," said Austin, which was true in a way. There was no need to say any more.

"How much do you owe?'

"Originally it was a hundred grand. Now it's a half a million."

"How come?"

"Penalty, interest and compensation for the death of his employee. Crawford said Conner Malloy had a wife, a kid, and a mortgage. Some of that money's supposed to be for them."

Jimmy smiled at that.

"You've been had," he said.

Austin frowned.

"Conner Malloy had none of those things. He was single and worked as a bouncer at a bar in Brooklyn."

Austin didn't like to be played. It made him feel dumb, which he was not. He was glad he'd decided to rat Crawford out.

"How do you get in touch with him?"

"He calls me."

"You don't have a number?"

"No."

"Email?"

"No."

"Where does he live?"

"I have no idea."

"Never went out for drinks?"

"No."

"How long's it been going on?"

"Six months, maybe a little longer."

"You've been paying him all along?"

"Yes."

"Where'd you meet?"

"Different places. Always on the street."

"In the City?"

"Yes."

"So what happened?"

"I got behind?"

"How far?"

"Very far."

"Then what?"

"Gillie Fader called me."

"And said what?"

"That Crawford wanted the matter settled quickly because it had been going on too long. On the phone Gillie sounds more like a stockbroker than a heavy. He's soft spoken and reasonable and makes it sound like it's a business deal you're working on. We agreed to meet at the Diner. I thought we could work something out till I laid eyes on him. The man's a monster."

"What happened?"

"I was short."

"How short?"

"Ninety eight thousand."

Jimmy's eyebrows lifted.

"You were just paying the interest?"

"Right."

"And they wanted the principal?"

"Yes."

"You never made a dent in the principal?"

"Right again."

"What happened then?"

"Gillie gave me a lecture on the value of my body parts."

Jimmy raised his eyebrows again.

"Because?"

"He said I wasn't coming out of this alive the way I was going and selling off my parts would be the right thing to do. He said there was a big market for them and right then I was worth more dead than alive. He told me my family would make out real good and I could feel nice about leaving them in such fine shape when I was gone. Naturally he said he'd take care of everything for me."

"And you said?"

"Fuck that and walked out."

"And?"

"That other guy was waiting for me in the parking lot with a baseball bat. You know the rest."

"You shot him?"

"I did."

"Where'd you get the gun?"

"I've had it for years."

"Why?"

"In case."

"In case of what?"

"Something like this."

"What did you do with it?"

"I threw it in the woods on the way home."

"Do you remember where?"

"Probably."

"It would be nice if we could recover it. All you need is for a kid to find it and do some damage with it and you'll never see the light of day again. We'll arrange for you to take a ride with Eddie and see if you can find it. Is that all right with you, counselor?"

The lawyer had no objection.

"You think you can help me get out of here?" said Austin.

There was a change in his tone. There was not so much bombast and he was heavy on the humble. It was almost a whine, but not quite. He managed to rein it in before it got pronounced, but he definitely almost whined.

"Let's see how much help you are," said Jimmy.

The first night was the worst. He was cold and miserable and hungry. The food was inedible. It was the same slop the prison body got and it was awful. He didn't know how he was going to make it. He shared a small area with twenty guys. Each cell opened out onto the communal space, which was not very big and had a table with a bunch of chairs around it. A TV was mounted on one of the walls and was on all the time until lights out. The only friction was who got to watch what and when. The guards usually supervised that. If you wanted to be alone you couldn't because everyone was hanging just outside your cell door. There was no privacy and no peace except after lights out and even then there was the occasional wail and the constant rumble of incessant farting.

He met them at breakfast; his new buddies. Not all of them were flight risks. Some were awaiting trial and couldn't raise bail and there were a couple of white-collar criminals who'd be at risk if they were in the general prison population.

They were taken to the canteen before the other prisoners and fed. Austin was the last on line. No one noticed him until he sat down at the end of the table. When they did they were friendly enough. A guy called Paco welcomed him to the 'twilight zone,' which was how he described where they all ended up.

His fellow jailbirds snickered at that.

Paco reached over and offered Austin a neatly rolled doobie, which Austin accepted gratefully and put in his top pocket.

"Getchoo whatever you want," Paco said with a toothy smile.

The others watched the exchange.

One of them said, "Paco's the welcoming committee here. Were you cold last night? Paco will get you another blanket. And that dope? He'll get you more if you want it. Make sure you smoke it after lights out and blow the smoke into the vent otherwise all hell will break loose. My name's Van by the way." He extended his hand.

Austin thanked him for the advice.

"How's he get paid?"

"Someone on the outside puts it in an account. He'll tell you how to do it. Right, Paco?"

Paco held out a meaty hand.

Austin slapped it and ordered a dozen joints to get his feet wet; also a blanket, some chocolate and a Big Mac, large fries and a milk shake. He figured he'd get the lawyer to make the deposit for him. He just wouldn't tell him what it was for.

Paco had an arrangement with a guard, he told Austin proudly. And there was nothing he couldn't get.

For a brief moment Austin actually believed this was going to work, but by lunchtime he was climbing the walls and sick of the sight of his newfound buddies.

"You've got to get me out of here," Austin begged Jimmy not caring how he sounded any more. He just wanted to get out of there. "You can see how it was, Detective. What was I going to do? Wait for him to take a swing at me? Did you see the size of that bat? Did you see it, I'm asking you? A fucking Louisville Slugger. Do you have any idea what that would've done to my head if he connected?"

Jimmy didn't say anything. He stared at Austin like he was examining him for flaws and imperfections. Trying to convey a lack of confidence in Austin's change of heart without saying anything and screwing up the dynamic.

"Let's see how you get on with the artist," he said doubtfully.

"Absolutely."

"We'll also need you to testify when we pull Crawford Taylor in."

"I will."

"And if you get out on bail you'll be wearing a bracelet. You know that, don't you?"

"Yeah, yeah," said Austin. "Anything."

They could wrap it around his dick for all he cared if it would get him out of this place. If he heard one more guy fart, he thought he'd go crazy.

CHAPTER 43

MAL FINKELSTEIN
TUESDAY

Mal Finkelstein was all of a tither. Was that the right word for it? Freaked out of his mind might be a better way to describe his demeanor. Austin Kenner had not shown up for work for three days. Neither had he called in and Mal was distraught. Not only was he distraught, he was crazed and out of his mind with worry. He'd called Austin's house. His cellphone. Sent emails. And nothing. He was sitting with Austin's worthless check for a quarter of a million dollars in his hands, which he'd tried to deposit. Asking the bank manager he'd known for fifteen years to see if the check was any good, which it wasn't. Mal was going nuts, and he still couldn't reach Austin. And what the fuck was he going to do now?

He's got bills to pay. He was in the middle of his launch. Every penny of it was accounted for, and now he was going to be short. A lot short, thanks to Austin Kenner. Checks will bounce and word gets around quickly. His partner Crawford Taylor will want to crucify him once he finds out what's happened. And he will find out. It's a small world out there. He'll want to know what happened to all the money he was supposed to be sitting on. Especially if he finds out he let Austin kite a check on him.

Not to mention how the lesser shys will react.

And everyone else he owes money to.

And Austin was nowhere to be found.

And no one was picking up at his house.

The intercom buzzed.

"There's a reporter here to see you," said his secretary in a sultry voice that was one of the reasons Mal hired her. The others were her hourglass figure and her gorgeous face.

Mal took a deep breath, unconsciously smoothed his hair, and plucked at the collar of his open shirt.

"Show him in," he said and composed himself.

The press release for the launch went out last week. Mal thought this was what the reporter wanted to talk about and got his head back in the game. By the time the secretary ushered the man in, Mal had a welcoming smile on his bottle-tanned face and looked as cool as a cube of ice.

The reporter did not look as cool as a cube of ice. He looked like a caricature of what a reporter was supposed to look like. He wore a scuffed leather coat with flaps and epaulettes and shiny metal buckles. It came down to his ankles this coat, and was cinched at the waist with a thick belt of the same material. He held a matching leather hat that was scuffed and beaten like the rest of the outfit.

Mal wondered why he didn't remove the coat, the office was warm, but then he did. Draping it on a chair by the door, and introduced himself.

"Connie Fieldstone," he said and handed Mal his card and shook Mal's outstretched hand.

Connie had a jump on the Austin Kenner story thanks to Jimmy, so he was ahead of the pack as to where Austin worked, as if his fellow reporters even cared any more. It was yesterday's news and the pack had already moved on to bigger and better things, but Connie had a follow-up piece to do. That's why he was there. It had taken him a while to track Mal down, some Googling and a few phone calls, but he'd managed to do it, and now here he was.

Mal started off by declaring that this upcoming Friday was the day of the official launch of his new line of women's clothes.

"There will be a fashion show at the Plaza," he declared and reeled off a number of 'A' list fashion luminaries who had committed to attending. Not to mention countless editors and some very hot stars who said they were coming and would, he assured Connie, make the event the talk of the season.

Connie had no idea what he was talking about, but he took a few notes to give the impression he did and to keep the ball rolling. When Mal seemed to run out of steam Connie stepped in.

Mal waited with a look of enthusiastic anticipation on his face. Set up in a crouch. Waiting to hit Connie's pitch over the fence with a crisp comment and an interesting insight. This was not Mal's first time at the ball game and he couldn't wait to show off all the moves he'd learned along the way. Even if he was bleeding to death he could always put on a good show. It's why he was so good at what he did.

"Can you tell me about Austin Kenner," said Connie leaning forward, pen poised, and his notebook at the ready.

Mal couldn't believe what he was hearing. His mouth dropped open and some sort of explosion was taking place in his head.

"I beg your pardon?" he finally said.

"Austin Kenner." Connie made a note of the shock on Mal's face and the confusion in his voice. "He was charged with murder the other day."

"There must be some mistake," Mal spluttered. "Are you sure we're talking about the same Austin Kenne here? My CFO? That Austin Kenner?"

"I am," said Connie and reeled off a couple of things from his notebook like Austin's address and what he looked like to make his point a whole lot clearer. "Don't you know about it? Didn't you see it on the news?"

Mal had not.

No one had seen it. They'd all been so frantic to get the new line out on schedule that no one had time for the news or anything else for that matter. They'd been submerged. Working through the weekend. All of them, except for Austin. And since no one from the real world had called him, Mal assumed that no one had made the connection. That was something, he supposed. But now it all began to make sense. Why he'd not heard from Austin for the last few days. And why he'd not been able to make contact with him.

Shit. Shit. Shit.

"He shot a guy in the parking lot of the Columbia Diner two weeks ago. He's in jail now. No bail's been set because they think he's a flight risk.

The color disappeared from Mal's face. He could see everything he'd worked so hard for pouring down the drain.

"Was he a good employee?"

Nothing.

"Did he give you any hint he was in trouble?"

Mal shook his head. As he did the gold medallion nestled in his graying thatch shook too, glinting in the light like some sort of warning beacon.

It was distracting this medallion and for a moment Connie was mesmerized by it. Then he couldn't help thinking how dated and gaudy it was. It looked like something from the '70s, or maybe what a pimp might wear. Not someone at the peak of his game about to launch an elegant line of women's clothing. He couldn't imagine Ralph Lauren, or anyone else with any taste for that matter, wearing something like that.

"Nothing you can give me here, Mr. Finkelstein? Some interesting little anecdote? Some little tidbit that might help me round out the story?"

Mal was frozen. He wondered if this was what having a heart attack was like? Paralysis. Heart pounding. Head throbbing with a big bass drum pulse. And there was that loud ringing in his ears.

"Nothing?"

It occurred to Mal that it wouldn't be long before the story was all over the place. If there was one reporter sniffing around there was bound to be others, and there went his launch.

Fuck. Fuck. Fuck.

Connie went on unperturbed.

"I believe he owed a shylock a great deal of money?"

Mal was far away now as his brain raced through the ramifications of his potential failure. He could see his parents knowing looks when they found out what had happened and he could hear that, 'I told you so,' tone they'd pour on him like water on a drowning man. And all of those people he'd borrowed money from. That trusted him. And believed in him.

"What did you say?" he mumbled, imagining himself floating face down in the Hudson River and washing out to sea after the shylocks had finished taking it out on him.

Connie pushed.

"I understand he owed a shylock a lot of money. Did you know that?"

He did not. He did not know anything about Austin's private affairs, except that he too owed a shylock a lot of money. He couldn't help thinking what a coincidence that was.

"Would you care to comment?" asked Connie,

Mal would not.

His mind shifted. Thinking about Austin now. Working side by side with him until last Thursday when he had to leave early because there was trouble with his kid. He was as cool as ice up until then and there was no sense that there was anything wrong. Austin was firmly in control and completely in charge, and all the time he'd killed someone. Mal couldn't help thinking how good he was and was forced to give him credit for a hand well played. He was sure he couldn't have given such a fine performance under the same set of circumstances.

Connie pushed on. Ignoring the obvious turmoil Mal seemed to be going through.

"How long has Mr. Kenner been with you?" he asked.

Mal's head was reeling. He didn't know what to think, or do, or say, so he said nothing. And told the reporter just that. Nothing. And sat there stony-faced and miserable and stared out of the window.

Connie looked disappointed.

"I'm going to write this story one way or another, Mr. Finkelstein. Are you sure there's nothing else you want to tell me?"

Mal thought about it then looked at Connie pleadingly.

"Look…," then his mind went blank and he couldn't come up with Connie's name. He searched for his card he'd tossed on his desk, and found it by the phone. "Mr. Fieldstone, I've got a big launch coming at the end of the week. I have everything riding on it, and I mean everything. Do you think you could you hold off on this story till after that? If this comes out before the new line does, the negative publicity will just about kill me. A couple of days are all I need, after that it won't make any difference one way or another." It might even help me, he thought. Any publicity is good publicity, but he needed the line to come out for that old adage to have any chance of working in his favor.

Connie made like he was thinking it over. The piece was for the weekend edition and had to be handed in by Friday so it was no skin off his nose to say yes and make himself look like a hero.

"What's in it for me?" he asked.

Mal was re-inflating. His face had begun to relax and you could hear a subtle exhalation of breath like a leaking balloon.

"Like what?" he asked.

"Something good about Austin."

Mal sighed.

"I really don't have anything for you," he said miserably, seeing his brief reprieve disappearing in the blink of an eye.

"You worked side by side with him for a week and a half after he'd killed a man and you're saying you didn't notice anything different about him?"

Mal nodded.

"He shot a man dead. It's not something you do every day of the week. Not a tremor or a twitch?"

Mal shook his head. The more he thought about it the more he couldn't believe it himself. And he thought he was cool. Austin was showing him moves he never thought he was capable of. Good old reliable Austin had killed a man. Imagine that? He worked side by side with a murderer. The idea of it suddenly made him shiver.

Connie said, "On time every day?"

Mal nodded.

"Not disheveled?"

"As a matter of fact quite the opposite."

"How so?"

And that was true too now he came to think about it; Austin seemed to have stepped up his game over the last week or so. He was early for work, and late to leave, and there was absolutely no hint that there was anything wrong or bothering him. For a brief moment Mal couldn't help admiring him.

"He was sharper than sharp and believe me, Austin always looked sharp."

Then he told Connie how hard Austin worked and how unconcerned he seemed to be.

Connie wrote it all down then looked up expectantly, waiting for more.

But there was nothing. Really. Except for Mal's closing statement, which he felt obligated to say because the silence between them was going on for much too long.

"Austin is an exemplary employee," he said regaining some of his earlier form. "Together we have grown this company from a bit player to a major force in the fashion industry. Together we have planned and worked tirelessly to bring this new line we're launching on Friday to the market place. It's because of his contribution I'm sure it will be a great success." He poked about behind him and came up with a press package, which he handed to Connie. "I'd be really grateful when you're putting this story together to mention us kindly." He also produced a press pass. "Come and see the show for yourself. I guarantee you'll be impressed. There'll be plenty of celebrities, good food and drink and, of course, the line itself which, if I do say so myself, is spectacular."

Connie raised an eyebrow. He couldn't help admire this man who was clearly blindsided by his CFO's transgressions and had managed to turn an interview that could be nothing but damaging to him into an eloquent sales pitch. That was pretty good in anyone's language.

"But nothing more to say about Austin?"

Mal shook his head sadly as he came to realize that not only was he out the quarter of a million dollars he gave Austin on the strength of a check not worth the paper it was printed on, but the chances of getting it back were between nil and zero.

"That's all I have to say," he said sadly. He thanked Connie for agreeing to hold back the article, and ended the interview.

Connie called Jimmy when he was out on the street to tell him what he found out. Nothing. Except that Mal had no idea Austin had been charged with murder and freaked out when he told him. And that he was going to a fashion show at the Plaza on Friday. Something he'd never done before.

After Jimmy finished speaking to Connie he went through some more of Kathy O'Brien's employment records. It was a tedious affair, especially the third agency. The Acme Agency. Kathy had a lot of short-term gigs there until she got to her third victim. She was with him for three years and he signed his stuff over to her half way through the second year. Chasing down the short-term gigs was hard work. Some of the people weren't around. Others you had to really work on to get something out of them. Either way no one had anything bad to say about her. After a lot of holding on and transferring, Jimmy was again able to connect with someone at the Acme agency who remembered her.

"She worked hard for her money. Isn't that a song?" said the woman. "Donna Summer, someone like that. 'She works hard for her money,' that's how it goes. Well that was Kathy O'Brien. We were all glad for her when we found out he left her everything. That guy was a bastard."

"What guy?"

"The guy that left her his estate. The first year she worked for him he ran her ragged. He was a very difficult patient. He'd already gone through three people we'd sent over before she got to him. She had to be a saint to turn that situation around. By the second year she had him eating out of her hand, it was the most remarkable transformation I've ever seen. After that it took him a year to die. She was there with him till the end. That's how good she was!"

"Huh," said Jimmy. Again, not hearing what he wanted, imagining Kathy putting a pillow over the old guy's face. That's why she was with him till the end. And that's how good she was!

CHAPTER 44
TUESDAY MORNING

Arple Shaw was an African-American hero with three Purple Hearts, two Bronze Stars and a Silver Star for valor. He served his country with distinction on the battlefields of Viet Nam, rising to the rank of sergeant in an army that had trouble with the integration of the races and the fairness of play. No one knew much about this solitary man who got on with his life by minding his own business and encouraging others to do the same. He never talked about his wartime experiences and no one knew of his heroic accomplishments. He lived alone, had few friends, and for the last twenty-five years supported himself by reading meters for the electric company in Copake, New York. He was soon to retire, this aging American hero with a hitch in his giddy-up and a bit of a stoop, and there were things lodged in the recesses of his mind he would rather weren't there.

Lurking like an evil curse.

Waiting for the moment.

That time.

To be prodded into life.

When Arple Shaw got to work on Tuesday morning it was raining, but by the time he got to the fourth house on his route it had turned into the most beautiful of days. Birds trilled loudly and a bright sun shone in a cloudless sky. Arple was preoccupied. He was thinking about his upcoming retirement and the river he was planning to fish, when he got a whiff of something he wasn't expecting.

And that's when it happened.

When those sublimated circuits kicked in by all themselves and there was nothing he could do about it.

The flashback ambushed him.

Suddenly shells were raining down all around him, and there was death and destruction wherever he looked. Screams of terror came from all sides, and there was that smell everywhere. That terrible odor that was stamped in his brain. The stench of death. And decay. And rotting flesh.

Then he blacked out.

An hour later the alarm was raised. Arple Shaw wasn't answering his cellphone. They couldn't reach him on the two-way or his beeper. Management called the cops. The cops, they were State Troopers, went to the last place of known contact, which was the first house on Arple's route.

Yes, said the elderly couple living there, they did have their meter read by Mr. Shaw. They had a quick exchange with him, they said, and then he was on his way. And yes, he looked just fine. And no they said after giving it much thought, he gave them no indication there was anything wrong or that there was anything on his mind.

The next two stops had not seen him, but that didn't mean he hadn't been there.

At the fourth house they found Arple collapsed on the stoop by the front door, but alive. He'd had a heart attack or so it seemed. They called for an ambulance, got blankets from the trunk and put one over him and rolled up the other one for his head.

It was after the excitement died down that they smelled it, an unpleasant odor that was coming from the inside of the house. They knocked on the door. Looked through the windows, and finally, when no one responded, kicked the door open. Inside they followed the putrid odor to a bedroom in the back of the house where they found a large, dead man lying in bed in his pajamas. His face was covered with insect life like something from a horror movie. It had been touch-and-go dealing with the stench, but the mass of insects on the dead man's face pushed the pair of Troopers over the edge. They both gagged and ran outside.

The first to recover called it in.

The good news was that Arple Shaw was going to be just fine. The ambulance came quickly. The medics stabilized him, gave him oxygen, and rushed him to the hospital where it was determined he suffered a mild heart attack brought on, as Arple described it, by "a big-ass flashback." There were no anticipated repercussions from his trauma and all of his parts were working the way they did before the attack. After a couple of days of observation and the royal treatment, they sent him home with some fresh medication and a brand new diet.

The local paper, while covering the story and after a little digging, came up with the details of Arple's heroic wartime exploits. Overnight he became a local hero. The electric company let him retire without returning to his job and laid on a magnificent dinner on his behalf. The mayor and all the local dignitaries were in attendance. They gave speeches as only politicians can do; you'd have thought they'd known Arple all their lives the way they spoke so glowingly about him. There were retirement gifts that before the incident would never have occurred to anyone. The company stepped up and instead of giving Arple the paltry pension he was entitled to after twenty-five years of dedicated service, awarded him the salary and health insurance he was currently receiving for the rest of his life. Plus, and this came from the president himself, a check for $25,000 on behalf of the company for his dedication to his work and a grateful nation for his service to his country.

The crime scene crew identified the corpse from his picture on the alert Jimmy put out as a person of interest in the Columbia Diner shooting. Six hours after he'd been discovered, the Troopers called Jimmy to tell him what they had: that Gillie Fader had been found dead in a house listed in his long deceased grandmother's name in a remote part of Copake, an hour north of Columbia in the great State of New York.

Jimmy said he was on his way.

The drive took him ninety minutes. When he left Columbia there were still some leaves on the trees. As he went farther north there were fewer and fewer until eventually there were none at all and the landscape looked bleak and wintery. He would have been there sooner only just outside of Millerton he got pulled over by a cop. He passed through the quiet little town studiously obeying the 35mph speed limit and began to go faster as he left the hamlet and approached a sign declaring the speed limit to be 55mph.

A cruiser peeled out of a parking lot with its lights on.

Jimmy was doing 45mph and figured it couldn't be him. But it was, so he pulled over.

The cop parked behind him and came over.

Jimmy rolled down the window.

"I'd like to think I was doing 45 in a 55mph zone," he said.

The officer, a kid really, wore a new uniform and had an Alfred E. Neuman face along with the freckles and the pug nose and the body.

He smiled and said he was afraid that was not the case.

"You were still in the town speed limit of 35mph so you were actually doing 45 in a 35mph limit."

Jimmy chewed on the side of his cheek.

"The 55mph sign's the start of the new limit?" he asked.

He already knew the answer. It was a speed trap. A cruiser lurked by the sign knowing drivers would speed up when they saw the sign thinking they were abiding by the law, but they weren't. It was a cheap trick. In the old days the cop that pulled you over would take the top note in your billfold and send you on your way. These days it's a municipal revenue source; a toll for the privilege of passing through the town. The locals know it's there. It's only the strangers that don't.

The kid said it was, but he was still in the town speed zone.

Jimmy handed him his license and his ID.

"I'm on the job," he said, expecting the universal cop courtesy that acknowledged they were all united in a common cause, and would be waved on.

"All the way up here?" the kid wanted to know. He was all wide-eyed and innocent.

Jimmy explained the situation.

The kid said he'd have to call it in.

He was very green, this cop, and he'd never come up against this situation before. Now he was nervous and was sure this was not going to turn out well for him.

Jimmy waited in the car. Drumming his fingers on the steering wheel, trying not to get mad.

Five minutes later the kid returned full of apologies. He said his boss said the rules were the rules and there were no exceptions. He handed Jimmy a ticket and a bunch of papers regarding procedure, apologized profusely, and sent him on his way.

But not before Jimmy said, "What's your Captain's name, officer?"

The kid straightened up. Not liking the question and not answering right away.

Jimmy waited.

The kid was trying to work out the ramifications of telling the man what he wanted to know. Would it be a black mark and make even more problems with the Captain who didn't like him in the first place? Or would it make him the object of derision? He was right in the first place. No good could come of this.

Jimmy took out his notebook and pen and looked up at the kid. Waiting.

The kid came to the conclusion that it was no a great secret. You only had to call the station and they'd tell you who he was.

"Captain Ardley," he said and sent a silent prayer to the patron saint of rookies.

Jimmy wrote it down, put the notebook back in his pocket and drove away.

By the time he got to Copake it was dark and cold, much colder than it was in Columbia. Winter had already arrived here. Going outdoors and working in the garden must have finished two weeks ago at least. Spring was probably the same way arriving two weeks later than it did in Columbia. Jimmy could never live in a place like this. He'd lose a month of his life cooped up indoors.

They met at Gillie Fader's house: the State Troopers who found him, Jimmy and the ME. Jimmy was the last to arrive.

They all shook hands, introduced themselves and exchanged cards.

When Jimmy told them why he was late the troopers cracked up.

One of them said, "We call him Capt. Canardly up here, because he can hardly get out of his own way."

Jimmy gave them a thin smile.

"My Chief will be calling him I shouldn't wonder. It's a pet peeve of his when locals act this way. We give cops a free pass when they come through our patch. The Chief thinks it's disloyal to the force to hand out tickets to them, especially if the cop's on the job. I have to agree with him."

They all smiled at that.

The ME handed Jimmy a copy of the autopsy report.

He was a kindly looking older man in a shabby dark suit, with a shock of white hair and bushy white eyebrows. He looked like he was enjoying the excitement. He got the call as soon as they found Gillie's body. Four hours later he was in the morgue, cutting him up. It's not like he had anything else to do. This was the most fun he'd had all year. The last autopsy he performed was six months ago when Cody Perkins OD'd on uppers, downers and scotch.

Before Jimmy could take a look at the report the ME said, "Mr. Fader had a lot of morphine in him, but that's not what killed him. Neither was it the gunshot wound in his shoulder, although that was pretty severe." He said it with an, 'aren't I clever' twinkle in his eye. It was a, 'go on and ask me,' kind of twinkle.

Jimmy obliged him.

"What then?" he asked.

"He was suffocated," said the ME proudly. "There were blotches on his eyes; it's a common way of determining if that method was used. He also received professional care for the shoulder wound. It was cleaned and bandaged by someone who really knew what they were doing."

"So it's murder?"

"Definitely," said the ME.

One of the Troopers chimed in, a young man with a peach-fuzz face and a tight buzz on his blonde hair. "That would explain what the crime scene crew came up with."

"What's that?" asked Jimmy.

"Nothing," said the Trooper. "We'll have their full report in a day or two, but they said the place has been gone over pretty good. It was vacuumed, and dusted, and all the surfaces have been washed down. There's no garbage anywhere. Not inside or out. The killer must've taken it with them. There was no wallet or identification. The car's plates were removed and there was no paperwork in the glove compartment. We traced the VIN number to a Hertz rental agency in the City. They confirmed the car was rented to Gillie Fader and it was long overdue. That and the match from the alert you put out confirmed who he was. This is the contents of his pockets from the clothes thrown over a chair." He handed Jimmy an evidence bag. "It's all there was, not even a tooth brush in the bathroom."

"He was on the lam," said Jimmy and chuckled.

They stared at him like he said something inappropriate.

Jimmy explained.

"A buddy of mine accused me of talking like I was in a Cagney movie and here I am saying he was on the lam."

They nodded like they knew what he was talking about, but they didn't. Not really. It would all have to be hashed out later when Jimmy was gone and they had beers in their hands. Especially since none of them had any idea what a "lam" was.

Jimmy emptied the bag on the table.

Some used tissues and small change, a toothpick and a set of keys that were probably to Gillie's apartment. Nothing.

"How long has he been dead?"

"I'd say five days," said the ME. "Give or take

"That fits. He got shot in Ossining by a guy called Lamont Dubois around 1:00 last Thursday afternoon."

"You think that's who did him?" asked buzz cut.

He told them how Lamont ended up floating in the river.

"Not possible. Lamont was killed a couple of days later. Gillie must've driven straight here after he got shot. That's why we couldn't find him."

"Who killed Lamont?" asked buzz cut.

"We're still working on that."

Jimmy told them about Kathy O'Brien and how a pillow over the face was her thing. How he thought she was responsible for five deaths, but they could only charge her for one. Shelly Barton. "Lamont was our main witness for that. Now he's gone and the charges are going to be dropped. "

The ME asked, "Do you think the same person who treated this guy's wound killed him?"

"I checked every hospital. No one saw him or treated him. The medical care Gillie got and the pillow over the face make Kathy O'Brien a pretty good suspect, but so far there's no proof. It's all conjecture."

Buzz Cut said they'd have the crime scene people go over the house again. There were places they hadn't spent much time on because they didn't think it was a murder.

The crime scene crew said they'd be there in an hour.

Jimmy said he didn't plan on waiting around for them.

"Mind if I look the place over?"

"Look all you like," this from the Trooper who had yet to speak. A burly-looking guy in his early twenties who must've played thc line in high school, he was that big. "We'll let you know what they come up with. We're gonna get a bite to eat now. It looks like it's gonna be a long night."

They shook hands and the Troopers left, but not before Buzz Cut reminded him to be sure to close the door and turn the lights off.

Jimmy chewed the side of his cheek, but didn't say anything.

Everyone had to get their licks in.

The ME handed Jimmy his card.

He said his day was over and he too had to be going.

"If there's anything I can do to help you, Detective, please don't hesitate to call on me." He said it sadly, like a kid being dragged away from an amusement park. Then he trudged out the door and was gone.

Jimmy stared around the living room. There wasn't much to see. A couple of old brown armchairs and a fraying maroon sofa were arrayed around a fireplace. A cherry sideboard sat against a wall with an oval mirror above it. There were bookcases full of the grandmother's books, a table and a couple of chairs against another wall by the kitchen, and an old TV with rabbit ears that sat on a rickety metal stand. The room was messy from people tramping in and out and searching the place, but there was nothing that looked unusual or out of place. He looked in the garbage cans. Checked the bedside table, the desk, the bathroom, and the backs of the pictures on the walls and the undersides of all the furniture. He didn't know what he was looking for, but you never know what you might find. In this case it was a book of matches from the Carlisle Hotel that was jammed in a drawer and had escaped attention. That was it. Nothing else. He was disappointed.

He called Mary and told her he was on his way home. When he was almost there, he got a call from one of the Troopers back at Gillie's house with the crime scene crew. He said they'd gone over the house from top to bottom and come up with nothing except for one pubic hair in the bathroom.

"Just the one?" Jimmy asked.

"Just the one," said the trooper.

"You'd think there'd be more," said Jimmy.

"You would, wouldn't you," said the Trooper.

The bathroom had been thoroughly cleaned, he explained, but on further inspection they found the pube stuck to the underneath of the toilet seat. They were sending it to the lab for DNA analysis. The lab was quiet, he said, and if they were lucky they'd have the result in a couple of days.

"Whoever was there left us an unlikely souvenir," said the Trooper.

"Unless it's Gillie's," said Jimmy.

"Unless it's his," agreed the Trooper.

By the time Jimmy got home it was 11:00. He was exhausted. Mary warmed something up for him and joined him at the table while he ate. They barely spoke. He was starving and bolted the food down like someone was after him. When he was finished, he staggered to the living room, plopped himself on the couch and put on the TV. And that's all she wrote. He was asleep before the picture came into focus.

CHAPTER 45

WEDNESDAY

JIMMY

The next morning Jimmy was late getting to the station house. He slept through the alarm. Mary turned it off and let him sleep. It was 9:30 when he woke up. To Mary's chagrin he threw on yesterday's clothes, though as a concession to her and a personal choice of his own he put on clean underwear, and rushed out of the house like a lunatic. It was going to be one of those days, he could tell. First came the lights: all red. Then he got behind someone who insisted on going 25mph and there was no place to pass them. And he tripped getting out of the car and ripped the cuff of his trousers on a suit Mary was dying to put in the poor box.

Score one for Mary.

The coffee at the station house was like mud and gave him heartburn that lasted till lunchtime. On top of all that it was bleak and cold and it was supposed to snow. If that wasn't enough to put him in a bad mood he didn't know what was.

Eddie slouched into the office with a long face.

"Wassup with you?" said Jimmy.

"Bad mood," said Eddie."

Jimmy waited.

"Gonna snow," said Eddie. "I hate the fuckin snow." Then he saw Jimmy's face. "Wassup with you?"

"I hate the fuckin snow too."

"What are they saying?"

"3 to 5."

"Whadda they know?"

Jimmy agreed.

"When's it supposed to start?" asked Eddie.

"This afternoon."

"I heard this morning."

Jimmy shrugged.

Eddie said, "I'm taking Austin Kenner out of the pokey to look for the gun."

"Better get going before it starts coming down."

"They're getting him ready. Gotta pick him up at...," Eddie looked at his watch, "11:30."

Jimmy punched the keys on his computer and brought up the weather.

"They're still calling for 3-5 starting in the afternoon, but you know how that goes. Take another uniform with you. If that stuff starts coming down and stays on the ground we won't find the gun till the spring."

Eddie agreed.

"Did you line up an artist?" Jimmy asked.

"I got Kelly Blake again. I'm meeting her at the lockup at 4:00, unless something comes up. Like the fucking weather."

Jimmy said, "I ran Crawford Taylor through the system. There's nothing on him, not even a driver's license. Be good if Austin gives us a picture to work with."

Eddie agreed.

Jimmy told him about Gillie Fader.

"You think Kathy did him?"

"She's the likely candidate. Gillie was suffocated."

"What a coincidence."

Then he told Eddie about the pubic hair.

"Just the one?"

Jimmy nodded.

Eddie said, "You'd think there'd be more."

"You would, wouldn't you? They said the place had been gone over pretty good."

"It's probably Gillie's," said Eddie.

"That's what I said."

"And nothing on Lamont?"

"Apart from being dead?"

"Apart from that."

"Nothing," said Jimmy. "Calum McHugh's people came up dry. Dupree's furious. He says Lamont was pushed. Trouble is Lamont liked his dope and you know what that's like. Dopers fall in the river all the time."

Eddie grunted. "You taste that coffee?"

Jimmy said he had.

"If I find out who made it," said Eddie, standing up, "I'll arrest him myself."

Jimmy smiled. It was the first of the day. Not a smile really, but the best he could do under the circumstances.

"Stay in touch," he said to Eddie's back as he slouched out of the door.

A little while later he took a call from Dupree.

"Lamont's funeral's today, James."

"What time?"

"2:30."

"Where?"

Dupree told him.

"Got a nice spot for him. You can see the River from there. Lamont loved the River."

"I'll be there."

"Be the only white face, James."

"Won't matter. It's gonna snow. We all look alike in that."

"Fat chance."

"Want me to pick you up?"

"Nah, thanks. Gonna be with my Moms. She's in a bad way. She loved that boy. She knew he was no good, but she loved him anyway." There was a pause. Then, "Got anything?"

"Nothing, Dupree. I'm sorry. The Ossining people asked around, and showed Lamont's picture, and went to their snitches and came up empty. I'm not sure we're gonna be able find out what happened."

"Yeah? Well fuck that James."

Dupree was of the street. He was not on the street any more, but he still knew where to go if you wanted to know what was going on there, especially if he spread some money around. And that's what he told Jimmy he'd done.

"Spoke to some of my old runnin buddies, James. Homie's know everythin that's going on down there. Everyone's watchin everyone else. S'all they got to do with their lives. Lookin out the window. High or straight, it don't make no difference. All you got is time down there to watch and see what's goin on. Good or bad, it don't make no difference. Word travels fast. That's why your guys don't know nuthin. Everyone knows who they are. See em comin a mile away. I'll find out what happened to Lamont, James. An you can take it from there."

Jimmy said he'd see him at the cemetery.

By the time Jimmy got to the cemetery the snow was coming down hard. Harder than they said it would and they'd changed the forecast to 5 to 7 inches. Maybe more. He found Dupree in the chapel with his Moms, who looked like she was in bad shape, sobbing and crying and hanging on to Dupree for dear life.

She was a large woman in a maroon coat with a black felt collar all buttoned up. She had bandy legs sheathed in gray support stockings and wore black shoes with heels that were too high and made her wobble unsteadily. It was probably the reason she was hanging on to Dupree so tightly. Her face was big and meaty and sad, and a black pillbox hat covered her head with a veil that came down to her nose.

They sat down in the front row, just the two of them. No one else was there. No relatives, or friends, or lovers. Such was the life and times of a street doper like Lamont. Not much to show for the 29 years he'd spent on this earth: an aunt, a cousin, and a cop that barely knew him.

Lamont's pinewood casket sat on a dolly draped in black at the front of the chapel. A young minister stood over it and incanted a prayer and a few words of sympathy, then a couple of workers stepped forward and rolled the carriage out of the open doors and into the swirling snow.

Dupree and Moms, who continued to cling to him for support, followed.

Jimmy brought up the rear.

At the gravesite the minister said a few more words then they lowered the coffin into the ground.

Dupree's Moms began to sob uncontrollably.

Dupree stepped forward and grabbed a spade that was stuck in a nearby mound of dirt and began shoveling earth into the grave.

There was a horrible thud as the dirt hit the coffin.

When she heard that awful sound, Dupree's Moms sobs became louder and more raucous.

And then there was Dupree, shoveling earth into that ugly pit. Crying now, snow swirling around him, and the wind whipping it up in sheets and whorls.

And there was that rhythmic thud as the dirt hit the casket over and over again like some prehistoric drumbeat until Jimmy stepped in and touched Dupree's arm.

Dupree stopped then, wiped his face with the back of his sleeve and angrily stuck the spade back in the mound of earth. Then he walked back to Moms who was supporting herself on a headstone, trying to get herself under control. He put his arm around her and gently led her back to the car.

After he got his car started, the heat pumping, and Moms settled in the back seat with a flask of brandy, Dupree went over to talk to Jimmy who was standing by his own car. Stamping his feet. Breathing into his cupped hands to keep them warm.

He thanked Jimmy for coming and excused his Moms for not saying the same, explaining she was in bad shape and barely knew where she was.

Jimmy waved his hand. It didn't matter.

Dupree had managed to pull himself together and, after giving his nose a healthy blow, said to Jimmy, "I got a call on the way over here, James. Corner boys are furious 'bout what happened to Lamont. They put the word out even before I did. Still took my money though," he said sounding slightly miffed. "But thas not the point here. Like I said, everyone knows everythin that's goin on down there an sometimes it takes a while to get to who saw what and when. Course if the corner boys are involved that tends to speed up the process some. Anyway, turns out a dude named Weasel did for cousin Lamont. It took the boys a while to find him and when they did it took a little more time to get it outta him. That, my friend, is nothin you wanna know about. Weasel got paid $500 for his trouble. A paltry sum in the whackin business you'd have to say. Lamont be furious if he knew how little it cost to waste him. They said some fancy black dude paid Weasel for the job. Cassidy Jones. A local boy made good in the City, first as a doorman at the clubs, then as a bartender. Now he's a hot DJ with quite the rep. He comes back to the hood every now and again to score some dope for him and his friends. Somehow Cassidy got to Weasel, who had a beef with Lamont from way back when and was only too happy to oblige. Weasel and Lamont were seen late Thursday night by all sorts a people hangin out their windows, headin arm in arm towards the river, smashed outta their minds. Only Weasel came back. Lamont passed out, was the story, but after some persuadin Weasel tells them he shot him up with H a couple a times to make it look right and shoved him in the river. Weasel be showin up where Lamont did pretty soon now, I shouldn't wonder. The street takes care of its own is the way that goes."

Dupree handed Jimmy a slip of paper. "This is the club Cassidy works at. If you find him, tell him not to come back to the hood no more or he'll end up like Lamont did. Thas what the corner boys say an I believe em. So should he."

"Why would Cassidy Jones want Lamont dead?"

"Weasel didn't know the answer to that one an believe me they asked him in a variety of ways."

Jimmy could only imagine.

They stood there for a minute looking at each other, snow swirling around them, and the cold seeping through their clothing.

Then Dupree shook Jimmy's hand and thanked him again for coming and headed to his car.

On the way back to the station house, Jimmy remembered he'd turned his phone off when he went into the chapel. When he turned it back on it rang immediately. He pulled over to the side of the road to take the call and got an earful for his trouble.

"Where the fuck have you been?" screeched Eddie, "I've been trying to get you for over an hour."

Jimmy apologized and explained where he was.

Eddie didn't seem to care. He had other things on his mind.

"We got the gun," he said excitedly. "Just as the snow started to come down. Lucky eh?"

Jimmy said it was.

"A little bad news though," said Eddie suddenly not as excited as he was before. "The artist baled on us on account of the weather. She said provided the roads were clear, we'd meet up at the lockup ten o'clock tomorrow morning."

"Nice, Eddie. Good work."

Eddie purred.

He loved the praise.

CHAPTER 46
CASSIDY JONES

Cassidy Jones loved to play cards. It was a weakness of his and he wasn't very good at it. You'd think he would've learned by now, but he hadn't. After all, he wasn't a kid any more. He lost small for a while, but that was a long time ago. Then he lost a lot more and that's been going on for some time now. The game was in the City and run by Crawford Taylor's old college friends. Crawford had the loan sharking action. He paid his friends a small percentage for the privilege because there were plenty of people like Cassidy who were getting out of their depth. That's how they met, Cassidy and Crawford, at the card table. And now Cassidy was in to Crawford for twenty-five grand that went up a thousand a month as regular as clockwork. There was a brief moment, not so long ago, when Cassidy was almost even, but he was falling behind again now.

Way behind.

Cassidy supplemented his payments with coke and weed and an occasional pretty girl and don't think Crawford wasn't grateful for that, but now he needed something else.

Cassidy Jones was a tall, lithe, African-American in his late twenties who prided himself on the fashionable clothes he wore. The skin-tight black trousers and black sneakers, the black tee shirt under the shiny silver grey mohair jacket, and the straw trilby with the black hatband. Think Bruno Mars here only taller, much taller, and Cassidy couldn't dance a step. There was something wrong with that and the jokes were becoming tired and annoying, but the truth was the truth. He couldn't dance a lick. Neither could he play cards. But music was an entirely different proposition and there was nothing he didn't know about that subject. Not a damn thing.

He was born in the shadow of Sing-Sing Prison in Ossining New York, and at an early age he vowed he would not turn out like everyone else in his family, and his class, and the neighborhood he lived in. He left school the minute he could and got a job on the door of a hip-hop club in the City working for peanuts and the thrill of being around a bunch of people who were cooler than he ever thought possible. He got a few modeling jobs because he was so good looking, and graduated quickly to a bartending gig at a hot club on the West Side of Manhattan. He still does some modeling jobs, but nowadays he's a DJ in the hottest nightclub in town.

It's a rare thing in a place like New York when an eighteen-year old, good-looking kid comes to town and makes his mark early and can sustain it and continue to climb the ladder. It's even harder to keep your feet on the ground when that happens and stay cool. Especially with all of those pretty girls flocking around you and all that money stuffed into your pockets. And the drugs, man. It's those drugs that will get you every time.

And so it was with Cassidy Jones.

Still sharp now and hot with one of the best gigs in town and a reputation to boot, but that nose candy, man. It was just too easy. It's everywhere. And I do mean everywhere. So by now all the money he makes is going up his nose and covering his losses at cards. He's a terrible player, but we've already covered that. He's one of those guys that keep coming back for more. An addiction, you might call it. Just like all the other addictions he's acquired along the way. He might as well have stayed in Ossining except that this was at a different level, a more glamorous level, but the pitfalls were just the same and he's fallen head first into all of them.

They let him win once in a while just to keep him coming back. It wasn't so hard really. There was no cheating involved. You just let him bid up a couple of pots and fold, but even with that he continued to lose heavily.

Crawford caught him at the end of a particularly bad night and took him out for a drink and a chat.

"Luck's not turning I see."

They were in a bar off of Third Avenue in the 60s.

Cassidy hung his head low and nursed his drink.

"How much are you into me for now, Hopalong?"

That was Crawford's name for him. No one else called him that. Not any more. In the old days they did it all the time, but not now. He's hot now. But if you owe someone a lot of money they can call you whatever they want. He was only glad it wasn't asshole.

"With tonight?"

Crawford nodded and ordered another round from the bartender.

"Around twenty-five grand," said Cassidy miserably. "I got some good coke. That should knock it down some." His eyes were wide. Selling eyes. Trying to push the idea without begging. "And that girl you liked, Anna. She was in the Club with a friend the other night." He put his fingers to his mouth and kissed them to the air to indicate how delectable she was. "I told her you'd be calling her soon."

The bartender put their drinks down. Macallan 25.

Cassidy took his down in a single gulp.

Crawford nursed his along.

Cassidy was pissed because he couldn't feel it. A fifty-dollar drink and there was no buzz. He'd been drinking all night. And losing all night. And doing coke all night. And he'd reached that stage where a fifty-dollar shot of booze gave him no buzz at all. What the fuck?

Crawford bought him another and got to the heart of the matter.

"Tell you what, Hopalong, I don't want your coke or your women. What I do need is a favor."

Cassidy's ears perked up. He took a sip of his drink and cradled it like it was a delicate piece of sculpture.

"In return for this favor," Crawford went on, "I'll wipe the slate clean including tonight's losses."

Cassidy's handsome face showed interest and concern.

Crawford told him about Lamont Dubois and how he needed the guy to disappear.

For normal people this kind of request would be a deal breaker, but not for Cassidy Jones. Such was the low he'd sunk to that he never lost a beat. Especially as he hailed from that neck of the woods his very own self and could probably get the job done for a song.

"I can do that," he said with all the confidence in the world.

Crawford filled him in on the details and at the end of his dissertation they clinked glasses, downed their drinks, and shook hands on it. Crawford paid the bill and told him he was looking forward to hearing some good news real soon, and the meeting was over.

As soon as Crawford was gone Cassidy called his Uncle Rolly who lived in Ossining and knew everything that was going on up there. Uncle Rolly got him to Weasel. Weasel hated Lamont from a long time ago and was only too happy to do the job for $500, plus expenses.

What are the expenses, Cassidy wanted to know?

A couple of grams of H.

Cassidy paid him in advance.

Now Lamont was gone. Done for by Weasel.

And so was Weasel. Done for by the corner boys.

Uncle Rolly heard they really liked Lamont. Who knew? He also heard they'd made Cassidy for putting out the contract, thanks to Weasel's loose tongue and low tolerance for pain.

Rolly told Cassidy he best not be coming to Ossining any more or they'd be doing for him too.

Cassidy said he was only too happy to oblige.

CHAPTER 47

THURSDAY

JIMMY

Breakfast was a bit of a bust. The girls were not their usual up-beat perky selves this morning. They hadn't had breakfast together since last week what with Jimmy being so busy and all, so this was a reunion of sorts.

And there were long faces at the table.

And glum looks.

"What's going on?" Jimmy wanted to know.

Lucy kept her eyes in her cereal bowl.

"Mary?"

Mary looked away.

"Lucy?"

Silence. Awkward, charged, silence.

"Okay," said Jimmy. "I know I haven't been around for a couple of days so I'm out of the loop and I'm sorry about that. Maybe someone would like to fill me in on what's going on."

Lucy looked at Mary.

Mary looked at Lucy.

Jimmy couldn't imagine what this was all about and went through his regular checklist of possible sins. Stuff left on the floor. Not rinsing his toothbrush. Toilet seat up, not down. There were so many rules to remember and he was still trying to learn them all: bowls on one shelf, plates someplace else, and the knives and forks had to be all facing the same way. It was an endless and constantly changing list and every other day there was something new to absorb. Last week he found out the spoons had to be separated and piled according to size and they all had to face the same way. Who knew? He was eager to please, what with being the new guy on the block and all, but sometimes. Sometimes. And maybe this past week he'd been so busy he hadn't been paying attention to the little things, and they were ganging up on him to give him a major head banging for some unintended transgression. Some mortal sin he was guilty of in the eyes of the feminine household. Some concept in the etiquette of living together he and every other guy in the world never even imagined existed.

"Tell him," said Mary.

Jimmy flinched. Waiting for the axe to fall. He'd already come up with a couple of speeches of contrition should they become necessary, but they weren't. Not this time.

Lucy's eyes teared up.

She took a deep breath and said, "Someone wrote RAT on my locker yesterday," and burst out crying.

Mary got up and went over to put a comforting arm around her.

Jimmy's face set in a grim mask.

"What else?" he wanted to know.

She shook her head. She didn't want to talk about it, but Mary encouraged her.

"Go on," she said. "Tell him."

Lucy sighed. She was just so sad.

"My friends won't talk to me," she said and began to cry some more.

Jimmy was shocked.

"Since when?"

"Since those boys were suspended for selling dope."

Jimmy was dumfounded.

"Is there anything else I should know about?"

Lucy looked in her bowl and shook her head like she didn't want to talk about it any more, but she did. Really. Because she was just so miserable.

"Tell him," Mary prompted.

Lucy puffed up her cheeks and blew out the air.

"I'm being shunned," she said.

"Shunned? By who?"

"Everyone."

"Everyone?"

She nodded.

"Define everyone."

"Well it was just a few people at first, the hard cases, I suppose. Those boy's friends, probably, but by Monday it had spread, which really surprised me. And by yesterday I didn't have a friend in the world. Then there was that writing on my locker."

"When did that happen?"

"At the end of the day."

"It wasn't there lunchtime?"

"No," she sniffled. "Or the afternoon break."

"Did you tell anyone?"

"No. I came straight home."

"On the bus?"

She looked at him like he was crazy.

"Are you kidding me? After that? I walked."

"And all your friends have turned their backs on you?"

She nodded.

"Christina too?"

She nodded.

Christina was one of her closest friends. She was a nice girl, but not very strong. She lived down the road. They'd been friends since Lucy came to Columbia. She was her first friend, so her best friend, right? Wrong. Not now. She didn't do anything bad, Christina. She just didn't do anything right and ended up hanging out with everyone else, and not her. Then her real best friend, Diane, did the same thing. And suddenly she was alone. It was like it was her first day at a new school. Something she'd experienced a lot before they got to Columbia, when you don't know a soul and no one wants to know you.

"Ah jeez Luce," said Jimmy. "I'm so sorry."

Mary said, "What are we going to do?"

"I'll go and speak to the principal," said Jimmy with a look on his face that meant trouble.

He was aching to tell Lucy to go at the person giving her the hardest time and beat the crap out of her, but Mary had a better way. Mary always had a better way when it came to Lucy, or anything else for that matter. Since moving in with them he'd learned to lie back and watch the situation unfold and not jump in with any of his male-oriented, antiquated ideas. It was like he was living in a sitcom only it was real life. His life. And he was learning a whole new way of doing things. Not like when he was a kid. You were on your own in those days. Sink or swim, it was all on you.

Lucy looked like she was going to puke.

"Please don't speak to the principal," she pleaded.

Jimmy asked her why not.

"It'll just make things worse."

"Worse than not having any friends?"

"It'll pass," she said. "I've seen it happen before. Next week they'll be picking on someone else."

"What if it doesn't?"

"Let's wait till next week," she pleaded.

Jimmy looked at Mary who was shaking her head.

"I don't think so," he said. "This is only going to get worse, Lucy. They've only just got going. This is what a mob does. They find a target and grind it down. It's what bullying is all about and it's got to be stopped. That principal of yours, if he believes in all that crap he spouts, has to step up here. One of his students is being victimized through no fault of her own. Lots of students helped us in that investigation. There's no reason that you should be the one who's singled out. This is a clear case of bullying. The crowd's gone wild and made you the target. It's not right and it's not fair."

Jimmy was looking for a fight. He was really mad now and was trying out his arguments on them to make sure he got them right.

Mary saw it.

"How about if I go?" she said, feeling a softer touch might work better under the circumstances. The chords on Jimmy's neck were sticking out like purple vines. She could only imagine how the principal would react to something like that.

"And say what?" said Lucy.

"All those things Jimmy just said," she gave him a soft smile, "only a little more diplomatically. Let's challenge the principal and see if he's got any balls on him. Oops. Sorry Luce, I didn't mean to say that."

Lucy let a grin show for a second, and then she went back to frowning. Not happy again and angry that her friends had turned their backs on her. And now she was anxious because the grown-ups wanted to get involved and what were the ramifications of something like that? Would it help her or just make things worse?

"And I'm calling Christina's mom and telling her what's going on," Mary said resolutely.

Lucy was horrified.

"I'm not sure that's such a good idea, mom."

"And why not?" said Mary indignantly. "How dare she do that to you. That girl's been in this house a million times and she treats you like that? Let's face em down, Lucy. Let's embarrass them. Let's make em take a stand one way or the other. And if they don't?" She looked at Jimmy and grinned. "Fuck em," and this time she did not apologize for her language.

Lucy blinked at the profanity, but agreed with the sentiment.

"What about Diane?" Mary wanted to know.

Lucy was mad at Diane, and hurt. She thought Diane would've had more backbone and shown her some loyalty. They'd told each other things along the way and shared some secrets. Lucy thought they had a friendship going. Not like Christina, who she never told anything to because she didn't trust her. Lucy thought it went deeper with Diane. It was something she'd never had before because they were always moving around so much. She was always the new kid on the block and she hated it. Trying to get people to like you. Or include you. Or even say hello. Except in Columbia. They'd been here the longest, so Lucy had some real friends now, or so she thought. And though she didn't count on Christina, she certainly thought she could rely on Diane.

Oh foolish girl.

And it's not like she crossed over right away. Diane. She waited to see if the fuss would die down and which way the wind was blowing. By Wednesday it was clear things weren't going to change, so Diane crossed over and joined the crowd. She had lots of friends and the loss of Lucy had no impact on her social life at all.

Lucy didn't, and now she was out of friends altogether.

"Diane's been avoiding me," she said.

Mary shook her head disgustedly and muttered, "I can't believe it." And said aloud, "I'm calling her mom too."

Lucy was panicked.

"And say what?"

"I'll tell her what's happening. There's a principle involved here, Lucy. Mob rule or common decency. I think those parents would want to know what's going on with their daughters. I know I would. I think they'll be disappointed to learn about their girl's behavior. They're nice people and I can't imagine they'll condone this. And if they do then I don't want anything to do with them anyway and neither do you. But I don't think that's the case. I'll suggest we do some stuff together over the weekend and try and force the issue. We have to fight this, Lucy. This is not right. You only need a couple of friends to stand by you to conquer this nonsense. And you should not be penalized because Jimmy's a cop, if that's what this is all about. This is bullying plain and simple and we have to fight it head on."

Jimmy said, "How about not going to school today, Lucy? Take the day off and have some fun before we start to fight back."

Lucy gave him a lopsided grin. Fight back. She liked that.

Mary thought it was a good idea.

"We'll do some cool stuff together," she said. "Maybe we'll take in a movie and get something to eat. How does that sound?"

Lucy said it sounded just fine and gave them the first real smile of the day.

CHAPTER 48

THURSDAY MORNING
JIMMY

The roads were slushy from yesterday's snow and everyone was going at a snail's pace. For once it didn't drive Jimmy crazy. It gave him time to chew things over and work them through, especially the idea that nothing happened in a vacuum. That one thing impacted on another and never failed to confirm the law of unintended consequences. Who would've thought that arresting those boys would have had such a negative impact on Lucy's life? From left field, he supposed, it made sense, but not really. The idea that everyone turned their backs on her was beyond his comprehension. He could see if she was a bitch, or the type of kid everyone hated, but she was none of those things. And even if she was, such behavior was unacceptable. But people are people. Young or old it doesn't make any difference. It's easier to go along with the crowd than take a stand. It's why he's not so crazy about people in the first place. You can't trust them was his experience. Until he met Mary, that is. Boy was she the exception to the rule. Like now for instance. How she decided to go head-to-head with those people. It's what he loved most about her. That practical, won't back down approach she applied to just about everything. He felt badly for Lucy, though. It was never nice to come face-to-face with a reality you'd rather not know. On the one hand it toughens you up; on the other you could've done without the experience.

When he got to the station house the results from the DNA lab in Copake were on his desk - a day earlier than promised. They weren't kidding when they said they weren't busy up there. The bottom line was they had a match. And surprise, surprise. The pubic hair they found in Gillie Fader's bathroom belonged to Kathy O'Brien. Her DNA was in the system from her arrest for the Shelly Barton murder.

There was also the report from the crime scene crew confirming what the Trooper said Tuesday night: Gillie's house was clean. There were no fingerprints anywhere. Not even Gillie's. The place had been given a thorough going over with Windex and vacuumed from top to bottom. But a girl's gotta pee, doesn't she? And who'd have thought you shed your pubes when you go to the bathroom? But she did. Kathy. Shed her pubes. Well, just the one. But that's all it takes, doesn't it? It was a fluke. Because it was clear that she'd gone to a great deal of trouble to clean up after herself. But this little sucker fell through the cracks and landed on the underneath side of the toilet seat.

So she missed it.

Kathy.

But the crime scene crew didn't.

Jimmy smiled and rubbed his hands together. It proved that Kathy had lied to him. She had been in Gillie Fader's house. A man she said she didn't know, in a place she said she never heard of.

He was sure she killed him.

He just couldn't figure out why.

He called her attorney and told him to have her at his office at noon. He had some questions for her that needed answers. When the lawyer spluttered the reasons why that would be impossible, Jimmy said it was either that or they'd arrest her for obstruction and he could visit her at the station house.

After that he called Eddie.

"Where are you?" he asked.

"At the lock-up with Austin and the artist."

"Right." He'd forgotten about that. "How's it going?"

"Wait a sec."

Jimmy heard Eddie excusing himself and a door opening and closing.

"You still there?" Eddie asked a minute later.

Jimmy wondered where else he would be.

Eddie said, "Austin's falling all over himself to get this right."

"And?"

"S'looking good."

"How long you gonna be?"

"Not long."

"You're in civvies, right?"

"I am."

"I need you to be at Kathy O'Brien's lawyer's office at 12:00. Can you do that?"

"I can," said Eddie. "What's up?"

Jimmy told him about the report on the pubic hair. That it was Kathy O'Brien's and he wanted to brace her.

"We've got a meeting at her attorney's office."

Eddie said, "Why don't we just haul her ass in for obstruction and toast her at the station house?"

"I want to see what I can get out of her on her own turf."

"Is this one of those detective things?"

"Just be there by 12:00."

CHAPTER 49
KATHY O'BRIEN

Kathy O'Brien was very upset. She'd spent the last couple of days putting her affairs in order so she could skip town. She'd just finishing packing when she got a call from her lawyer telling her to get to his office as soon as she could. The fat cop wanted to talk to her again. She was hoping to be on her way by the afternoon. First to the Cayman Islands to loosen up some money and from there, anywhere; she just hadn't made up her mind yet. Now here was this new bump. From Fatty. Again. Boy that guy was getting to be a pain in the ass. She thought about leaving anyway. Why not? She was free and clear and no one would know she was gone until it was too late. But there was always the chance she might not be able to come back, and she didn't want that. And so far as she could see they had nothing on her anyway. She'd covered her tracks pretty good. This was probably some formality. She didn't want to leave any loose ends. She wanted to be able to go with a clear mind. So she took a quick shower. Threw on a pair of jeans and a sweatshirt. Bundled her wet hair up in a bun. Grabbed her coat and rushed out of the apartment.

"It's a mistake," she said furiously twenty minutes later in her lawyer's office when Jimmy told her about the pubic hair they'd found in Gillie's bathroom.

"That's the beauty of DNA," said Jimmy. "It's infallible. That's your pubic hair they found there, Ms. O'Brien. There is no doubt about that."

Jimmy and Eddie sat in the same chairs as the last time, facing the lawyer's desk. Eddie was looking a little crumpled. His wardrobe was not extensive. He wore the same outfit he'd worn every time Jimmy told him to wear civvies: a sport jacket, a two day old white shirt, no tie, and brown slacks that were rapidly losing their crease.

Jimmy was faring better thanks to Mary. He was wearing his new blue single-breasted pinstripe, a clean white shirt with a light grey tie, and highly polished black shoes. He felt good about his appearance. Especially because he looked so much better than Kathy's lawyer in his blue serge suit with a collar full of dandruff.

The attorney knew it too. Jimmy could tell by the way he kept looking him up and down when he thought Jimmy wasn't paying attention.

It's moments like this when Jimmy realized how far he'd fallen before he met up with Mary. How much he'd let himself go and what a great job she'd done in cleaning him up. He resisted, of course. He liked being a slob and reverted to it from time to time for the sake of it. Especially on Fridays. But it was this feeling he liked most of all. When he knew his appearance added five percent to his argument and maybe, in this case, a little bit more.

"Rubbish," Kathy snarled. She was standing next to the attorney who was sitting at his desk. "Someone must've put it there."

"Where?" asked Jimmy.

"Wherever they found it."

"In a house upstate."

"I wouldn't know."

"Who would go to that sort of trouble, Kathy? Someone must really dislike you, don't you think? Putting it in a place you say you don't know."

"I don't," she barked. "I just told you that."

"So let's be clear. You don't know this guy or where he lives in spite of this earth-shattering discovery we've come up with?"

Kathy was nodding.

"And you want me to believe this other thing you're telling me. That someone put it there, the murderer maybe, to throw us off the scent and put it on you. A pubic hair of all things. You gotta wonder how he got it?"

"How should I know," she said angrily. "You're the detective, you figure it out. All I know is I have no idea who this person is or where he lives."

"The person who got your pube, or Gillie Fader?"

"Both."

"Well, the pube guy has got to know you pretty good it seems to me. He either has access to your privates or your bathroom, or both."

She looked at her lawyer.

"You gonna let him talk to me like that?"

The lawyer shrugged. What was he going to do?

"So who is it?" asked Jimmy.

"Who is what?"

"The guy. Who's the guy?"

"What guy?"

"The guy that has all that access?"

"There is no guy."

"That's right," said Jimmy. "There is no guy. Because you've been lying to me all along, haven't you?"

She shook her head.

"I have not." She glared at him. "I keep telling you I don't know this man and have never been inside his house. Neither do I know who took one of my pubic hairs."

He told her how Gillie Fader was found with a gunshot wound in his shoulder.

"That's the hole Lamont Dubois put in him."

"I told you," she said. "I don't know anything about that."

Jimmy looked skeptical.

"The Medical Examiner says Mr. Fader received professional care on his shoulder. No hospital or doctor reported treating him. You're a nurse Ms. O'Brien. You would have the knowledge to treat such a wound, especially because the evidence says you were there in that house. And if you were there, it seems logical to me that you were the one who killed him. Especially because he died of suffocation, a method you seem to favor."

"Now wait just one minute," said the lawyer. Standing up. Adding some drama to his performance to make up for his previous silence. "You have no evidence that says any of that and there's no proof my client ever killed anyone, let alone having a favorite method. I should be very careful throwing around these accusations if I were you, Detective."

"I'm not at liberty to say what evidence we have or haven't got, counselor. Not yet, anyway. But let's say Kathy's right, and she doesn't know Gillie or where he lives. Whoever planted Kathy's pube up there was trying to frame her. Who would do that to you, Kathy? Put you in a box when you were free and clear. I bet you were on your way out this afternoon. Bags packed. Future before you. And why not? No one's got anything on you and you're as free as a bird. Well not any more, Kathy. I'm afraid something's come up."

She could have smacked him. She looked at her lawyer as if to say, "Do something."

But there was not much he could do.

"The State Troopers will want to question your client," said Jimmy to the lawyer. "They're handling the investigation." He looked at Kathy. "What's your connection to Gillie Fader? I can't figure it out. You were home free, Kathy. Lamont's gone. The murder charges in the Shelly Barton case were dropped, even though we've got you on a disc saying you did it, and four other people too. You were home free, Kathy. You got away with everything."

"I don't know him," she growled.

"Someone put the pube there to frame you?"

"Right."

"Who? And why? It makes no sense. You don't even look angry. You've got one foot out the door, and now this. You must be really be pissed. Why did you kill this guy and put yourself at risk again?"

"Don't answer that," cautioned the lawyer and sat down.

"Don't worry," she said snarkily. "I don't have the faintest idea what he's talking about."

Lawyer and client conferred.

Then the lawyer said, "Either charge my client with something, or this interview is over."

Jimmy thought about it.

"How about obstruction of justice in the course of an investigation?"

"What investigation?" asked the lawyer.

"Gillie Fader's murder. What do you think we've been talking about here?"

"We've been through all this," he said tiredly. "She's told you she wasn't there and doesn't know him.

"DNA says otherwise," said Jimmy. "I think I can make a case."

He stood up to go.

Eddie too.

Jimmy said, "Does the name Crawford Taylor mean anything to you, Ms. O'Brien?"

Bingo.

The blood drained from her face.

Jimmy raised his voice.

"How much do you owe HIM?" he asked.

"Do not answer that," said the lawyer. "Like I said, Detective. Either charge my client, or leave."

Jimmy figured why not? As far as he was concerned the pubic hair proved she was at Gillie's house. He was sure she fixed up his shoulder and was equally sure she killed him. He also knew the pubic hair was not enough to convict her. It was a thin reed that needed support and they had nothing else. No fingerprints or any other evidence to prove she was there. Barring some miracle, she was going to get away with it.

The DNA evidence gave him the right to arrest her for obstruction and let the court figure it out. It would also keep her around for a while longer and maybe, during that time, something else might show up. If he didn't, she'd skip town and they'd never find her again. So he went for it and charged her with obstruction of justice in the investigation of the death of Gillie Fader. He read her her rights and had Eddie cuff her and take her to the station house for processing.

She was out by the end of the day of course, but not without having to surrender her passport and put up ten thousand dollars bail.

The DA convinced the judge she was a flight risk, considering the controversy that was swirling around Gillie Fader's murder and the fact that Mr. Fader took a run against Lamont Dubois, their main witness against Ms. O'Brien in the Shelly Barton murder case. The DA said he wasn't asking for Ms. O'Brien's incarceration, only that she surrender her passport.

The judge went along with the DA's request and had her passport confiscated and set the date for a trial.

Kathy was furious. Every time it looked like she was safe something else came up. Now this obstruction of justice shit. What a crock.

Her lawyer said she had nothing to worry about.

They were talking in the courthouse, waiting for the paper work to be completed for her release.

"They've got no case," he said soothingly and patted her arm like a father does a child. "He's just trying to drive you crazy."

"Well he's done a fine job of it," she declared.

The lawyer patted her arm again.

Kathy thought if he patted her arm one more time she was going to kill him.

"The pubic hair proves nothing," the lawyer whispered. "They have nothing up their sleeve. And this obstruction thing? I can't see them proving you know Gillie Fader if you say you don't. They've got no one who saw you with him, otherwise he'd have said so. It's your word against theirs."

He never asked her if she knew Gillie Fader or whether she had, in fact, killed him. He didn't care. So long as she paid him, he was her champion. That was his job. That's what he signed up for. Guilt or innocence played no part in the equation. Not so far as he was concerned.

Kelly Blake, the artist, faxed Jimmy the likeness of Crawford Taylor she had worked on with Austin Keller that morning. He got it right after Kathy's arraignment at the courthouse. Jimmy snatched up the fax, rushed outside, and caught Kathy and her lawyer as they were coming down the courthouse steps.

He waived Crawford's picture in her face.

"Do you know this man?" he asked her. "Do you know him?"

She stiffened, but kept on walking. Down the steps. Game face on until she got into the lawyer's car. Then, as they drove off, she began to freak out. If they could link her to Crawford Taylor, Crawford would link her to Gillie, then the shit would really hit the fan. This was not good. She had to see Crawford right away and sort it out.

They watched her leave. Jimmy and Eddie. Standing together in the street. Eddie was passing as Jimmy was waving Crawford's picture in her face. It was getting late. Jimmy hadn't worked so hard since he was in Brooklyn and that was a long time ago. He was older now and out of shape. It's not like he yearned for the quiet because he didn't, but all of this running around was taking its toll on him and he was beginning to feel it. His body ached and his joints were starting to creak. He stifled a yawn and wondered whether he should join that gym Mary was driving him crazy about?

The thought of it made him tremble.

He said, "Well, we got her passport. That's something."

"What's so good about that?" said Eddie.

"She was leaving town."

"How do you know?"

"Go over there. I bet you'll find packed cases."

"What are you, clairvoyant?"

Jimmy smiled.

"She can still run," said Eddie.

"She can," Jimmy agreed, "but it's more difficult now. Skipping bail's a bad thing to do. It shows up when you go through security and immigration. She'll be a fugitive and she doesn't want that. She wants to be able to come and go as she pleases."

"How do you know that?"

"She's got investments here. Real estate. She needs to be able to come back and check them out once in a while."

"That's it? That's all we're doing is stopping her from running?"

"The Troopers can't put a case together. They're working on it, but I don't hold out much hope. The pubic hair doesn't make a case and that's all they've got. No fingerprints or anything else. Frankly, I don't see that changing."

Eddie asked him not to call him Frank.

Jimmy smiled. Weakly.

"We can't prove she knew Gillie Fader. Neither can we prove she knows Crawford Taylor. You should've seen how she reacted when I waived his picture in her face, but where he fits in this thing is beyond me."

"So what are we doing apart from spinning our wheels?"

"Stirring things up."

"What happens then?"

Jimmy yawned and stretched.

"Things have a habit," he said tiredly

CHAPTER 50

CRAWFORD TAYLOR
THURSDAY

Crawford Taylor was shaken to the core. He wondered if it was possible for things to get any worse; so much for everything falling into place for him. Those days were gone now. He'd seen Austin's arrest on the news and read about it in the newspapers. He couldn't reach him and that was very troublesome. Austin could finger him for loansharking, and even though he didn't know where he lived or how to contact him, he could come up with a description of him and that was a very bad thing.

Think. Think. Think.

Then they found Gillie Fader's body. That was another blow. He thought they'd never find him. A fucking meter reader stumbled on him, and what are the odds on that? What, he couldn't read the meter a couple of weeks later, when he was long gone? That's when he knew his luck had really turned. Because that's what he was planning to do now - take a vacation to anyplace until the heat died down.

He didn't believe in coincidences.

But here was one that just occurred to him.

Austin Kenner told him he worked in the garment center. He said his boss was loaded up with cash to pay for a big launch, something about a new line that was a major move on his employer's part. This was long before he ever met Mal Finkelstein, so there was no reason at the time for him to make the connection. But the way his luck was going, it was entirely possible that Austin Kenner's employer was Mal Finkelstein, something he never thought about until just now. Looking back, he can't believe he made such an elementary mistake.

Crawford leaned over the coffee table and snorted another line of coke. It did his paranoia no good this last hit, and doubled down on his miserable state of mind and sent him on a cocaine-fueled worry jag.

He was furious with himself for making such a stupid error.

But how could he have known?

And did he know now?

Maybe not.

Maybe he'd got himself all worked up for nothing? Austin never said much about where he worked. Only that he'd kited checks on them for the last twenty years.

And he never asked him.

That's right.

He never asked him.

So maybe it's not Mal he works for?

Maybe.

He always asked every one of his clients where they worked as a matter of course, but not this time.

"And why was that?" Crawford asked his reflection in the coke mirror.

Because it was a time when he could do no wrong and the money was pouring in. This was before the bubble burst when they were all so cocky, and hot, and sashaying around town like they owned the place. He and people like him: the players, the movers, and the big time shakers.

They were making millions.

And so was he.

Then one day they weren't.

And neither was he.

That's when the lights went out on Broadway.

In the movie *Billy Bathgate* there's a scene where one guy says to the other, "I hate to see a time when the money stops going around." Well this was one of those times. It's what caught Austin Kenner short and the reason he came to Crawford in the first place. Now it was happening to him. Money was hard to collect and nothing was going out. He'd closed up shop and the money had stopped going around. Everyone owes everybody else and it's everyone for themselves, boys. Man the lifeboats.

"So what went wrong?" he asked the mirror.

Austin was going to give him a half a million dollars, that's what went wrong. Then the stupid fucker went and got himself arrested. He should've let Gillie pop him when he wanted to, then he wouldn't be in this mess.

Think. Think. Think.

Then there was Mal Finkelstein.

It was looking more and more like the stupid fuck gave Austin a quarter of a million dollars on a worthless check. How could he be so dumb? What a fuck-up. Or was he? Or had he? Or did he?

Crawford snorted another line of coke, took it all the way down, and shook his head. Then he did the same for the other nostril.

Pacing. Pacing. Frantic. And grinding his teeth like crazy. Coke can do that to you; make you grind your teeth, especially if you do enough of the stuff and you're freaked out of your mind.

If it was Mal who gave him the quarter of a mil, he must be shitting bricks by now for getting gulled by the likes of Austin Kenner. But had he? Did he? And there was no way to get in touch with Austin to find out.

What to do? What to do?

The best play, so far as he could see, was to see if Mal was guilty as charged, because it was entirely possible that Austin didn't work for him and it was some other schmuck Austin kited a check on for a quarter of a million dollars. If that was the case, he'd got himself all worked up for nothing.

But if Austin did work for Mal, then it was his quarter of a million Mal had loaned Austin, and if that was the case he was going to be really pissed off. And if it was Mal, what the fuck was he thinking? Why would he do such a thing? It was beyond Crawford's comprehension that someone could be so stupid. His raging brain could make no sense of it, which led him to think he was wrong.

But what if he was right?

If he was right then he might be able to squeeze Mal for some money. Mal was always bragging about how rich his folks were. Maybe they'd cover his losses if he put a little hurt on him? He'd never done any rough stuff before; he'd always had Gillie to do it for him. But this time was an exception. And Gillie was dead. And it was just a matter of time before the boys in blue came calling on him from the description he was sure Austin had given them. Or Kathy. No. Not Kathy. She wouldn't do that. They'd known each other much too long and besides, they were tied at the hip weren't they? If he goes down, she goes down too. She knows that.

Or does she?

Maybe he should have had Kathy done as well?

His brain was on fire.

Frying.

Sizzled by the coke.

242

He was thinking on Mal now; how just a little hurting should do the trick, and he was certainly capable of that. The guy was such a pussy, a three year old could frighten him to death.

There was a lot going on. His head was swimming, and bubbling, and boiling over. He poured himself a tumbler of Johnny Walker Blue to calm himself down and take the edge off the coke. His head was groaning from the possibilities.

He looked out the window onto Central Park. It always soothed him when he did this. It reminded him how well he'd done, living on Central Park West with all the big shots. He'd had a decorator design the place for him and no expense was spared on his elegant furnishings and tasteful art. There were extravagant plantings on the terrace and fresh flowers in every room that were replaced twice a week by a service that cost him a fortune.

The scotch was beginning to do the trick. He could feel the warmth reach down through his body and his heart had begun to slow down.

The phone rang, startling him.

It was Kathy O'Brien.

She said, "I'll be in the neighborhood tonight. I'm coming up. We have things to talk about."

"What time?"

"About 8:30."

"See you then."

He was pleased she was dropping by. It would clear the air between them and give him a chance to remind her how vulnerable she was.

One problem solved.

Now for the other.

He called Mal Finkelstein, who sounded nervous. No, that was not true. He sounded freaked out of his mind. Crawford had a radar that was always tuned to tone and rhythm, and Mal had none of it. He was rattled, which put a chill up Crawford's ass and forced him to excuse himself while he did another line. This last hit doubled down on his insecurities and raised his threat level to major proportions, because even though Mal was trying hard to act natural, he was doing a miserable job of it.

"How you doing?" Crawford asked him.

"The opening's tomorrow," said Mal nervously. "You know how that goes, Crawford. I'm freaked out of my mind. There are so many details to take care of I don't know where to start. My head is about to explode."

It was a reasonable excuse, but Crawford wasn't buying it. He was too coked up and his paranoia was working overtime.

"I can just imagine," he purred. "Stop over for a drink tonight, Mal. You're sounding very tight. I've got some good coke and I'll call up a couple of honeys and we'll have us some fun. That should relax you."

Mal begged off.

Crawford insisted.

Mal did the math.

He figured there was no way that Crawford could know Austin's check had bounced on him. Or that Austin was in jail. Or that Austin worked for him. How could Crawford know any of these things? It was impossible. Crawford didn't even know that Austin existed. And checks won't start bouncing till next week, or maybe later if they wrote enough business tomorrow. As far as Crawford was concerned, everything was copacetic. So Mal let himself be persuaded because, even though he was worried shitless, there were two things he really enjoyed. Good coke and good pussy. And Crawford had both.

He said he'd be up around 9:00.

CHAPTER 51

THURSDAY

JIMMY

It was getting late. Jimmy was back in his office. He shuffled a few papers around, but he didn't have the energy to accomplish anything. Man he was tired. He gave Mary a call to find out how Lucy was doing. Okay, as it turned out. They were at the mall getting a bite to eat. They'd done some shopping and taken in a movie and after they finished eating they were going home.

Jimmy asked what happened with the school principal.

"I've got an appointment with him tomorrow morning."

"And the parents?"

"I'll call them tomorrow. I figured we'd keep it light today."

Jimmy agreed with her.

Mary said their food had arrived and ended the call.

Before he left for home, Jimmy called Morgan to see if he'd ever heard of Crawford Taylor.

Morgan picked up on the first ring, which was unusual.

Jimmy said, "Nothing to do, Morgan?"

"So now you're a wise-ass?"

"I'm fine, Morgan. How's by you?"

"Fuck you."

Wassup?" cooed Jimmy. "Someone piss on your shoes?"

"Worse."

"What could be worse?"

"Getting dumped."

"You got canned?"

"I got dumped by my girlfriend."

Morgan was a stud muffin. Sharp clothes. Slick hair. The works. Guy's like Morgan didn't get dumped, they were usually the dumpee.

"Ah man," said Jimmy sympathetically. "You two have been together for a while."

"We have," said Morgan. "In fact you know her."

"I do?"

"Well, not actually know. You know of her. She manages the beauty salon on Madison Avenue that the guy who had a house up your way owned. The one who got himself killed."

"Roberto Angelini?"

"That's him. She's running the place now. We started going out not long after we closed the case."

It was the last case they worked together.

Jimmy said, "What happened?"

"She says she wants to see other guys."

"Why?"

"That's what I said."

"And?"

Morgan didn't mean to get into it. He wasn't looking to cry on someone's shoulder, but here he was. Telling Jimmy stuff he hadn't told anyone else. Not even his partner.

"She says she doesn't see herself married to a cop. Time's getting on, she says, and she's got to find herself a husband."

"Ah, man," said Jimmy.

"So I say, but we're going out now, right? And doing all of that good stuff?"

"What did she say?"

"She didn't and it died down for a while. Then it came up again yesterday. She said she had a date and she couldn't see me. When I said that was no good, she dumped me."

"Huh." said Jimmy. He didn't know what else to say.

There was one of those pregnant pauses. A long one.

Then Morgan said, "So what's going on?"

"Ever hear of Crawford Taylor?"

Morgan said he hadn't, but that didn't mean anything. There were a lot of people he never heard of.

Jimmy filled him in. How Austin Kenner owed Crawford Taylor money. How Gillie Fader and Conner Malloy came to collect and Austin popped Conner in the diner parking lot.

"Now Gillie's dead."

"How'd that happen?"

Jimmy told him the Kathy O'Brien story. How Gillie Fader came to kill Lamont, their star witness against Kathy for the murder of Shelly Barton, and how Lamont put a hole in Gillie's shoulder.

"Lamont turned up dead four days later and Gillie three days after that."

"Who did Lamont?"

"Some local for $500. But someone put him up to it."

"Who?"

"A guy called Cassidy Jones."

"Why?"

"I don't know. I've got an address in Yonkers. I'm going to talk to him."

"You think someone put Cassidy up to it?"

"I do."

"And who would that be?"

"The same person who put Gillie up to it."

"Kathy O'Brien?"

"She's the one who benefits. We had to drop the murder charge when Lamont turned up dead." Jimmy told him about Kathy's pubic hair in Gillie's bathroom.

"Just the one?" asked Morgan.

"Just the one."

"You'd think there'd be more?"

"You would, wouldn't you?" said Jimmy and told him how well the place had been cleaned. "They were lucky to find that. And Gillie was suffocated. Kathy's stock in trade."

"So you got her?"

"Nah, not really. One pube does not make a case. There's nothing else to tie her to the place. The suffocation thing is a coincidence that can't be proved and there's no other trace of her. Not a fingerprint or a strand of hair."

"Huh."

"And I still can't figure it out."

"What?"

"The connection between her, Gillie Fader, and Crawford Taylor."

Morgan chewed on that for a while.

Then he said, "So you got Jack Shit."

Jimmy grimaced, but that was about the size of it. He had nothing.

"I got Kathy for obstruction on the Gillie Fader investigation, but it's a bullshit charge. She wouldn't say a word when we got her to the station house and she was out by the end of the day. I said she lied to me and the pube proved it. It was worth a shot, if only to keep her around for a while. My boss just called. The obstruction charge is being dropped."

"So where does Crawford Taylor fit?"

"That's what I can't figure out," said Jimmy, frustration sounding in his voice. "Except that he's a shylock and he loaned Austin money. More than that I've got nothing. We got Austin to work with an artist. I'm sending you Crawford's picture."

"YOU are?" asked Morgan incredulously.

"The clerk is."

"I won't have you lie to me, Jimmy."

Jimmy sighed.

"I gotta learn this stuff," he said sadly.

"When?"

"Soon."

"You're falling behind."

"I know. I know. Lucy's helping me."

Morgan felt sorry for her.

Jimmy told him about the book of matches from the Carlisle Hotel he found at the house where Gillie was killed.

"Can you show their pictures around for me, Morgan? Gillie and Crawford. Maybe it's where they meet."

"My pleasure," said Morgan and hung up.

CHAPTER 52

AUSTIN KENNER

Austin thought he was going to go crazy. How did people do this, he wondered? The boredom was crushing, there was no privacy, and everyone was on top of one another. Maybe none of them knew any better, but that wasn't true. The guys seemed nice enough and were not what you'd call hard-core criminals. Most of them were waiting for their trials. Some of them had been there longer than others. Paco had been there for a year and a half on a drug beef. There was always a delay for Paco, always some continuance. It didn't seem to bother him though, and why should it? He ran the floor like a general and made out like a bandit. He even looked like one; stocky with a round pockmarked face, beady eyes, a pencil mustache, and jet-black hair. He looked capable of just about anything, though there was no need for that in their section. The pussy section is what the guards called it. They were white collar criminals mostly. Austin was the only murderer. There were a couple of stock fraud guys, a con man, and the rest were flight risks. There was no one to fear except for Paco, who never showed that side of himself because he didn't have to. It was there though, just below the surface. A quiet menace that was hard to mistake.

"No need for rough stuff," he confided to Austin when he was delivering his order. "You not gonna pay me? Fuck you, man. No more goodies for you and I got people outside who will go to your house and take what I'm owed. You get what I'm saying here, Mr. Austin?"

Austin got it. A message nicely delivered with a big toothy smile.

Then Paco told him a story about someone who stiffed him and how his friends took their time with the guy's wife and daughter and stole everything that wasn't nailed down.

Peter Green

"Don fuck with me, Mr. Austin. Bidness is bidness. Even in here. There's always consequences."

Another message this time not so nicely delivered.

There were messages at home too, Shirley from Great Neck told him. Calls from Mal Finkelstein pleading and whining things like, "How could you do this to me?" Or, "I'm dying, Austin. You have to help me. Send me something. Anything."

"Fuck him," thought Austin. He needed that money for his 'dream team,' who would only go as far as his money would take them, which was fair enough, he supposed.

Crawford Taylor called once and left a message saying he'd be patient but not for long and spent some time reminding him about his wife and kid and the beautiful home they lived in. When Shirley told him this he thought Crawford must've been talking to Paco, but not really. They were all the same these people; leverage and fear, fear and leverage. It's the only language they knew, and how are you gonna beat that, Austin wondered?

The lawyers were upbeat.

Gillie Fader was dead, they told him. He'd been found upstate with a gunshot wound in his shoulder. It made their self-defense case easier because it was obvious that Gillie was a bad man. And it buttressed their argument that Gillie and Conner had come to the diner to harm him. Add that to Jimmy, who said he was willing to say the same thing, and there was already talk of a deal. Austin would plead guilty to a lesser charge. An unregistered gun, something like that. The DA, they said, was hinting at grabbing what he could. A $10,000 fine was brought up and a year in jail. The lawyers thought they could do better; probation and no jail time. Dangling some cheese now to show Austin what a good job they were doing.

And by the way, could you cut us another check please?

Shirley came to visit him as often as she could. Her eyes were always red rimmed from crying. She was no longer bordering on fat. Now she was bordering on thin and looked very much like she did when they first met. Sweeter too. And more loving.

Now where did that come from?

Having no money. That's where that came from.

For the first time in her life she was living on a budget and quickly found out what he brought to the party: money honey and plenty of it. And now there was very little of it left, or so she thought. She got dressed up for him and talked nice. And here was the funny part. He missed her when she was gone and was

250

pleased to see her when she showed up. His dick had died, it was only good for pissing now, so it's not like it was lust he was feeling for her. He actually liked her was the thing.

Who knew?

He was starting to think there was something wrong with him. You could hear guys jerking off as soon as the lights went down and there he was with a limp dick. Not that he wanted to choke the chicken, but it would have been nice to have had the option. They even had a couple there who were choking each other's chickens. They were two businessmen who were battling fraud charges and fucking the life out of each other. You could hear them going at it all the time and they didn't seem to care who heard. They were actually proud of it. At least they were getting laid, they said, which was true if you wanted to look at it that way. And here was the punch line. They both had wives and kids on the outside and had never done anything like this before in their lives.

Go figure.

In the *The Sopranos* Tony Soprano told his wife they gave you a free pass when you were in jail. "What you gonna do stuck in there for years," he told her, "so long as you don't bring it out with you when you get back on the street." That was the rule.

Austin figured even if he was tempted, which he wasn't, he'd be no fun. He'd "outlived his dick" was a Willie Nelson line that now seemed to apply to him. He hoped it was a temporary thing, a 'Pokeyitus' type of condition, but for now he was as limp as a wet noodle.

"Sit tight and be patient, we got it covered", the lawyers kept telling him like it was the easiest thing in the world to do.

In this madhouse.

Where every second was an hour and every hour was a day.

"It's going to take a while," they told him sweetly. "These things always do. And by the way, here's another invoice. And have a nice day."

CHAPTER 53

FRIDAY

CASSIDY JONES

The rain stopped before dawn and the roads had dried out. What was left of the snow had been washed away, except for the higher elevations where there was a frost line. Below it was wet and bare. Above it was a world of frosty white where trees were covered in ice and snow that glistened and sparkled in the morning sun. Jimmy wished he had a camera. Then he remembered his cellphone. Lucy had been helping him move into the 21st century and taught him how phones were used for other things besides talking. Like taking photos. But by the time he got the thing out of his pants and figured out what button to press, he was at the station house, and that was the end of that.

The address Jimmy had for Cassidy Jones was in Yonkers. He rounded up Eddie, who was preaching to a bunch of guys in the parking lot, and together they went to talk to him. On the way Jimmy cleared it with the locals who said they were so rushed they didn't care what he did on their turf so long as they didn't have to do it with him.

Cassidy Jones lived in a door-manned apartment building that overlooked the Hudson River. It was cheap too, especially by City standards. He had two bedrooms and a terrace that looked over the Palisades and the Hudson River where there was always something different going on to look at. Ships passing. Eagles soaring. And trains that ran on both sides of the river. Snowstorms were the best. Whipping up the Hudson and banging up against the bluffs. Or a rainstorm, watching it sweep across the water before it got to his side of the river.

Cassidy was feeling pretty good on this this sunny Friday morning. He'd gotten Crawford Taylor off of his back and the only person who could testify against him was stupid Weasel, who was dead. Killed by the corner boys as warning to others not to take outside contracts against locals. If someone needed to be done they were the ones who'd be doing the doing. Especially if it was someone they liked.

The desk called.

Two gentlemen wished to speak with him. One was wearing a police uniform. Should he send them up?

A shock wave went through Cassidy's body that sobered him up and ruined his good mood. What did they have on him? Nothing. And that's what he told the dumpy looking one with the sidekick who looked like he just got off the, *Car 54 Where Are You?* lot. They asked themselves in, sat themselves down, and asked him a bunch of questions about Lamont Dubois and Weasel.

He'd admit to nothing is what he told them, and why should he? Weasel was dead. Sorry about that, but he had nothing to do with that. And the $500 they said he gave him may or may not be true, but it was on them to prove it, and they couldn't. So like he said, he would admit to nothing.

"What does that mean, admit to nothing?" asked the fat cop. "No one's asked you anything yet."

They sat there in silence.

Jimmy and Eddie on the couch.

Eddie with his notebook at the ready, pencil in hand.

And a barefoot Cassidy Jones sitting in an armchair, facing them. Wearing skin-tight jeans and a black tee shirt. Leaning forward. Anxious. And nervous. And chewing on a fingernail.

Jimmy got to work.

"This is what we've got on you, Mr. Jones. A recorded interview with this guy Weasel saying he was hired by you to kill Lamont Dubois for $500. Hiring someone to commit a murder is considered a major crime in this great country of ours. We also have several witnesses who saw you talking to Weasel in Ossining two days before Lamont was found floating in the river. In other words, Mr. Jones, we have enough to arrest you as a suspect in the murder of Lamont Dubois. If we do that I will personally make sure that every newspaper and news broadcast are made aware of it. I can see the headlines now, 'Hot NY DJ arrested in murder investigation.' So long modeling career and big time DJ gig. Neither of those industries enjoy the kind of scrutiny you're about to expose them to."

This was not going the way Cassidy thought it would. It was no longer a question of telling them nothing. It was now a question of what could he tell them so that they'd leave him alone.

"What do you want?" he said wearily.

"As much as you've got."

"In return for what?"

Jimmy had nothing on him anyway. He'd made it all up. He was rather pleased with himself for coming up with such a great improv.

Eddie was too. He'd been scribbling away for all he was worth when he suddenly realized what he was writing and looked up at Jimmy full of admiration.

"I'll rip up everything," said Jimmy magnanimously. "But what you tell me better be good."

Cassidy was on an emotional roller coaster. One minute he was finished and maybe going to jail, the next he'd been thrown a lifeline he was desperately clinging on to.

"A free ride, right?" he asked. "Nothing comes back on me or is leaked to the press?"

"Right," said Jimmy.

They shook hands on it. Solemnly. And with great purpose.

Then Jimmy said, "Why'd you pay someone to whack Lamont Dubois?"

"Not me."

"Who then?"

"Someone else."

"Who?"

This was it. That 'aha moment' Jimmy had been waiting for. He was sure Cassidy Jones was going to implicate Kathy O'Brien and then he'd finally have her, but he was wrong.

Cassidy wanted to make sure.

"A free pass?" he repeated. "Nothing in the press and I go on with my life like nothing happened?"

Jimmy stiffened.

"It's got to be good, Cassidy. You can understand that, can't you?"

Cassidy could. He was cornered. If he didn't do what they wanted he was done for. And if he went along with them he could go on like nothing happened. It was a no brainer.

"Crawford Taylor," he said.

Jimmy was amazed how the same names kept cropping up. Before it was Kathy O'Brien. Now it was Crawford Taylor. This guy seemed to be at the center of everything. If he could only find him there was a good chance he could tie everything up in a neat little bow and be able to nail Kathy O'Brien for something that would put her away for a while.

"You know him?" asked Cassidy, raising his perfectly shaped eyebrows.

"I do," said Jimmy. "The question is, why do you?"

Cassidy told him about his gambling problem and how Crawford Taylor loaned him the money to cover his debts. And how Crawford recently needed a favor in return for wiping the slate clean.

"How much did you owe him?" asked Jimmy.

"$25,000, give or take."

'What did you do for him?"

"Put him in touch with Weasel."

"Not you?"

"Not me what?"

"Not you who found Weasel and paid him to do the job."

"No, not me."

"We've got witnesses that say otherwise.

"They're lying."

It was Cassidy who was lying, but Jimmy let it go. He had nothing on him anyway. He was lying too.

"But it was Crawford who wanted Lamont done?"

Cassidy nodded.

"Why?" Jimmy asked.

"For a friend."

"Who?"

"I never knew."

"Ever hear of Kathy O'Brien?"

He did not.

"Nurse Kathy O'Brien?"

"No."

"And Crawford never said it was a 'she' who wanted Lamont done?"

"No."

Jimmy was disappointed. It's not what he was hoping for. They talked a while longer. How Cassidy knew Crawford Taylor. How Crawford had the loan-shark action at the card games. And how Cassidy knew a bunch of people who'd been into Crawford at one time or another and might be willing to talk to him. These were fellow card players he'd met along the way.

"Whose games?"

"These guys. They've got a couple going every week, sometimes more, always at a different location. There's coke and booze and whatever else you want. They call and give you an update at the beginning of the week. The schedule. Whether you play or not is up to you, but if you don't show up at least once a month they cut you loose. You can't just get in, either. You have to be sponsored, and then they check you out. If they don't like you, you don't play. Another thing is you can always score good dope there."

"What sort of dope?"

"Anything you want, and as much as you want within reason. Good prices too."

"So let's recap," said Jimmy. "Crawford Taylor hired you to set up a hit on Lamont for an unknown person."

Cassidy shook his head.

"That's not right. He hired me to find him someone who could do it and he made the deal."

"And that would be Weasel?"

"Correct."

"Crawford Taylor is a loan shark. This you know because he's loaned you money and you know of others he's provided the same service to?"

"Correct."

"And you'll sign a statement to that effect?"

"In return for a free ride on whatever you think you have on me for Lamont's death."

Jimmy said, "Correct."

He thought Cassidy had the makings of an excellent snitch. He couldn't wait to tell Morgan what he'd got for him. Apart from the information on the card games, he was also plugged into the club life in the City. It was hard for law enforcement to meld in with those people. Snitches were always the best way to find out what was going on down there, especially if you've got something on them. Like Cassidy here. Who was trading his freedom from a threat that wasn't there because he believed Jimmy had something on him he didn't.

"Where does Crawford live?" asked Jimmy.

Cassidy didn't know.

"How do you reach him?"

"He reaches you."

Jimmy told him about Morgan, his friend in the NYPD who would want to talk to him. "The same deal," Jimmy assured him. Whatever Cassidy told Morgan he was free and clear from the Lamont Dubois affair. No charges no matter what he fed them, but he had to tell Morgan everything.

Cassidy agreed. How could he not? He thought he was in deep shit.

Oh foolish man.

They had him write a statement on a legal pad Eddie brought along just in case. It was part of the drill whenever they went on an interview. They had Cassidy sign it. And date it. And told him they'd be in touch. And left him wondering whether he was having a good day or a bad one. It was hard to tell.

Back at the office, after some coffee and a cruller at Dunkin's, Jimmy called the fourth agency Kathy O'Brien worked for. The Crown Agency. This one took a while. He had to call back a couple of times to get to someone who remembered her working there. And yes, this person did recall something about a patient leaving his house and possessions to Kathy when he died.

"Was that a bad thing?" asked Jimmy.

"No," said the woman. "It happens all the time."

He went through the short-term patients with her and got the same story. Kathy was a saint. A saint that killed five people, but he couldn't find anyone who'd say anything bad about her. They'd come to the end of the short-term assignments. It was the name of the last short-term patient that caught his eye. It was on a separate sheet of paper that was underneath everything else. That's why he hadn't seen it before. And now he was annoyed with himself for not finding it sooner. The pile of faxes had been on his desk for two days just sitting there. He could say he'd been busy, but that wasn't the point, was it?

This was Kathy's last assignment with the Crown people. Her last patient for them. A herniated disc. A three-week posting. Nine years ago.

For one Crawford Taylor.

Jimmy had to laugh at the luck of the thing. If he'd started with her recent jobs instead of the oldest, he would've gotten there sooner. A day earlier for sure. It was likely that she and Crawford were still friends. And that was probably how she got to Gillie Fader. Through Crawford. If only they could find him they had enough on him from Cassidy Jones and Austin Kenner's statements that he might want to roll over on her, and that would be just dandy.

But first they had to find him.

The phone rang.

It was Morgan.

Jimmy said, "That was quick," thinking he was calling to say he'd found Crawford Taylor, which, in a manner of speaking, he had.

"Do you believe in coincidences?" Morgan asked him.

Jimmy did not.

"And neither should you," said Morgan. "Because at approximately 11:30 this morning Crawford Taylor was found dead in his apartment on Central Park West by his cleaning lady."

"Son of a bitch," said Jimmy. "Every time I get close to someone they either die or get off scot free."

"You wanna explain that one to me?"

Jimmy told him about the tie he'd just discovered between Kathy O'Brien and Crawford Taylor, him being her patient and all, and how it looked like Crawford set her up with Gillie Fader to take Lamont out. And about Cassidy Jones. How he'd signed a statement implicating Crawford's loansharking business and how he was hoping they could use it, along with Austin Kenner's statement, to get Crawford to roll over on Kathy O'Brien.

Morgan said, "Anything else?"

"Nah. This whole business is turning out to be one big pain in the ass. Was he murdered?"

"We're not sure. Drugs, maybe. There's coke on the table and booze."

"Not murder then?"

"I didn't say that.

"A different theory?"

"Not so far. The doorman and the front desk both have a woman visiting him last night around 8:30. She told the desk she was visiting Mr. Taylor. They announced her and Crawford said to send her up, meaning he was still alive at that time. Crawford didn't ask what she wanted, so it's reasonable to suppose he knew who she was and was even expecting her."

"Anyone after that?"

"Not that we know of. The desk backs that up. By the time you get here we'll have more from the ME and the crime scene crew."

"I'm on my way."

Morgan gave him the address.

"No need to rush. We've got it under control. The crime scene people have only just started. It's gonna take them a while and you know how that goes."

Jimmy did.

He said he'd be there as soon as he could.

CHAPTER 54

JIMMY

Just because he was in a hurry Jimmy caught every light on the Saw Mill River Parkway, and every light after that. Not his usual eighty percent, then? No sir; a hundred percent this time. Every fucking light. How is that possible, he wondered? And he managed to get behind every slow driver and every van driver who was on the clock. As soon as he got past one of them another one popped up. It took him two hours for a ride that was supposed to take an hour. By the time he got there he was a nervous wreck. He'd even used the lights and the siren and it still took him two hours. Oy!

He parked in front of Crawford's building in a spot that said 'No Parking,' left his 'Police Business' card on the dashboard and told the doorman where he was in case there was a problem.

The doorman gave him a look that said, "Everyone knows there's been a murder here. You really think I can't figure out where you'll be, asshole?"

Jimmy headed for the elevator. He caught the look, but he was too stretched out to fight.

When he entered Crawford's apartment he thought he'd stepped onto a movie set. A murder movie set. Lying on the couch in a peaceful repose was the star of the show. Mr. Crawford Taylor. A battery of floodlights surrounded him along with a gaggle of people photographing, examining, and chatting to each other about this thing or that. The only one not participating in the proceedings was Mr. Taylor because he was dead. Someone had closed his eyes so he looked like he was sleeping. If you didn't know he was dead you'd wonder why he didn't wake up what with all the noise that was going on all around him.

In front of the couch was a glass coffee table cluttered with an ashtray that held two half smoked joints and few cigarette butts. One joint had lipstick on it, so did some of the butts. There was a half empty pack of Marlboros with a gold Dunhill next to it, a half empty bottle of Johnny Walker Blue, an almost empty bottle of white wine, a scotch glass with a half finished drink, and two empty wine glasses that sat on rattan coasters. One of the wine glasses had lipstick on it. There was a dish of peanuts, a small pile of cocktail napkins and a couple of screwed up used ones. One of them had lipstick on it. Resting on a round mirror was a pile of cocaine, a razor blade, five evenly spaced white lines of coke and a rolled up $100 bill. The table was covered in white dust, cigarette ash and dried moisture rings where glasses were put down without coasters.

The apartment, or what Jimmy could see of it, was exquisite. A massive terrace overlooked Central Park. The furnishings were of a masculine nature all leather and wood, and thick and chunky. There were sculptures and paintings that must have cost a fortune and a thickly carpeted drop living room that featured a picture window with a panoramic view of Central Park.

A uniform asked Jimmy his business. When Jimmy told him, he was handed a pair of white booties to put over his shoes to protect the crime scene, and was directed to where Morgan was holding court.

It had been a while since he'd been to a murder scene in the City. In Brooklyn he'd see one of these every week, sometimes two, but that was a long time ago. He breathed in the atmosphere and savored the memory like a long lost friend, but he was glad he didn't do it any more. The tension was excruciating. He was good at it back then, before they rained on his parade, but not now. He didn't have the energy for it any more.

"Some place," he said to Morgan.

Morgan agreed.

He looked cool in a blue mohair suit, white shirt and narrow black tie. His thick black hair was buzzed at the sides with a spikey-gelled front. He had a swarthy, clean-shaven face, with chiseled features and deep blue eyes that were tense and alert. What spoiled it for Jimmy were the white booties that covered Morgan's black suede loafers. They looked kind of silly on such a sharp looking dude.

Morgan said, "You wanna get something to eat? We've got time. They're still working."

And so they were, which added to the movie set visual of lights, action, and a whole lot more besides. The ME's people wore white booties and white coveralls with ME written on the back in black letters. They were pouring over the body and surrounding area with cameras, magnifying glasses, and tweezers. Sheets of plastic protected places of interest from incautious feet even though everyone wore coverings. Detectives in booties wearing suits with badges clipped to the top pocket, were reporting to Morgan, or conferring with him, or obeying his instructions. Uniforms covered the front door and the hallways. They were not wearing booties and were not allowed into the crime scene area. Colored extension cables snaked this way and that attaching themselves to a variety of electrical appliances. The Crime Scene people, wearing booties and blue and white overalls, measured, dusted, and tested everything that caught their attention.

It was an organized chaos Martin Scorsese would have been proud of.

Jimmy said he'd eaten.

He'd grabbed an Italian combo and coffee from Gino's across the road from the station house, and ate it on the way down. The car smelled of onions and salami. He did too. A little. There were crumbs everywhere and some of them were still on his suit. A spot of salad dressing had landed on his tie. And coffee. He'd spilled that too and smelled of it. Luckily it hadn't got on his clothes, but it wouldn't have made any difference. He still looked like yesterday's mashed potatoes.

By Friday, any Friday, he'd had enough of looking neat and tidy. Mary was still working on Fridays with very little to show for it. She'd cleaned him up four days out of five and kudos to her for that, but Fridays were proving to be difficult. Jimmy took a delight in making a suit go one more day, or a shirt. Shoes were polished on Monday and the shine was gone by the end of the week. What are you gonna do? Four days out of five is a victory in anyone's language, but that fifth day was turning out to be a bitch on wheels.

Morgan looked around the apartment.

"Crawford owns it," he said. "I'm putting in a bid."

"And here I thought you were an honest cop."

"I could've inherited."

"And that's why you're working like a dog for a pittance and a pension."

Morgan shrugged.

"Believe what you want, but if they accept my offer this place is mine. Back to coincidences."

"I don't believe in them."

"Neither should you because they've found your, who now turns out to be our, Kathy O'Brien's fingerprints all over the place. Neither did he die of natural causes, or OD. He was murdered. Suffocated with a pillow." He pointed to a pillow in a plastic bag sitting on the dining room table. "They also found a bunch of pubic hairs in the bathroom. We've got to wait for the DNA report on that. It can take a lot or a little time depending on how busy they are. The cleaner says she scrubs the place every other day so you've got to believe the pubes are fresh. They're also the same color as the one they found in Gillie Fader's upstate place. It's the first thing I checked."

"What's the deal with that?" Jimmy wondered.

Morgan said he didn't know.

Jimmy said, "Maybe she's got a bladder condition?"

"What's that got to do with it?"

"You have to go to the bathroom a lot with that, and she's shedding. We're lucky she doesn't have a Brazilian down there."

"I don't understand that," said Morgan.

"Me neither," said Jimmy.

"It hurts. Did you know that?"

Jimmy did not.

"They put wax down there," said Morgan sounding like he was going to be next in line for one. "Then they rip those little suckers out by the roots."

"Ouch! Why would you wanna go through that?

"I wouldn't."

"Me neither," said Jimmy. "You think she knows she's shedding down there?"

"I don't know, but I'm sure gonna ask her," said Morgan. "I never asked anyone that before."

"How will you do it?"

"Come right out with it, I suppose."

"No lead up?"

Morgan thought it over.

"I could say something like, bladder infections are a pain in the neck, then bleed into the idea that she's shedding her pubes all over the place and what's up with that?"

"Suppose she doesn't have a bladder infection?"

"I thought you said she did."

"I said she might have one, which would explain why she goes to the bathroom all the time."

"They all do that." Morgan waved a hand at him dismissively. "Half the time I'm with Acushla I'm looking for a bathroom and the other half I'm waiting for her to come out of one."

Acushla was his girl friend.

"We're back together, by the way."

Jimmy hadn't wanted to ask.

"What happened?"

"That date she went on, the guy wanted to bang her. She figured if she was gonna do that she might as well do it with me."

Jimmy said, "I'm glad to hear you're good at something."

Morgan gave him a noogie.

"According to the ME, Crawford's approximate time of death was between 8:30 and 9:30 last night. The desk log shows Kathy O'Brien arriving at 8:32 and leaving at 9:05. There's no record of anyone else visiting him before or after that. Neither the desk nor the doorman saw anyone they can't account for coming in or going out around that time. We're still canvassing the building to see if anyone saw anything unusual. I think we've got her, Jimmy. There's a lot of evidence here."

Jimmy agreed. There was.

Morgan said, "Can you have Eddie pick her up?"

Jimmy took out his cellphone, called Eddie, and told him what he wanted him to do.

Eddie said he'd call in as soon as he had her.

Jimmy said to Morgan, "She got her passport back, I told you that didn't I? Her lawyer got all hot and bothered about my bullshit obstruction charge and called a connection, who knew someone in the DA's office, who spoke to the big boss, who spoke to my boss, and that's why the obstruction charge was dropped. A dollar says she's not at home."

Morgan wouldn't take the bet.

Eddie called Jimmy twenty minutes later to say she was gone. Witnesses saw her putting cases into her car yesterday afternoon. The super let him into her apartment. It was cleaned out.

Morgan put some people on it.

"Airlines, car rentals, bus stations, planes, boats, trains and hotels, they'll check em all and find her," he said, "but it's gonna take some time."

They'd moved to Crawford's terrace to get out from under everyone's feet. A setting sun they couldn't see bathed everything in a pinkish hue. There were long shadows and a skyline that differed in size and shape. The City was spread out before them like a patchwork quilt of architectural wonder.

Another movie set, thought Jimmy. Cue the strings and 'Rhapsody In Blue.'

From where they were standing they could see all the way up to Harlem and beyond. Looking south was a jumble of skyscrapers and neon signs. Straight ahead was LaGuardia Airport where the planes kept up a constant rhythm disappearing or rising from behind this building or that in a majestic splendor.

The thing about a great view is you never look at the person you're talking to; you're always looking at something out there, some aspect that's so unusual you can't take your eyes off it. So there was Jimmy and Morgan having a serious discussion without making eye contact, fixated on this view or that while they talked or listened to whatever the other one was saying.

Morgan said, "Tell me about the Shelly Barton case again."

"Lamont Dubois was my friend's cousin. Lamont's banging Kathy O'Brien. She gets too high and tells him she gets old people to sign over their stuff to her, then kills them. She says she's done it five times. She's a caregiver and lives with them. Lamont hates anything to do with scamming old people, so now he hates this woman. He gets her high and records a Q&A where she tells him all this and how she puts a pillow over their face to finish the job. Lamont tells my friend. My friend tells me.

"Mary knew Shelly Barton. He's the last person Kathy O'Brien took care of. When he died Kathy got his house and whatever money was left. Our ME didn't do an autopsy on him figuring Shelly died of old age. The DA exhumed Shelly on what Lamont told us. They said he'd been suffocated. We charged Kathy with his murder based on what she told Lamont and his willingness to testify. Next thing we know Gillie Fader takes a run at Lamont. Incidentally, Gillie was sitting with the shooter who popped Conner Malloy in the Columbia Diner. Lamont shoots Gillie in the shoulder and Gillie disappears. Three days later Lamont's found floating in the Hudson along with our case against Kathy O'Brien. Three days after that Gillie's found upstate, suffocated. One of Kathy's pubes is found in the bathroom. She says she was never there and doesn't know Gillie Fader. There are no fingerprints, witnesses, or any other trace of her up there. The pube is not enough for a conviction. She'll walk. I arrested her for obstruction. So far as I'm concerned the pube says she was up there and she lied to me. Those charges were dropped yesterday."

A hawk flew by. A hawk, can you believe such a thing? Jimmy lived in the sticks where there were hawks all over the place, but he'd never got this close to one. The hawk was close enough to touch. It gave them the eye as it wafted by twisting its mottled head to check them out. And it was beautiful, this hawk. Close up. With its reddish tail and proud beak. Drifting by them on unseen currents and outstretched wings. Near enough for eye contact and to see its feathers ruffling in the breeze.

Jimmy said, "Did you see that?"

Morgan said he did and was suitably impressed.

"And why do we think she killed Crawford?" he asked. Watching as the hawk disappeared behind a building. Going through it again to make sure they had it right.

He'd worked with a lot of out of town police over the years. They were usually pretty good for wherever they come from, but they couldn't hold a candle to a City cop. Jimmy was different. Morgan checked him out when they first worked together. Just because Jimmy was a little rough around the edges, it didn't mean he was a Rube. He was good, and sharp, with a track record to prove it, especially from the old days. Morgan had checked that out too. Jimmy's jacket was full of praise and commendations until the end, when his world fell apart. Except for that, Jimmy looked a lot like Morgan did now. Sharp, and hot, and ready to go.

"He's the only one left who could point a finger at her," said Jimmy. "The rest are all dead. Lamont. Gillie. Now Crawford."

Morgan nodded in agreement. It made perfect sense.

The morgue people came for Crawford's body.

The crime scene people were wrapping it up. Literally. Rolling up the huge sheets of plastic they'd put down earlier.

It was getting cold so they went inside.

A crime scene guy came over.

"Kathy O'Brien's prints are the only ones in the system, but there are a lot of others you may or may not want us to identify. It'll take us a while to sort them out and figure how many sets we've got."

Morgan thanked him.

The man went back to his team.

Morgan's partner Tim joined them.

'Timmy from Brooklyn.'

Jimmy shook his hand and thanked him for helping to find out who Gillie Fader was.

Timmy said he was happy to help.

He had things to report.

They'd interviewed everyone in the building. No one saw anything odd between the hours of 7:30 and 9:30, or any other time for that matter. Neither did anyone hear anything unusual. No loud voices, or shouting, or mysterious thuds. It was a quiet building. The desk guy and the doorman positively identified Kathy O'Brien from a picture he showed them as Crawford Taylor's visitor last night. The desk guy showed him the entry in and out, 8:32 and 9:05. Tim double-checked the register to make sure there were no more entries. The garage people, two guys, also saw nothing unusual around that time. Street cams from the adjoining buildings see her coming and going at those times. This building has no security cameras. They say they're definitely going to have them installed.

Morgan brought him up to date on his end.

When he was finished Tim asked, "How did she do it?"

Morgan looked at the pillow on the table.

"I know that, but how? What, he just lay there and let her put a pillow over his head?"

"He probably passed out," said Jimmy.

They all nodded at that. The autopsy would tell them more.

"We've got his computer," said Morgan. "They found it in his study. I've got a good tech guy at the station. I'll have him look it over. Maybe Crawford keeps his life on that thing."

Timmy said he'd take it back with him, he was going anyway. He'd call them the minute he had something.

It took the tech guy a while. These things always do. A uniform, the low man on the totem, went out to get everyone coffee. He came back with a cardboard box with twenty coffees, forty little plastic containers of milk and packets of sugar and Sweet'n Low, but he forgot the stirrers. A moan rose up from the apartment as people found out and were forced to use pencils and pens and anything else handy to stir their coffees.

Jimmy and Morgan went out on the terrace to drink theirs. It was getting dark. The City was beginning to light up. The Park began to twinkle then a few of the buildings lit up. Then all the lights came on at once as if they were all on the same switch.

It got darker quicker.

And the City changed into something else.

They talked about the Giants and the Mets and went back inside for more coffee. Two containers sat in the cardboard box. They were cold and bitter and hard on the breath. Then they went back out to the terrace for a heavy dose of bullshit and another noogie for Jimmy.

Jimmy told him more about Cassidy Jones.

"I said you'd want to talk to him about the information he gave me, and the gravity of his situation."

"How grave is it?"

"I told him I had information I didn't."

"You lied to him."

"I did," said Jimmy. Shame faced, but not really. "And he believed me. So in return for giving him a clean bill of health on what I didn't have on him, he told me a bunch of stuff about a floating card game I thought you might be interested in. I said you'd give him the same deal. A free ride on the stuff we don't have on him providing he tells you what you want to know. He can't wait to help you. I think he'll make the perfect snitch."

"And he thinks I have the same stuff you do, only you don't."

"And neither do you."

"What exactly did you tell him?"

"I had statements and witnesses who saw him with Weasel, and a signed statement from Weasel saying he paid him $500 to kill Lamont."

"And he believed you."

"He did."

"He must be very dumb."

"Not really. He doesn't want any trouble. Cassidy's a male model and a hot DJ. If anything bad comes out he's done for, that's how fragile his world is. So yes he believed me. He can't afford not to. Now he can't afford not to with you. You'll like him. He's just a kid from the hood trying to survive in this wicked world of ours, though he did do for poor Lamont, there's no doubt about that. We can't get him for that, but it would be nice if you ran him ragged. You know, stretch him out a little and make him feel scared. He deserves that at least."

Morgan said he'd be happy to and thanked him. A good snitch was hard to come by.

Tim called.

The tech guy got into Crawford's loansharking business. He had a lot of clients. All those accounts had been closed in the last ten days and he was sitting on a lot of money. Three accounts were still open. Austin Kenner owed him a half a million dollars. Mal Finkelstein owed him $350,000, and he'd put the company up as collateral. There was $500 owed by someone called Skip. And there was no account for Kathy O'Brien or any trace of her so far.

Jimmy suggested poking around his bank accounts.

A little while later Tim called back. The tech guy came up with a lump of money going to an attorney in Tarrytown two weeks ago.

"Name?" asked Jimmy.

"Keddlestein and Adler."

"That's Kathy's lawyer. A weasely looking guy you could really take a disliking to."

"I hate him already," said Morgan.

Jimmy asked, "How much?"

"A half a million."

Jimmy said, "I'd say that's Kathy's bail and something for the lawyer."

Morgan told Tim to have the guy keep digging.

"Tell me again," he said to Jimmy, just to be sure, "why you think, apart from the evidence, she killed Crawford Taylor."

"Because he knew she killed Gillie. He was a threat to her."

"But she killed Gillie for Crawford."

"Yes."

"And not for herself?"

"No. She did it for herself too."

"Because?"

"Okay let's take it from the beginning. Gillie worked for Crawford. Crawford had him take care of Lamont. But instead of killing Lamont, Gillie got shot. That makes both Crawford and Kathy vulnerable, because if Gillie gets caught he could turn on them. He knows he was doing Lamont for her. So Crawford asks her to do Gillie for both of them. And Kathy owes Crawford because he put up her bail and got Gillie to go at Lamont for her.

"You think?"

"I do," said Jimmy.

They noodled it over and agreed it sounded right. They'd run it by Kathy when they got her, to see if it fit.

"What about the other two names the tech found on Crawford's computer? Mal Finklestein and Austin Kenner. You know anything about them," Morgan asked.

"Austin Kenner is the guy who killed Gillie's partner Conner Malloy in the Columbia Diner parking lot."

"Right," said Morgan. "And Mal Finklstein?"

"Mal Finkelstein?" Jimmy said taking that in. "Mal Finkelstein is Austin Kenner's boss. Now that's a surprise – or a coincidence. And we both know what we think about coincidences. I gotta to talk to him. There's something weird about them both being connected to Crawford and owing him so much money."

"When do you want to go at him?"

"Not today. I wanna dig a little deeper. There's gotta be something I'm missing."

Morgan sounded shocked.

"More than murder and mayhem? Whatever could it be?"

Jimmy smiled.

"As well as murder and mayhem."

"Like what?"

"I have no idea, that's why I wanna see Mr. Finkelstein and shake him up a little. Maybe something will come loose. Or not. I've got nothing else to do."

Morgan said, "Be my guest."

It was 7:30 by the time they got out on the street. It was dark and chilly, and the traffic had thinned out. Morgan was laughing at a car parked in the wrong spot in front of Crawford's building. There was a sheaf of tickets tucked under its wipers and it looked like it had been driven from Alaska.

"Can you believe this guy?" he said to Jimmy, shaking his head in wonder.

"That's my car," said Jimmy sheepishly and explained what a state he was in when he got there. "I caught every light, Morgan. Every fucking light. I thought I was gonna have a heart attack."

Morgan took the tickets off the window.

"I'll take care of them," he said and started to laugh some more.

They headed for the Carnegie Deli on 7th Avenue. On the way Jimmy filled him in on what was going on with Lucy. How, because of her, they got to Austin Kenner because his kid was selling dope at school. Now she was being shunned. Shunned. What the fuck was that all about? Next they'll be burning people at the stake.

Morgan was sympathetic. Bullying was everywhere. People were more aware of it these days and quicker to act, but it still happened a lot.

At the Carnegie they had kreplach soup and corned beef sandwiches with orange sodas, pickles and coleslaw. For dessert they had apple strudel with vanilla ice cream, coffees, and a lot more bullshit.

Then Jimmy went home.

CHAPTER 55

JIMMY

Jimmy's drive home was uneventful, which was just as well because it was late, he was tired, and it was dark. He hated driving at night. His night vision was getting worse as he got older and he thought, not for the first time, he better get his eyes checked out again. He tucked himself behind someone in the slow lane and let them lead the way. He was pleased to see he was back to his 80% red light ratio. The 100% on the way down freaked him out. Nothing was 100%. And Morgan's laughing at him didn't help any.

He was listening to Beethoven's *Pastoral Symphony* to calm himself down and work through the events of the day. It was one of the beauties of a long drive home. He could let his mind wander and alight on things he didn't see, or not, as in this case because he was so full he could hardly move. Deli food did that to him; left him bloated and filled with gas. It was a good thing no one else was in the car with him.

His mind finally settled on Lucy. He'd called home several times and the phones were always busy. He called when they left Crawford's building and again when he left the Carnegie Deli and the phones were still busy. He left messages. But no one called him back.

He couldn't help thinking something was wrong.

But when he got home there were hugs and smiles waiting for him. A big surprise, all things considered. It's not like he was dreading it, but because he'd had no contact with them his thoughts had blossomed into a full-fledged worry fit. All he could think of was doom and gloom and he certainly wasn't expecting to find happiness in all of its glory.

And why was that, he wanted to know? Why were they so happy?

The day after Jimmy arrested the two boys the principal had a meeting with the school superintendent to go over everything that had happened. A re-enactment, if you will, to see if mistakes were made. What they were? And how they could be rectified? It was smart management on the superintendent's part. It's one of the reasons he got the job in the first place; he was very good at managing things.

They met in the principal's office, the scene of the crime, and agreed, when all was said and done, that they could have done a much better job of it. They got off on the wrong foot with Det. Dugan, they agreed, and things went downhill from there.

The principal thought he was to blame. No, not thought. Knew. He'd behaved badly and let his prejudices get the better of him and read the detective wrong. It was Jimmy's appearance that gave the principal no confidence. And that was the root of the problem right there. Judging a book by its cover. This superiority complex of his has done him no good. And look what it's got him now. Nothing, that's what it's got him; it's lost him this encounter. Lost him a step in the eyes of the superintendent and lost him the respect of Det. Dugan. He can still see the way Dugan looked at him when they arrested Mike Kenner.

Like he didn't exist.

What did he expect with his haughty manner and his toffee-nosed attitude?

And the rumpled detective took him on.

And won!

The superintendent was gracious enough to shoulder the blame himself and not point the finger. The principal would never have done such a thing and it inspired him to look at things differently. He became introspective and self-appraising and changed the way he dealt with people, shelving his superior attitude and moving from obtuse and aloof to someplace in between. The faculty noticed the difference immediately and reacted accordingly. Energies were spent on their duties instead of dealing with the principal's idiosyncrasies and pomposity. It was an unexpected pleasure.

So when Mary walked into the principal's office and told him about Lucy's situation, apart from being outraged and appalled, he saw it as a chance for redemption in the eyes of Det. Dugan and another step forward in his personal reclamation project.

And then there was the bullying issue.

He'd been bullied at prep school, so he knew all about the trauma such actions can cause. It didn't break him and he managed to survive it, but it took its toll and helped form the distant and aloof part of his personality, that unapproachable coldness he projects that has had such a negative impact on his relationships and working situations.

When Mrs. Harwood finished telling him Lucy's story, and, after expressing his heartfelt sympathy, the principal called a lunchtime assembly.

The assembly was held in the auditorium. All the students were required to attend. The principal stood behind a lectern in the center of the stage flanked on either side by a seated and puzzled faculty. No one could ever remember having a lunchtime assembly.

The principal was breaking new ground.

The students filed in and sat in the seats that were assigned to them at the beginning of the semester. There was not much noise, an occasional whisper or the scuffing of shoes as they settled in, anxiously waiting to see what was going to happen.

The principal, after a short preamble thanking them for attending and apologizing for breaking into their lunch time, launched into an impassioned speech about the power of bullying and what it leads to. How a student, never mentioning Lucy by name, was being bullied for something she did not do. How this student got into trouble for using drugs and how drugs do not belong in their school. Period. And how this unnamed person and others helped them rid the school of this scourge. He talked about shunning and what it meant. How there were many ways to bully someone besides violence, and shunning was the leading example. He talked about how this type of ostracism can, in extreme cases, lead to suicide. How, with cellphones and computers, it was so easy these days to make someone crazy and drive them into the ground.

He challenged each one of them to look into their hearts and wonder what they'd do if it happened to them. Everyone turned against them. Not a friend in the world. How would they handle it? What would they do?

He compared them to a lynch mob. A pack of dogs. He railed at them like an old time preacher waiving a clenched fist in the air to make this point or that. Accusing them of not thinking. Of not using their heads. Of going along with the crowd. The mob. And not willing to take a stand. He told them that was how they should see themselves. Judges and jury. Sheeple. And he railed at them for being gutless. For not standing up for their ideals and guilty of the sin of neglect. Of looking the other way. Of mob rule and heartlessness. Pointing his finger at them. Accusing them. Thrashing the air with his waving arms.

It was a masterful performance.

When the principal finished there was a moment of silence. No one moved or breathed. Then the hall erupted in wild cheering as the students were caught up in the principal's passion. Applauding, and whistling, and stomping their feet in approval.

The principal dismissed them while they were still on his side, giving them no time for reflection and hoping it would stick.

Which it did.

Almost immediately.

The phone in Mary's house did not stop ringing. People Lucy barely knew were calling to apologize. Her dearest friends, Christina and Diane, were distraught. There were tears. And recriminations. And forgiveness. And a date for the six of them, mothers and daughters, for manicures and pedicures and general primping at this great place someone knew about.

Tomorrow.

Can't wait!

Cuddling in bed at night was the best part of Jimmy's day. Mary spooning into him and holding him tight made him feel safe and secure.

"That principal stepped up," she whispered. She loved to whisper in the dark. "You should've seen him, Jimmy. Like one of those old-time religion guys. I never figured him for passion. He always looks like such a tight ass, but not today. He looked like he was going to make the lame walk today."

"And the phone hasn't stopped ringing?"

"Well has it?"

"Not since I've been home."

"Well there you are."

"Nice," he said.

And it was, because Lucy seemed so happy.

He told Mary about Kathy O'Brien. How they got her for Crawford Taylor's murder, as soon as they could find her.

"Where is she?"

"We don't know," said Jimmy sadly.

CHAPTER 56

KATHY O'BRIEN

She was home free. She was drunk and she was home free. She was drunk on a plane to the Cayman Islands, and she was home free. Flying first class. Out of her mind and drifting in and out of an alcohol induced euphoria. She had all her ducks in a row now. Finally. The properties were under a concoction of corporations and cutouts that ended up in a holding company in the Caymans. Her Tarrytown lawyer was authorized to manage the company's assets for a percentage of the income. All her money had been moved around until it came to rest in her Cayman bank account.

She could not get over herself.

The idea that she got away with it. All of it. And escaped the clutches of that fat cop who was beginning to drive her crazy. Who's on their way to the Caymans now and who's stuck in Columbia, answer me that, Fatso? She was up and away and free as a bird leaving a trail of dead bodies behind her like an ugly wake.

After she left Crawford's apartment Thursday evening she drove to the Sheraton Hotel on Conduit Avenue near Kennedy Airport and checked in for the night. In the morning she dumped the car in the Kennedy long-term parking lot, and good riddance to that piece of junk, then took the shuttle to the American Airlines terminal. It was 12:00pm. The flight was at 1:30. There was plenty of time, so she decided to have a feed up at Bobby Van's, a restaurant in the middle of the terminal. She ordered a big steak and a baked potato with all the fixins, and slab bacon and mushrooms and onions and mmm, mmm, mmm. It was like she'd never eaten before as she wolfed it down like a homeless person. Smacking her lips a little too loudly for her fellow diners who gave her glances of displeasure and frowns of scorn. For dessert she had a parfait that was creamy and gooey and tasted just wonderful, and washed it all down with a triple Stoli with a dash, just a dash mind you, of freshly squeezed orange juice.

After that she was good to go.

She has a lay over in Miami. It would be late by the time she got to the Islands.

"Yes please," she said to the flight attendant's offer of a refill.

She was on the last leg now. She had to wait around in Miami. The plane was late coming in, so the plane was late going out. But now she was on it. An hour in and a little less than an hour to go. Drifting in and out. Drinking since mid-day. Her buzz could've powered the plane. The Miami layover hadn't helped her any. She had a light snack there and a few doubles to keep the fires banked.

She was on the first step of living out her fantasy and she could hardly believe it. After all she'd been through. Where should she go? Where should she live? It was the first time she'd let her mind go there since she'd been charged with Shelly Barton's murder. She'd spent so much time dodging and weaving she thought it was bad luck to think about it, but now she could. She'd heard in Thailand you could buy yourself any fantasy you could come up with. Apparently making westerner's dreams come true was the country's largest industry. And she certainly had the money to make that work.

"Thanks," she said to the attendant who brought her the drink.

This was the one that pushed her over the edge. This drink. She'd been pacing herself all day, if you can call double and triple vodkas pacing, and she'd managed to walk that fine line. But there's always a straw, isn't there? And this one was it. So after a couple of belts it was 'hello there,' and she took off like a rocket ship. Scurrying from one fantasy to another. Crisp beaches and bright sun. And men, lots of men, all sturdy and handsome and hard.

She was out of it. Mumbling and humming and singing gospel songs about freedom. Because she was free now, wasn't she? She'd pulled it off. She was liberated. And safe. And rich. And she never felt better in her life. She began singing louder, becoming imbued with the spirit of her emancipation.

Hallelujah baby she was free at last, free at last, almighty dollar she was free at last.

First class was empty except for the guy sitting in front of her. She must have been kicking his seat because that's what the flight attendant asked her to stop doing as she woke her from her stupor. Kicking his seat. Not singing. She never mentioned anything about the singing.

Kathy told the guy she was sorry and took another slug of her drink.

She was flying high now. Zooming. Star rockets in flight. Rejoicing it was finally over. She was safe. And floating. And warm and cozy all wrapped up in the funk of the booze and the blankets they had given her.

She slurped on her drink.

Drifting. Drifting. Safe. And free.

She must have passed out.

The next thing she knew the attendant was shaking her, telling her they'd landed. It was time to leave the plane.

Her head was throbbing and her vision was slightly blurred. They'd landed. She was there. She had this idea of kissing the tarmac, then dismissed it as too dramatic; the result, she concluded, of being drunk and not thinking right.

She stepped out of the plane and onto the steps. The heat hit her like a blast furnace. Hotter than New York, and humid. So humid. She was wearing the wrong clothes and began to sweat like she was fully dressed in a Turkish bath.

The area was brightly lit with floodlights. She walked down the stairs breathing in the hot dank air. Still high. Basking in her freedom and the new life that lay before her. Descending those stairs like an old time movie star. Sideways and slowly, one step at a time. Hips swaying. Wearing dark glasses. A floppy white hat. Jeans. A white tee shirt. A fur jacket, and a knit scarf that reached the ground. It's a well known fact that wool and fur in ninety-degree humidity don't mix.

Now she was halfway down the stairs.

Proud and confident.

Hot.

And sweaty.

And horny?

Who'd have thought she'd be horny? Sweaty horny. Lusty horny. High horny. The taxi driver would score her some dope and a guy for sure. Those boys will do anything for a twenty-dollar bill. The last time she was here the cabbie got her the most incredible weed and a guy that wouldn't stop. It was gonna be sooooo sooooo good; she could taste it. And felt it, between her legs. A tingling. An electricity. And a dampness, she was sure of it. Even wet.

She was almost to the bottom now.

Hot.

And horny.

And high.

Oh my.

CHAPTER 57

SATURDAY
JIMMY AND DUPREE

Saturday. Lunchtime. The girls were on their mani-pedi beauty extravaganza. Christina, Diane and their mothers, and Mary and Lucy. Everybody was having a good time was the last update. Everyone, Mary whispered down the phone, was trying to put the shunning behind them and thank goodness for that.

Jimmy wondered what was going to happen on Monday when Lucy went back to school? One day at a time was his thinking on that one. And the kid was happy, wasn't she? And suddenly she had friends up the kazoo.

Things certainly have a habit.

Jimmy was at the Magic Wok in Pleasantville, meeting Dupree. It was his call this time and off their regular schedule. He needed a service only Dupree could provide him. Jimmy liked the Magic Wok. The owner always remembered him no matter how long it was between visits. He couldn't remember how he found the place, but he'd been coming here since he got to Columbia.

"Hello Mr. Jimmy," said the owner as he walked in the door.

She was always there. The owner. Sitting at the counter by the till. A small Asian woman in what looked like a housecoat but wasn't, with a kind, almond shaped face, and thick graying hair that was tied up in a bun. Every now and again she'd flit through the restaurant to pick up a take-out from the kitchen; smiling or stopping at a table to say something before scurrying back to her station behind the counter.

Dupree was already there, working on the noodles and the duck sauce.

They exchanged hellos and, after ordering, Jimmy told him everything that was going on including Crawford Taylor's murder and how they had enough evidence to charge Kathy O'Brien for it. How Austin Kenner worked for Mal Finkelstein and they both owed Crawford Taylor a lot of money. When he'd finished he told Dupree how he felt there was something missing. Some piece he couldn't figure out.

The wonton soup came. And more noodles, a big bowl of them.

Dupree scattered a fistful into his soup and got to work.

So did Jimmy.

For a while they slurped in silence. They came from the "hot food" side of the argument. If you talk, the soup gets cold. They both knew this. Mary did not. Neither did Lucy. Hot food meant nothing to them. Was that a girl thing, he wondered? He'd have to ask Morgan about it. He knew all about that stuff.

Dupree was the first to finish.

Just because he was slurping soup didn't mean his brain had gone to sleep. The hacker on a white horse feigned confusion.

"And you want me to do what?" he asked.

"Nose around Mal Finkelstein's stuff and see what you can find."

Dupree feigned surprise.

"You want me to break the law?"

Jimmy feigned indignation.

"I most certainly do not."

Dupree feigned reasonableness.

"What then?"

Jimmy feigned patience.

"I'm describing a situation to a friend where there's absolutely no doubt his talents could help me find out what the fuck is going on here."

"A favor, then? You're asking me to do you a favor and you're trying to influence my decision by plying me with Chinese food and outlandish compliments."

"I am not."

"What would you call it then?"

"I'm trying to enlist the help of someone who feels the same way I do about the bad guys and who could, because of his previously stated talents, help me nail another disgusting breaker of our laws."

"Why didn't you say so in the first place?" said Dupree feigning pique. "Tell you what. For the same price I'll take a look at Austin's stuff too. Is that enough of a declaration of our friendship and proof of my commitment to helping good conquer evil?"

Jimmy said it was.

"When we do this stuff," said Dupree, "shouldn't we get suited up?"

"A Batman and Robin thing?"

"Well?"

"You wanna wear a cape?"

"I'm the one getting dressed up?"

Jimmy said he was already dressed up."

"Not today you ain't," sniffed Dupree.

Jimmy's Saturday dress code was an extension of sloppy Friday: unshaven, dirty jeans, scuffed sneakers, frayed denim shirt and a cast-off black hoodie Mary didn't wear any more. He loved the hoodie. It was from J. Crew. Black and bulky. Something he'd never buy for himself because he was too cheap.

The soup bowls were removed and their food was placed in the middle of the table. Eggrolls. The duck special. Shrimp with fried noodles. Well-done spare ribs. Ten ingredient fried rice. Broccoli with oyster sauce. More duck sauce and noodles. Chinese beer for Dupree, and a Coke for Jimmy. It was a little different from their order at the place in Columbia, but change is good don't you think? And so was the food, which they gobbled down like they hadn't eaten in a week, clucking and pecking and commenting on this dish or that as they stuffed their greedy faces.

"What am I looking for?" Dupree asked between mouthfuls.

Jimmy said he didn't know.

"I'm figuring a crafty fellow like yourself will know it when he sees it."

He was all tongue and teeth and sucking noises, trying to dig out a bit of sparerib caught between his teeth.

Dupree told him to stop doing it. He looked ridiculous and it was making him sick.

They talked about Dupree's cousin Lamont and how lonely Dupree's Moms was. Lamont slept on her pullout. He was her nephew and she treated him like a son. Especially since Dupree didn't live there any more. She liked Lamont's company and now she was alone.

Jimmy was sympathetic.

"Where you at with Cassidy Jones?" asked Dupree.

Jimmy told him how he made him think he had stuff on him he didn't.

"So?"

"We've got no proof he set the contract on Lamont, but he did get me to Crawford Taylor and threw in all sorts of other stuff my friend Morgan's interested in. I handed Cassidy over to him with the same deal. A free ride on stuff he thinks we've got, but don't, in exchange for - and this is where it gets good - a lifetime as Morgan's snitch."

Dupree made a face.

"What?"

Dupree made the same face.

"Dupree," said Jimmy sympathetically. "Morgan's gonna run him ragged and none too gently I promise you. That was a special request from me. It's the best we can do under the circumstances. There's no way we can charge him with anything unless you can convince one of the corner boys to testify."

Dupree chuckled at that and nodded. He understood.

They talked about Dupree's business.

And Jimmy's Lucy story.

"You ever get bullied?" he asked Dupree.

"Nah. Lamont always got my back."

Jimmy was sympathetic some more.

Then he said, "Check out the money, Dupree. They both owed Crawford Taylor a lot of it."

Jimmy pried open his fortune cookie, read it, shook his head and put the little piece of paper in his back pocket.

"What did it say?" asked Dupree.

"I'm a lucky man."

"That's what it said?"

Jimmy nodded.

Dupree said, "Show me."

Jimmy handed him the little piece of paper.

"Son of a bitch," said Dupree.

"What's wrong with that?"

"I never get fortunes like that," complained Dupree.

To prove it he cracked open his cookie and read the fortune out loud. "Hold the middle ground and help others who strive to do the same."

"What's wrong with that?" Jimmy wanted to know.

"I don't usually get em like that. They're usually stupid and make no sense."

Jimmy signaled for the check.

He handed the waitress his credit card.

"Tomorrow?" Jimmy asked wanting to know when Dupree would call.

"Why not. Where you at?"

"Home."

Jimmy signed the receipt, left a big tip, and the two of them filed out, but not before the owner gave them a toothy smile.

"Thanks, Mr. Jimmy. See you again soon, yes?"

Yes.

It was later in the day when Dupree got back to him. Jimmy was watching a college game. Wisconsin and Ohio State. Go Badgers. He had a bag of chips on his lap, a soda in his fist, and the game on loud. Naughty boy stuff he couldn't do when the women were around. The girls, with their different way of doing things. There was so much to absorb he wondered if he'd ever get the hang of it. And there was always something new to learn. Spoons here. Glasses there. Don't stack them like that. Like this, see. And napkins. And place mats on trays. Who knew?

He was really into the game when the phone rang.

It was Dupree.

They went through their hellos and how they were still stuffed from lunch, which, they agreed, might have to be revisited they liked the place so much.

"Mal Finkelstein gave Austin $250,000," said Dupree. "It came out of Mal's business account and shows up in Austin's personal account as cash, so it had to be a cashier's check. And it went into Austin's personal account, not a joint account with his wife. Then the money goes into a TD Ameritrade account also in Austin's name and he uses it to buy tens of thousands of out-of-the-money options."

"What's that?"

"It's a stock market thing. What it is isn't important. What is important is that three days later the options were up by a factor of ten and Austin made a bundle. Four million give or take. That money now sits in his lawyer's escrow account. His lawyer has power of attorney and dribs money out to his defense team whenever they present an invoice. It looks like Austin has not paid Mal back the $250,000. It doesn't show up in Mal's books, or his personal stuff, neither does it come out of Austin's account. No one's drawing on Austin's money except his attorney. I'll bet the wife doesn't even know it's there."

"Mal Finkelstein just launched a new line of clothes," said Jimmy. "Why would he give Austin a quarter of a million dollars when he needed every penny for the opening?"

"Blackmail?"

"Could be. I'm gonna take a run at him on Monday and see what shakes loose. All that money's sitting in the lawyers escrow account?" he asked. "He's not giving any to his family?"

"Not that I can see and the Mrs. is running short. The joint account is low and she's maxing out the credit cards."

"What a piece of shit," said Jimmy. "I heard he's gonna get a slap on the wrist for popping Conner Malloy. They're working on a probation deal for having an unregistered firearm. Normally I wouldn't give a shit, but the guy's such a prick, you know? Be nice if we could extend his stay with us for a while and show the wife where the money's at."

Dupree couldn't agree more.

"So, to be clear," said Jimmy. "Austin's sitting on close to $4 million. He hasn't paid Mal Finkelstein back the loan or whatever it was, or Crawford Taylor who's dead. And we think Austin's wife has no idea this money exists." Jimmy paused to think it through. Then, "It sounds like he's gonna run as soon as he gets out of jail."

Dupree agreed. It did sound like that.

"Mal wrote a lot of orders at the launch. Enough to pay off Crawford Taylor, but he doesn't have to do that any more does he. Crawford's dead."

"How lucky can you get?"

"Well, not so lucky," said Dupree. "Austin still owes him a quarter of a million and it doesn't look like he's gonna get any of that back."

"If Austin's blackmailing him, Mal never thought he'd get it back in the first place. Crawford's death has certainly helped him out of a hole, though. I wonder what Austin's got on him?"

Dupree couldn't imagine.

Neither could Jimmy.

Dupree's voice got serious.

"Kathy O'Brien's not gonna walk on this one, is she, Jimmy?"

He was sure she was responsible for Lamont's death and it pained him every time she got away with something.

"It's iron clad," said Jimmy. "And when was the last time you heard me say that?" He didn't tell him they hadn't got her yet. He figured it was just a matter of time, so what was the point in upsetting him. "You've been a big help, Dupree."

"Aw shucks, Jimmy. You makin me blush."

Jimmy said he hoped it would help him nail Austin for blackmail. He couldn't imagine why else Mal gave him that money at such a crucial time.

Wisconsin scored again. They had the game in the bag. Jimmy flipped to another channel. And another one after that. And kept on flipping. Bad boy stuff. Stuff they wouldn't let him do when they were around. The girls. And that's fair because flipping's a guy thing isn't it? Everyone knows it drives women crazy. But they weren't around were they, so he could flip to his heart's content.

CHAPTER 58
JIMMY

Sunday morning. Jimmy and Mary were lying in bed. Mary made Jimmy promise not to do anything. He was to relax and take it easy after the vigorous week he'd been through.

"No pottering around the garden and lugging heavy things. You look like shit," she said kindly.

And he supposed he did. He certainly felt that way. Running around all week had worn him out and he was happy to comply.

She had a surprise for him, she said, and hopped out of bed, put on her robe and went downstairs. Not long after that mouthwatering smells wafted up from the kitchen, and not long after that she called out, "BREAKFAST."

Lucy emerged from her room.

Jimmy from his.

"Ta da," said Mary when they came into the kitchen.

Each place had a plate full of steaming food.

"An English breakfast," Mary declared. "Or 'a cooked breakfast,' or maybe it's a 'full English breakfast,' I can't remember which is which. Whatever they call it it's guaranteed to clog up your arteries."

They all sat down.

Jimmy wanted to know where she got it from.

"There's an English shop in Wilton. We're always watching those English detective shows where someone's saying, "Would you like a cooked breakfast, sir?" I wanted to know what it was. The lady in the store told me and made me buy all this English stuff. I drew the line at something called blood pudding. She was going to tell me what was in it. I said stop right there, because it sounded so disgusting. This food will give you a heart attack. I can only imagine what blood pudding does to you."

Jimmy looked at his plate then touched it. It was hot. A hot plate meant the food would stay warm longer. It also meant that Mary went to a great deal of trouble for him. She never warms the plate and always laughs at him when he asks her to do it. There were two perfectly fried eggs. Two sausages. Bacon of a type he'd never seen before, all meat and very little fat. Back bacon, it's called. Fried potatoes and mushrooms, a couple of fried tomatoes, fried bread and baked beans. Baked beans? For breakfast? Mary said the bread was fried in the bacon fat, hello emergency room. And toast and marmalade, orange juice, and a mug of tea. Jimmy tucked in, humming and smiling and chewing and never picking his head up till his food was gone. Then he looked over at Lucy's plate.

"Gonna eat that?" he asked her, pointing at a sausage, some bacon and fried bread that she hadn't eaten yet.

She wasn't.

He harpooned them, put them on his plate and then ate them himself. And chugged down his orange juice. And munched on his toast. And purred with delight. That's right. Purred. And the two women burst out laughing when they heard him doing it.

It got better.

Everyone thought it was a good idea if he stayed in his bathrobe and stretched out on the couch and watched the pregame show and the three football games that came after. When he agreed, because you'd have to be a moron not to go along with them, they brought out all sorts of goodies for him to pick at. Cheese and crackers, pepperoni, and chips. And dips. And vegetables. And fruit. And salsa.

They sat with him for as long as they could stand it, because neither of them cared very much for football, then wandered off to do other things. Checking in from time to time to see how he was doing.

Midway through the second game the phone rang.

The Giants were playing the Packers. Jimmy was a Giants fan. The Giants were up by twenty. Could it get any better?

Apparently it could.

It was Morgan.

"We got her," he said. Meaning Kathy O'Brien. "They found her on a plane going to the Cayman Islands last night. We had a warrant sworn out and they arrested her when she landed. A U.S. Marshal's on his way to bring her back. They figure it'll take till tomorrow till they get her out of there. Nothing's easy, you know that."

Jimmy did.

"They're booked on a flight into LaGuardia supposed to land at 12:00pm. If all goes well we should have her here by 1:00, 1:30 something like that."

Jimmy said he'd be there.

"Any change, I'll let you know. What happened with Lucy?"

Jimmy told him.

"Well that's good news. You don't get many happy endings when it comes to bullying. That's just great."

Morgan was pleased he had no kids of his own. If there was any doubt, Lucy's little problem confirmed it. The challenges of parenting were endless and if it wasn't one thing it was another. That's why he didn't want them. Neither did Acushla. They weren't cut out for that sort of thing and they both knew it.

They kicked around the Giants for a while.

Morgan hated Eli.

"Today's a good day," he said sagely. "Next week he'll look like shit again. The guy's erratic. You can't count on him."

Jimmy reminded him of the Super Bowl he'd won.

It was hard to argue with that.

Morgan did the best he could.

CHAPTER 59
KATHY O'BRIEN
THE CAYMAN ISLANDS

Kathy was halfway down the stairs. The heat was beating down on her like a blast furnace. At the bottom were a couple of policemen checking passports. Kathy saw them when she stepped out of the plane, but paid them no mind. Why should she? They were checking everyone's passport so there was no reason to be concerned. In fact the thought never entered her mind. All she could think about was getting high and laid.

They were coal black, these policemen, with gleaming white teeth and bright white eyes, wearing open necked white shirts with epaulettes, creased white shorts with black belts, and white caps with black peaks and red bands. They were starched and polished and sparkled and shone in the brightness of the floodlights.

Kathy handed her passport to one of them, a young man with a smile that melted her heart. He looked at it and his beautiful smile disappeared. He said something to his partner she didn't understand and the next thing she knew she was being led away with a policeman on either side of her, guiding her towards a white, two-story building with an orange tiled roof.

She asked them what was going on?

Why was she being arrested?

Was she being arrested?

No one would talk.

She thought it was for being drunk and disorderly. It was all her fogged up brain could come up with. What else had she done?

They put her in a locked cell and left her there without saying a word.

An hour later the American Consul, a courtly looking older looking man in a white linen suit and a Panama hat, came to see her and explained the situation. She was being extradited to the United States, he told her in a patrician voice. A warrant had been issued for her arrest.

"On what charge?" she wanted to know.

"Murder."

"And who am I supposed to have murdered?"

A rustling of papers as the consul consulted his notes.

"Crawford Taylor," he said.

She sat there in silence staring at the man in the linen suit, processing the predicament she'd found herself in.

Then she said, "Lawyer."

And that was all she said.

Over and over again.

It took the NYPD two days to get her out of there. She spent most of that time in a Cayman Island Immigration holding cell along with a middle-aged Russian woman with gas problems, a white American college student stoned out of her mind, and two attractive looking Jamaican hookers. She was the oldest, Kathy, by far. And the biggest. So they left her alone. Not so the American student. They cleaned her out that first night and took everything off of her including her underwear and left her with cast offs and a black eye. Kathy might have been able to help, but she was passed out on a bench in the corner of the cell and didn't wake up until morning. By then the damage had been done. Everyone pretended nothing happened, the American student included. And life, such as it was, went on.

They had one toilet between them, but at least it had a door. The food was inedible and no one ate it. The coffee was black and they existed on that. There was no shower and after two days the smell in the holding cell was not to be believed.

On Monday morning Kathy was put on a plane back to New York in the company of a U.S. Marshal. He was a huge black guy, an ex-football player and Marine who served two tours in Iraq. U.S. Marshal Creasy Robinson was 34 and a recent divorcee with no children. Reason for the divorce? Creasy couldn't keep his dick in his pants. Enough said.

When Kathy O'Brien set eyes on Creasy Robinson those horny feelings she had just before she was arrested rekindled themselves in the form of a hot flush and a moistness in her nethers.

They were seated at the back of the plane. The plane was empty and there was no one sitting near them. Kathy was starving. All she had since her arrest was black coffee. The plane offered nothing free except coffee, tea, and soda. She got Creasy to part with $50 and selected a fruit plate, two chicken sandwiches, three packets of chips and three sodas. When she finished she was still hungry, but Creasy was tapped out so that was the end of feeding time.

She needed to go to the bathroom. Once inside she cleaned herself up as best she could. A 'strip wash' was what her daddy used to call it. He'd strip to the waist and use a washcloth to clean himself. There was no washcloth so Kathy used paper towels, but she didn't stop above the waist. She pulled down her jeans and panties and polished up her privates, just in case.

Back in the seat she said she was cold and needed a blanket, then another, and that's when the campaign began in earnest. First an accidental arm touching. Then one of the blankets got draped over his leg. Then she feigned sleep and ended up resting her head on his shoulder. Then a hand found itself on his knee. Then began moving higher.

U.S. Marshal Creasy Robinson was horny as hell. Since the divorce pussy had been hard to come by, probably because his head wasn't in the game. But that had nothing to do with him being horny. He was always horny, wasn't that what the divorce was all about? But he'd been experiencing a dry spell. He figured it was lack of effort. He missed his wife was the truth of the matter and he was sorry for the cluster fuck he'd made of their lives.

Enter Kathy O'Brien.

He was aware of what the prisoner was up to from the get-go. The way she looked at him when the authorities handed her over. Her faux-sexy walk when they got on the plane. The softness of her voice whenever she spoke to him. The fluttering of her eyes when she made conversation. And the lightness of that first brush against his dick that was bursting out of his pants. And he would have let her, you know, do whatever she wanted. It's not like he's never done it before. But Kathy O'Brien was hard to look at. She was over forty and had that mean look on her jowly face whenever he wasn't looking at her. And there was that big ass of hers and those floppy titties. No sir. This girl was just plain ugly and on top of that she smelled bad. He wanted no part of her and that's exactly what he told her as she was going for her second pass at his aching Johnson.

Just as she was about to make contact, he leaned over to whisper in her ear.

She closed her eyes dreamily, waiting for those magic words.

And he said, "If you touch my dick again I'm gonna break your fucking arm."

Those were the last words they exchanged until U.S. Marshal Creasy Robinson handed Kathy O'Brien over to the NYPD who were waiting for them at Kennedy Airport.

CHAPTER 60

MONDAY

It was a big day for the family. Lucy was about to make her reentry into the school world and it looked like she was going to have a lot of support, judging by the calls she was getting. She was starting to feel positive about the whole experience. What a turn around that turned out to be. Everyone was upbeat and Lucy was almost giddy with excitement. She'd never been a popular kid and suddenly she was the center of attention, in a nice way. She only hoped it would last.

So did Jimmy.

Mary too.

They'd know soon enough.

And it was a big day for Jimmy too. He was going down to the City today, he and Eddie, for Kathy O'Brien's interrogation and take down. There was no way she was getting out of it this time. No sir, not this time. The evidence was too overwhelming. This time they had her for sure.

Breakfast was great: pancakes and fruit salad, and bacon. Lots of bacon. Syrup. Butter. Coffee, juice and jelly.

Everyone was upbeat.

And smiling.

And excited.

At the office Jimmy futzed about and drank a lot of coffee as he anxiously waited for Morgan's call, which came at 12:00.

"Kathy landed," he said. "You still in?"

"Sure."

"They're processing her as we speak. If you leave now you'll get here when she does.

"I'm on my way," said Jimmy. "I'm gonna see Mal Finkelstein later in the day, you wanna come along?"

"I'll pass on that. We got a lot going on here."

"I'll have Eddie with me."

"I like Eddie."

"Me too."

The boys looked good for this one. Jimmy was in another new suit he'd put off wearing. Don't ask why. In Yiddish it's called a mishigas. A craziness. Which is exactly what it was. So today Jimmy looked cool. Dusting off the old moves. Feeling even better than he did when he looked sharper than Kathy O'Brien's lawyer, and that was pretty good.

Mary helped him get it right. Fluttering around him like a moth around a flame. Fixing this. Pulling that. A three-piece dark blue pinstripe. Wool and mohair. We're talking sharp here. With his new Banana Republic white shirt with the up-to-date collar. And the blue silk tie. And the shoes, let's not forget the shoes. Kept in the box for that moment, like the suit, when he got a chance to put on the cape. Like today, for example. Nailing Kathy O'Brien. You want to look good for something like that.

Eddie must have felt the same way because he was all dolled up too in razor-creased grey slacks, a crisp white shirt, a black sport coat and shiny, shiny shoes.

What a pair.

Jimmy put a disc in the player when they got on the road. Muddy Waters. The blues. Music to contemplate to. If it were up to Eddie they'd be listening to oldies. Jimmy was tired of the oldies. There were only so many of them and they seemed to be playing them all the time. The Beatles. The Stones. Some Elton John and Pink Floyd. Enough already. How many times can you hear the same stuff? They were on the jukebox in the diner. And a couple of the bars. The same songs wherever he went. He turned up the volume to drown out Eddie's moaning and dissatisfaction with the driving world around him.

Eddie put the light on the roof and got off on driving up to slowpokes and flashing them. He had a way with the traffic lights too. Green 80% of the time. The same ratio as Jimmy only in reverse. It hardly seemed fair. They made record time too, which added insult to injury, and got to the station house just as Kathy O'Brien arrived.

An assistant DA got there at the same time. A young looking 35-year old with fair hair that was thinning prematurely.

Morgan and Tim greeted everyone at the desk and, after introductions and handshakes, led them to an interview room and ushered them inside.

Morgan walked Jimmy to a corner of the room out of earshot and whispered in his ear, "Nice threads."

Jimmy had been a small blip on Morgan's happiness radar. He wondered what the consequences would be if Jimmy looked like he did on Friday. Would it rub off on him? Did he care? And how would the ADA see it? It was nothing he'd talk to Jimmy about because he didn't think it was any of his business. Jimmy was entitled to do whatever he wanted, including how he dressed. Which was the reasoning he'd settled on before Jimmy showed up looking so cool.

"What happened on Friday?" Morgan whispered.

Jimmy didn't know what he was talking about.

"Friday?" he asked.

"You looked like a train wreck."

Jimmy made a face. He'd forgotten what he looked like on Friday.

Morgan hadn't.

"I didn't know I was coming to the City," Jimmy said feeling his face begin to flush.

"What's that mean?" said Morgan.

"Friday's slob day," Jimmy whispered. "If I knew I was coming to the City I'd have dressed better."

It sounded ridiculous even to him.

Morgan thought there was a lot about Jimmy he didn't understand.

They were all looking at them. Eddie, Tim, the ADA, Kathy and the lawyer. Waiting. Some sitting. Some standing. No one talking. Just looking at them.

Morgan smiled.

Jimmy smiled.

They walked over to the interview table. There was an exchanging of cards and the scraping of chairs, as everyone got comfortable.

Morgan got the ball rolling by reading Kathy her rights. The Marshal did it when he got her from the Cayman authorities, but Morgan wanted to have it on record. He informed everyone the meeting was being recorded.

Lawyer and client huddled.

The lawyer said, "For the record, can you tell me why my client has been brought here?"

Morgan said, "Your client's been arrested for the murder of Crawford Taylor."

"I did no such thing," Kathy spat contemptuously.

The lawyer patted her arm.

She gritted her teeth. If he did it again she'd kill him.

"Were you at Crawford Taylor's apartment last Thursday night from 8.32pm to 9.05pm?" asked Morgan.

Kathy looked at her lawyer who nodded she should answer.

"I was," she said.

"Why?"

"I wanted to say goodbye."

"Goodbye?"

"I was leaving for the Cayman Islands. I wanted to thank him for his help and say goodbye."

"Thank him?"

"He put up the money for my bail and got me my lawyer," she turned to her attorney and gave him a brief smile. "He really helped me out."

"Why?"

"We're old friends."

Jimmy smiled at that. They were old friends.

"How so?" he asked.

"I was his private nurse for his back, knee and neck surgeries. We've known each other for years.

Jimmy said, "So it was Crawford Taylor who got you to Gillie Fader?"

"Again with the Gillie Fader," said the lawyer angrily. "She's already told you she doesn't know any Gillie Fader.

Morgan said, "But you agree you were in Crawford's apartment on Thursday night."

"I do."

"What happened?"

She looked at him quizzically.

"What happened?" asked Morgan. "Did you have a fight?"

"No we didn't have a fight."

"What then?"

The meeting with Crawford did not go the way she'd planned and, after a big fight, ended up with her telling him not to get cute. She told him she'd put a package together and left it with a friend as an insurance policy in case something happened to her.

Crawford said, "You don't have any friends."

She said, "You'd be surprised."

Crawford said, "Let's just be clear here. We're both vulnerable to each other. So there's no point in one of us ratting out the other. We agree on that, right? "

"Agreed" she said, liking the 'we' part. Enjoying her sudden elevation to an equal with this man she considered to be a genius. They could each destroy the other. But not, she thought if something happens to you first. Then I'll be free and clear.

"I did not do this," she said to the room. Looking from one to the other. Trying to make them believe her.

Morgan checked his notes then looked at the lawyer.

"The doorman and deskman positively identify your client as Crawford Taylor's visitor at the time he was murdered. Her prints are all over the apartment. We just got the DNA report. The lipstick marks on the cigarettes and the joint we recovered from the scene are hers. The lipstick on the wine glass and a screwed up napkin also recovered from the scene are hers. Her pubic hair was found in Crawford's bathroom." He looked up from his notes. "What's the deal with that, Kathy? Jimmy here thinks you've got a bladder infection. He says that's why you're always going to the bathroom. I'm more concerned with whether you know you're going bald down there. We're talking about a lot of hair in Crawford's bathroom."

She glared at him.

"We figured if it was us we'd know. How about you? Do you know you're molting down there like a parakeet?"

Kathy did not.

The lawyer said, "Does this have anything to do with anything?"

Morgan said it did not. Really. He was just curious.

Kathy figured she'd better get herself tested. Hair loss was never a good sign. She thought it could be stress. She'd definitely been under a lot of stress recently.

"Crawford had no more visitors after you," said Morgan. "You're the last person to see him alive. Now he's dead. Suffocated with a pillow. A method you seem to be comfortable with."

"What does that mean, Detective? My client has yet to be found guilty of any crime. I repeat, any crime. So to my knowledge there is no method of killing that my client is 'comfortable with,' and I object most strenuously to you suggesting there is. We've had this argument before with your colleague." He looked at Jimmy. "There is no evidence my client has killed anyone, so lay off the cheap shots."

Morgan ignored him. They were not in court and he could say what he liked. He looked at Kathy dispassionately.

"All the evidence points to you killing him."

She looked horrified.

"I did not," she said and looked at her attorney imploring him to say something, but there was nothing to say.

Tim said, "Then who did?"

"How should I know?"

"But not you?"

"No."

"In spite of this overwhelming evidence?" said Morgan.

"What evidence?" asked the lawyer skeptically.

Morgan didn't answer him. Instead he gave Jimmy the nod and the two of them went outside.

"Whaddya think?" Morgan asked him in the hallway.

Jimmy said, "She's good isn't she? Butter wouldn't melt in her mouth. The only thing that bothers me is why so clumsy? She's been so careful up until now."

"People do crazy things after they kill someone," said Morgan. "She probably didn't plan it. Maybe he got aggressive and scared her, and that's when she slipped him the Ketamine."

"What Ketamine?"

"He had Ketamine in him, enough to put out an elephant. It's in the ME's report. I got it just before we went in." He fumbled around in his inside pocket and produced a fax and handed it to Jimmy.

Jimmy scanned it and handed it back.

"So they fought. He gets violent. She gets scared. Slips him the K. He passes out. She helps him on his way with a pillow, panics, and gets the hell out of Dodge."

"S'about it," said Morgan. "I like it."

Jimmy did too.

They went back inside.

Everyone watched them as they sat down.

Morgan handed the ADA the ME's fax, then started up again.

"Tell me about the Ketamine?" he asked.

Kathy said, "What Ketamine?"

"The Ketamine you slipped Crawford."

"And why did I do this?" she asked. Belligerent now.

"So you could put a pillow over his face and kill him."

"Why would I want to do that, he was my friend?"

"He knew you killed Gillie Fader."

"Again with the fucking Gillie," she said angrily. "I told you before, I don't know who this Gillie Fader is."

"I really must protest," said the lawyer. "My client stated under oath that she has no knowledge of Gillie Fader. This line of questioning must stop."

All eyes fixed on him. This mousy looking lawyer with dandruff on his collar and skin tags on his face.

"You've got this all wrong," said Kathy. Looking each one of them in the eye. "I stopped by Crawford's to say goodbye and thank him. That's it. End of story. I love him. He's my friend. Why would I want to kill the only friend I have?" Then the ice broke and she teared up. Then she began to cry. Softly. No act. Real tears. Real emotion. "Why would I want to kill him?" she asked them. "He was my friend."

Morgan passed her a tissue.

After she cleaned herself up he said, "So let me get this right. You say you met with Crawford in his apartment between 8:30 and 9:00 last Thursday night. There was no fight between you or any other unpleasantness. Neither did you put any Ketamine in his drink. And he was alive when you left?"

"Yes."

"And you saw no one in the hall after you left or while you were waiting for the elevator."

"Correct."

"What about the lobby?"

"It was busy when I left."

"What's that mean?"

"There were a lot of people in the lobby."

"Like who?"

She thought.

"Some restaurant delivery guys. A couple of dog walkers." Her eyes floated to the ceiling as she thought about it some more. "People were leaving, people were coming in. The doorman was outside trying to flag a cab. It was busy."

"Why do they know what time you left?"

"I waved to the desk guy and made sure he saw me, and when I got outside I waved at the doorman. Those boys were real nice to me on the way in. A girl likes that sort of thing."

The people on the law enforcement side of the table looked at her like she was crazy.

Jimmy said, "I don't believe you."

"What's not to believe? Ask the desk guy, or the doorman. They'll tell you."

"That part's true," said Jimmy. "We have their statements to back it up. It's the rest that's crap. All the evidence points to you killing him. I think you had some sort of fight with him. Maybe he threatened you, or intimidated you. Something got you scared. That's why you slipped him the K. You put it in his drink to knock him out because you were frightened of him. You might even be able to convince a jury it was self-defense. That he was going to come after you and hurt you or maybe even kill you and you had no alternative. When he passed out you put a pillow over his face and got out of there."

Everyone on the law enforcement side liked it. They all nodded like bobble-heads on the back of a car.

The lawyer did not.

Neither did Kathy.

"This is a frame up," she declared. "If I killed him why would I draw so much attention to myself when I was leaving?"

"You got me," said Morgan. "People do strange things after they kill someone. It's like kryptonite. They think it gives them powers of invincibility. Conversely some people, the most organized and calculating, get freaked out of their minds and barely know what they're doing."

"Well I never killed anyone," she said petulantly.

"So you say," said Morgan.

"It's a frame-up," she said.

"No it's not," said Morgan. "Find me someone else that was there. Give me a witness that saw someone besides you. We spoke to the delivery guys. And the dog walkers. And the people coming and going in the lobby. Everyone is accounted for. No one saw anyone else there except for you. And everyone remembers you."

"What about the security cameras?" said the lawyer.

"What about them?"

"Did they show anyone else in the lobby?"

"The building doesn't have security cameras. They say they're getting them soon, but they don't have them now. Next door has security cameras. They show your client coming and going at the times we've already established and your client has admitted to."

Morgan kept coming at her from different directions. Then Jimmy had a turn. And Timmy from Brooklyn followed up, but they couldn't shift her. She kept saying she didn't do it and the lawyer kept objecting to everything they asked her. What else were they going to do? Deny everything and admit to nothing. SOP. But this was a tight box they had her in and the evidence against her was overwhelming. While a jury might find reasonable doubt with one piece of evidence or another, when all the pieces were knitted together they made a compelling case.

Morgan called a recess.

Everybody on his side of the table trooped outside.

In the hallway Morgan said to the ADA, "So whaddya think?"

The ADA gave the knot of his tie a confident pinch and said, "Open and shut."

The ADA looked at Jimmy.

"You?"

Jimmy said he thought they had her cold.

'Timmy from Brooklyn' piped up.

"If we found someone who saw something I'd be tempted to believe her, she really seemed to like this guy and those tears were genuine and she did appear to be all choked up, but no one did. In which case you gotta believe she killed him. There is no one else."

They all looked at Eddie.

Eddie hated her from the minute he clapped eyes on her at Magdalena's house. She'd managed to slip out of everything they'd thrown at her. All he cared about was if she could she wriggle out of this one. He didn't think so and he told them so.

The ADA was pleased and gave his tie knot another pinch. They were all on the same page with no objections. When they went back inside he took over the meeting and, after a few cursory questions, charged Kathy O'Brien with Crawford Taylor's murder.

Kathy went berserk and had to be restrained. After she'd calmed down, she was processed and eventually arraigned where she was denied bail as a flight risk and sent to the Tombs to await trial, all the time professing her innocence and insisting she'd been framed.

Morgan wanted to celebrate and take them to Katz's Deli on the lower East Side, but Jimmy begged off. He had that appointment with Mal Finkelstein and he didn't want to be late. He took a rain check and told Morgan he'd let him know what went on, then he and Eddie drove down to the garment center.

CHAPTER 61

MAL FINKELSTEIN

Jimmy made the appointment with Mal Finkelstein earlier in the day under the guise of needing to cover a couple of details on the Austin Kenner murder case. The drive downtown was hard to endure because of Eddie's constant swearing at his fellow drivers, especially the cabbies who knew no fear.

But then neither did Eddie.

On the way Jimmy told him why they were going, that he thought Austin Kenner was blackmailing Mal.

"Who told you that?" said Eddie as he swerved to miss a cyclist.

Jimmy's heart was in his mouth. If they didn't get there soon he thought he'd have a heart attack.

"A little birdie," he said.

"Birdie my ass," said Eddie. "Dupree told you, didn't he?"

Jimmy was looking up, down, and sideways, anything not to look straight ahead at obstacles that seemed to be hurtling towards them at an alarming speed.

"I can't tell you that."

He was about to tell him to slow down when Eddie slammed on the brakes to avoid breaking a light.

Eddie looked at him and smiled.

"S'gonna be fine Jimmy. I'll get you there in one piece, I promise you."

Jimmy wasn't so sure. He cracked open a window to get some fresh air, but it didn't help any. He was sure he was going to throw up.

Eddie said, "What else did Dupree tell you?"

They started up again, but now the traffic was jammed up and Eddie could only crawl along with everyone else. Jimmy was silently grateful and began to relax a little.

"I never said it was Dupree. And even if it was, it's best you don't know."

"And why is that, Kemosabe?"

"You know why. If it ever gets into court you can say you don't know and it'll be the truth."

Eddie saw a gap in the traffic and punched the accelerator, narrowly missing a pedestrian who was trying to cross the street. Jimmy's stomach heaved but he managed to hold it together. Eventually they made it to their destination in one piece, albeit a little worse for wear. They put the car in a lot and marveled at the cost of such an exercise, wondering how people could afford to do it on a regular basis.

When they got to Mal Finkelstein's office they almost had to put Eddie away when he laid eyes on Mal's voluptuous receptionist. She spoke to them in her syrupy purr and it was all Eddie could do not to make a complete fool of himself. He was well on the way with his open-mouthed gawk and the glaze in his eyes.

Jimmy stepped in to avoid any more embarrassment, but not before the receptionist gave Eddie a wink in appreciation of his appreciation. She got up to show them into Mal's office, wiggling her way ahead of them to announce their arrival.

Mal's office was filled with so many orchids and flower arrangements the place looked like a greenhouse.

"From people wishing Mr. Finkelstein congratulations after the show," the receptionist confided when she saw their reaction. Then she vamped her way back to the reception area, taking Eddie's heart along with her.

Mal looked like a man without a worry in the world.

He wore brown slacks and a tailored white shirt that was, as usual, open a button too many, showing off his hairy chest and the gold medallion. He stood up to greet them, shook hands and indicated they should sit in the chairs on the other side of his desk. He offered them coffee or Snapple or anything else they might want.

Eddie wanted the receptionist, but he kept that to himself.

Jimmy declined for the both of them and gave Mal a card.

"How did the launch go?" he asked.

Mal beamed and looked around the office at the greenery and color that graced every surface and took up a lot of the floor.

"Great, thanks."

And so it was. A big hit. And that was not just him talking. *Women's Wear* loved it. So did the *Times*. The fashion magazines were over the moon and several shoots had already been booked featuring his clothes. And orders? Beyond anyone's expectation. He was the hit of the season and the toast of the town and it was nice to be back on Broadway again. Everything about him screamed winner from the bounce in his step to the quickness of his smile. All the worries and fights to bring the line to market had disappeared to produce the man they were seeing before them. Oozing self-confidence and glowing not only from his bottled tan, but from what a win will do to anyone.

Make them seem larger than life.

Even to themselves.

They exchanged a little banter and even Eddie got in a line or two, then Jimmy moved on to the mission at hand. Austin Kenner. Did Mal have any idea he'd killed a man while he was working side by side with him? Was there any inkling? Some hint?

And Mal telling him what he told Connie, that there was no sign. And how Austin had stepped up his game during that period. Looking sharper than sharp. And so on. And so forth.

Jimmy leading him on and getting him comfortable, which is when he slipped it in. When Mal was full of his success and bonhomie.

"How come you gave Austin a quarter of a million dollars a couple of weeks ago Mr. Finkelstein?"

Mal swallowed hard. Caught off guard. There was an ominous silence as he worked it through. That he'd done nothing wrong here. Austin was the one who'd kited the check on him. Kiting's against the law, especially if the fucking thing bounces. He owed Austin no loyalty or anything else for that matter. What he owed Austin was the same thing Austin gave him. Nothing.

Jimmy said, "We got the impression he was blackmailing you?"

Mal had to smile at that.

Then he said, "No he wasn't blackmailing me."

"What then?"

"That money was against a post-dated check he gave me for the same quarter of a million dollars. Austin said he had a real estate deal and his investor's checks hadn't cleared. He wanted me to cover it. I know, I know. It sounds risky." He saw the skepticism on their faces. "But I've done it many times before for him."

"Why?"

"Well, he's a loyal employee for one thing, and because I could."

Jimmy said, "How many times?"

Mal thought.

"It's got to be at least a dozen. Probably a lot more over the years, and I have to tell you Detective, there's never been any trouble. Until now, that is. It's always a real estate deal. He's got a line on foreclosures, so he's got to move quickly. He does his deal, we deposit his check and everyone goes home happy."

"Huh," said Jimmy.

"Anyway. This one bounced. He kited a check on me. Isn't that the term? I've got it here someplace," He rummaged around in a drawer and came up with an envelope and handed it to Jimmy.

Jimmy smiled. So that was it. Not blackmail. Check kiting. It wouldn't send Austin away for life, but it would put him away for a while and that was a good thing. No slap on the wrist for this one, Austin. This time you're going down.

He gave Eddie a satisfied grin.

Eddie grinned back. He didn't like Austin very much either.

Jimmy said, "Austin didn't buy real estate with that money, you know that, don't you Mr. Finkelstein?"

Mal leaned back in his chair looking puzzled.

"What did he do with it?"

"He bought options."

Mal couldn't believe it.

"He doesn't have a real estate portfolio?"

"Not as far as we can tell."

"Never?"

"Except for the house he's living in. Other than that he's got nothing."

"You're saying every time I fronted him some money, he bought options with it?"

"I can't say what he did in the past, sir, but he certainly did this time."

Mal ran a hand over his face. Then he called the receptionist on the intercom and asked her to bring him a Snapple. He was addicted to the kiwi strawberry flavor. When something came up that jarred him, he liked to chug one down.

He looked at Jimmy and Eddie.

"Is there anything she can bring you?"

Eddie was thinking something crude. He'd fallen in love with her and was trying to come up with a way to ask her to marry him.

Jimmy shook his head.

"We're fine, thanks."

The receptionist came in with Mal's Snapple and left with Eddie's heart.

Mal drank his Snapple down and appraised Jimmy. Stewing on what he'd just been told.

"So what happened?" he said angrily.

"Happened?"

"Yeah. Where's my quarter of a mil?"

Jimmy had to be careful here. He'd already said things he shouldn't have. If push came to shove not only could he get into trouble, so could Dupree. People might want to know how he got this information.

"I'll ask him next time I see him," he said waving the envelope around. "Which will be very soon thanks to you. I'm assuming you'll be willing to testify if it ever goes to trial?"

Mal thought about the torture Austin put him through. Not returning his calls. Leaving him to twist in the wind after all he'd done for him. So much for loyalty.

"What happened to the options?" he asked.

"He seems to be sitting on a lot of money," said Jimmy. "So you have to assume they went up."

Mal would have his attorney look into it. There was a lot of money at stake here and it would be just great if he could get it back.

"I'll testify," he said. Furious that Austin put his launch in jeopardy and happy to do anything to get him back for that.

"We'll also need a statement from you," said Jimmy. "Speak to your lawyer and have him help you put one together, then send it to us. Either that or we'll take it from you now."

Mal said he'd speak to his attorney, if they didn't mind.

They did not.

"You need to have your receptionist make a copy of this for your records." Jimmy handed him the envelope with Austin's check.

Mal called the receptionist and told her what he wanted done.

She swept in and out leaving behind a refreshing slipstream of her delicate fragrance.

Eddie's heart soared.

Jimmy said, "There's a good chance it won't get to court, Mr. Finkelstein. They usually cop a plea on something like this. It saves a fortune in legal fees and gets them a reduction in sentence. At least that's what usually happens, unless the accused gets feisty and believes he can get away with it. How Austin thinks he's gonna get away with this is beyond me."

Everyone grinned at that. Mission accomplished. The guilty would be punished and justice would be done.

Mal was all smiles and happiness.

There was even a chance he'd get his money back. That was something he never considered. There was something about payback that was really a delight.

All those people who thought he'd fail now had to eat his shit. And the same went for Austin. How dare he play him for a sucker and hang him out to dry.

Jimmy moved on.

"I wanna show you some pictures, Mr. Finkelstein. See if there's anyone you recognize or heard Austin talk about."

Mal had no objections. He was still gloating over the chance he was going to get his money back

Jimmy reached into the envelope he'd brought and produced an 8x10 glossy of Gillie Fader.

He placed the photo in front of Mal.

"Do you know this guy?"

Mal picked it up for a closer look and shook his head.

"His name is Gillie Fader. Does the name mean anything to you, Mr. Finkelstein? Did Austin ever mention him?"

Mal said, "Never," and handed the photograph back to Jimmy.

Jimmy followed up with a picture of Kathy O'Brien.

Mal looked at it and shook his head.

"Her name is Kathy O'Brien. Nothing?"

Mal said no and handed the picture back.

"How about this one." Jimmy handed him an 8x10 of Lamont Dubois.

Mal gave it a quick look and handed it back.

"I've never seen him before."

"Lamont Dubois. Does that name ring a bell?"

Mal didn't even have to think about it.

"'Fraid not," he said.

Jimmy took out an 8x10 of Crawford Taylor and passed it to him.

"Ever see this guy? This is Crawford Taylor."

Mal looked at it.

A siren went off somewhere. No. It wasn't a siren. It was a ringing in his ears. He shook his head to try and clear it. Then he told them he'd never seen the man before.

"We understand, Austin had some dealings with him. Did he ever mention it to you?"

"No," Mal said. "He did not."

"Crawford Taylor's a money lender," said Jimmy. "Austin owed him a lot of money. That's what the shooting was about in Columbia. Crawford sent his goons to collect and Austin panicked. Why do you think he had to go to Crawford Taylor for money, Mr. Finkelstein?"

Mal had no idea, because he had no idea. He couldn't imagine why Austin needed money. He got paid a fortune and so far as he was concerned was well off. Or was he?

"You know," he said giving it some more thought, "this was the first time Austin asked me to cover a check so close together. Normally it's about once a year, sometimes longer. Six months ago he asked me to do the same thing. I put his check in four days after I fronted him the money and it cleared. He said he had a property lined up and needed to act fast."

Jimmy asked, "How much for?"

"A hundred thousand."

That was the original amount Austin said he owed Crawford Taylor, thought Jimmy.

"That's about the time the market took a nosedive," he said.

Mal agreed, it was.

"Would you remember what his demeanor was like back then?"

Mal shook his head. He did not.

"There's been so much going on I can't think that far back. I've got enough trouble thinking about last week."

Jimmy said he understood. "But maybe, if he was playing the stock market and got caught short, he went to Crawford to help him cover the check. If that check bounced he'd run the risk of losing his job and his credibility and he's got a wife and child to support not to mention his mortgage and whatever else he owes. You can see why he'd go the shylock route if he couldn't cover it."

Mal agreed. It made sense.

"I would've fired him," he said.

"And you?"

"Me what?"

"Have you ever heard of Crawford Taylor?"

Mal hesitated.

Then, "No. I never heard of the guy.

"Austin never mentioned him to you?"

"No."

Jimmy looked at Eddie.

Eddie looked back at him and took out his notebook. Making a show of it. Then, slowly and deliberately, he reached for one of Mal's pens stuffed in a mug on his desk.

They stared at Mal. Waiting for him to say something.

Mal was unsettled by this sudden display of officialdom. The ringing in his ears stopped, but now he was having a hard time swallowing. He took a long gulp of Snapple and emptied the bottle. He wished he had another one and contemplated asking Jill to bring one in.

Jimmy said, "Mr. Finkelstein, when I asked you if you knew Crawford Taylor you said no. That was a lie wasn't it?"

Jimmy waited for his answer.

When none was forthcoming he said, "Mr. Finkelstein, your name came up on Crawford Taylor's computer as someone who owes him $350,000."

Mal was picking at the label on the Snapple bottle. It was a habit of his when he was under pressure. The paper was damp from the condensation and it was easy to peel off. He liked to twiddle bits of it between his fingers and found it soothing. He continued to stare into space. Not saying anything. But his head had begun to pound.

Jimmy said, "Care to comment, Mr. Finkelstein?"

Mal did not care to comment. His body had become a mass of sensitive nerve endings all tingling and sizzling at the same time.

"You must have met him if you owed him money?"

Mal still didn't speak. Instead he turned his chair slightly and stared out of the window. It was as if he was being spoken to from a long distance and he was having a hard time hearing. Pulses started up, especially in the corner of one of his eyes. He rubbed it to make it stop, but it didn't seem to make any difference.

"He's dead," said Jimmy. "You know that don't you?"

Mal appeared shocked, although he'd been looking that way for a while now. Jimmy thought it was since Crawford Taylor's name came up.

Eddie did too.

Ever since Crawford's name came up.

Mal said he did not, in a strange and distant voice.

"Did not what, Mr. Finkelstein? Did not meet him? Or did not know he was dead?"

Mal licked his lips. God, they were dry. And his throat; it felt like a vice had a hold of it."

"I didn't know he was dead," he croaked.

Jimmy and Eddie looked at each other.

What was going on?

"It was in all the papers," said Jimmy. "How could you not know?"

Mal turned back to face them.

"I've been busy," he said. "The launch. The parties. Who's got time for the papers?"

"The TV then. It's been all over the news."

"I don't watch TV."

"But you owed him that money, didn't you? And, as I understand it, he also had an ownership position in your business? You put it up as collateral, isn't that so?"

Mal nodded. Slowly. Eyes darting from one to the other.

"So you lied?" said Jimmy.

Mal looked cornered. Then he looked contrite. Then he went for his best posture. Sympathy. Not for nothing was he a great salesman. He sighed then took a deep breath like he was about to dive into the deep end.

"Look, Detective. If people know a shylock has a piece of my business they'll never work with me again. It's not the sort of thing I want to get around, you can understand that, can't you?"

"I do," said Jimmy. "But I've got nothing to do with your business. Why would you lie to me?"

Mal spread his palms out in a gesture of helplessness.

"I don't want to see this on the front pages of *The Post* or *The Daily News*, especially now I'm on a roll. Just the hint of a scandal can stop my forward progress like that." He snapped his fingers. "I've seen it happen. Lots of times. A leak. A word. Things get out and people talk. It's human nature. And not to be rude about the police department, but those places are like sieves when it comes to stories like mine. Information leaks out all the time and this is the kind of stuff people love to read about. If that happens, I'll be ruined. So it's better to lie and hope it goes away."

Jimmy looked at Eddie.

It made sense.

Eddie put the notebook away and the pen back in the cup. There was nothing going on here.

"So, was Crawford a friend of yours?" asked Jimmy.

"Not really."

"What then?"

"Business associate."

Mal began to twiddle the Snapple label some more. His desk was littered with little rolled up pieces of paper. He licked his lips. God he was thirsty. He picked up the phone and asked for another Snapple and to bring Austin's check back for the Detective.

He looked at them.

"Something?"

Jimmy said they were fine.

The girl came in, gave Jimmy the envelope and Mal his Snapple. She cleaned up the mess on her boss's desk and left.

Eddie stared after her.

Mal guzzled the Snapple down. A calmer look returned to his face.

"I gotta say, Mr. Finklestein, for someone who didn't know his partner was dead, you don't seem very surprised, or upset for that matter."

Eddie was nodding. He'd noticed the same thing himself.

Mal asked, "How did he die?"

"He was murdered."

A beat.

Then, "Oh."

And there it was. If you've been around a while you know stuff. What that is is hard to explain, but every now and again it comes to the fore. Like now, for instance. After the word murder and Mal's reaction to it. How he gripped the Snapple bottle and the narrowing of his eyes. There was a body language too, a tensing, subtle, but there to someone who knows about such things. Someone who wasn't looking for anything, but found it just the same.

"That's awful," said Mal with a little more emotion and gulped down the rest of his Snapple.

A sheen of sweat appeared on his brow. He peeled more paper from the label and began to twiddle it. He crossed his legs and a foot went up and down in a rhythm that made no sense. Was this the same guy they were talking to when they first came in? It didn't look like him. This person was sweating and twiddling and fidgeting and fussing and his face had clouded into a mask of forced confidence.

Eddie wondered what was going on?

So did Jimmy.

"Tell us about Crawford Taylor. Mr. Finkelstein," he asked.

Mal looked uncomfortable.

"What do you want to know?"

"Did you like him?"

"Sure."

"How long have you known him?"

"No so long. A couple of months or so."

"Where did you meet him?"

Mal told him how they met at Balthazar and became friends and hung out and partied.

"When was the last time you saw him?"

There it was again; a subtle catching of the breath and this pause. Not a pause really, more like a skipping of a beat. Another beat.

"Last week sometime," said Mal.

"Could you be more specific?"

Mal made a show of thinking.

"Tuesday, I think."

"Where?"

"Where what?"

"Where did you see him?"

Mal shifted in his seat and screwed up his face. Then he shook his head.

"You know," he said. "I really can't remember."

"That's all right," said Jimmy. "It's not important. When did you talk to him last?"

And there it was. Again. A half beat so feint it almost wasn't there, but Jimmy caught it. He'd caught them all and they didn't add up.

"Well," said Mal, trying to come up with an answer. "We speak on the phone all the time."

"Okay," said Jimmy. "When was the last time you spoke to him?"

Mal shook his head. He couldn't remember.

Then, "Probably Thursday."

"That's the day he died, you know that, right?"

Mal said he didn't.

"Would you remember what you talked about?"

"I'm sure it was about the opening. It was the next day. Friday."

Mal was in fidgeting overdrive. Twiddling. Leg bouncing. A hand worked its way through his hair and there was a look on his face of extreme discomfort.

It made no sense. Unless….

But that didn't make sense either.

He turned to Eddie and looked at his watch.

"It's getting late, Eddie," and gave him a wink. "We're right in the middle of the rush hour. It's gonna take forever to get the car out. I'm thinking you should get it now while I finish up here and I'll meet you in the front of the building."

Eddie knew what that meant. He'd seen it before, a lot of times. Jimmy wanted to be alone with Mal and Eddie could see why. The man was falling apart before their eyes and Jimmy wanted a little one-on-one time to get to the bottom of it. People don't like facing two people in a situation like that. It's intimidating and frightens them, which makes them less likely to open up.

Like now for instance.

With him gone Jimmy would find out what was going on. That was what usually happened. Eddie stood up, shook Mal's hand, and was out of there. He lingered at the front desk to chat up the receptionist, listen to her husky voice, and inhale her delicate fragrance. But the phone rang and she had no more time for him save for another wink that drove him wild and would, he was sure, keep him going for months to come.

CHAPTER 62

JIMMY AND MAL

After Eddie left, Jimmy leaned back and looked at Mal, trying to decide what to say and how to say it. You could hear the hum of the City outside. Cars honked. A police siren went off close by. Then two. A fire engine's klaxon blared in the distance. He could hear the phone ringing in the reception and the receptionist answering it with her sexy spiel.

While Jimmy was looking at Mal, Mal was looking at him. His face was a blank. His tan seemed to have faded leaving him with a greenish pallor that didn't look quite right. The sheen of perspiration was a little more obvious and he was holding onto the Snapple like it was a life itself.

Jimmy was picking up a vibe here. You'd have to be blind not to.

"Tell me more," he said, "about that last conversation you had with Crawford on Thursday, Mr. Finkelstein. When exactly did that take place?"

Mal froze. Everything stopped. The twiddling. The leg bouncing. Even his breathing, for a second.

Then, "Why?"

Jimmy didn't answer.

Instead he asked, "Did he seem anxious to you, would you remember that?"

Mal didn't answer.

"Did he say he was expecting someone? A woman, maybe?"

"I… I can't remember."

"What about his tone?"

"What about it?"

"Did he sound nervous? Or scared?"

"I don't know," he snapped. "For God's sake it was last week and so much has happened since then. How can you expect me to remember something like that?"

Jimmy ignored the snit.

"What time was it?"

Mal didn't answer. Again.

"Was it late in the day? Does that sound right?"

"I don't know."

"You don't know?"

"No."

"Earlier then?"

"Oh for God's sake," Mal huffed. "What's the point of this? I've told you everything you want to know. I can't see what this has got to do with anything."

"Well it has, sir. Really. We're trying to get an accurate picture of Mr. Taylor's last moments before he was murdered. This phone call could be very important to our investigation. What exactly did he say to you?"

Mal stared out the window. His leg was bouncing again. He was twiddling again. And he didn't answer Jimmy's question. Again.

"All right," said Jimmy, "What did you say to him?"

No answer.

Jimmy was going around in circles, so he decided to lower the boom.

"Could you tell me where you were last Thursday night Mr. Finkelstein?" and watched Mal's reaction.

But Mal rallied. Again.

Or tried to.

He turned to face Jimmy. Grim.

"Aren't you a little out of your jurisdiction for a question like that, Detective?"

It was the wrong thing to say. It was a product of *Law and Order* or *CSI Anyplace*. An attempt by an amateur to turn the tables on his accuser. It was revelatory and by definition confirmed what Jimmy was beginning to suspect all along: that Mal knew more than he was saying. The thing about amateurs is just that, they're amateurs. They don't know what they're doing. Amateurs commit half the crime in the country, maybe more. Pros know how to handle an interview or a cross-questioning without giving anything away. That's why they're called pros; it's part of their job description and they're pretty good at it. Not so the amateurs. They've got no experience lying to cops except what they've seen on TV or the movies, and that's not the real world. It's a good reason why everyone should stick to what they know.

Jimmy smiled.

"You're right, Mr. Finkelstein. I have nothing to do with this investigation except that Det. Morgan Flynn, the person in charge, is a friend of mine and I'm helping him out. With that in mind, I'd still like to know where you were last Thursday night?"

Mal's heart was jumping out of his chest. He was surprised the detective couldn't hear it, the banging was so loud.

How to answer?

What to say?

Jimmy pressed.

"Tell me about Thursday night Mr. Finkelstein. What were you doing?"

Jimmy wasn't sure what he was going to hear. He was flying on instinct, but you only had to look at Mal to know he was holding back something. Hiding it. Concealing it. But what could it be?

They had Kathy cold for Crawford's murder, or did they?

"I was here," said Mal. Finally. Figuring he had to say something before everything flew completely off the rails. He pealed off another sliver of paper and rolled it between his finger and thumb and looked at Jimmy like a man who was waiting for the officer in charge of the firing squad to say 'Fire'.

"All night?"

"All night."

"Is there anyone who can verify that?"

There was not. There was more twiddling and more sheen on his brow. A big bass drum was banging in his chest and the ringing in his ears had come back.

Jimmy was patient. He sat there looking at Mal. Non-committal. Non-judgmental. Wanting to hear the story and waiting patiently for it to come out.

Mal looked like he was either going to drop dead or spill the beans; there wasn't going to be a middle ground.

He shook his head. No, there was no one who could verify he was here.

"Crawford Taylor was murdered between 8:30 and 9.30 last Thursday night," said Jimmy. "Did you know that?"

A pause. Then a rally of sorts.

"How could I know that if I didn't know he was dead?"

Jimmy nodded. That made sense.

"You know the one thing you haven't asked me, Mr. Finkelstein?" He was going for a 'we're on the same side' tone here, like he was trying to help him.

Mal made a face. Not knowing the answer. Not knowing that thing that would make all of this stop and the cop go away.

"What's that?" he said finally. "What haven't I asked?"

"You never asked me if we caught who did it?"

Mal didn't know what to say. He was having trouble thinking straight. Everything was crowding in on him. Rather than Jimmy making like they were on the same side, Mal was thinking he was looking more like the elephant in the room. A huge fucking elephant sucking every ounce of air out of his office, so he was having a hard time breathing what was left.

Jimmy leaned forward. Like he was sharing a confidence.

"Do you know why I sent Eddie out, Mr. Finkelstein?"

Mal looked perplexed. More questions. What was this, a fucking quiz show? Leave me alone, his brain screamed. Get the fuck out of here and leave me alone.

Jimmy waited for an answer.

Mal said, "To get the car?"

Jimmy shook his head.

Brrrrrrrrrrrrrrrrrp. Wrong answer.

Fuck, fuck, fuck.

"No, sir," said Jimmy and stared at Mal long and hard.

Mal shifted in his seat. The bouncing foot started up again and kept hitting the side of his desk, which made an annoying noise, so he stopped.

"So there'd be no witnesses."

"I beg you pardon."

He was not sure what the detective was saying here or why he was saying it.

"So no one can hear what we're talking about," Jimmy explained.

Mal screwed up his face. Not getting it.

"Why would I give a rat's ass if someone heard what we're talking about?" he said petulantly.

"Because if you told me something to get it off your chest, it would be inadmissible in court."

Ah jeez, thought Mal. Here we go.

"I have no idea what you're talking about," he said unconvincingly.

And that was another thing about amateurs. They have a need to tell someone what they've done. It's so horrible, so out of the ordinary, that they have an overwhelming desire to unburden themselves and get it off their chests. Guilt grows inside them like a cancer. It invades their sleep and their waking moments and they can't get it out of their minds Not for nothing is the act of confession the most artful tool the Catholic Church has in its arsenal to keep the flock tied to its apron strings. Who else could you tell this stuff to with impunity?

Mal made another attempt at a rally.

"I want you to go now." Stiffening in tone and manner. Figuring he'd come up with a way out, and oh God what he'd give for a line of coke. That would help him see things properly, instead of this panic that was rising up in him and taking over his body.

Jimmy continued to work the friendly thing.

"If I go now, I'll have to come back with Det. Flynn. Like I said, he's the guy handling the investigation. If that happens the press will most definitely find out because they're following this story and Det. Flynn around like bees on a honey pot. Then what, Mal? What's that gonna do to your business when it comes out?"

"When what comes out?" Mal challenged. Fucking bumpkin coming here and rattling his cage. Who the fuck is he anyway?

There was a staring contest.

Mal's eyes were hard and unmoving. Inside he was freaked out of his mind. Bits of twisted label were all over the desk. His pallor was no longer tan but wan and he was beginning to look like he had a bad case of jaundice.

What to do? What to do?

His mind was racing.

Jimmy's eyes were relaxed and amenable. Trying to convey trust and camaraderie. He was beginning to wonder if it was working.

"When the press finds out you're involved in a murder investigation and the dead man was your shylock, business partner and friend, and you were the last person to speak to him before he was murdered, well sir, one can only imagine the field day that pack of wolves is going to have ripping your ass apart.

Murder.

There was that word again. Why did he keep saying that word?

"Tell me about Thursday night, Mal."

"I told you," said Mal truculently. "I was here."

"All night?"

Silence.

"Tell me what's going on Mal?"

Think. Think. Think.

"Tell me about it Mal. You'll feel better when you do. Whatever you're holding back is going to eat you up alive. You've got to tell someone, it might as well be me. It's on the tip of your tongue. I can see it even if you can't. Let it go, Mal. No one will know. I give you my word. This conversation is off the record. That's why I sent Eddie out. So there'd be just the two of us and whatever you tell me can't be used against you. "

Mal squirmed in his chair and ran a hand through his hair. Then he came up with a brainwave straight from TV land.

"How do I know you're not wearing a wire?"

Jimmy smiled. It was a come to Papa sort of smile. If he could have hugged him he would, but it would have destroyed the moment. The momentum. The big MO that was beginning to move to his side of the argument. He stood up and held his arms out from his sides.

"Help yourself, Mr. Finkelstein. Frisk me if you want. I've got no tape recorder. My phone's turned off," he reached into his pocket and handed it to him to examine. He emptied his pockets on the table and patted himself down to show Mal there were no lumps and bumps.

There was a long silence while Mal thought it through, then he seemed to come to a decision.

He talked into the intercom.

"Jill, bring me in a couple of Snapples," he looked at Jimmy. "Something?"

"Water would be good, thanks."

"And a couple of bottles of water. Then you can go home. Turn the phones off. I don't want to be disturbed."

She was in and out in a flash.

Mal gulped the first Snapple all the way down and opened the second one just in case.

Jimmy sipped his water.

Calm and relaxed.

Two friends talking without a care in the world.

CHAPTER 63

MAL FINKELSTEIN
THURSDAY NIGHT

When he got to Crawford's apartment all Mal had on his mind was coke and pussy. That's what he'd been promised and that's what he was expecting. That's why Crawford invited him over. That's what the phone call was about; Crawford saying he thought Mal was tense and needed to relax.

He agreed and said he was coming over. That he was all wired up because of the launch tomorrow

When he got there the doorman was hailing a cab and didn't see him go in. The guy at the desk was busy with deliveries and the people in the lobby, so he didn't see him come in either. There was a big African-American woman swishing her hips and waving at the desk guy, trying to catch his eye. All eyes were on her so no one saw him. It was a fluke, really.

Mal moved quickly to catch the closing elevator.

No one saw him get in.

The elevator was empty.

No one was in the hall when he got out.

When Crawford let him in, Mal could tell things weren't going to go the way he thought they would. Crawford was very high. There were half-smoked joints in the ashtray, coke on the coffee table, and a half empty bottle of scotch.

Crawford had been going at all three.

And he was angry.

They'd spent a lot of time together, but Mal had never seen him like this before. He was usually so buttoned down and cool. This new Crawford was scary. Mal was no fool. He knew Crawford was a shylock, but he'd begun to think of him as a friend. People were calling him The Shadow because wherever Crawford turned up he was right behind him.

But this guy?

This was someone he'd never seen before.

"Where's my fucking money?" said Crawford and slammed Mal up against the wall.

Mal was terrified.

Crawford went into a rant about Austin Kenner and why did he let him kite a check on him for a quarter of a million dollars?

Mal denied it of course, but he wondered how he knew? Who told him? Then Crawford let slip that Austin owed him money too. Mal thought that was how Crawford had put it all together, but he was wrong. Crawford didn't know, because Austin never told him. Crawford was just fishing. But it didn't matter anyway. Crawford was too far out of control for the truth to get in the way.

Crawford glared at Mal.

Mal was scared shitless. He'd been caught in a lie, or so he thought, and he didn't know what Crawford was going to do about it.

Crawford did another line and chased it down with a slug of scotch.

He didn't offer Mal any.

That's when Mal knew he was really in trouble.

That's when he figured how to fix it.

He always carried tabs of Ketamine around with him. In his business you never knew when you were going to need it. The models loved the K. It made them all warm and fuckable and after they popped one of those babies all they wanted to do was cuddle up and screw. So while Crawford was parading around the apartment ranting and raving about what he was going to do to him, Mal slipped a couple of tabs into his drink. Those things are strong. Two are enough to knock out an elephant, which is what Mal thought he was dealing with. A big fucking scary elephant.

Crawford finished his marching around and flopped down next to Mal, took a slug of his drink and shoved his face into Mal's. Eyes bugging. Lips snarling.

"I want my money," he growled, "and I want it now. Call your folks and tell them what's going on. Tell them what a tight spot you're in. And tell them this from me: 'If I don't get my money by the end of business tomorrow, I'm going to tear their little boy limb from limb.' I'm talking about you, Mal. Tell them that will you, and I want you to know old buddy, I mean every word of it."

He did too. You'd have to be crazy not to realize it. And if that's what he wanted to do, there wasn't much Mal could do to stop him.

Mal told him he was expecting big things at the launch. He thought they'd be writing a lot of orders. If that was the case, he'll be able to pay him off next week, way ahead of schedule. Which made the business with Austin's check irrelevant, didn't it? Even though it wasn't true.

It did not.

Crawford wanted his money and started in on another rant, this one scarier than the last. Cataloging what happened to people who'd stiffed him. It was awful to hear and terrible to imagine.

Mal figured he had no choice. Really. What else was he going to do? What would you have done?

Eventually the Ketamine kicked in.

Crawford began to slur his words, leaned back on the couch, closed his eyes and was gone.

Out like a light.

Mal knew what to do next. There wasn't a moment's hesitation. He stretched Crawford out on the couch then put a pillow over his face until he stopped breathing.

Mal hoped they'd think he OD'd. Then he got out of there. He hadn't touched anything, at least he didn't think so, but he wiped down the door handles just in case. There was no one in the hallway and no one in the elevator, which he took down to the garage. There was no one there either. Another fluke. He walked up the ramp into the street, hailed a cab, and went home.

No one saw him. What are the odds?

When he read they extradited Kathy O'Brien from The Cayman Islands for Crawford's murder he thought he was home free.

Until this asshole showed up!

Jimmy waited patiently as Mal fiddled some more. He was relaxed and exerted no pressure, but there was nothing forthcoming and Mal had begun to look at him strangely. Finally Jimmy couldn't take it any more. He had to ask, otherwise they'd be staring at each other all night.

"We were talking about Thursday night, Mr. Finkelstein? What happened then?"

And the fish slipped the hook.

Jimmy saw it.

Mal changed and backed off.

In the time it took him to order his Snapple and chug one down, he'd sorted it out.

319

What was he thinking anyway?

This bumpkin with his syrupy ways had almost got him going. He was about to spill his guts. About to open up. Almost. Was he crazy? Was he mad? They had nothing on him. They already had someone for Crawford's murder. Kathy O'Brien. It was a slam-dunk is what the papers were saying.

This guy, Mal suddenly realized, was on a fishing trip.

If he held his ground everything would be all right.

So he held his ground.

And everything was all right.

CHAPTER 64
JIMMY AND EDDIE

Eddie was parked outside Mal's building. It was 5:15, the middle of rush hour. To get to the car Jimmy had to cut across a river of humanity streaming out of the office buildings and heading for home. If you're not used to it, this can be intimidating. People were everywhere. Crowds backed up at the lights waiting to cross the street. Vast conga lines disappeared down the subway station entrances. The sidewalk had eight and in some places ten people across in a kaleidoscope of brightly colored clothing and different lengths of hair. Most were going one way, a trickle went the other, all of them were jostling and bumping into each other in their frantic rush to get home.

Jimmy figured there were more people in the space he was crossing than in all of Columbia put together.

"How'd it go?" said Eddie when he got inside the car.

Jimmy was dejected.

"I lost him, Eddie."

"Lost him?"

"He got away."

"From what?"

"Telling me what happened."

"We know what happened. Kathy O'Brien killed Crawford Taylor."

"I don't think so."

"We've got her cold, Jimmy. You were there at the meeting."

"We've got the wrong person, Eddie. Mal Finkelstein killed him, I know he did. I had him Eddie. I got this close," he held up a finger and a thumb. "It was on the tip of his tongue," he shook his head sadly. "Then he slipped away."

"What happened?"

"He got a Snapple."

"That's it?"

"It broke the momentum. After he chugged one of those babies down he came out a different person. What the fuck do they have in those things anyway?"

Eddie didn't know.

"But you think he did it?"

"I know he did it. You saw him, Eddie. Twitching and squirming every time Crawford's name came up."

"He certainly did that."

"After you were gone it got worse. That's when I had him."

"Till he had the Snapple."

"That changed everything."

"Did you tell Morgan?"

"Not yet."

"He's not gonna like it."

Eddie was right.

Jimmy punched out Morgan's number and had to hold the phone away from his ear Morgan was yelling so loud when he found out why he was calling.

When he stopped Jimmy said, "He did it, Morgan. If you were there you'd know it too."

"Well I wasn't," Morgan barked, "and I don't. Neither will the bosses. They like Kathy O'Brien for this one and so do I. They're getting their creds for it as we speak and a press release has already gone out. I'd leave it alone if I were you, Jimmy. It's not like we don't have a solid case. And what have you got?"

"Not much," Jimmy allowed. "But if you were there Morgan you'd think twice about going with Kathy. At least not without taking a closer look at this guy."

"We got it all tied up, Jimmy. And I'm not seeing any light for anyone else."

Jimmy told him how close he got to Mal confessing.

"But he didn't, did he?"

Jimmy had to agree. He didn't.

"I really like him, Morgan."

"Well I don't."

"Check the prints in Crawford's apartment. I bet some of them are Mal's."

"So what? He'll say he's been there before, and then what? Let it go, Jimmy. You've been after Kathy for weeks and she keeps slipping away. Now we've got her in a box she can't get out of. You should be cheering."

"But…"

"No buts old buddy. You're not thinking straight. We've got her, Jimmy. Iron clad. And this guy Mal? We'll never get anything that'll stick. He'll get some slick lawyer and it'll all slide away, that's how these things work. And if, for some reason, we were to go in that direction, Kathy O'Brien would be laughing at us from some tropical paradise, and fuck that, Jimmy."

"That's what we care about now, being laughed at?"

"It's not and you know it."

Jimmy did. That wasn't fair. And it wasn't like he didn't agree.

"Check the street cams..."

"We did already."

"You were looking for Kathy, not this guy. He'll show up, you'll see."

"That's why I'm not gonna look."

"You have to.'

"I don't have to do anything." He was getting angry. "Look, I've got four murders I'm working as we speak. I've got no time to go looking for maybes."

"This is no maybe."

"What if we see him on the cams? He was taking a walk. Passing by. Anything. A good lawyer will punch a million holes in it. Take a step back, buddy, you're not seeing it right. What is it you told me your old man used to say?"

"Things have a habit."

"Yeah. Well? Things have a habit and you should be pleased. You've got someone who killed five innocent old people and one mobster, had Lamont done, and got away with it all. So she didn't do this one. What's the diff?"

There was none. Really. Morgan was right. If they went after Mal, Kathy would walk. And if they went after Mal, he'd walk too.

So he went along.

Jimmy.

What else was he going to do?

What would you do?

Morgan was pleased.

"Take it off your list, Jimmy. You've got nothing to do with this decision, your conscience is clear. You've done your job and thanks for your help. Go home, get a good night's sleep and put it behind you."

"How'd that go?" Eddie asked when he got off the phone.

"You know how it went. You're sitting right next to me."

"Not his side," Eddie persisted.

Jimmy put a disc in the player.
Muddy Waters.
The blues.
Good thinking music.
And turned it up real loud.

CHAPTER 65

JIMMY AND MARY

In bed.

Lights off.

Mary spooning into him.

Arms wrapped tightly around him.

"What happened today?" She whispered.

She loved to whisper in the dark.

It was the first chance they'd had to talk. The chatter, when Jimmy got home, was about Lucy and how great her day had gone. The bullying thing was over, now it was about how many new friends she had. Jimmy never saw her like this before. She never stopped talking in a breathless avalanche of names, 'she said,' 'I went,' and 'he goes.' But it wasn't just the talking he'd never seen before, it was the smile on her face that went along with it.

Now they were catching up on Jimmy's day.

Jimmy and Mary.

Spooning in the dark.

"They charged Kathy O'Brien with Crawford Taylor's murder."

"That's good," she said. "They finally got her on something that'll stick."

"That's what Morgan said."

"What's that mean?"

"She didn't do it."

He told Mary what he thought happened with Mal and Crawford at the apartment that night and about his conversation with Morgan.

"If we go after Mal, Kathy walks and Mal walks too. We'll never get him for this. And we know for sure Kathy murdered six people.

"So you're all right with this?"

"I guess so."

They were silent for a while.

Then Jimmy whispered, "My dad was right about one thing, though."

"How's that?"

"Things have a habit…"

Made in the USA
Middletown, DE
17 July 2015